ISBN 978-0-6157-1666-4
Website: janicelanepalko.com
Twitter: @janicelanepalko
Blog: thewritinglane.blogspot.com
Facebook: JaniceLanePalko.writer
Pinterest: Janice Lane Palko

This is the message of Christmas: We are never alone. —
Taylor Caldwell

To my husband, my source of magic.

A Shepherd's Song

By Janice Lane Palko

Chapter 1-1992

I didn't belong here. I sensed it. But if I were truthful, I didn't belong anywhere. But I wanted the money so I ignored that bowel-clenching sense of dread that has come over me and shut off my Sentra's engine. Picking up the note my roommate, Rob Bubash, had left me, I re-read it, wondering what a graphologist would make of his handwriting. It spiked on the page like a printout from a Richter scale.

Tom—

Got to be at work by eight. Deliver a Sammy to some chick named G. Davidson at three, 1000 Perry Highway, Ross Township. Man, she was desperate. Squeezed her for $150!!!

When my eyes saw that figure this morning, they bungeed out of their sockets. In a matter of days, the toy's price had skyrocketed.

I stretched across the seat, wiping a porthole on the foggy window. The car's heater had broken back in October making it a meat locker on wheels. This last Sunday in November, Perrysville was deserted: everyone was either indoors watching the Steelers or at Ross Park Mall Christmas shopping.

Last year we were robbed in a parking lot during one of our deals. Since then, we'd made it a practice to meet buyers at public places. As I scoped out the street, the place looked safe, but hey, you can get killed anywhere these days. Why would Rob agree to make a delivery here? One hundred fifty dollars probably had something to do with it. Through the condensation, I made out the address on the The Nuts and

Bolts Hardware store across the street. It said 999 Perry Highway. One-thousand Perry Highway had to be nearby.

My hands were not only cold now, but also clammy when I opened the car door, put a foot outside, and stood, looking over its roof. The sign stuck in the small, snow-dappled lawn beyond the sidewalk, stopped my heart.

It read: *Holy Redeemer Church. 1000 Perry Highway.*

Oh, this had to be a mistake! Maybe this was Rob's idea of a joke.

I ducked back inside the car and moved my fingers to the keys, which were still in the ignition. I wanted to get the hell out of there. But what if it wasn't a joke? I'd lose $150.

My hands dropped into my lap. Holy Redeemer? It sounded like a congregation of coupon clippers. I snickered. Ah, this is ridiculous to be afraid of a place. It was only a church for God's sake. What could happen to me?

Pushing up my fatigue jacket's sleeve, I glanced at my Timex—three twenty-five. I was late. I got out of the car, scanned the street, and wished I were an animal so I could sniff the air for the scent of danger.

The church, a red brick giant, sat back from the street, squeezed in among the smaller buildings.

I shoved the note and my keys into my pocket, grabbed the black garbage bag containing the Sammy from the back seat, and closed the door.

Snow flurries fell in slow motion from the dust-rag colored sky, but they were too sparse to freshen the mounds of old, gritty snow lining the curb, which was all that remained of the Thanksgiving eve blizzard we'd had four days ago.

Hanging in the air with the snowflakes was a palpable creepiness. Something was strange. Who at a church would want to buy a toy?

I walked to the far side of the building. No sign of a buyer. A driveway ran along it and led to a rear parking lot, which was filled with cars. I didn't see anyone milling about waiting for me.

I hurried back to the front of the church and decided to give my buyer a few more minutes to show.

Then I had a thought. With this lousy weather, maybe my buyer had gone inside to wait.

I climbed the limestone steps and set the bag down. Pressing my nose to the glass doors, which were etched with some kind of crazy religious symbols, I cupped my hands around my eyes and peered inside. All I could make out were some flickering candles.

4

I pulled the door's handle. Damn, it was unlocked. I stuck a foot inside but quickly withdrew it. No way was I going into a dark church alone. I released the handle; the pneumatic door closed with a sinister hiss as it slowly shut.

Glancing over my shoulder, I checked to make sure no one had sneaked up from behind. Then I looked at my watch—3:28. I'd give the buyer two more minutes, and then I'd be out of there.

I watched the Timex's digital readout form the numbers 3:30. Time was up. No one was going to come now. If this wasn't a joke, Rob was going to go ballistic that I'd been late and botched the deal. I'd have to lie and make up some kind of an excuse.

Annoyed at the weather and that I may have screwed up a deal, I picked up the Sammy bag to leave.

"They're in the church hall," boomed a voice from behind me.

"Jesus Christ!" I cried, nearly jumping out of my Doc Martens. Whirling around, I saw a chubby man in a Steelers jacket standing there. His face was as red and round as the bulb end of a thermometer, and thick, unruly white hair stuck out all over his head.

"Sorry, wrong guy," he said.

"Huh?"

"Jesus Christ? You called me— Get it?"

When I didn't laugh at his lame joke, he waved his hand. "Ah, never mind. Sorry to scare you." He patted my shoulder. "Come on, follow me."

And like an idiot, I did. Holding onto the plastic bag's drawstrings, I trailed along after him as he walked around the side of the church.

Perhaps I followed him because he seemed so harmless. His jacket barely covered his gut, and he walked on the toes of his suede shoes, swinging his arms happily at his side, reminding me of one of Snow White's dwarfs, you know, Fatso, going off to work.

When we came to a side door, he opened it for me. I could see that it led to a staircase. He smiled a dopey grin and swept his arm aside like he was a doorman at the Hilton or something.

Ignoring my instincts to run and get the hell out of there, I stupidly went in. As I passed through the doorway, I rummaged in my pocket for Rob's note.

The door closed behind us with a loud thud, like the sealing of a vault. Inside the stairwell, an odor of dust, coffee, and stale Coke lingered in the air while a droning, like the buzzing of a thousand bees, rose up the shaft.

5

Midway down the stairs, I found the note and pulled it from my pocket. I could barely read the name on the paper my hand was trembling so badly. "I'm looking for a G. Davidson," I said to Fatso. I didn't want him thinking I was there to join in on some Bible class or something.

Fatso pulled open the door at the bottom, releasing a sonic boom of chattering voices. As he walked into the hall, he said something.

"What?" I yelled, stepping in after him. But if he answered, I didn't catch it. Then what I saw inside the room made my ears ring and sent my other senses into overload. Blood. It was everywhere. As were people lying on gurneys hooked up to tubes. What the hell is this? A damn Robin Cook novel?

My vision dimmed as my legs turned to blubber. I wanted to run, but blubber legs don't respond well to terror. Feeling myself starting to sway, I dropped the bag, reached behind me for the wall, and braced myself against it, preparing to black out.

As I waited to faint, the tidal wave of adrenaline pulsing in me ebbed, and my sight slowly returned. And then I felt like a complete ass.

A table to the right was draped with a huge banner that read: "Pittsburgh Metro Blood Bank." Two nurses were seated there, while a line, hundreds of people long, snaked away from it.

I straightened up and caught my breath. "It's a blood drive," I whispered repeatedly to keep from passing out.

I looked around, and Fatso was gone. Obviously, he'd mistaken me for a donor. My legs gradually changed back from liquid into solid, and I quickly picked up the bag. As I was about to bolt, he reappeared.

"This is Ginny Davidson," he said, presenting a dark-haired woman.

Fantastic! I hadn't lost the sale.

The woman was petite and looked to be about thirty. I could tell she was young because her body still had that youthful snap—like a green twig has when you break it. But her face looked much older, and her dark, straight hair hung limply on either side of her colorless cheeks.

Don't get me wrong, she wasn't ugly; she just seemed tired or worn out. Her brown eyes were fixed on me, and looking into them, I was reminded of burned out light sockets. They had no juice.

"Will you excuse me a moment," Fatso said, and left us.

The woman continued to stare at me while I waited for her to say something. After all, she'd been the one who called to buy the toy. Then she arched her brows, opened her palms, and said, "Yes?"

"OK, hold on a sec . . ." Turning my back on the crowd, I loosened the bag's drawstrings. "It's in there," I whispered.

Puzzled, she glanced inside the bag and then her eyes shot to mine. Electrical service restored. Shock registered first on her face then a broad smile took over.

She looked into the bag a second time. "Oh, praise God," she said, covering her heart with her hands. When she raised her head, tears were glistening in her eyes. "I can't believe it. Oh, God bless you." She threw her arms around my neck, hugging me so tightly, I swear she knocked my spine out of alignment.

Man, the way she carried on, you'd have thought I was giving her the toy. For $150 bucks, I should have been crying and hugging her.

One of the nurses at the table rose and called, "Mrs. Davidson, is something wrong?"

She released my neck and turned around, wiping tears from her cheeks. "Wrong? Oh, good heavens no." She picked up the bag containing the toy. "You'll never believe it. This young man is here to give Christo a So Big Sammy!"

Give a So Big Sammy? Is she out of her mind?

A murmur rippled through the crowd.

What should I do? What I should have done when I first got to this creepy church. Run. I'll rip the toy out of her hands and get the hell out of there.

As I was about to snatch it away, the mob suddenly burst into applause. Surprised, I halted. A collage of eyes focused on me, nailing my feet to the spot. If I grabbed it and ran now, they'd nab me and kill me. My intestines coiled into a giant knot.

All I wanted was to get my money and get out of there. The woman clung to me, mumbling, "Thank you! Thank you!"

"Excuse me, ma'am," I whispered, as I pried her arms from my neck. "I'm afraid there's been—"

A voice like a shovel scraping cement pierced the thunderous applause. "Quick, film this!"

Film? What the hell is going on?

"What's your name, young man?" That voice again.

I jerked my head so that my hair fell in front of my face. Through the screen of hair, I saw that a woman in an expensive navy suit was standing next to me. She was all made-up like those cosmetic counter ladies in Kaufmann's who spritz you with cologne, and her honey-colored hair was short and puffy and so heavily sprayed, her head looked like a shellacked walnut shell. She held a notebook, and for some reason, she looked familiar.

A man with a camera perched on his shoulder like a flamethrower was aiming his lens at me. Then I realized that Walnut Head was a reporter, and I was going to be filmed by the Channel 6 News crew. I wanted to puke.

Walnut Head called to a young woman in a Channel 6 News sweatshirt. "Melody," she commanded, "get the kid over here. Let's get a shot of him," Walnut Head was pointing at me and talking to the cameraman, "giving the kid the toy."

Why did everyone think I was giving the Sammy away? Oh, I have to get out of here.

The crowd wandered out of the orderly line and surged toward the camera, hemming me in.

"What'd you say your name was?"

"Huh?" I mumbled.

"Push the hair out of your eyes and speak up," she commanded. Her tone scared me, and like an ass, I obeyed. When I pushed my hair behind my ears, I saw that she'd traded in the notebook for a microphone. *Uh-huh, no way was she interviewing me.* I pulled my arm away but her French-manicured nails dug into my flesh.

"I got the kid," Melody shouted as she threaded her way through the swarming crowd.

Ginny Davidson called out, "Someone please find Joe."

"I'm coming," yelled a husky, bearded man as he emerged from what appeared to be a kitchen on the left. In front of him, an apron-clad old lady walked carrying a tray of doughnuts. The man reached over her shoulder, plucked two from the tray, and strode toward us, licking jelly filling from his upper lip. When he saw the TV camera, he looked as confused as I felt.

He swallowed hard. "What's going on?"

The intern put her finger to her lips and shushed him. She took the bag with the Sammy from Ginny Davidson, and shoved a small boy forward.

When I saw the kid, my heart deflated like a steamroller had run over it. The boy had no hair. Did he have the mange or something?

I tried to move away but the crowd was too thick. Trapped, I constricted my nostrils, so as not to breathe in too deeply. If this kid had something contagious, I didn't want to be sharing the same air.

Walnut Head stepped in front of us and her transformation as she morphed into her on-air persona stunned me. Throwing her

8

shoulders back, she raised her head, and began to speak. The annoying voice was gone. Instead one as sweet and smooth as fudge flowed from between her glossy lips.

"As you recall," she said, "yesterday during our six o'clock broadcast, we introduced you to four-year-old Christopher Davidson, who is battling leukemia."

Leukemia! Man, this kid is *really* sick.

"We're here at Holy Redeemer Church in Ross Township, where a blood drive and tissue typing is being held with the hopes of fulfilling his Christmas wish of finding a bone marrow match."

Bone marrow? I've walked into a frickin' nightmare.

"We also told you that Christopher had another item on his Christmas wish list—a So Big Sammy. He is hoping Santa will bring him one. His parents, Virginia and Joseph Davidson, told us yesterday that they cautioned Christopher to not be too disappointed if Santa doesn't bring him one as this toy has become quite popular. In fact, Channel 6 News at our noon broadcast reported that all the local stores have been sold out of the popular toy and that toy scalpers are demanding upwards of $50 for one."

Toy scalpers? That's what they're calling us? It sounds so . . . so criminal.

Walnut Head continued to gush into the microphone. "But we're happy to report that one of Christopher's wishes has come true." She paused for effect.

The intern nudged Ginny Davidson, who then moved in front of the camera, bent down, and put her arm around her kid's thin waist.

"Christo," she said, "this nice young man has something to give you." Her last few syllables were punctuated by sobs.

The intern kicked me in the shin, snapping me out of my disbelief. She handed me the Sammy, cueing me to give the kid the toy. As much as I wanted to run out with it, I couldn't. There was no way to escape. I had no choice but to give it to the kid.

"Here," I said, grudgingly handing it over to the boy and making sure I didn't touch him.

The package was nearly as tall as he, and Ginny Davidson helped him unveil the bag's contents. When he saw the toy, color filled his pale cheeks, and his eyes lit up like a neon beer sign. "It's Sammy!" he shrieked, grabbing for the box.

Quickly, his mother took his small hands and held them tightly while she looked into her son's face. "What do you say to this kind young man?"

9

The kid looked up at me, and smiled, revealing baby teeth no bigger than grains of rice. Then he wrapped his arms around my leg.

I flinched; I felt like shaking him off like you do a dog that's humping your leg, but I couldn't because everyone was watching.

"*Fanks* so much," he said, butchering the "th" sound. "Now all I need is a *twanspwant*."

A transplant? I felt a squeezing sensation in my chest and hoped I wasn't having a heart attack. What kind of world is it, I wondered, when a kid too young to pronounce transplant correctly needs to have one?

Staring down at the boy with hair like the fuzz on a peach, I waited for him to release me, but he hung on tightly, and it scared me that now he'd gotten hold of me, he'd never let go.

"Welcome," I squeaked. Finally, he relaxed his grip on my leg to inspect the toy. When Walnut Head knelt to get Christopher Davidson's reaction to his gift, I made a break for it.

A collective gasp from the crowd followed me as I ran to the door. I hit the handle and shot out of the hall, climbing the steps two at a time. When I burst through the door at the top of the stairs, frigid air hit my face.

While I'd been trapped in the church basement, the snow had intensified, covering the driveway. I slipped as I sprinted alongside the building, skidding the last ten feet to my car.

As I stuck the key in the lock, I heard Melody calling after me from the doorway, "Stop! We didn't get your name."

I hopped inside and fired up the Sentra's engine. My back-end fishtailed as I pulled out, the snow covering the rear window blowing off, trailing behind like a comet's tail. In the rearview mirror, I saw Melody run toward the street, waving her arms like she was Gilligan trying to flag down a rescue plane.

Walnut Head came running up beside her in her pumps, skidded, and fell on her ass. I laughed as I floored the pedal.

The last thing I saw in the mirror as I sped away from Holy Redeemer was Walnut Head sitting on the snow-covered sidewalk scribbling something in her notebook.

Chapter 2

I headed south on I279. Rounding a curve in the East Street Valley, I came upon a line of cars strung bumper-to-bumper, stretching all the way into downtown Pittsburgh. As soon as a snowflake falls, everybody panics and forgets how to drive. I pumped the brakes. My tires slipped some and then grabbed the road as the car slid to a stop.

The storm had intensified, obscuring the city's skyline, softening the hard lines of the USX Tower and completely erasing the turrets atop PPG Place.

I punched the buttons on the radio, searching for some music. Only warmed-over rock songs and blather from that idiot talk show host, Mark Thornton, poured out. After ten minutes of him, I switched off the radio and sat listening to the snow crunching under my wheels.

The earth's land area is 57 million square miles, and of all the places in the world I could've been, don't you know I had to show up at Holy Redeemer at precisely the wrong moment. But that's how my whole life has been. If I believed in that mystical garbage, I'd think I was born under a bad sign.

Lately though, I'd been convinced that maybe my luck was changing. Since Thanksgiving, I'd been happier and more optimistic than I could ever remember. See where that got me.

I'd spent a miserable Thanksgiving Day in the dorm. Rob had taken pity on me and invited me to his family's place in Mars, a small town about fifteen miles north of Pittsburgh, for dinner. But I declined. Last year, I went home with him, but it made me feel like a charity case.

So I spent this Thanksgiving hibernating in my room. Very few people remained in Stephen Foster Hall; a handful of foreign students had gathered in the lounge to eat a meal of rice and lamb. They said I could eat with them if I wanted, but their menu sounded like something prepared by Purina, so I passed.

I spent the time studying and listening to the Detroit Lions lose to the Houston Oilers on the radio. Unlike the rest of the rich brats in this place, Rob and I were too poor to afford a TV. Periodically, I took breaks to watch the falling snow as it buried the campus.

My holiday feast consisted of two hotdogs and a carton of chocolate milk I'd picked up at the 7-11. Afterward, I settled back on my bunk to enjoy my après dinner liqueur—an Iron City beer.

As I popped the tab, the six o'clock news came on the radio. "Heavy snowfall across most of the country has stranded holiday travelers."

My Thanksgiving had been no Norman Rockwell painting, but I guess it could have been worse. I could have been marooned in some airport. I took a gulp of beer, savoring the way it stung my tongue before it slid down my throat. At least I had beer and a bed.

"And in financial news," the radio crackled, "industry analysts released their annual report forecasting this year's list of hot toys for the upcoming holiday shopping season."

At the word "toy," my ears pricked up.

"Topping this year's list is So Big Sammy, the purple plush monkey that plays the game 'So Big.'"

I hopped out of my bunk to turn up the volume and spilled beer down my chest.

"Seems analysts are on target with their prediction," said the newscaster, "because retailers all over the tri-state area are reporting that they can't keep the So Big Sammys on their shelves."

The voice continued: "Gee Whiz Inc., the manufacturer, has gone into round-the-clock production in an attempt to keep up with the demand. Even so, a company official cautions that they still may not be able to satisfy all the orders for the toy in time for Christmas.

"Consumers are reportedly paying as much as $100 a piece on the black market for the toy—more than triple its retail price. Wall Street analysts are predicting that if current indications hold forth, So Big Sammy could be the next Cabbage Patch Kids, earning record profits."

"Yes!" I thrust my fist in the air. Finally, something has gone right in my life.

"In a related story . . . " I cocked my ear toward the radio, holding my celebration in check for a moment. "This morning, a Steubenville woman sustained a concussion and broken nose when

12

frenzied shoppers stormed a Toys 'R Us. The store had just received thirty of the coveted purple primates, when a mob rushed security guards and broke into the shipment. State Police were called in to restore order." Disbelief colored the newscaster's voice.

"Turning to world news. . . In Somalia, the Red Cross reports that thousands of people starving in Mogadishu have—"

I shut off the radio and unleashed my joy, dancing around the room. "Martinique, here I come," I shouted. I unlocked the door, and screamed down the hall, my voice echoing off the institutional green tile walls.

One of the Asian students peeked out from his room, saw it was me carrying on, shook his head, and slammed his door. I ducked inside and laughing, collapsed into the orange vinyl chair.

My eyes darted around the room. The decor was hideous—a cross between early psych ward and nouveau-Brady Bunch. Splashes of orange, avocado, and harvest gold assaulted my eyes. And the furnishings—cheap metal bunks, Naugahyde and chrome couch and chairs, pop-art daisy curtains, and out-of-date lamps—offended good taste. But tonight this small, rectangular room, this decorator's nightmare, looked like a palace because every available square foot of it was crammed with boxes containing So Big Sammys. We'd snagged fifty of them.

Everywhere I turned, the frozen grins of the purple monkeys stared back at me from behind their cellophane windows, looking like a troop from a psychedelic rain forest.

I ran to the desk, ripped a sheet of paper from my notebook, and as I searched for a pencil, I grabbed Rob's dirty sock that had been sitting on the window sill for over a month and mopped up the beer I'd spilled down the front of my shirt.

I loved this sweatshirt. Rob gave it to me last Christmas after dubbing our toy selling partnership Scrooge and Marley, Inc. On it was a picture of Tiny Tim sitting by a fire, his hands curled around a mug, his crutch propped beside him. The caption said: "Let's Get Drunk and Scrooge!"

God bless us everyone. I chuckled as I blotted the beer. This was going to be a great Christmas!

Tossing the wet sock back onto the sill, I took a seat at the desk, and began calculating. If we sold the toys for $100 a piece, we should have enough money to get to Martinique during spring break. I raised my head and looked out the large window above the desk. Martinique sounded pretty good right now.

Three Rivers University, home of the TRU Bluejays, clung to a ridge on Pittsburgh's North Side that overlooked the downtown area. From my window in Foster Hall, the silvery cityscape shivered in the night.

Since last evening, six inches of snow had fallen, draping everything in a bolt of white flannel. Late this afternoon, it had stopped. Now approaching six-thirty, it was cold, and I knew windy by the white caps curling on the black glass waters of the Allegheny and Ohio Rivers. Out of habit, I checked the sky—it was clear and starlit.

Grabbing a box, I took out the Sammy. Turning it over, I flipped on its switch. As I grasped the silly-looking simian by its hands, a cartoonish voice cried, "How big are you?" The toy paused then asked, "Are you soooo big?" Then it raised its arms like it was doing the wave. "I'm sooooo big toooo!" It giggled and lowered them.

Sammy repeated the game until I turned it off. As I set it on the desk, I shook my head. What parent in their right mind would buy their kid one of these ugly, annoying toys for Christmas? But then again, what did I know about parents and Christmas?

The room was quiet now, and I hated to admit it, but I was lonely. Even though Rob sometimes gets on my nerves, I couldn't wait until he returned tomorrow so I could tell him the good news—that Scrooge and Marley were on their way to Martinique.

Neither Rob nor I was loaded. He worked part-time at the Toy Trunk, while I collected chump change from toiling in the campus bookstore. I survived on a small academic scholarship, loans, and the infrequent check from my father.

We've never been able to afford a trip at spring break. In October, we pooled our money and began making the rounds of area stores, buying toys to sell at inflated prices. At each, we bought two or three toys, stockpiling them in hopes of making a killing at Christmas.

The rest of Thanksgiving evening, I spent composing a classified for the *Post-Gazette* offering Sammys for sale and daydreaming of lying in the sun on the beaches of Martinique.

Late on Friday afternoon, Rob exploded through the door and slung his backpack on the chair. "Ebenezer, my boy," he called, crossing the room and pulling a small neon-printed cloth out of his jacket pocket. He twirled the swatch on his index finger. "While I was at home, I dug out my thong because, man, we are headed to Martinique."

I plucked the fabric from his finger. "This isn't a thong."

"It certainly is."

I held up the bathing suit. The back of it was nothing more than a string.

"You'll look like a praying mantis in a diaper."

Rob paid no attention to my remark as he took off his jacket. He's aerodynamically designed so that insults flow without resistance right over him. He bent his long legs, sat on the lower bunk, and leaned forward on his elbows, reminding me of an origami bird I'd once folded in Mrs. Osborne's fourth grade art class. At 6'4", he was all angles and points from his beaky nose to his knobby knees that jutted out beneath his jeans.

"I swear I'm not going anywhere with you if you wear that thing." I shot the bathing suit at him slingshot style.

He snatched the suit out of the air and put it on his head. "You may jest, Thomas, but I've been doing my mother's 'Buns of Steel' video."

I've seen his mother. "Buns of Tapioca" was more like it.

He stood, turned his backside to me. "You must admit, *mon derriere* looks perkier all ready. Oh," he growled, "I'm going to be a babe magnet in Martinique."

I didn't want to look at his *derriere* let alone comment on it, so I changed the subject. "I take it then you've heard how hot our friend Sammy is?"

"Hot?" Rob cried, picking up the toy that I'd left on the desk last night. "Hot? He's sizzling! This dude should be classified as an alternative energy source. Forget nuclear, man. We got Sammy. Last night, Tommy, I watched the news, and people were killing each other for this guy." He stroked the toy's head. "He was the only bright spot in my Thanksgiving."

"Why? Something happen?"

"Nah, same old stuff."

"Was it Fat Head?"

Fat Head Michalski was Rob's mother, Chickie's, latest live-in. A long-distance trucker, he had a head the size of the Pirate Parrot's. Or at least his head used to be that big. See, Fat Head had asthma, and one night after washing away the miles with some Wild Turkey in an Indiana Motel 6, he passed out. During the night, the weather changed and his asthma flared. In the darkness, Fat Head fumbled for his inhaler on the night stand, but in a drunken stupor, picked up the pistol he kept for protection by mistake and shot off his upper lip and the ridge of bone above his right eye. The bullet and subsequent surgery reduced the circumference of his head by a quarter.

15

"Who else?" Rob said. "The doofus insisted on making the gravy. Man, you know how he can't control his spit. Well, I looked over and his drool was dripping into the pan. I yelled, '"Hey, divot head, that pot ain't a spittoon.' But the moron didn't care. He just kept on stirring his spit into the gravy." Rob shook his head. "Be glad you weren't there."

Believe me, I was.

"What'd you do for Thanksgiving?"

"Ah, not much. Studied. Watched the snow pile up. Oh," I said, grabbing a paper off the desk, "and I wrote that classified. I phoned it into the *Post-Gazette* this morning. It'll be in tomorrow's paper."

Rob read it over then handed it back to me. "Looks great. Be prepared, Tommy. I'm warning you, the phone's going to be ringing off the hook."

I grinned. "Oh, I'm prepared—prepared to make a lot of money. I swear, when I saw that stupid monkey the first time, I thought you'd lost it. I thought it'd be a dud like last year's toy."

"No, Ebenezer, my boy," Rob said, thrusting the monkey in my face, "Sammy's the man. He's your ticket to paradise."

Now, as my car inched along in the storm, I was mad at myself for ever thinking that things could change for me. My life is one giant game of *Sorry*. Just when I think I'm getting ahead, someone yells "Sorry," and I'm sent back to square one.

Thinking about what happened back at Holy Redeemer, how I'd been swindled, how I'd been made a fool, how I'd have to invent some excuse for Rob on why I'd blown the sale, I wasn't so sure anymore about what he'd said about Sammy.

A headache was forming above my left eye. As it gathered fury, I had the sickening feeling that Sammy was not my ticket to paradise but more like my passport to Hell.

Chapter 3

My father is like a virus; he strikes when your resistance is low. I shouldn't have been surprised then when he called after the incident at Holy Redeemer. You see, we share a special connection like those bonds identical twins have. You know the kind—they always make the headlines in *The Star*. WOMAN RUPTURES APPENDIX. TWIN FIVE HUNDRED MILES AWAY FEELS PAIN. My father feels my pain all the way in California. Then calls to inflict more.

When I returned to the room, I had the mother of all migraines, and although I was hungry, I ate nothing because I knew if I did, it would only come back up. I needed to lie down.

Taking off my fatigue jacket, I walked over to the desk and stuffed the wad of bills I'd made from my other sales into the manila envelope in the top drawer.

Kicking off my Doc Martens, I crawled into my bunk, and tried to quiet my racing mind and pounding head.

I closed my eyes and tried to fall asleep, but the vessels in my head throbbed in time to the bass beat of the rap music pulsing through the wall next to my bunk.

Charles Parkhurst Barnes III, on the other side of the wall, was heavily into ghetto music, which I found ironic. Chaz (I call him Chaz to annoy him) grew up in Fox Chapel, one of Pittsburgh's most affluent suburbs, and I bet he's never even seen a ghetto or ever will unless his old man, goes out and buys him one.

My fist pounded the wall for a good minute until he realized I was doing the banging and not the song.

"Kiss off, Shepherd," he yelled before lowering the volume.

As I massaged my temples, scenes from Holy Redeemer exploded in my mind. The blood. The crying woman. The sick boy. The boy smiling at me. Aw, no. I rolled over, the bunk frame rattling like a cage, and faced the wall. I covered my head with the pillow, but that sick kid's face haunted me.

I must have dozed off because the room was dark when the phone rang. Submerged in sleep's deep end, I only surfaced to consciousness when the phone trilled a second time. The third ring jump-started my headache. I felt like letting the answering machine take it, but I was afraid it might be someone wanting to buy a Sammy.

Crawling from my bunk, I shuffled to the desk as if my head were a beaker of nitroglycerin and would explode with too brisk a step.

"Hello," I said weakly. The drowsiness clouding my brain made the words sound more like a question than a greeting.

"T.P?"

At the sound of his voice, my gastric juices curdled. No one calls me "T.P." except my father, and I hate it because all I can think of is toilet paper. But I guess it's appropriate since he just uses people and flushes them from his life.

He and my mother were college radicals and thought it cool to name me after Thomas Paine, the great American revolutionary. My mother gave me my father's surname because her name was Linda Pell, and Thomas Paine Pell was a little too strange—even for people who thought names like Moon Unit, Rose Hips, and Sea Urchin were great. I've always thought the Paine part of my name was especially appropriate.

I cleared the sleep from my throat. "Yeah?"

"Keeping out of trouble?" He snickered.

Will he ever let me forget about my arrest? I sighed and sunk into the desk chair, picturing the wise guy-grin on his face, the gap in his smile where a bicuspid had been knocked out by a club in an antiwar demonstration. I lay my head on top of the cold metal desk. *"Yeah."*

"Sorry we couldn't get you out here for Thanksgiving, but hey, with Jeffrey now, cash is tight." Voices squawked in the background. "Amber and Jeffrey say 'Hi.'"

Amber is my father's main squeeze, old lady, bed-buddy, live-in, significant other—whatever you want to call someone you think is good enough to sleep with but not good enough to marry—and Jeffrey is my half-brother. Amber is twenty-eight—young enough to be my sister— and I'm old enough to be Jeffrey's father. No wonder I get migraines.

18

When I went to college, he quit his job and moved to San Francisco. Capitalizing on his graduate degree in geology, he went into business supplying New Age stores with crystals. Seems there are a lot of people who believe curling up with a mineral will help everything from impotence to eczema. I swear those people could save themselves a ton of money if they just mined and polished the rocks rattling around in their heads.

"Ah, no problem," I said. I didn't want to argue with him tonight; I was too tired to fight. "I'm kind of busy anyway with finals coming, and besides, Christmas will be here soon."

I was looking forward to the trip to the Coast; it'd be nice to get a break from winter.

He paused. "Ah, that's what I'm calling about. Hey, ah T.P., Christmas plans have been altered a little."

I straightened up. "You couldn't get the direct flight? A connection's OK. I don't—"

"Ah, it's not the flight." He paused again, and I knew from the silence that he was gearing up to lay some lame excuse on me. I waited, tapping my fingers on the desk.

"See, well, you know Amber's parents?"

Know her parents? I've only met them once, and I'm still trying to forget them.

"Yeah?"

"Well, they offered to take Jeffrey for the week between the holidays. And well . . . Amber and I haven't been away for so long—not since before he was born. This kid stuff is murder. So I thought, I mean, we thought we'd go to Mexico—sort of take a second honeymoon."

There it was—the excuse. I knew it was coming. He pitched it to me; it came in over the plate, and sailed right past me for a strike. I expected something else—a three-connection flight, or a booking on a fly-by-night airline—not a complete cancellation of my trip. I shook my head in disbelief.

My cheeks burned with rage. *Funny, you couldn't find the money to fly me out for Thanksgiving, but you found it to go to Mexico. Blow me off again, Dad. I don't care anymore.*

"Hey, ah, Amber's parents said you're welcome to come and spend the holidays with them."

How thoughtful. Amber's mother, Garnet Williams, has a set of ill-fitting false teeth that click like Scrabble tiles when she laughs, and her idea of a good time is parking her polyester-clad butt in her La-Z-Boy

19

and ordering faux gemstones from QVC. And her father, Harry Williams, has a passion for walking the beaches with a metal detector, scanning the sand for nickels. He wears his pants slung low under his massive gut, and whenever he bends over to uncover a coin, his big white ass moons the whole beach. From the looks on the sunbathers' faces, I think they'd pay him a buck just to stay out of sight.

"Ah, I think I'll just stay here." I don't know why, but I always think my father's going to change, but he never does. I guess I'm just an idiot.

"I told them you'd probably want to stay there." His tone was so casual, if he'd been in the room, I'd have strangled him. "Amber was so worried you'd be upset about being alone for the holidays, but I told her you wouldn't care. I told her that you and I never got into that Christmas garbage like she does. I told her that Christmas is no big deal. Right, T.P.?"

"Yeah, right," I said, embossing my reply with sarcasm. "Christmas is no big deal."

While he talked about Mexico, I sat in the dark watching *The Gateway Clipper* sailing up the Allegheny. No doubt the boat was packed with people, probably a Christmas party. On its upper deck, a tree strung with multicolored lights twinkled. And beyond it, downtown Pittsburgh had suddenly broken out in a severe case of decorations. And above it all, the sign on Mt. Washington blinked in red letters, *Happy Holidays.*

Yeah, Christmas is no big deal.

The call went on for another five minutes while my father rambled on about Amber and Jeffrey. How smart Jeffrey was. How Jeffrey knew his colors. How Jeffrey knew the difference between a pterodactyl and a pteranodon. How Jeffrey loved *Sesame Street.* He talked so much about Big Bird, you'd swear he'd personally flopped his ass down on Big Bird's egg and hatched him.

He babbled about how much he's enjoying a parenting class that Amber enrolled them in at their local college. A class taken twenty-two years too late, I'd say.

Every so often I contributed a lackluster "Does he?" or a "That's nice" as punctuation to his monologue, but in my mind, I'd disconnected the call right after he bagged me for Christmas.

"Well, talk to you after the New Year, T.P.," he finally said. I guess that meant not to expect a gushy call at midnight on New Year's Eve telling me how much he loved me and how much he missed seeing me.

"See ya," I said, and I would have slammed the phone down, but I was afraid the noise combined with the rage swelling in me would cause my head to explode like those watermelons David Letterman tosses out windows.

Dragging myself back to bed, I gently placed my head on the pillow. Pulling the blanket up, I curled into a ball, and wished I'd fall asleep and wake in the morning to another life.

But I couldn't sleep. Instead, I lay staring at the luminous dial on the clock. It was only a little after seven. So many hours of darkness yet ahead. Oh, I can't tell you how many nights I've spent alone in the dark staring at a clock.

Chapter 4

Rob came in at eleven. While he rattled around undressing, I pretended to be asleep because I hadn't made up a good excuse for botching the Sammy deal.

Rob shut off the light and crawled into bed. In seconds he was asleep, snoring like a sow. Then he was silent. After a while, I became drowsy. And just as I was about to cross the border into sleep, he let out a snort that a sounded like the starting of a snow blower.

When I finally fell into a deep sleep, I dreamed I was a meteor whipping through the universe, speeding along the Milky Way. When I cruised past the moon, instead of seeing the crater-pocked face of the man-in-the moon, I saw that Davidson kid's smiling back at me. He winked.

Startled, I veered off course and was captured by the earth's gravity. I was falling. Wispy clouds swirling around the world loomed larger as I plummeted. I hit the atmosphere, but instead of dropping through the clouds, I bounced off them like a pinball. Thump. Thump. Thump.

When I ricocheted off one in the shape of Sammy, my level of consciousness rose, and I realized I wasn't ping-ponging off clouds, but that Rob was pummeling my head with his pillow.

I opened a bleary eye and saw him winding up for another strike. Covering my head, I took the blow, but before he could hit me again, I grabbed the pillow by its grungy slip.

"What the hell is wrong with you?" I cried, trying to wrestle the pillow away. Still lying in bed, I had no leverage. His face was in mine, and before he got the better of me, I broke out the heavy artillery. Gulping air, I burped so loudly my tonsils vibrated.

"You pig," he said as my timed-release stink bomb, a combination of morning breath and onions that had been fermenting overnight in my stomach, detonated. He recoiled, relaxing his grip on the pillow.

I snatched it from him and flung it across the dark room, toppling the Sammy boxes stacked on the CD player.

Rob came at me, in a cartwheel of fists armed with a blue bolt of four letter words. Then I got angry and threw a headlock on him.

With his neck pinned under my armpit, his face turned red, like my finger when the dental floss gets wound too tightly around it. "What's wrong with me?" he choked out the words. His breath was laced with maple syrup. "You're the nut who's giving Sammys away."

"What?" I tensed, unconsciously tightening the hold around his neck. "How do you know about that?"

"How do I know?" His tongue hung out the side of his mouth. "The whole damn world knows." I dropped the headlock, and he scrambled away.

I watched him in the gray morning light seeping through the crack where the curtains failed to meet. I was afraid, he might go at me again, but he moved away from the bunks, bobbing and weaving and grasping his neck. "You held a press conference."

"Press conference? I don't know what you're talking—"

"Oh yeah, right." He swiveled his neck the way Roberto Clemente did on old game highlights. "Like you didn't know you were going to be on the news this morning." He switched on the overhead light, sending my eyes into convulsions of pain.

"No! I'm not." I squinted and clutched my pillow in front of me like a shield. I hadn't even had time to draft an excuse. "You're lying."

"The hell I am. Coming back from breakfast, I glanced up at the TV in the lounge and three guesses whose ugly mug was on the screen?" He walked to the bunk, pointing a crooked finger at me. His knuckles were covered with black hair. "Yours—playing Mr. Big Shot, handing out Sammys like Santa Claus, while the crowd oohed, and aahed. That was $150 you gave away, idiot!"

I batted his furry finger away. "I wasn't handing out toys."

"Well, then why was that woman crying and hanging all over you? And why did that reporter call you a hero?"

"Hero? She didn't."

24

"Yeah, she did."

"Aw, no." I fell back on the bed. "That stupid Walnut Head."

"Walnut Head?"

"Yeah, the reporter. Her hair was hard . . . " I waved a hand across the air. "Oh, forget it." *How did she find out my name?* Then I remembered her sitting in the snow scribbling in her notebook. I kicked the wall, sending needle pricks of pain up my instep. "Yow," I said, rubbing my arch. "She must have traced my license plate."

Rob leaned over the bunk, and I flinched. "Relax, jerk face, I'm not going to hit you again, although I'd like to slap the snot out of you. You're telling me a reporter traced your license plate?" He arched his black caterpillar brows. "Why did she do that?"

I rose and swung my legs over the side of the bunk. "I ran into a problem yesterday."

"No kidding, Captain Obvious."

"I was going to tell you all about it this morning. I didn't even give her my name. I swear, I never dreamed she'd be able to use that tape without me signing a release or something."

"Let me get this straight." His neck was still fire red from the headlock. "You were giving away toys anonymously then?"

"No, moron." I hopped down from the bunk. "That address you left me . . . Well, it was a church."

"A church?"

"Yeah, a church."

I filled him in on everything that had happened yesterday afternoon, editing out the part where I nearly fainted and how bad I felt for the sick kid.

"If I'd demanded the money, Rob, the crowd would have freaked and killed me." I walked to the desk chair and sat. The linoleum was ice-skating rink cold under my feet. I fished a pair of dirty socks from the heaps of cruddy laundry strewn on the floor and slipped them on. Their soles were stiff and crusty and smelled like an expensive cheese. "Before the reporter got my name, I ran."

Rob shoved some Sammy boxes aside and sat on the couch, smirking. "You ran?"

"Well . . . yeah."

Last night's migraine had diminished to a dull ache that danced on the edges of my skull, taunting me to get upset again so it could return and finish ravaging my brain.

"You would've too." I sounded like a kid justifying why he'd run from a bully. "They might have arrested me or something."

25

Rob snickered. "They can't arrest you, Tommy. You weren't doing anything illegal."

"I know. But have you read the papers? Or listened to the talk shows?"

"No, I've been too busy working."

Trying to defend myself while sitting in my underwear left me feeling disadvantaged. I picked up my jeans from where I had dropped them on the floor last night and pulled them on.

"You know a lot of people are furious about what we're doing." I buttoned the fly. "While I was stuck in traffic yesterday, I listened to the radio, to that talk show. You know, Mark Thornton? Well, they were talking about the So Big Sammy craze. Everyone was calling in ranting about what a disgrace it is the way people are acting over this toy. And what assholes the people who sell them are."

Rob looked dubious. I leaned forward for emphasis. "I'm telling you, they hate us. Why some old lady called in and said, now get this, Rob, that 'we should be taken out to the woods and castrated.'"

Rob's hands flew to cover his crotch. "A little old lady said that?"

"Yeah, and she said she'd personally like to have the honors."

Rob's face puckered as he contemplated his fate as a eunuch. Maybe now he'd understand the pressure I faced at Holy Redeemer and why I'd run out without getting the money.

"And guess what those people on the radio called us?" I asked, driving home my point.

"Financial wizards?" he grinned.

"No. Scalpers! Toy scalpers!"

Rob's shoulders shook with laughter. "Toy scalpers. Man, that sounds like someone who slices off the hairdos from Mattel dolls." He began to beat his hand against his mouth. "Wooo Wooo Wooo. I can see it now." He rose and thumped his breast with his fist and said in a stereotypical, Indian voice that would offend every Native American, "Me scalp'em Star-Brite Sparkles. Add to scalp from Barbie and Baby Go-Bye Bye." He fell onto the couch, holding his middle, roaring.

"OK, laugh. But you won't be when I tell you what else they said."

He wiped tears from his eyes. "What?"

"Representative Watson is sponsoring a bill in Harrisburg that'll make toy scalping illegal in Pennsylvania." I dropped my hands to my side, shaking my head. "Rob, everyone thinks we're scum."

He walked over to me, patted my shoulder, and gave me his evil, sly Grinch smile. "Everyone except the people who are buying our toys, Ebenezer. The Sammys are flying out the door."

Rob went to the pile of toppled boxes in the corner and began stacking them. "Listen, they can pass a million laws, but if people want something badly enough, they'll do anything to get it."

After reassembling the pile, he picked his pillow off the floor and stood. "You've been outside Three Rivers Stadium before a Steelers game. It's illegal to scalp tickets, but people still do it. It's like prostitution, drugs," he paused, smirked, and plumped his pillow with a punch, "like running numbers."

"Oh, thanks for reminding me," I said. I knew he was trying to be funny, but that chapter of my life was something I'd prefer to forget.

"Look, I'm sorry I didn't get the money," I said, "but I just couldn't ask." I rooted through the laundry for a T-shirt, found one, and sniffed the armpits. It reeked of fermented sweat, but with a lot of Right Guard, it'd do. I slipped it over my head, walked over to the dresser, and searched through the top drawer for the Tylenol.

Rob sat quietly for a minute then whistled. "Man, do you believe the nerve of that chick. We discussed price and everything, and then she goes and sets you up with a news camera. We were conned, big time, my friend. They talk about us being scum—that woman is lower than the stuff growing on the shower walls."

I fought with the child-resistant lid. "I don't know. The whole thing was strange. She looked as confused as I was." Too weary to be annoyed anymore, I said, "Deduct the loss from my share of the profits."

Rob walked toward me, and I must have looked terrible because he seemed to take pity on me. He punched my arm. "Ah, don't worry about it, Tommy. Scrooge and Marley are going to make so much money—one lousy toy won't matter. Chalk it up as a business expense."

"Business expense?"

"Yeah, a publicity stunt." He walked over to the orange vinyl chair near the door, sat sideways in it, throwing a long leg over its chrome arms. "Who knows? I bet this'll even help business. Every time Sammy's name is in the news, people go nutty." Then a wide smile broke over his face. "And the price skyrockets."

I wrenched the lid off the Tylenol bottle. White pills flew out and spilled all over the floor. "Oh man," I said, grimacing and dropping to my hands and knees, scrambling to retrieve the caplets from the mess of dirty clothing. But even if I'd found and swallowed every last tablet, they couldn't have prevented the headache that was waiting off in the distance for me, beating like war drums.

Chapter 5

After Rob left for class, I put on my shoes and gathered my books. I wanted to get to the cafeteria before there was nothing left but bran muffins and prune juice. I threw on my fatigue jacket, closed and locked the door, and rushed across the small lawn to Caliguiri Hall. My hollow stomach pitched and groaned with hunger as I fought my way in the howling wind.

When I opened the cafeteria's double glass doors, a thick curtain of grease enveloped me and coated the back of my throat. I grabbed a green plastic tray. Still warm from the dishwasher, it felt great on my frozen hands. Bacon spit and sizzled on the grill behind Wilma, the cafeteria lady.

"What'll it be?" she asked in a monotone, slapping eggs, in regular intervals, on the student's plates ahead of me. An automaton would have been more enthusiastic.

Amber lights warming the toast gave the bread the appearance of having been dipped into iodine. Nothing appealed to me. The bacon and eggs seemed the least offensive to my stomach. As I reached to take the plate from Wilma, someone smacked me hard on the back; my bacon slid off the dish.

"Hey," I growled, as I retrieved the errant strips. I turned around and saw Wally Brickley, the offensive tackle who'd sat next to me in Physics I freshman year, (he's still taking the class) leap in front of me. When I saw it was Wally, I changed the tone of my voice. "How you doin', man," I said, letting him go ahead.

Wally reminded me of a dinosaur. Everything about him was huge except for his head—it was tiny like a T-Rex's. His brain was the only part of his anatomy that was underdeveloped.

"That was really cool, man," he said, taking two plates of pancakes and sausage from Wilma.

I shook my head, agreeing with him. I have a simple rule about guys twice my size: Always agree with them. Wally had taken a lot of blows to the head. God only knew what he was talking about.

I went to my usual table, the one near the window that no one else ever sat at because it wobbled. A draft whistled in between the window's casement and sleet pinged off the glass. I buttered my toast and watched the students outside scurrying across campus, their heads hunkered down inside coat collars, looking like a mutant race born without necks. I shivered and gulped the coffee, hoping the mega dose of caffeine would dilate my blood vessels and relieve the migraine.

Scattered on top of the table was a copy of *The Post-Gazette* someone had left behind. I gathered the sections and bit into a bacon strip, which shattered because it was overdone.

I scanned the classifieds for our ad. It was there along with six others. Sammy was making a lot of Christmases brighter this year.

Shuffling through the other sections of the paper, I then glanced at the front page. An article on the starving Somalians made the headlines once again. I stuck my fork into the eggs and they were so rubbery, I swear they bounced. I wished I could pack them up and ship them to Africa.

Popping another bacon shard into my mouth, I opened the paper. When I saw the picture below the fold, I swallowed the bacon whole, its sharp edges scoring the back of my throat.

On the bottom of the front page, in full-color, was a photo of me with that Davidson kid glued to my leg. A bold black headline leapt off the page: THE GOOD SHEPHERD

"Son of a—!" I pressed the picture to my chest and looked over my shoulder, to see if anyone was watching me. Luckily, no one was.

I glanced at the photo again. Folding the paper, I tucked it under my jacket, and stuffed the rest of my breakfast in my mouth. Grabbing my backpack, I dashed into the men's room across the hall and locked myself in a stall. There, I slipped the paper out of my jacket and studied the picture.

My hair was hanging in my face, concealing one of my eyes, and the layering of the color printing process was slightly out of sync making my only visible eye appear bugged-out. The photo was so awful, maybe no one would be able to recognize me. Of course, the Davidson kid looked angelic, smiling up at me. I ran my hand over my thigh where he had latched onto me yesterday, and I still felt the pressure of his hold there today.

The caption under the photo read:

Christopher Davidson, in a battle for his life, shows his appreciation to Tom Shepherd, who surprised the boy with a So Big Sammy yesterday. Story on page A-6.

Anger churned in my gut. "I could kill Ginny Davidson." I kicked the stall door.

Flipping to page six, I found the article.

Christopher Davidson, four, son of Joseph and Virginia Davidson of West View, has two hard-to-come-by items on his Christmas wish list this year—a bone marrow transplant and a So Big Sammy. Yesterday, during a blood drive and tissue screening held on his behalf, one of his wishes came true.

On Saturday, the day before the blood drive, his parents filmed an interview with reporter, Sandra Creighton, of WGRK, Channel 6 News, encouraging people to donate blood at their church, Holy Redeemer. While interviewing the Davidsons, Ms. Creighton asked Christopher what else he wanted from Santa. Christopher told her he would also like a So Big Sammy.

Santa must have been listening because during the blood drive and bone marrow donor screening for Christopher, a mysterious young man appeared at the church and gave the boy a So Big Sammy. The Channel 6 News crew had just finished filming a follow-up segment on the blood drive when the young man arrived with the toy. Fortunately, the whole episode was caught on tape. However, before anyone could get the philanthropist's name, he fled, leaving the crowd of 700 stunned.

Ruth Lawson, a neighbor of the Davidsons who was waiting in line to donate her blood, witnessed the scene.

"It was something out of a storybook—like Cinderella," said Mrs. Lawson, "only he left behind a toy instead of a glass slipper. From out of nowhere this strapping, handsome young man, appeared, gave the toy to Christo, and just vanished."

Wow! She said I was strapping and handsome. At least that was some consolation. The article continued:

"Others in the crowd speculated that the young man was an angel. Not one to let a story get away, Sandra Creighton followed the young man out of Holy Redeemer church and copied down the mystery man's license plate number as he sped away. The car belongs to Thomas P. Shepherd, 22, of Pittsburgh, a senior physics major at Three Rivers University."

Man, not only did she find out my name, but my age, my major, and where I go to school. Why did she stop there? Why didn't they

31

print that I favored boxers over briefs and had no cavities at my last dental checkup?

The article concluded with quotes from the kid's parents, telling how grateful they were and the boy's reaction to his gift. The last paragraph of the piece made the eggs and bacon in my stomach turn a somersault.

The pastor of Holy Redeemer, Rev. Robert Moran, remarked that, "truly this young man is filled with the spirit of God and follows His command to love one another."

I deposited my breakfast in the toilet.

After rinsing my mouth at the sink, I crumpled the paper and threw it into the trash on my way out of the bathroom. Cutting across campus, I made my way to the bookstore for my nine to noon shift.

As I walked into The Three R's Book Store, Rajiv Venkataraman, the middle-aged manager, was standing near the front rubbing out fingerprints on the store's windows.

"Good Morning to you, Thomas," he said in that high-pitched questioning way that is distinctive to Indians. He always sounds like he's tiptoeing over hot coals.

"Morning," I grumbled. He smiled, his white piano key teeth dazzling in contrast to his brown skin. "You will be pleased to know that a large shipment arrived early this morning."

Only he would think I'd be happy to know that a ton of boxes were waiting for me in the stockroom. I certainly was *not* pleased to know that. Not this morning.

I walked into the stockroom, hung up my jacket, and punched the time clock. Boxes stacked everywhere made it difficult to move. This was not the day to be hauling boxes around. Since I hadn't had a decent meal since yesterday, I was a quart low on blood sugar. I found a utility knife, tucked it into my back pocket, and began to make sense of the mountain of cartons.

I was alone in the stockroom. Bob and Jean, the other students who worked at the store, were manning the cash registers. I needed some time, pardon the pun, to digest what had happened.

A little after ten, I lugged a carton from the stockroom, slit the packing tape, and pulled out some Anthropology books to shelve when I heard a commotion in the front of the store. Three reporters, each accompanied by cameramen, were storming up the aisle. "No! Pardon me!" Rajiv cried, waving his arms and trying to push them back out the door.

"Tom Shepherd!" At the sound of her voice, I froze. It was Sandra Creighton, Walnut Head. Dropping the books, I reached around to my back pocket, pulled out the utility knife, and went into a crouch, hoping the sight of a weapon would deter her. But she kept on charging.

"Aaaaah," I screamed and dropped the knife, it clanked on the tile floor and skittered away as I ran into the stockroom and locked the door behind me.

Boom. Boom. Boom. Fists beat the door. "Tom Shepherd." Sandra Creighton and the others were shouting my name.

Rajiv, his voice so shrill it almost evaporated in the air, called, "This will not do. I am sincerely sorry, but I must ask you to please leave."

I braced my back against the door, feeling the force of their pounding through the wood. Then the cavalry arrived in the form of Willis McGee, the store's security guard. His baritone voice thundered above the chaos. Willis moonlights at the bookstore when he's off duty from his other job, guarding the cons at Western Penitentiary. He's a six-foot, five-inch solid block of black marble, who used to scare the daylights out of me until I discovered him one day in the back of the store reading romance novels. Willis was politely instructing the reporters to leave.

After much squabbling, things quieted, and then I heard a knock on the door. "Little pig, little pig, you can come out now." Willis laughed. "I done chased the big bad wolf away."

Slowly, I opened the door and slunk out. Rajiv stood next to Willis, his hands folded in front of his chest like he was praying. "Is there some problem, Thomas?" Rajiv asked. "Why is the news media so interested in you?" His onyx eyes lit up. "Ah, perhaps you have won the lottery?"

"This is why they're after Tom," Willis said, handing Rajiv a copy of *The Post-Gazette*. "I was standing by the racks checking out this morning's headlines when the reporters came bustin' in." Willis turned to me. "Seems, ol' Tom, here is a regular Andrew Car-nay-gee."

Rajiv quickly scanned the article. When he looked back at me, his eyes were misty. "This is a good thing that you do, Thomas," Rajiv said, patting the picture of me and that kid. "You know, there is an old saying—"

"Oh, Rajiv, save the karmic crap for another day," I said. "I'm in no mood today for quotes from '*The Gita*' or *The Upanishads* . . . ."

"There is an old saying . . . " he continued. "What goes around comes around." Both Willis and I laughed. "This good deed that you have done, it will someday return to you."

"Well, Rajiv," I said, "there's another old saying: 'No good deed goes unpunished.'"

"Ah, Thomas, all the time you are so negative. It is not good. You should strive for the middle road, for balance."

"I was born negative, Rajiv. I can't help it."

"Oh, but you can. Perhaps if you looked deeply within yourself. Yoga might—"

"I told you before, Rajiv, I have no desire to twist myself like a pipe cleaner in order to discover the meaning of life."

Rajiv shook his head. "Ugh, you may think this amusing, but I am speaking to you in earnest. You are a scientist, Thomas? That is correct?"

"Yeah."

"Then surely you realize that nature must have balance. Man is balanced with woman, summer with winter, protons with electrons, life with death. And you, Thomas, what is your balance?"

I shrugged.

"What happens when a negative encounters a positive?"

"When a negative meets with a positive," I replied snottily, "they annihilate one another."

"Annihilate? No! No! No! They complement one another. You too, Thomas, one day you will meet your positive. Fate will see to it."

"Well," Willis said, slapping Rajiv on the back, "You're not the first to say ol' Tom's off-balanced."

"Someday you will learn," Rajiv said, spreading his hands like some Hindu god. "The universe is bound by strict laws, laws that cannot be denied."

"Hey, you don't have to tell me about the universe," I said. "I've been studying it all my life."

"Stars and moons and planets are not what I refer to." Rajiv closed his eyes, and the look of serenity that settled on his face led me to believe that he'd entered that "middle state" he talked about so much. "There is a subtle universe, Thomas. One of peace, love, and joy. Only an enlightened few have ever fully experienced it. Most of us, while in this existence, only achieve mere glimpses of that realm. Still, it is very real, more real than the physical plane you experience now. Strive for moderation. Find the balance, Thomas. Then you will see."

May the force be with you too, Obie-won Kenobi.

He opened his eyes and glanced toward the front of the store where the reporters had encamped outside on the sidewalk. "Unfortunately, Thomas, I do not think you will find that balance with the press swarming about like hungry locusts." Rajiv patted me on the shoulder. "Today, I think you will not be able to work. Perhaps it is best for you to go back to your dormitory." He then turned to Willis. "And you, Mr. Security, I will rely on you to keep the reporters out of the store so that they do not drive away our poor customers." Rajiv turned and walked away.

"I think you'd better sneak out the back, Tom," said Willis. He escorted me to the stockroom where I put on my jacket and pulled up my collar. Willis punched my time card and opened the back door for me. As I was about to step out into the alley, he cleared his throat. "Ah, I never told any of you this, but I had a younger brother, Derrick. When I was eleven, he died. From leukemia."

Willis peered down the alley, pretending to look for reporters, so that I couldn't see his eyes when he spoke. I may not have been able to see them, but I could see the crack in the marble; it ran straight to his heart. He shifted his gaze to me. "Stuff like you done, Tom, makes a big difference to sick kids and their families. Let me tell you. Ol' Willis has been there." He pushed me out the door. "Now you better get your sorry ass out of here before I have to rescue it again." The door slammed behind me.

Chapter 6

When I walked into the dorm, Phil, the Security Guard, waved me over to his station adjacent to the lounge. As I stood at the chest-high counter, the "Price Is Right" blared from the mini TV he kept hidden beneath the ledge. He's not supposed to watch the tube while on duty. "Hey, wanted to warn you, Shepherd. There was a babe here asking about you." His eyes never left the screen.

"What'd she look like?"

Phil flew back in the chair. "Will you look at that." He stabbed a finger at the TV. "Any moron knows Rice-A-Roni don't cost no $3.50 a box. Where'd they get this lunkhead from?"

"Phil, the woman?"

"Oh, it was that news broad from Channel 6. What's her name? Cindy . . . Sandy . . ."

"Sandra Creighton?"

"Yeah, that's the one." I hoped he was never called in to ID a criminal. "I didn't let her in," Phil said with an air of authority. I felt so secure with him on duty. "But, hey, she wasn't too bad lookin'. Maybe I should a let her in, huh?" Phil laughed, the buttons on his uniform working overtime to keep his shirt together over his quaking belly. "What she want with you, Shepherd?"

"Thanks, Phil," I said, but he didn't hear me. He was too busy screaming at the TV, yelling at Bob Barker and the little yodeler to stop before the yodeler fell over the cliff's edge.

When I arrived at my room, I found a note sticking to the door written in Rob's unmistakable handwriting. It said: *I'm your agent.*

37

"Agent? I plucked the note off and heard the phone ringing inside. I riffled through my pockets for my keys, unlocked the door, and as I stepped into the room, the answering machine clicked on.

"Hey, we're not in right now." Rob's voice said. *"If you're gorgeous, leave a number. If you're a dog, call the pound."*

He thinks that message is hysterical; I think it's embarrassing, but no one calls me anyway. So what can I say?

At the beep, a perky voice filled the room. "Hi! Um . . . I'm calling for Tom Shepherd. This is Cassandra at the Pittsburgh Zoo. We're shooting some new promos, and we'd be interested in your doing some publicity photos for our primate house. Please call 1-800 SEE-APES. Thanks!"

Publicity photos? What was she talking about? I went over to the machine to replay the message and on top of the desk was a mosaic of yellow sticky notes left by Rob.

There was "Call Randy, *River Watch* wants an interview." *River Watch* was the school newspaper. There were four messages from Sandra Creighton and one from the mayor's office about me being Grand Marshall of the city's St. Patrick's Day parade. *The North Hills News Record* called requesting an interview as well as *The Tribune Review* and *USA Today*. Someone from the Penguins' office left a message about me dropping a ceremonial puck in a face-off for an upcoming game, and the Steelers also called to invite me to be their guest at this Sunday's game against Seattle.

There were messages from someone named Quinn Cavanaugh from the VFW. He wanted me to speak at their meeting. Radio talk show host, Mark Thornton, left a message as well as a nun named Sr. Mary Euphemia. Her message said she wanted me to address her youth group on the subject "How Important Young People are in the Body of Christ."

Everyone wanted a piece of "The Good Shepherd." Too bad there was no such fool. I threw the messages into the trash and took off my jacket.

On Mondays, I didn't have a class until two o'clock, so I locked myself in the room. The phone rang constantly, but I didn't dare answer it. My headache threatened a resurrection, so I downed another dose of Tylenol, and to stave off my hunger, ate a stale bag of potato chips that had been sitting on the dresser for over a week—the perfect lunch for a queasy stomach.

At 1:45, as I was putting my jacket on, a thought occurred to me. Opening the window above the desk, I stuck my head outside into the winter air and craned my neck to see the entrance to the dorm. My instincts were right. Five stories below, a huddle of people and a camera with the Channel 6 logo had staked out the front of the place. Thank goodness Phil hadn't let them upstairs. Wouldn't they have had a great lead for the nightly news if they'd come up to my room and discovered the stash of Sammys and that I scalped them? From now on, I'd have to be very careful.

I rooted around in the bottom of our closet until I found a scarf and cap. The cap had a mask knitted into it, and I considered wearing it, but I was afraid I might be mistaken for a terrorist or a bank robber and wind up getting shot. I pulled the cap over my head and wrapped up my face with the scarf. To avoid the reporters, I went down to the first floor lounge, opened a back window, and crawled out.

I made it to class without any of the press-vultures spotting me. Relaxing a little now that I was in a classroom, I began to unwind— literally.

My Theoretical Physics class was soothingly boring until the President of the University, Dr. Dillington, walked in, interrupted my professor, and called me down to the front of the hall to shake my hand. Then he made a speech about how "Three Rivers University has always taken pride in its fine students and the citizens it molds."

Funny, the only other sign of pride Dr. Dillington has ever shown in me before this was the overdue tuition bills he sent.

The students in my class clapped, but it wasn't in appreciation of me. It was that wise-guy kind of clapping. I know when I'm being made the butt of a joke. I wished that I'd kept my face wrapped to hide my red cheeks.

When class was over, Tiffany Ruckles, the 250-pound girl who sat in my row of the lecture hall, that we referred to as Tough Tiffy, squeezed past me and placed a note on my desk. I unfolded the slip of paper. She had scrawled her phone number.

Shuddering, I shoved the note in my folder. As I stood to leave, I noticed her lurking in the doorway at the bottom of the hall. She waved at me. I turned and ran to the top of the lecture hall and left through the upper exit.

All over the campus, wherever I went, people baaed like sheep in reference to the "Good Shepherd" headline. My stomach rumbled. I was running on fumes. Desperate for food, I headed to the nearest place to eat, The Student Union, where there was a deli in the basement

When I entered the boxy glass and metal Union building unnoticed, I thought I'd escaped my tormenters. I pushed the elevator button and waited, watching the numbers above it light in descending order.

The elevator doors parted. I started into it but stopped—it was packed full of girls. As I backed up so they could exit, one of them recognized me and yelled, "Hey, he's the guy from the paper." Another one grabbed my arm, giggling, "Come on in here, Shepherd, and we'll see just how good you are!"

I yanked my arm way and ran as the girls erupted in laughter.

Sprinting to the nearest exit, I found myself standing inside a cold stairwell. Looking up the ladder work of metal and concrete stairs, I wondered where I should go? What I should do? And then another, more crucial question, the girls' question, *How good are you?* blotted out all the others.

And over the next few weeks, that question would be one I'd come to ask myself over and over.

Chapter 7

I couldn't stay in the cold stairwell forever. Then I remembered—the fourth floor. At one end of it were campus club offices, but on the other was a small lounge situated outside a chapel. No one ever goes in there; they should turn it into a something more useful like a pinball arcade. I've hung out in that lounge a few times before when Rob was getting on my nerves.

After climbing the four flights, my quadriceps felt loose like the elastic on an old pair of underwear. I'm in good shape; years of running high school cross-country and track left me fit, but even Roger Kingdom can't function without food. After it got dark, maybe I could sneak to my car and hit a drive-through.

I tiptoed down the corridor past the campus offices. Some of the doors were open. Voices echoed from inside the *River Watch* office, but no one noticed me creeping by.

When I reached the lounge, it was deserted as I'd expected. Outside the chapel, a labyrinth of couches and chairs sat clustered in small conversation groups. I selected a leather love seat that faced the chapel's door and plopped my books on it.

The Tylenol was wearing off. Before the throbbing intensified, I needed to calm down, figure out a way to get back to the dorm, get something to eat, and deal with this "Good Shepherd" garbage.

I took off the hat, the scarf, and unzipped my fatigue jacket, but kept it on in case I needed to make a fast getaway. Hiking the collar up around my ears to prevent anyone from recognizing me by the back of my head, I collapsed onto the couch, sinking deeply into the spongy cushions. If this is what fame is like, then Andy Warhol can have my fifteen minutes back.

I sighed. How did I wind up in such a mess? All I wanted to do was make a few bucks and enjoy a nice Spring Break. Who would have dreamed this would happen?

Suddenly, my face felt warm. I touched my cheek, checking for a fever. Maybe it wasn't a migraine after all. Maybe I was getting sick. Maybe all this stress had impaired my immune system, and I was getting the flu.

Then I noticed columns of light slanting in through the Union's floor-to-ceiling windows, spilling over my face and the couch. Ah, the sun. The day had been so insane, I hadn't noticed that the cloudy, ferocious morning had mellowed into a cold, but sunny afternoon.

I gazed out the window, across campus, toward downtown Pittsburgh, and it sparkled like a fairy tale city as the sun reflected off the building in sharp diamonds. So crystal clear was the day, it seemed as if with one tiny tap the whole world might shatter into a million glassy shards.

Circling my neck, I loosened my knotted muscles, and my spine let out a series of cracks that sounded like they came from a ratchet. The sun on my face was the medicine I needed.

Specks of dust floated on the sun's beams. I liked watching the dust; it was soothing, like observing a parallel universe—a universe that always existed but was only revealed by the light.

As I watched the motes sliding down the rays, I felt unnaturally relaxed, as if someone had tapped one of my veins and dripped in Valium. My eyelids sagged and closed and my muscles slackened as the tension flowed out. And I felt as if I'd evaporated, that I'd been dissolved into the smallest particles and had been absorbed into the light, until I was no longer me but part of the light too.

"Tom Shepherd?" A female voice was calling my name. Relaxed now, it sounded as if I were hearing the call from deep inside a well.

"Tom Shepherd?"

My muscles kinked, breaking the spell. Why can't they leave me alone? I didn't want to open my eyes for fear it might be Tough Tiffy, so I pretended that I was asleep.

"Tom . . . Tom Shepherd?" The voice was drawing closer.

"Yeah?" I raised my lids. The glare burned my eyes. I squinted, making out a figure standing before me in the dazzling sunlight. From her slender silhouette, I knew it wasn't Tough Tiffy.

42

Shadow concealed the girl's features, but around her profile a golden aura glowed and her long blond curls captured the light; her hair radiated around her shrouded face like a corona.

At first I thought that an aneurysm had burst in my brain, that I was dying. As she approached, the halo around her shimmered, making the girl seem more like a mirage.

I dug my heels into the floor, scooting up straighter in my seat. Beneath my hands, I felt the cushions, so I knew I was still alive.

When the girl stood directly over me, she turned slightly and the sun struck and illuminated her face. I gasped. She was otherworldly beautiful, and every cell in my body rushed at my skin wanting to break free of me and cling to her.

Her face was princess-perfect, with creamy skin, full, pink lips and delicate features. And her green eyes, as they smiled at me, sparkled like a Rolling Rock bottle set on a sunny window sill.

"Oh, I can't believe I've found you!" she exclaimed. I tugged at my jacket to keep it from riding up around my ears. "Do you mind if I take a seat?"

Mind? Take a seat! A kidney! My heart! Whatever this goddess wanted from me, she could have it.

"Ah . . . no," I said, hoping she didn't hear the tremble in my voice. I quickly made room for her beside me on the love seat. Sweeping the hair out of my eyes, I watched as the Incarnation of Beauty herself flung off her backpack and sat.

She wore a bulky white, full-length down parka, but instinctively I knew that underneath was a body that could make your teeth ache with desire. After a few seconds of gazing at her, I turned my head. She was like looking at a solar eclipse; I was afraid I'd damage my retinas.

"Oh, this is absolutely incredible!" she said, laying her hands on her cheeks. A wonderful scent, sweet and vanilla-like, rose from her. She smelled delicious like a bakery. "This is awesome. You've been on my mind all day."

Me? I'd never even seen this girl before.

"In fact, you'll never believe this, but I was just in the chapel praying that I'd find some way to get in touch with you. Then lo and behold, I come out and there you are, sitting right outside the door." She shook her head. "It's like I was supposed to find you. There's a name for that . . . " She bit a nail and thought for a moment. "Oh, what's it called?" She snapped her fingers. "Synchronicity. I think that's the word. Well, whatever you call it—isn't that wild?" Her eyes blazed like solar flares.

"Yeah, that is." I wanted to ask her why I'd been on her mind, but she never gave me the opportunity; words flowed from her before I could ask.

"Oh, I'm so happy I ran into you. Now I can thank you."

"Thank me? For what?"

"Christo Davidson is my cousin."

My jaw dropped. How could someone so perfect be related to that sick kid? Too shocked to come up with an intelligent reply, I stuttered, "R-really?"

"Yes. And you don't know how much your giving Christo that toy means to him and to our family." She touched her fingertips to her lips, hesitating before speaking.

Tears welled in her eyes giving them a watery look like an impressionist's painting of spring grass that I'd seen in one of my mother's old art book. She moved her hand away.

"Yes," she said, her voice brimming with emotion, "it's so hard watching him suffer. But . . . but thanks to you, you've made things a little easier for him."

Her long, slim fingers dabbed at the corners of her eyes. Her nails were short and painted pink.

"I'm sorry," she said, fishing a tissue from her pocket and blotting the tears. "What you did was so beautiful. It makes me cry."

I looked at my hands, and picked at an old paper cut on my thumb. I knew I should say something, but I didn't know what. I couldn't tell her it was all a big misunderstanding, that I had no intention of giving the toy to her cousin, that I had been at the church only to sell it. That I'm really the bad shepherd. She would think I was scum. And how could I disappoint her? After all it was synchronicity, wasn't it?

"Oh, it was nothing," I said quietly. And that wasn't a lie. I really had done nothing. It had all happened to me. I'd been the victim.

I don't know if the sun became more intense or what, but as she spoke about the episode at Holy Redeemer, moisture began collecting under my arms, reconstituting the old perspiration dried into the fabric of my dirty T-shirt. My b.o. rose out of the jacket. Of course, I meet the most beautiful girl in the galaxy and don't you know I smell like a sweat sock. I hoped my jacket trapped the odor inside so she couldn't smell it too.

"Oh, yes it is," she said. "You don't know how much Christo wanted that toy. But we couldn't find one anywhere. And wow, the prices those scalpers were asking . . ." She rolled her eyes. "But thanks to you, he has one now."

Taking a deep breath, I raked my hands through my hair and then crossed my arms, tucking my palms into my armpits, in hopes of containing my stench. "Well," I said, "I have a half-brother who's small and seeing little Christopher on TV—well, it just ripped my heart out."

I tried to conjure some tears, and the fumes emanating from inside my jacket made them easy to produce. As I blinked back the phony droplets, I made my voice somber, "I had to do something."

"Oh, how kind of you. When you gave the So Big Sammy to Christo, I was in the kitchen pouring orange juice. All I saw was the back of you running out the door. Afterward, my family felt terrible that they never got your name."

I looked off into the distance, trying to appear humble. "I prefer to remain anonymous."

"Wow, how admirable. I haven't met many guys like you. Most are so selfish. You're a real humanitarian like . . . like Mother Theresa."

Heat rushed to my cheeks. I have a propensity for blushing and it annoys me to no end. "Thank you," I said meekly, picking at the paper cut again.

"Oh, I've embarrassed you. I'm sorry."

"That's OK. I'm just not used to the attention. That's why I like to keep my charity work a secret."

I felt terrible for b.s.ing her, especially since she was so sincere, but I had no other choice. She was too beautiful not to lie to her.

"Well, it's selfish on my part," she confided, "but I'm glad Sandra Creighton tracked you down. And when I read in this morning's paper you went to TRU too, I just about flipped."

"You go to school at TRU? And your cousin is Christopher Davidson? That's . . . " I couldn't find a word to explain it. Then it popped into my head.

"Synchronicity." We said the word in unison and laughed.

She sat for a moment, looking out the windows, and then she pivoted on the couch, so that she faced me. I expected her to speak, but she said nothing. She only gazed deeply into my eyes like she was searching for something, hunting for the core of me. Then suddenly, she placed her hand on top of mine. Her skin was soft and smooth, and when she touched me, all my fidgeting stopped as if she possessed some supernatural power that enabled her to drain all the tension from me.

Hypnotized with desire, I stared into her eyes. Her pupils were black holes that attracted and consumed everything that fell under their gaze. I felt myself being sucked into them, swallowed by them. She squeezed my hand. "Thank you, Tom."

Her words struck the essence of me and rang throughout my heart.

She released my hand, patted the top of it, and said, "I'd better go now."

Dumbstruck, I sat there staring at my hand. She had unleashed a power surge in my body, short-circuiting my electrical system. My neurons misfired and my synapses sparked as my heart pounded out of sync with my breathing. As I watched her rise and sling her backpack over her shoulder, the nerves in my body arced wildly like downed utility lines. I wanted to react but was paralyzed.

She turned and walked toward the elevator, disappearing back into the sunlight from where she had come to me. And like an idiot, I sat watching as this wonderful creature walked out of my life.

Then something clicked and turned over in my brain. A whooshing sound filled my head as a drawing of power gathered energy and then released it in a great tingling rush throughout my body. Springing to my feet, I cried, "Wait!"

She pressed the elevator button and looked over her shoulder.

"Wait! Please wait," I sprinted after her. When I reached her, I was breathless. "I don't even know your name."

She threw her head back, laughing, revealing straight, pearly teeth, that St. Peter would have been proud to have adorning the Gates of Heaven. "Now, I'm the mystery person, dashing out without leaving a name. It's Gloria . . . Gloria Davidson."

Gloria. Ah, what a perfect name for her.

I've never been suave with girls, but the new energy pulsing within me made me bold. "Can I walk you to your dorm?" I asked. "I'd like to see you again." I didn't want to sound too desperate; I was afraid she'd realize what a geek I really was, so I quickly added, "and to hear how the little guy, Christopher, is doing . . . his progress."

"I don't live on campus," she said. "I commute." She glanced at her watch. "And if I don't get moving, I'm going to miss my bus." She opened her backpack and found a sheet of paper and pen. "Here's my number," she said. "What's yours?"

Her phone number, the Holy Grail, I had it in my hand. I was so shook up, my brain had trouble recalling my number. Pushing my hair back, I recited it while she copied it down.

"I'm sorry, but I've really got to leave now," she said. "I can't wait for the elevator." She shoved my phone number into her coat pocket and started toward the stairs.

I trailed behind. "When can I call you? Can we meet for lunch? How about tomorrow? Twelve-thirty is fine with me, if that's fine with you?"

As Gloria tap-danced down the steps, she looked over her shoulder and said, "I can make it. Where will we meet?"

I thought for a moment. "How about The Parlor?"

When we came to the landing, I hoped that the door was locked and that we would be trapped in the stairwell together forever. But when I pushed on it, the stupid door opened.

"Sounds great," Gloria said, as she hurried past me in a cloud of vanilla scent. "My class is finished at noon. Sometimes it runs over. I'll call if I'm going to be late."

I smiled. "OK, see you then."

She pulled on her gloves and turned back to look at me. "You know you should smile more often," she said as she walked way. "That picture of you in the paper was terrible. You've got great dimples; they light up your whole face." She turned, threw the hood of her coat up over her head, waved goodbye, and scurried off.

Holding the door, I watched her walking away until she was only a dot of white on the horizon. And then she vanished like a shooting star.

I stepped back inside, and the metal door closed behind me with a loud thunk. I looked at the slip of paper in my hand to make sure it was real. The paper was real. She was real. All of this was real. I pounded the door and let out a "whoop" that echoed up and shook the four flights of stairs.

Chapter 8

I went upstairs, gathered my books, and stuffed the scarf and hat into my jacket pocket. I no longer cared who recognized me. I had a date.

If people stared or baaed at me as I made my way back to the dorm, I didn't notice. To tell you the truth, I don't even remember how I got back there. I could have flown. The way I felt after meeting Gloria, anything seemed possible.

Arriving at my room, I switched on the lights and the spot on my hand where she had touched me pulsed with a mystical beat. I swear Gloria altered me genetically.

The answering machine's red light was blinking, but I ignored it. As I was taking off my jacket, the phone rang, but I ignored that too. Throwing my jacket on the bed, I stripped off my ripe T-shirt, gathered the laundry, and hurried down to the laundry room where I loaded the bank of washing machines. Tomorrow I didn't want to be sitting at lunch with Gloria wondering if my clothes smelled.

I had a date. When I thought of Gloria, my blood effervesced as if someone had pumped carbon dioxide into me. A date with her was more than payback for what had happened to me at Holy Redeemer.

After returning from the laundry room, I popped a Pat Metheny CD into the player, opened my books, and began studying, but my brain drifted from quantum mechanics to Gloria.

The doorknob rattled. Rob opened the door, strolled in, and before he told me, I knew from the smell of French fries and the aroma

49

of fresh bread that he'd made a run to Primanti's. He placed a bag before me on the desk.

"You haven't eaten, have you?"

"No," I said, closing my books. My stomach growled. Until I smelled the food, I'd forgotten how hungry I was. "Thanks. How much do I owe you?"

Rob glanced around the room. "You doing laundry?"

"Yeah."

He looked surprised. "What's up?"

"Nothing's up." I pulled out my wallet and extracted a five-dollar bill. "I needed clean clothes, that's all." I didn't want him to find out about my date in case things didn't work out with Gloria.

"Yeah. So. That never made you do laundry before." He tossed his coat on the chair. "What's really going on?"

"*Nothing.*" I waved the money in front of his face, hoping it would divert his attention the way it usually does.

"It's on me."

"Huh?" He never treats. He always figures out my share down to the penny, including the tax. Maybe this was a peace offering, his way of smoothing over this morning's argument.

"Yeah, we're celebrating."

"Celebrating?" My eyes shot to the Mellon Bank calendar hanging on the wall to see if I'd forgotten a holiday.

"Yeah, man." He slapped me on the back. "Everywhere I went today people were talking about 'The Good Shepherd,' asking me if I knew you. You da man, Ebenezer." He moved my books aside. "Where'd you put the messages?"

I pointed to the trash. "In there."

"What did you do that for?" Rob began digging around in the can. He pulled out the crumpled wad of messages and held them in front of my face. "You're a hero. Your public is crying out for you."

"I'm no hero." I pulled the sandwich from the bag and unwrapped it. The smell made my mouth water. Primanti's made their sandwiches by piling the cole slaw and French fries on top of the meat. I picked up the enormous sandwich and opened my mouth to take a bite.

"According to *Good Morning America* you are."

My jaw froze, the sandwich suspended in front of my face. I turned my head. "What'd you say?"

"*Good Morning America.* They called. Didn't you see the note?" Rob went to my bunk, lifted my jacket, and pulled a sheet of paper from under it. "I purposely put this note on your bed so it wouldn't get lost in

50

the other messages." He slapped the paper down in front of me. "While you were out, a producer called. They heard about 'The Good Shepherd.' Joan Lunden wants to interview you. They want to fly you to New York."

"No." I set the sandwich down. "No way." I pushed the note off the desk. "I can't."

"Can't?" He picked the paper off the floor. "What do you mean, you can't?" The phone rang. Rob reached behind me to pick it up.

"Don't answer it," I cried, throwing my body over the ringing phone like it was a live grenade.

"What is wrong with you?" he yelled, stretching around me to reach the receiver. I grabbed his wrist and we wrestled on the desk until Rob kicked me in the shin and broke free.

"You jerk," I cried as my leg gave out. He lifted the receiver, but I quickly lunged and hit the disconnect button.

Rob slammed the phone down, looking at me with murder in his eyes. A harpoon of four letter words shot from his mouth. I collapsed into the desk chair, rubbing my leg.

Throwing his hands into the air, he turned his back on me and stormed across the room. When he faced me again, his complexion was the color of grape juice. He marched over to me, huffing. I smelled grease on his breath. Stabbing a finger in my face, he spoke with fragile control: "I don't know what's going on, but as your agent, I'm advising you that you've got to do that interview."

"Agent? Are you insane? I don't need a agent."

"Oh, yes you do. Listen, Tommy," he said, "if you play this thing right, we could make a killing." He rubbed his hands together greedily, reminding me of a horsefly sitting on a pile of dog crap. "I see book deals and movies."

"Get out of here." I turned and faced the window.

"No. I'm serious. It's a great story. Young college student gives toy to dying kid. Remember that baby Jessica, who fell down that pipe? They made a movie about that. You're a sensation. I say we demand Tom Cruise."

"Demand him for what?"

"Your part. He's shorter than you, but they can work magic in Hollywood—put lifts in his shoes or something."

"You've totally lost it."

"No, I'm serious. You're the Tom Cruise type."

"Tom Cruise?" I looked over my shoulder at him. "You really think so?"

"For sure."

I swiveled the chair and scrutinized my reflection in the window, and I must admit there was a resemblance.

"Does Tom Cruise have dimples?" I asked, smiling and regarding my cheeks.

"As deep as the potholes on West Carson Street."

"Girls are wild about him too, aren't they?"

"Oh yeah. All he has to do is wink and the babes keel over." Rob came and stood behind my chair, his face joining mine in the window. "And for me, I was thinking along the lines of Jeff Goldblum." He turned his head from side to side, admiring himself. "He's tall, dark, and handsome. Like me. Now, all we need is a beautiful girl—a love interest."

Beautiful love interest? Suddenly, I remembered Gloria and that broke Rob's seductive spell. I shoved him. "What have you been smoking? There's not going to be any movies because I'm not doing any interviews, public appearances—nothing."

"You're crazy. Opportunities like this don't come along every day, pal."

"Look, get this through your thick skull," I stood and rapped on his head. It sounded hollow like a coconut. He backed away, but I followed. "I don't need an agent! I'm not going to New York! I'm not doing interviews! Period! I just want to be left alone." I slumped back into the chair.

Rob stood there staring at me. I'd never flipped out on him before, and to be honest, my outburst had shocked me too. Clasping the back of my neck, I wrapped my elbows around my ears, like I was bracing for a bomb to detonate. "Oh man, if anyone ever finds out that I'm selling Sammys, I swear, I'm dead."

Rob sighed and sat on his bunk. I felt bad for screaming at him after he had bought me dinner. I dropped my arms to my side. "Look, Rob, I know you're trying to help, but I can't do interviews, appear at Penguin games, be parade marshal—nothing. And I can't deliver Sammys anymore either. I'll do everything else—negotiate deals over the phone—but you're going to have to deliver them by yourself. No one can find out I'm involved in toy scalping."

"OK," Rob said, shaking his head, "don't do the interview. Don't do anything." He pursed his lips and sat quietly for a few seconds. "But what I can't understand is why you care if people find out that you sell toys."

"Why do I care?" My teeth hurt from clenching them. "I'll tell you why. You have no idea what this day's been like."

I stood and began pacing. "Everywhere I went today, people were treating me like I'd walked on water or something. Do you know what it feels like to be congratulated for something good that you didn't intend to do? I'll tell you—you feel like crap. Then there were the idiots. People baaing, making a fool out of me." I went to the desk, reached for a piece of paper stuck inside my folder, and pulled it out. My voice grew shriller. "Just look at this," I shoved the paper under his nose. "Even Tough Tiffy is after me." I crumpled the paper and fired it at the bunks and drained, fell back into the chair. "And then Gloria comes along, and she's thanking me, telling me to smile, and touching me."

Rob walked over and grabbed my shoulder. "Calm down, man. OK, if you don't want to deliver Sammys anymore, then don't. You can play it cool."

Rob walked over to a brown bag he'd left sitting on the chair near the door. He pulled out a Rolling Rock from the plastic packing rings and handed it to me. "I bought this too, and man, I'd say you sure could use one." He opened a beer for himself and took a sip. "You know what your problem is, Tommy," he said, waving his can at me, "you think too much. You got too much of a conscience."

The insanity of the last two days had left me exhausted; I didn't feel like discussing my character flaws.

Rob picked up the paper I'd thrown at the bunks. "Hey, who's this Tough Tiffy? Do I know her?"

"You know her," I said, popping the top on my beer. "She's that chick whose old man owns that Harley dealership in Wexford. She rides a bike to school."

"You mean that heifer? That's the chick that's after you?"

"That's the one."

"Ugh," Rob said, dropping her note as if it had been contaminated with radiation.

I took a sip of beer and heard it splash when it hit my empty stomach.

"No wonder you're upset."

"Oh, that's not all. Then there were all these girls laughing at me, saying dirty things." I leaned the cold can against my temples.

Rob's eyes widened and made his voice as soft as a golf commentator's. "Ooh, what'd they say?"

"I'm not telling you." I set the beer down and picked up my sandwich again.

Rob turned and walked away, shaking his head. "I don't get you, Tommy. Most guys would love to have girls talk nasty to them." He took a seat near the door.

"Not if they're doing it to make a fool out of you, you wouldn't."

Rob thought about that comment. We both knew he'd still like the girls to talk dirty to him no matter what.

I opened my mouth to take a bite of my sandwich when Rob asked, "So who's this Gloria you mentioned?"

A French fry fell from the end of my sandwich, plopping onto the wrapper. I'd hoped he hadn't heard me before when I was shooting my mouth off and Gloria's name had slipped out. I picked up the fry and stuffed it back into the bun. "She's just a girl I met today." Merely mentioning her name made me tingle all over. Against my will, I felt the corners of my mouth curling into a smirk.

"What do you mean 'just a girl'?"

"She's just a girl."

"Yeah, right," Rob said, slapping his thigh. He pulled his chair over to mine; its legs scraping the tile floor. "Tell Dr. Ruth all about her. Is she a babe?"

"Get out of here." I kicked the chair away.

He pulled it closer again. "Must be a real bow-wow."

"So much you know. Babe doesn't even come close." I unleashed the smile I'd been restraining. Rob leaned in like an old woman sitting under a dryer in a beauty salon straining to hear the latest gossip. "She's awesome—

"Awesome? What does she look like?"

"Well, she has long blond curly hair . . ."

"Blond," he repeated zombie-like.

"And big green eyes . . . "

"Green eyes."

"She's tall and—"

He bolted upright in the chair. "What does she want with you, Tommy?"

I ignored his question, but I'd been asking myself the same thing.

"The sick kid I gave the Sammy to. . . Well, he's her cousin. She came to thank me. She thinks I'm some kind of saint."

"She doesn't know that you were there to sell the toy?"

"No. And if I can help it, she never will."

"How'd you explain what you were doing at that church then?"

"I kind of led her to believe that I came there to give it to him."

"You lied to her?"

"Well . . . no. I didn't lie to her. I just sort of went along with her and exaggerated a tiny bit. I had to." Rob waited to be spoon-fed more information. I closed my eyes, imagining Gloria. "Ah man, Rob, she's like no one I've ever met before. I felt lit up just sitting next to her. Oh, and then when she touched my hand— It was metaphysical."

I opened my eyes. Beads of sweat glistened above Rob's upper lip like rain on a newly-waxed car hood. He gulped, his pointy Adam's apple bobbing in his neck, and let out a big puff of air. "She touched your hand? I bet you were lit up." He tugged at his T-shirt. "Wow, I'm on fire just hearing about her." He chugged the rest of his beer.

"Now you see why no one can find out what I was really doing at Holy Redeemer and why I can't deliver Sammys anymore? I feel bad, Rob, sticking you with all the deliveries, but I have no choice. There's one good thing though. I never said anything while the camera was on me so no one knows what my voice sounds like. I can still make deals over the phone, but that's it. No one can connect me with toy scalping. She can never find out."

"But what do you care if she finds out? You're never going to see her again," he said.

I leaned back in the chair and smiled. "Oh, but I am. She goes to school here . . . and I'm taking her to lunch tomorrow."

Finally, I sank my teeth into the sandwich, biting off a large chunk, stuffing my mouth so full that I could barely chew.

Rob jumped out of the chair and held up his hand for a high five. "Way to go, Romeo!"

When I slapped his hand, I began to choke. I'd stuffed my mouth too full. And soon, I'd find out that the sandwich wasn't the only thing from which I'd bitten off more than I could chew.

Chapter 9

I swear I have a date about as often as Comet Arend-Roland orbits the sun—every 10,000 years.

When morning arrived, I shaved, showered, and made an extra effort to do something about my hair, going so far as using mousse, a blow dryer, and hair spray. I wanted everything to be right when I saw Gloria again, and I needed all the help I could get.

I settled on my Levis and white cotton shirt. The shirt was wrinkled, but I didn't have an iron, so there was not much I could do about that. But the biggest source of anxiety was my earring. Should I keep the gold loop in? Gloria didn't seem like the type of girl who would go out with guys who had a pierced ear. Gloria didn't seem like the type of girl who would go out with me. I was afraid to change anything, so I wore it. For good measure, I splashed on some of Rob's Polo cologne.

As I loaded my books into my backpack, Rob, who had a later class, rolled over in bed. "You know, Tommy," he said, his voice thick with grogginess, "you don't look half bad when you're all cleaned up."

My wet towel was lying on the floor, and I picked it up and draped it over his head. Rob swore and threw it off. As I pulled the door closed, he called, "I want a full report."

The morning sun greeted me and to my relief, news cameras didn't. I went to class, and a few people teased me about my attire, commenting that since I was now a celebrity, I'd have to dress the part. Watching the classroom's clock, I swear its hands had been weighted they moved so slowly around the dial.

After classes, I stopped back at the dorm to do a final inspection of myself, drop off my books, and check the answering machine. It was 12:10 and there were messages from Sandra Creighton, Mark Thornton, and some people wanting to buy Sammys, but none from Gloria. A good sign. The Parlor was only a short walk, and I left at twelve-twenty.

I arrived at the restaurant five minutes later. Although it was clear, a strong wind blew down Western Avenue, threatening to destroy my hair. A few times I had to cover my head to protect it.

The Parlor, an old red brick Victorian row house, sat on the shadowy side of the two-lane street. Across from it, Waldman's Bakery, Alioto's Shoe Repair, and the Tres Belle Beauty Salon were bathed in cheery light, their gutters gurgling with melting snow. I bounced on my toes to keep warm.

A brass plaque fastened to The Parlor's bricks caught my eye. It stated that the building had been designated as a historical landmark. At the turn of the century, the North Side was known as Allegheny City and until 1907, had been a separate entity from the City of Pittsburgh. During that time, The Parlor had been the residence of industrialist, Simon Witherspoon until the late fifties, when the only surviving relative died. Over the years the house had become rundown and was eventually abandoned.

A few years ago, two TRU grads bought the building, renovated it, opening a restaurant and banquet hall. Its proximity to campus, delicious and generous portions, and cheap draft beer, made it a favorite among TRU's student body. The restaurant was sandwiched between the law offices of Meyers, Hamilton & Oglethorpe and a floral shop, Josie's Posies.

Near the door, displayed in a glass case, was the menu. I studied it for a while and then began pacing, waiting for Gloria. As I passed the law office's windows, I caught my reflection in a pane of glass. Gazing at myself, I practiced my smiling while saying "Gloria." I wanted to make my dimples as deep as possible. I stood there squeezing and relaxing my cheeks until a gray-haired woman, whose glasses hung from a chain around her neck, walked over to the window, gave me a dirty look, and dropped the blinds.

Embarrassed, I walked away and checked the time again—twelve thirty-five. She should be coming soon. I walked to the end of the block. The wind tore at my face as I peered around the corner. No Gloria.

Like a sentry, I marched the length of the block, back and forth, until I noticed that the other side of the street was no longer sunny. The wind picked up, sending a crumpled McDonald's bag skittering down the sidewalk. The Christmas flag hanging outside the flower shop snapped in the air.

I eyed the sky. Thick, black clouds, herded across the sky by the wind, had trampled out the sun. The automatic streetlights clicked on, coloring everything a sickening, jaundice shade. The wind stung my cheeks and slashed through my jacket.

Perhaps Gloria had arrived earlier and was waiting inside. I hurried to the restaurant and opened the old wooden door. The wind caught the wreath hanging on it and sent the circle of evergreens swinging like a pendulum.

What a relief to be inside. The old house's foyer now served as the waiting area. I saw no hostess and no Gloria. Two women in their fifties were the only people in the waiting area. Sitting on the tapestry settee, they were deep in conversation, oblivious to me and to the turn the weather had taken. The grandfather clock in the corner chimed twelve forty-five. Although the restaurant smelled delicious with grilling beef, my appetite was fading. I peeked into the bar—no Gloria. She probably went home yesterday, realized what a jerk I was, and bagged me.

The door rattled. I whirled around. Entering were two middle-aged men in dark wool overcoats. Oh, why did I ever tell Rob about Gloria? To have to go back to the dorm and admit that she was a no-show would be humiliating.

I headed to the window, searching for any sign of Gloria.

"Evans party," a voice called from behind. The hostess must have returned. The decrease in chatter in the waiting area told me that the two gabby women were being led to a table.

Outside, a snow squall throttled the street, reducing visibility to a few feet. Snowflakes streaked horizontally past the window. I looked at my watch. Seventeen minutes late. I felt like I'd swollen an anvil. I promised myself I wouldn't wait any longer than one o'clock; I had some self-respect. But I'd already extended my waiting limit to one thirty, when I heard the hostess speak again. "One for lunch?"

When she repeated the question, I realized she was addressing me. I turned around. The hostess held a menu. Her bleached hair was the color and texture of rattan and her thin face had tiny lines around the mouth, probably the result of too many breaks spent sucking on cigarettes.

"Oh, no. I'm waiting for someone," I said. "I think the weather's held her up." At least, I hoped that was the reason.

The hostess squinted and looked outside. "Ew, does look wicked out there." Then she disappeared into the bar. I resumed my post at the window.

"Excuse me." It was the hostess again.

I looked over my shoulder. "Yeah?"

"Is your name Tom?"

Slowly, I walked toward her like a kid called to the blackboard to solve a tricky algebra problem.

"Yeah, why?" Please don't say Gloria's not coming. *Please.*

She read from a slip of paper. "A Gloria just called." I held my breath. "She said to tell you she's on her way."

My shoulders fell as I let out my breath. I smiled, "Great."

The hostess made a notation in her reservation book. "From her description, I knew you had to be Tom." The wrinkles around her mouth fell into pleats as she smiled back. "You do have gorgeous dimples."

"Thanks," I mumbled and embarrassed, I bit the insides of my cheeks to keep from displaying them. I walked back to the window and leaned my forehead against the cold pane of glass. *Oh, thank God she was coming.*

At twelve fifty-six, Gloria's white figure materialized out of the whirlwind of snowflakes. Not wanting to appear desperate, I ran to the settee, picked up a copy of the *Green Sheet,* and pretended to read.

The door opened. Gloria entered preceded by a gust of cold air and an entourage of snowflakes. She closed the door, threw off her hood, and brushed the snow from her shoulders. As the flakes fell to the floor, they sparkled like fairy dust in the light from the Tiffany chandelier. She stomped her feet on the mat and looked around.

When her eyes fell on me, my heart lurched against my rib cage. The sight of her in the flesh so overwhelmed me, I nearly giggled. Taking a deep breath, I reigned in my hysteria, and walked toward her. "Hi," I said.

With a vicious yank, she opened the snap at her collar. "I hope you got my message," she said. "My class ran late. I called your room, but no one answered." She pulled off her gloves with short little jerks and shoved them into her pockets.

When she spoke, she seemed to be looking past me, avoiding my eyes. She thinks I'm repulsive. Yesterday, she'd probably been swept up in the emotion of finding me and thanking me, and now that sense had gotten hold of her and she'd seen me again, she's regretting this date.

"I'm fine," I said. "Don't worry about me." I tried to catch her eyes, but they were locked on the chalkboard listing the daily specials.

The hostess came and led us past the bar, up a flight of carved mahogany stairs, and down a narrow hallway. You could tell the building was old because the floorboards were warped and they creaked. Following Gloria, I felt disoriented like I was walking in a fun house.

The hostess stopped in the doorway of a small dining room in the front of the building. "This OK?"

The room overlooked the street and was empty except for the two chatterbox women in the "Evans party."

"This is fine." I said, and I waited for Gloria to give her approval, but she said nothing.

"Looks like you'll pretty much have the place to yourselves," said the hostess. "Would you like a table by the fire or the window?"

"You pick," I said to Gloria.

"I don't care." She shrugged her shoulders. "Oh, window—I guess."

The hostess led us to a small wooden table. "The storm's keeping people away," she said as she put menus at our seats. "I've had so many cancellations." Then she stepped back and pointed her pen at me. "Hey, wait. You look familiar."

Gloria pulled out her chair. "You've probably seen him on TV. He's a big hero." Was it my imagination or was it guilt, but her tone sounded sarcastic? I began to blush.

"Oh, yeah," the hostess said, the light of recognition flickering in her eyes. "You're The Good Shepherd, the guy who gave that little boy the toy." She struck a match and lit the hurricane lamp on the table. "That was so sweet. I cried when I saw that story on the news." Before she left, she told us to enjoy our lunches.

A fire crackled and hissed in the grate of the old marble fireplace, while in the corner, a Christmas tree, decorated with antique ornaments twinkled. It was a cozy place in which to pass a winter storm.

I took off my jacket and hung it on the back of my chair, and I watched as Gloria unzipped her bulky coat and peeled it away. Suddenly, I was no longer cold. I turned my head toward the window before she caught me leering at her.

The storm obliterated the view, making me feel as if I were trapped inside a whirring blender.

Gloria took a seat, unwrapped the silverware from its napkin bunting and set her place, making sure the bottoms of the utensils were all on the same horizontal plane. A tan rubber band encircled her wrist.

She'd probably forgotten that she'd put it there. Without saying a word to me, she opened the menu. My palms were sweating.

"It's certainly nasty out there," I said in an attempt to start a conversation. How clever—opening with a line about the weather. What a loser.

She looked over the top of the menu. "It sure is." Her eyes went back to the menu.

She couldn't bear to look at me. Right after lunch, she's going to dump me.

She spoke to me while looking at the Christmas tree. "It's nice in here though. I love Christmas, don't you?"

"Christmas?" I plucked a Sweet 'n Low packet from its porcelain holder. "Yeah, I guess so."

Her head snapped back, and she glared at me. "You guess so?" The tone of her voice gave me the feeling that I was being tested and that I had failed the first question. "What do you mean, 'you guess so'?" She measured and sliced her words as if she was putting them through a paper cutter.

I began flipping the sweetener packet over and over between my thumb and index finger. "Well, I've never celebrated Christmas much. When my mom was alive, she celebrated it." I stared at the candle's flame flickering between us. "But she died when I was four. My dad never got into the Christmas scene."

Why did I tell her about my mother? Did I want pity? I guess when you're not getting anything else, pity will do.

"Oh, how sad. You never had a tree or anything?" Her green eyes were wells of compassion.

"My memories of that time are hazy. I think we had a tree and I got gifts, but it was so long ago and I was so young," I said. "I don't know if it really happened or if I wished so much that it had, that now it seems real." I shrugged. "Anyway, after she died, I went to live with my father, and he never got into Christmas."

"He didn't celebrate it at all?"

"He made an attempt for a while, but each year he did less and less. Then when I was around seven, he just didn't bother any more."

"Do you mind if I ask what happened to your mom?"

"No, I don't mind." I stared at my silverware. It was still wrapped in the napkin. "She was killed in a car accident."

Gloria gulped. "How terrible! It must have been awful for you."

"Yeah, I guess it was. I was so small, I don't really remember. Anyway, I'm over it now. Life goes on."

Like the weather, her mood had suddenly changed. Even the way she spoke was different. Her tone was softer now and she was more like the Gloria I'd met yesterday.

"Why did your father forget about Christmas?"

"I'm not sure. Guess he thought it was a capitalistic plot or something."

"So he just dropped it completely?"

"No, not at first," I said. "He more or less phased it out. I remember being seven and still believing in Christmas. But you know that's the age when you start to realize that there's no way one man can visit every house in the world in one night. I was skeptical, but I was afraid not to believe. But my dear old dad set me straight." I picked up the menu and stared at the selections. "I'd made up a list for Santa. My father found it, sat me down, and said, 'You know there's no Santa.' Then he handed me the Sears catalog and told me to pick out two or three things I wanted." I looked up at Gloria. "Sometimes I wish he'd abandoned Christmas altogether rather than going along and sucking all the fun out of it."

"Were your parents divorced?"

I had no choice but to give her a brief synopsis of my screwed up life. "No, they were never married. They met in college. My mother was an art major and he was a grad student studying geology. I guess you could call them hippies. I think I was a side effect of free love. After I was born, my grandmother got cancer, and my mother and I moved in with her. My dad never bothered with me until he had to take me in after my mother died and my grandma got too sick to take care of me."

She closed the menu and frowned. "How traumatic. And to abandon Christmas. That's terrible—to take away all the magic."

"Oh, I don't know," I said, placing the wrinkled sweetener packet on the table, "sooner or later everyone loses the magic."

She leaned across the table. The black pupils centered in her green eyes beckoned me, magnetized my whole being, and dared me to draw near just like they'd done yesterday. Never taking her eyes from me, she picked up the sweetener packet, smoothed out the wrinkles, and placed it back in the holder. Then she whispered, "*I've* never lost the magic."

And looking into those eyes, I believed her.

Chapter 10

"Hi," said the waitress, "I'm Mandi and I'll be your server." Thank goodness she brought a pitcher of ice water because Gloria had me so overheated, I swear I was about to set off the sprinkler system. I chugged my glass as she went over the day's specials. "Oh," she gushed, "and I almost forgot. We're featuring a special drink during the holiday season—hot buttered rum. So yummy!"

Gloria flashed her eyes at me. "Oh, they're delicious. Ever had one, Tom?" I shook my head. "They're just the thing on a day like today." We both ordered one.

After Mandi wrote down our selections, she said, "By the way, your lunch is on the house."

"It is?" I said. Gloria looked at me confused, and I shrugged.

"Yeah, the manager heard that The Good Shepherd was here, and he wanted to show his appreciation."

"Oh . . . thanks," I muttered as Mandi bounced away. Embarrassed, I lowered my eyes and pretended to be interested in the menu. After skimming it for a while, I stole a glance at Gloria. She, too, was studying her menu. I swear she was even more beautiful than yesterday. Most of the girls came to school looking like . . . well, like slobs like me, pajama bottoms and sweatshirts. But not Gloria. She was wearing a pair of gray corduroys that complimented her blue turtleneck.

She looked up and caught me staring at her. "What?"

"Nothing." I felt like a voyeur nabbed in the act.

"No, what is it?"

"Well, it's just funny," I said, picking up the napkin and unwrapping my silverware, "that I've never seen you on campus."

Keeping my eyes on my hands as they arranged the napkin on my lap, I added, "And I know I would have remembered someone as pretty as you." That sounded so pathetic, I cringed.

Blushing, I slowly raised my eyes and was pleased to find Gloria smiling back at me. "Thank you," she said, as she played with her earring, a gold snowflake. "I guess our paths have just never crossed. TRU is a big school, and I read in the paper that you're a physics major?"

"Minoring in astronomy."

"Wow. I've always wanted to take an astronomy course. Tell me something about the universe that'll blow me away."

"What do you mean?"

She leaned across the table. "Oh, you know. Something astonishing. Like, it would take three hundred million hot dogs laid end to end to reach from the earth to the sun."

I laughed. "Something astonishing? Hmm. . . ." I scanned my mind for something clever to impress her. "OK," I said, pushing back my hair, "here's one. The gravitational force of the universe is so precise that the slightest increase or decrease in it either way would destroy us. A decrease would send the earth spinning off into space and an increase would pull us into the sun."

"Wow," she said, gripping the table's edge, "I didn't know that. That's awesome."

I felt as if I were trying to maintain the same delicate equilibrium with her. I needed to tell her enough about me to interest her, yet not so much that she'd see what a jerk I really was.

"There truly is an order to the universe," she said.

I'm glad she thought so. I've never found any.

"What's your major?"

"Music. I play the piano. I want to be a music teacher. In fact, I already have five students that I teach from my home. It gives me some extra money."

I was impressed. I had no artistic abilities. "Music, huh?" I chuckled. "Talk about opposites."

The waitress brought our drinks, and we placed our orders. Gloria raised the steaming mug of buttered rum to her mouth. She puckered her lips, blowing on the hot liquid, and her pink mouth in kissing position entranced me. The cinnamon-spiced pat of butter melting on top of the drink formed a whirlpool under her breath. Watching her, I felt as disoriented as the twirling butter.

I raised my mug. "Here's to opposites." She clinked hers with mine, and then I took a sip and felt the warm drink slide down my throat and radiate throughout my body. It was like liquid phosphorus; I glowed all over from it.

She took a sip and after she swallowed asked, "Do you really think physics and music are opposite?"

"Well, yeah," I said, shifting in my chair. "I mean physics deals with principles and music. . . . Well, I know music follows principles, but it's rooted in creativity. I'm not creative at all." I didn't want her to think I thought physics was a superior major, so I added, "Don't get me wrong. I admire creativity immensely. It's just that I'm not comfortable with the abstract. I do better with the tangible—things that are concrete. Absolute."

Gloria set her mug on the wooden table. It made a small thump. "I think they're very closely related."

"You do? How?"

She paused a moment and closed her eyes, while she formulated her response. When she opened them, she extended her right hand, palm up. "On one hand," she said, "we have physics—based on laws." She extended her left hand in the same manner, acting like a scale. "On the other, music—full of creativity." She looked straight at me. "Who makes the laws, and who inspires the creativity?"

Stumped, I shrugged.

"Well, God, of course," she said bringing her hands together.

"I don't believe in God."

As soon as the words left my mouth, I wanted them back.

Gloria's face fell and a small "oh" escaped her lips. She picked up the cardboard tent on the table that had pictures of Mississippi mud cakes, sundaes, and pecan balls on it.

"What I meant to say," I quickly added in an attempt to salvage the conversation, "is that I've never found concrete evidence that He exists."

Gloria wrinkled her nose and set the dessert card down. "Don't tell me you're one of those fundamentalists."

"Huh?" I've been called many names before but never a fundamentalist.

"Oh, you know. One of those by-the-book scientists. If it's not in a text or some science journal, then it's not true."

She was not only beautiful, she was bright and witty. I laughed.

"What's so funny?"

"I've never been called a fundamentalist before. I thought you had to be religious."

"Same blind faith, different creed."

"What do you mean?"

"Only that some scientists are so closed-minded they shut themselves off to other possibilities."

"What other possibilities?"

"That there's a whole other plane of existence beyond the physical."

I thought of my conversation yesterday with Rajiv. "You know," I said, "it's weird, but you're the second person in two days to tell me that. I take it you've experienced this 'other plane,' then?"

"Of course."

"*You have?*"

"Sure. Haven't you?"

"No."

She took another sip of her drink and then said, "Probably because you're not open to it."

"Jesus, I'm open-minded," I said, sounding defensive. "I'm the most open-minded person I know.

"I didn't say you weren't," Gloria said. "Look, the way I imagine it is that our minds are like radios able to receive certain frequencies. You have to know how to tune into this other plane or God, whatever you want to call it. Some people have attuned themselves to a spiritual frequency."

"Why don't I receive these frequencies?"

"You could if you wanted to."

I shook my head. "Nah, I don't think so."

"Look, Tom," she said, "did you ever read *Highlights* when you were a kid?"

"The magazine?"

She nodded.

"Sure."

"Remember the Hidden Pictures?"

"Oh, God yes. They drove me crazy. I could always find every item except for the stupid pencil."

"Me too. But the pencil was there, wasn't it?"

"Well, yeah. But you had to look really hard. Sometimes I had to turn the page upside down to find it. So what's that have to do with anything?"

"But the pencil *was* there, wasn't it, Tom? Just because you couldn't see it, didn't mean that it wasn't there, did it?"

She was setting a trap. "Yes, but—"

"Well, God is like the pencil. Just because you haven't found Him yet, doesn't mean He's not there. No one knew about microorganisms until we developed microscopes. To find God, you have to have the right perspective or attitude. Sometimes you have to turn the page upside down."

"I take it then that you're tuned in, that you've found Him, that you believe in God?"

"Certainly."

"OK, so you believe in God. Fine. That's great for you, but I'm a scientist. I need proof."

"I think you believe in Him too."

"I do not."

"Then why do you bring Him up so much?"

"What?"

"Have you ever listened to yourself, Tom? It's constantly 'Oh God,' or 'Jesus this' or 'Christ that.'"

"But I don't mean it in a religious sense."

"Oh, so you're just taking His name in vain then?"

"Jesus—I mean, jeez . . . I don't know. I was just talking."

"Well, God happens to be a good friend of mine, so I'd appreciate it if you'd stop talking about him in such a disrespectful way."

"Hey," I held up my hands. *"Sorry."* Angry now, I thought I'd turn the tables on her. "Well, can you teach me to tune into the spiritual? Can you prove God's existence?"

Gloria rested her elbows on the table, folded her hands, sitting her chin on her delicate knuckles. Then she leaned across the table, and her eyes shone as brightly as beacons. "Let me ask you this." She paused, and I knew I'd walked right into her trap, but the lure of those eyes left me helpless. "Do you believe in love, Tom?"

What kind of question was this? How do you answer such a thing, especially from a girl that looks like Gloria?

I tried to wrap myself around an intelligent thought, but she left me speechless again. "Well, yeah," was all I could muster. I looked at her and a shiver sashayed up my back, feeling as though her finger had been playing my spine like a xylophone, like she was playing me like a xylophone. No matter how annoying she was, her beauty rendered me powerless. "Sure, I believe in love," I said softly.

She tilted her head, coyly. "How do you know love exists, Tom?"

A long time ago, I'd sealed up such thoughts and emotions and jettisoned them deep into the blackness inside of me. Her eyes blazed

69

like a searchlight as she spoke. "Can you capture it in a test tube? Or weigh it? Or heat it until it boils?" She was approaching that space in me, my universe of sadness and pain.

"No," I said quietly, staring at my silverware that lay scattered on the table. I tried to straighten it but couldn't remember if you put the fork or the spoon with the knife. "You just feel it. Or see its results."

"Where do *you* feel it, Tom?"

Mission Control we have touchdown. Startled, I dropped the fork; it clattered on my plate. Gloria made a perfect landing in the center of my agony, discovering the vast world of darkness within me, leaving the terrain of my soul exposed for her exploration.

Where did I feel love? In this black void in the center of me that ached for lack of it. Perhaps at one time my heart had been alive, running with love, but like the Martian landscape, now only dry gullies and rivulets remained etched on its arid surface.

I was afraid to speak for fear she'd hear the emptiness of my soul clanging in my reply. So I pointed feebly to the center of my chest.

"Tom, I know you're smart and you're a logical person."

Nervous, I reached for the fork I'd dropped, but she intercepted my hand. My heart stopped. "If you believe in love, Tom, then you believe in God. Because God is love. And if you can feel love, you don't need proof. The feeling is the proof. It's absolute."

I sighed. "Ah, it all sounds so simple coming from you." The warmth of her hand soothed my fears, and like the butter in the mug, I melted under her gaze.

She squeezed my hand. "Love was never meant to be complicated, Tom."

That was so far from the truth, I wanted to take her by the shoulders and shake her. Maybe for people like her love came easily, but I knew love to be the most elusive element. But I wasn't up to another debate; I was drained.

We sat silently, mulling over our conversation until the waitress brought our lunches. Then we ate in silence, too. Obviously, a gulf separated us, one of belief and attitude. I was sure it could never be spanned. As I put the pickles on my burger, I knew that this would be my last date with beautiful Gloria.

"You've got a quick mind," I said to break the unbearable silence. "Have you ever thought about switching your major to law?"

She looked sheepish. "Oh, I'm sorry, Tom," she said. "I did interrogate you, didn't I?"

"No! No, I didn't mean it that way. What I meant is that you're very persuasive."

"But still," she said, "I apologize. It's rude to bring up religion with someone you hardly know."

"Really, I didn't mind," I said. "I enjoyed the debate."

"No," she said. "I come on too strong. The thing is that ever since Christo got sick, I've had lots of time to evaluate my life, find out what's really important. It's a fault, but I no longer have patience with game playing. I want to know what makes a person tick."

"Well, I bet you're really disappointed in me then. As you can tell, I don't tick all that well. I guess this is our first and last date."

Gloria looked confused and put down her fork. "Now, why would you think that? Because we have different beliefs?"

I found myself in the awkward position of supplying reasons why we shouldn't see each other again. "Well, sure. You're spiritual and I'm a heathen. What could you possibly want with me?"

She tilted her head and played with her earring, smiling provocatively at me. "Tom, don't you know? Believers have always wanted heathens. It's been that way for centuries. Where do you think believers come from in the first place? We recruit."

God, she was flirting with me. She wanted me. *Wanted me!* And the way she said "wanted" made my toes curl with desire.

A huge smile broke over my face, and I felt my dimples showing. "You mean you're out to convert me?"

"Oh, Tom," she laughed. "Hang around me long enough, and you'll have no other choice."

"Let me warn you," I flirted back, "you've got your work cut out for you."

"Oh, I don't know about that," she lowered her eyes flirtatiously. "I sense there's more to you than you lead others to believe. Maybe more than even you yourself know about."

"Oh, really."

"Yes, all that nonsense about not being creative and needing things that are tangible, I think that's a cover," she teased. "I sense a lot of beauty and passion in your soul."

I took another bite of my hamburger, and this time, I could taste it.

She picked up her fork. "How else could you have done something as kind as giving Christo that So Big Sammy?"

The burger stuck in my throat. I wished she'd forget about Holy Redeemer. I wished everybody would. And most of all I wished I'd

71

never had to lie to her in the first place. I swallowed and tried to change the subject. "How is little Christopher?"

"OK. For now. We're waiting to hear if they've found a bone marrow match. We should know in a few weeks. Meanwhile, we're all busy praying for our second miracle."

"Second? You've already had one?"

"Yes. You were the first."

"Me?" I pointed to myself. "I'm a miracle?"

"Well, not you exactly. Your bringing Christo the Sammy—that was a miracle. Those toys are so hard to find. Where in the world did you ever get one?"

Thank goodness I was chewing, so I had a second to invent an answer. I took my time chewing and swallowing, then said, "I bought it for my half-brother, Jeffrey. He's going to be two in January. He lives in San Francisco with my father. Rob, my roommate, works at the Toy Trunk. He picked the Sammy up for me before everybody went crazy over them. During the holiday break, I planned to go to California, and I was going to give the toy to Jeffrey for his birthday."

I was ashamed at how easily I could lie to her. Grabbing the Heinz bottle, I focused my attention on the ketchup, watching it glug out onto my fries. I'm a terrible liar, and I didn't want to look at Gloria while I spun my tale.

"But when my father told me he was spending the holidays in Mexico," I continued, "I just held on to it because the box said 'Ages 3 and Up,' and Jeffrey's too little for it. " She looked like she was buying the story. I put the cap back on the ketchup. "And then when I saw the report on the news about Christo, I decided to give it to someone who would really appreciate it."

She rolled her eyes. "It's disgusting how crazy Christmas has become anymore. My family has been trying to get a Sammy for Christo for the past two weeks. But every store was sold out. Do you know those toy scalpers are asking more than $150 for the toy? A hundred fifty dollars for a $30 toy! Jeez, we've been holding bake sales and spaghetti dinners to raise enough money to finance this bone marrow typing and transplant. There just wasn't money to spare for a toy."

She buttered a roll, smoothing the pat until it was spread uniformly. "Those people who scalp these toys should be ashamed of themselves. They're a disgrace."

Gloria's words stung. I tried not to sound defensive. "Well, I guess they're only giving people what they want."

"Oh, but that's what's really sickening. People act like they *need* these toys, like their life depends on them, like they're insulin or something, and they'll lapse into a coma without one." She pointed the knife at me. "I believe people would kill for them. Did you see the news this morning?"

"No."

"Well, some woman at a truck stop near the Somerset exit on the Turnpike pulled a gun on a sleeping trucker. He was transporting a shipment of So Big Sammys. She stole five of the toys, and when the other people there saw her running away with them, they beat the trucker and stole the rest of his load. He's in serious condition."

"No kidding?" My voice sounded too gleeful, so I shook my head in feigned disgust. The price for Sammys would surely rise again. Gloria was right. People would kill for them. Not only would I have to be careful that she didn't find out I sold them, but for my own safety, as well.

"My family would never have gotten involved in such insanity, but the circumstances with Christo were special. Anything that boosts his spirits might be the edge that helps him to survive all this."

I wanted to keep her away from the subject of So Big Sammy. I pushed my hair behind my ears. "He has leukemia, right?"

"Acute lymphoblastic leukemia or ALL to be specific." Gloria looked out the window, and I noticed she ran a finger under the rubber band on her wrist. Sadness washed over her face as if she were watching something heartbreaking taking place outside the window.

I turned and looked outside, but only saw the storm's handiwork. A dusting of snow on windshields and in the cracks and edges of the sidewalks was all that was left behind. The storm front, for all of its bluster, had passed through quickly, leaving only traces of snow.

"Christo was perfectly normal, healthy, a beautiful little boy until his second birthday," she talked as she gazed out the window. "Ginny, his mother—you met her at church—took him to the doctor's for a regular checkup. When he examined Christo, he discovered that his spleen was enlarged. The doctor immediately sent him to Children's Hospital where they ran tests. The tests confirmed what we feared most." Then her voice cracked, "Nothing's been the same since."

She turned and faced me, wearing a sad smile that made me want to get up and hug her. But of course I didn't. She whispered and played with the rubber band, "And I've never been the same since."

I said nothing, knowing that she had paused only to gather strength to continue the story. "He's only my cousin, Tom, but he's

73

more like my brother or even my child. I'm his godmother, and I've babysat him since he was born."

Huge tears waited in the corners of her eyes. "They started treatments." She took the napkin from her lap. "It was awful," she closed her eyes and the tears skipped down her cheeks.

I reached out to touch her hand, but quickly withdrew it. I'd never comforted anyone before, and I was afraid I'd do something wrong.

Then she shook her head like a child swallowing a putrid medicine. "He went into remission. We were so happy." She brushed her cheeks and set her napkin beside her plate.

"He relapsed this summer and had to undergo treatment again. Thankfully, he's back in remission, but his doctors aren't sure how long he'll remain there. The cure rate for kids with ALL is around seventy-five percent. Unfortunately, Christo's cancer seems to be very aggressive. His doctors recommended a bone marrow transplant—they think it would be his best option. We hope to find a match while he's still in remission. We're playing beat the clock."

What do you say after someone tells you a story that rips your guts out? I stared at my plate wanting to offer some words of encouragement, some hope. But I couldn't. No one could.

Gloria tossed back her hair. "Are you busy Friday night?"

I shook my head. "I don't think so." If I was, I'd cancel whatever it was to be with her. "Why?"

"How about coming with me to visit Christo? Everyone in my family feels indebted to you. When I told them that I'd found you, they were thrilled. I know Ginny and Joe, Christo's parents, would love to meet you again and thank you properly."

I was so concerned about asking her out again and here she was asking me. I hesitated before I answered. As much as I felt sorry for Gloria and Christo and his family, I didn't want to be near that sick little boy again. I only wanted Gloria not the rest of her family. And what would I say to Christo's parents anyway? Then another, more frightening thought entered my mind: What if Ginny Davidson knows that I was at Holy Redeemer to sell her the toy and tells Gloria? I couldn't risk it.

"They don't need to thank me again," I said. "Meeting you has been thanks enough."

"Oh, please come," Gloria begged. "Please." She touched my hand. "Please." If it meant being with her again, I'd go. It'd be worth the risk.

"OK," I said, and as I did, a log in the fireplace shifted and thunked against the grate, startling me. Sparks like fireworks sizzled and crackled as they shot up the chimney. Gloria reminded me of the fire—warm and bright. And dangerous. As I watched the fire blazing, the flames leaping and licking at the log, I hoped that when she was finished with me, something would still remain of me—something more than a heap of dried, gray ashes.

Chapter 11

Friday seemed light years away. I had to see Gloria before then. As we walked back to campus, I asked her to meet me after classes the next day and she agreed.

On Wednesday morning, I leaned out from my bunk and saw that Rob's bed was empty. The holiday shopping season was in full swing now, and the Toy Trunk had overloaded his work schedule. As Rob had predicted, the attention I'd received only made Sammy hotter. The demand was so great, we were able to drive the market up and double our asking price to three hundred dollars a toy.

As I lay in bed, calculating the enormous amount of money we were going to make, I began tossing around the idea of going on to grad school. I knew if I told my father I wanted to continue my education, he'd scream bloody murder that he didn't have money to support me any longer. Who knew? With the way the Sammys were selling, I might be able to swing a trip to Martinique and enroll in grad school.

The phone rang, and not wanting to miss out on a sale, I hopped out of bed and answered it.

"Is this Tom Shepherd?"

I gritted my teeth. It was Walnut Head. Making the pitch of my voice very higher, I answered, "You must have the wrong number." I hung up the phone and resisted answering it when it rang again.

After classes, I met Gloria outside Benson Music Hall. The day was chilly with the sun snooping over slatted clouds. The weather service was predicting a snowfall for late tomorrow night, but the forecasters were being elusive on how many inches we might receive.

Gloria and I decided to walk to Burger King for a couple of Whoppers. "So," she said, as we made our way across the quad, "tell me another incredible fact about the universe."

It was great to have someone take an interest in the things I found fascinating. My father, the geology major, never cared about astronomy. He was happier crawling through and excavating the bowels of the earth rather than exploring the sky. And every time I asked Rob to come stargazing with me, he replied: "The only stars I want to watch, Tommy, are ones on the tube."

"OK," I said, pushing the hair out of my face, "here's a fact that will blow you away. Did you know that there are more than a thousand million stars in our galaxy alone and that there are more than a million galaxies each with that many or more stars?"

She stopped in mid-stride. "Really?"

"Really."

"Wow, that's so cool. We're so insignificant. How comforting."

Comforting? All my life, I've been insignificant, and I've never found it comforting. There's nothing I'd love more than to be the center of the universe, anyone's universe. "Wait a second," I said. "How's being insignificant comforting?"

"It makes my problems seem small. And it's nice to know that someone who can create something that enormous is in charge." She walked away.

What problems could she possibly have looking like that? She was probably referring to Christo. I quickened my pace to catch up to her. "So, we're back to God again?"

"Well, isn't that where everything begins?"

"Tom Shepherd." I heard someone calling.

Our conversation had been so intense, I had failed to notice Sandra Creighton, her camera man, and the intern standing outside the administration building. But she had seen me.

Walnut Head hustled over to us and stuck a microphone in my face. "What was it about Christopher Davidson that prompted you to give him a toy you could have sold for hundreds of dollars?"

"No comment," I said and kept on walking. I looked at Gloria and chuckled. I've always wanted to say that. It made me feel like a big shot.

Sandra and her crew followed at our heels shouting questions. "Where did you get the So Big Sammy? Do you plan to give away any more toys?" When she got no response from me, Walnut Head shoved the microphone in Gloria's face. "I remember you from the interview we did with Christopher's family. You're his cousin, Gloria. Right?"

Being polite, Gloria said, "Yes."

"I've done some checking around campus and people have seen you two together. Are you dating?"

While Gloria looked at me to see whether she should answer, Sandra peppered her with more questions, crowding her, pushing the microphone closer. "Did you know each other before the blood drive? Did you have your blood tested? Have you heard any results? What's it like waiting and watching while someone you love suffers? Does Christopher know that he could possibly die?"

By the shock on Gloria's face, I knew Sandra's aggressiveness and callousness had offended her. This was none of Sandra's or anybody else's business.

I pushed the microphone away from Gloria's face. "Leave her alone," I roared, "or you're going to eat this microphone." Putting my arm around Gloria's shoulder, I said, "Come on!" We stomped away, but Sandra Creighton pursued us, hurling questions at our backs like snowballs.

As we neared my dorm, I looked at Gloria. Our eyes met, a spark of an idea jumped from my mind to hers, and I knew we were thinking the same thing. I slid my arm from her shoulder and picked up her hand. "Now," I whispered, and we broke into a run, holding hands as we sprinted to the parking lot.

Sandra Creighton followed, her high heels clicking on the cement walkway. But her dress shoes and the heavy camera made her and her crew slow. We ran to my car. I fumbled in my pocket for my car keys and unlocked the Sentra. "Get in quick!"

Gloria jumped in the passenger seat; I hopped in the driver's and started the car. As I shifted into reverse, Sandra Creighton caught up to us. Pounding on Gloria's window, she shouted questions. I threw the car into drive. The tires screeched as I zoomed out of the lot. In the rearview mirror, I saw Sandra and her crew running for their news van.

I headed across the West End Bridge to the West End Circle where exits branched out from it like spokes around a hub. If she tracked us across the bridge, she'd still have to guess which exit we'd taken.

I looked over at Gloria, and her cheeks were pink from running and she held her stomach, laughing. Inside the car, it was cold, and every time she exhaled plumes of frosty breath came out of her mouth. The windows steamed.

"Where should we go?" I asked. "Pick an exit."

Gloria leaned forward, wiped the condensation off the windshield, and scanned all the road signs. She pointed. "That one. There. Let's go to Mount Washington." I turned the car and headed for the mountain that presided over the city.

"Wow, this is exciting," she said. "I feel like Bonnie and Clyde."

As the car passed the restaurants lining Grandview Avenue, Gloria, who had now caught her breath, asked, "This is fun, but why are we running from Sandra Creighton, Tom?"

"Aw, ever since that report aired, she's been nothing but a pain. She calls me nonstop, harassing me, wanting me to give her an interview."

"Why don't you want to speak to her? I know she's abrasive, but in all honesty, she's been very helpful to my family. If you granted her an interview, she'd probably leave you alone."

I found a parking spot in front of St. Mary's church. "I didn't give the Sammy away to become a celebrity," I said. "I just wish she'd leave me alone." We got out of the car and crossed the street.

An observation deck stuck out like a tongue from high atop Mount Washington. It always puzzled me why the city fathers dubbed the downtown area of Pittsburgh "The Golden Triangle" when all the skyscrapers were in various tones of silver and gray. But tonight as I approached the observation deck, I understood how it had acquired its nickname. The setting sun had spilled liquid gold over the city.

We walked onto the deck as lights were clicking on everywhere giving the city a jeweled appearance.

The overlook was deserted. Gloria strode all the way to the end of the concrete platform and grasped the wrought iron railing. She leaned out and inhaled, taking in the view of the city as if it were a fragrance. I noticed the stillness as I joined her at the railing. Only the faint sounds of distant traffic and the rustle of wind in the treetops below us broke the peacefulness.

I looked down into the steep ravine beneath us, and when I saw how small the cars looked below on McArdle Roadway, my legs melted beneath me. I moved back and stood behind Gloria. She glanced over her shoulder, and if she had any inkling of the unbridled terror unleashed in me, she didn't let on.

The view of the city didn't interest me anyway; the one of her did. The setting sun had coppered her hair and turned her skin the color of peach sherbet. She leaned back from the rail, looked over her shoulder at me again, and spoke in a tone that was as mellow as the twilight. "You're a paradox, Tom. For an agnostic or atheist . . . What are you anyway?"

"I don't know," I said, preoccupied by the height and my racing heart. "I'd never given it much thought before. Let's just say I'm an agnostic—it sounds more open-minded. And I'd never want to be accused of being a closed-minded fundamentalist."

Catching the little jab I threw her, she bumped me with her hip, and it felt as if the earth's axis had shifted and that I was falling over the side. I grabbed for the railing and held on tightly.

"As I was saying, Tom, you're a paradox. For an agnostic, you certainly behave like a believer."

My fingers ached, they were clutching the rail so tightly. I raised an eyebrow. "I do? How?"

"Giving without expecting a reward. That's a religious concept."

"I'm sure charity isn't limited only to believers." I wondered if the railing was anchored properly to the deck. "Unbelievers can be charitable too."

Gloria chuckled. "Well, if they are. They need a better publicist."

"What do you mean?"

Gloria turned, looked out over the city, and raised her arm. Her hair whipped in the breeze. "Look at Pittsburgh, Tom," she said as her hands swept across the skyline.

I wished she'd stop waving her arms around and just stay still. She could fall over or something.

"Out there, we've got Presbyterian, St. Francis, and Mercy Hospitals. Then downtown there's the Salvation Army, Saint Mary's Soup kitchen, and on the North Side the Light of Life Mission. I don't see any 'Our Lady of the Doubtful Hospital' or 'Brotherhood of the Uncertain' soup kitchen."

"OK," I conceded. Who cared about hospitals, when the whole observation deck could break away and send us hurtling down the side of the mountain? "You've made your point. Perhaps I'm just inherently good without believing in God." I tugged at the railing, making sure it was secure. "We should probably go now."

"Not yet!" Gloria exclaimed. "I want to watch the rest of the sunset, Tom." She turned back to the view. Taking a deep breath, I tried to enjoy it too, and I found that if I held on tightly to the railing and stood very close to Gloria, I was not as anxious.

We were quiet as we watched the sun leave the sky and ignite the clouds with crimson fire. I knew thousands of facts about the sun—its diameter, how long it took for its light to reach the earth, its surface temperature—but until today, I'd overlooked something. I never knew its beauty until I watched it set with Gloria.

I let go of the rail with my right hand and put my arm around her. Inching closer, I took in the smell of her hair and waited for the right moment to kiss her.

She sighed. "Ah, Tom, when you see a beautiful sight like this, I don't know how you can't believe in God." She turned her head and looked up into my face.

We were so close I felt the warmth of her breath on my cheek as she spoke. The pale flesh of her neck tantalized me, tortured me. What would it feel like to touch her skin? To kiss it?

"Isn't it amazing," she whispered, "that in every one of those houses there isn't one person who is exactly alike?" The sun reflected in her eyes; they blazed with fire, hypnotizing me. "Can't you see it, Tom? God's hand—it's in everything." I moved my lips closer toward her. I wanted her to stop talking, stop talking about God, so I could kiss her.

"And it was God, Tom, who designed you to be a male, so that you'd be so preoccupied with kissing me, you wouldn't hear a word I'm saying."

Embarrassed, I backed away as my cheeks turned the color of the sky. Laughing, I raked my fingers through my hair. "Ah, how did you know that?"

She grinned. "Because He made me female and designed me to wonder why in the world you're taking so long to do it."

Before I could move, she touched my cheek and kissed me. Our lips fused and set off a glow in me brighter than any sun.

"Jesus, I mean gosh, I think I'm designed to like that," I whispered in her ear afterward.

She smiled and turned back to the sunset.

Standing behind her, I grasped the railing on either side of her, trapping her in my arms. My knees began to wobble again, not from fear, but desire. I didn't care if she worshiped Golden Calves or Moon Rocks; I wanted her like I'd never wanted anything in my life. I closed my eyes and leaned my head against hers. She was annoying, outspoken, brutally honest, and more than I could handle, and I couldn't get enough of her.

"Ah, Gloria," I said softly, "I marvel at all that, too, but I don't connect it to a God. Maybe I'm just a cynic."

She whirled about in my arms. I opened my eyes to see a pained expression contorting her face. "Don't say that, Tom!" She gently punched my chest. "You can be skeptical. I can handle skepticism."

82

She closed her eyes and shook her head. "Ah, but cynics—Tom. Cynics have no hope."

I put a hand on her shoulder. "OK, then I'll be a skeptic." I'd be anything she wanted me to be.

I slowly stroked the side of her neck. Her flesh was warm and soft, soft as my mother's old buckskin jacket. I pulled Gloria to my chest and hugged her.

Maybe I wasn't a cynic as I had thought. For the first time in my life, I felt as if I did have hope. I was holding it in my arms.

Chapter 12

As the days drew nearer to Christmas, our stockpile of So Big Sammys dwindled. The picture on the front page of Thursday, December 3's, *USA Today* featured two women, wrapped in headlocks, wrestling in an aisle of a Virginia Wal-Mart over the store's last toy. Sammy mania was sweeping the nation. Rob and I were now commanding $400 a piece for the toy. I had no problem arranging deals over the phone, other than the fact that I felt terrible doing it behind Gloria's back.

Thursday morning, I met Gloria for breakfast in the cafeteria. Outside, the sky looked threatening. If clouds could have teeth, these would have had them. Earlier in the morning, The National Weather Service had issued a winter storm warning for Western Pennsylvania.

Sitting across the table from her, I watched as she spread cream cheese on her bagel. She swirled and smoothed with the deftness of a cement mason, leveling the cream cheese to the bagel's edges. She looked wide-eyed and fresh, like a kid just up from a nap. Somehow she'd retained the childlike ability to appear vibrant in the morning, and from the looks of her sitting poised in a red turtleneck and tartan plaid flannel shirt, and black jeans, I imagined that she probably woke this morning pink-cheeked, sweet-breathed, with her golden curls tossed about her pillow.

I, on the other hand, had lost that. I think it disappeared about the same time that I took up cramming for tests and drinking beer. Now I awoke looking like I had been on the losing end of a WWF match. And unfortunately this morning, I looked particularly whipped. Last night, I slept on my stomach, and when I looked in the mirror this morning, my eyes were puffy, red creases lined my face, and my hair—well, let's just say it was a bad hair day. I showered this morning with the hope that the water would perform a miracle on my appearance. But as I sat watching the storm clouds gathering in the sky, out of the corner of my eye, I glimpsed a strand of hair, sticking out at a right angle to my head. Only some holy water could have exorcised the demons tormenting my hair.

I drank my coffee, savoring it as if it were a magic elixir and fussed with the unruly strand, eventually giving up and tucking it behind my ear. Gloria continued swirling and smoothing the cream cheese until I finally said, "If you want, I could run to the hardware store and get you a trowel."

The knife froze. She looked at me and laughed. "You sound like my brother. He used to kid me that he was going to buy me a sable brush so I could paint the mayonnaise on my sandwiches." She wiped the plastic knife clean with her napkin. "You know what I like about you, Tom?"

I hoped it was everything. "What?" I asked, knowing it was not going to be this morning's stylish coiffure.

"Your tolerance." She bit the bagel, ruining the layer of cream cheese she had so artfully applied, and then placed it on the plate. It seemed a shame the way she had worked so long and hard, and now it was ruined.

"My tolerance? The other day you called me a fundamentalist."

"Yes, but you're only a fundamentalist toward God and science. What I mean is most people," she said between swallows, "especially guys, aren't nearly as understanding."

"What's there to understand?" I spun the plastic stir in my coffee.

"Oh, you don't have to be tactful with me of all people. I know very well, that you wish I'd shut up about your religious convictions."

"Or lack of them," I added, taking another hit of the coffee. The caffeine was working its magic; I began to feel half-alive. "Honestly, I don't mind the discussions," I said, "but I won't lie. I wouldn't mind talking about something else once in a while."

"Well, at least you're honest." She slipped her index finger under the cuff of her flannel shirt, and pulled down a rubber band that was trapped inside her sleeve. "Most guys just dump me."

"Dump you? You're kidding. I bet you've never been dumped in your life."

"I have. More times than I'd like to remember." She teased a tea bag in and out of the hot water. "Most guys who ask me out are football players—jock types. All they see is blond and think Barbie doll. They assume I'm an airhead who's content to adore and adorn them."

"Adore and adorn? I don't know what you mean."

"Sure you do." She pulled the soggy tea bag out of the water and set it on the edge of her saucer. "They want me as a decoration, a trophy. You know, someone cute to hang on their arm, and worship them." Gloria rolled her green eyes. "Well, you know me. I can't keep my mouth shut, and I detest big egos." She shrugged. "They never call back."

My rebel lock of hair sprung free, and I pushed it out of my eyes. "It's their loss." I said. *And my gain.*

"Thanks." She glanced up at the cafeteria line. "Do you think they have any lemon for the tea?"

"If they do, it's probably moldy."

"Discrimination," she said through clenched teeth. "Restaurants should have a selection of teas and lemon and sugar cubes . . ." She picked up one of the small plastic containers, read the label, and grimaced. ". . . and real cream." She pulled back the lid and dumped in the non-dairy creamer and stared into the cup as if the leaves were still in there steeping and she could read something from them. "You know," she said, taking the stirrer from my cup and sticking it into hers, "sometimes, you start to wonder if it's just you that's out of step with the world." She looked up at me. "Do you ever feel that way, Tom? You know, like you're a square peg?"

"Square? Oh, Gloria, most of my life I've felt like an octagon."

She put the stirrer back into my cup and smiled. "Octagon, huh? Maybe that's why we've hit it off so well. We're a pair of irregulars."

I found it difficult to believe that she felt so out of step. "Yeah, I might be an irregular, but I don't care, Gloria. I've never wanted to be like everyone else." Everyone else was my father, and I certainly didn't want to be like him.

Gloria sipped her tea. "That's so weird. I've always felt like that too. I hate blending in. And since Christo has gotten sick, that feeling has intensified. I can count only one true friend, Mary Beth. We've known each other since first grade. She understands me, but she's away at school. I have a hard time relating to others."

Gloria began to pluck the rubber band on her wrist. It snapped against her skin. I flinched.

"A lot of the things girls my age are interested in seem trivial or boring," she said. "Ever since Christo got sick, I couldn't care less how weird Madonna looks in her latest video, or whom Josh Lewis is sleeping with on the *Guiding Light*." She picked up the bagel. "I don't want to sound like I think I'm better than other people. I don't know how to describe it exactly, but I feel like I operate on another level of awareness. Do you understand what I'm saying?"

She'd put into words, how I'd felt all my life. "I understand completely," I said.

A welt rose on her wrist where she had snapped the rubber band. Curious, I asked her, "Why do you wear that?"

Puzzled, she glanced down at her clothing. "What?"

"That," I said, pointing to her wrist.

She blushed. "You mean the gum band?" Like many people in Pittsburgh, she referred to rubber bands as "gum bands."

"Yeah, the gum band. I noticed you wore one at lunch on Tuesday and that you had one on yesterday. I thought maybe you put it on your wrist and forgot about it, but it's always there. Why?"

"Behavior modification."

"What?"

"I wear it to change my behavior, or change my thoughts to be precise."

"I don't get it."

"I'm trying to improve myself. I want to think positive thoughts. When I think negative ones, I snap the gum band and the pain acts as a deterrent, conditioning my mind to avoid negative thinking."

"Like Pavlov's dog?"

"Yeah, I guess so."

"And it works?"

"Yes, it does. When Christo first got sick, my thoughts were very pessimistic, but I read about this gum band technique, and it really helps you monitor your thought processes. Now, I think much more positively about him, and I've adapted the technique to other areas of my life."

"Like what?"

"My piano playing for instance. If I think 'I'm going to botch this piano piece,' then I just snap the gum band and repeat in my mind 'I'm going to play this piece perfectly.'"

"And then you play it right?"

"Most of the time. But even if I don't, there are only benefits to thinking positively. Thoughts have a direct link to the body. You know, Tom, it's not: You are what you eat. Rather, you are what you think."

"But doesn't it hurt?"

"A little. Depends how often you have to snap yourself. Hey," she said, flexing her biceps, "no pain, no gain."

If I snapped a rubber band every time a negative thought crossed my mind, my skin would be in tatters and my hand would be hanging from my wrist by a tendon.

"You might want to try it, Tom," she teased. "Every time you swear, you could just . . ." She stretched the rubber band on her wrist and let it spring back. The noise it made as it struck her skin made me cringe.

"No thanks," I said. "I'm not into self-flagellation. I don't want to change my behavior that badly."

"Maybe now you don't." She diverted her gaze, looking out the window at the stewing clouds.

The way she avoided my eyes made me feel she was hiding something.

"But someday," she said sadly, "you might get sick of being the way you are, and you'll want to."

I couldn't tell if she was talking about herself or me. The sickening feeling eating at my gut told me she was talking about both of us.

Chapter 13

Thursday's clouds not only threatened snow they delivered. On Friday morning I awoke to seven inches and the revelation that I was no longer a media darling. Sandra Creighton and the rest of the press had abandoned "The Good Shepherd," for a bigger story. President Bush had ordered U.S. troops to Somalia in a deployment dubbed Operation Restore Hope.

When I heard that, I thought, good luck, Georgie. You've got your work cut out for you. Restoring hope to this sorry old world seemed . . . well . . . hopeless.

As I hung on the telephone arranging deals for the Sammys, guilt plagued me. Maybe Rob was right. Maybe I did have too much of a conscience. I hated selling Sammys behind Gloria's back. I resolved that after they were gone, I'd never lie to her again.

On Friday night, I waited for her to pick me up out in the dorm parking lot. The moon danced in and out of clouds that moved rapidly across the sky. I inhaled the brisk, clean December air, and I felt purified.

A green Dodge Caravan pulled up near me, the tires crunching the thin layer of snow left covering the asphalt. Gloria tooted the horn. I opened the door and climbed into the passenger seat.

"Hope you weren't expecting a Porsche," she laughed, as I pulled the door closed.

"Hey, I'm not complaining," I said. "At least this has a heater."

"Put your seatbelt on," she ordered. "I don't want anything happening to you while you're still a heathen. You'd spend eternity in hell."

91

"Ha, ha. Very funny."

Gloria drove out of the lot and headed off campus toward I-279. I liked being the passenger; I could stare at her as long as I wanted unnoticed.

"How're the roads?" I asked.

"Not bad. I took it easy. Luckily, we don't have to drive too far," she said as she got on the entrance ramp.

Rush hour was over and the traffic had carved ruts into the snow, making it seem as if the van ran on rails as it followed the tracks left by the other cars.

"Too bad my parents are at a Christmas party tonight," Gloria said as she accelerated, "or you could have met them too."

"Maybe another time." I tried to sound disappointed. I was nervous enough without adding her parents into the equation.

We left I-279 at the Bellevue/West View exit, and our speed decreased as we traveled over the slicker side streets. She turned onto Cornell Avenue. The limbs of the trees lining both sides of the street were flocked with last night's snowfall.

Gloria pulled the van over to the curb in front of an older red brick home with a large front porch. Heaps of snow left by the plows sat along the curb.

The sidewalk in front of the house was chalky-white from too much rock salt. Strings of lights blinked in the shrubs hugging the house, and in the bay window a Christmas tree sparkled. From the street, the muted barking of a dog interrupted the snowy silence.

As Gloria led me up the front steps, I realized the barking was coming from inside. She rang the doorbell and the yapping grew louder. Sprigs of holly gathered in a red velvet bow decorated the front door. Gloria plumped and straightened the bow's loops.

I stood behind her rocking on my heels. In the porch light, our breath was visible, and I noticed my puffs were coming out twice as fast as hers. What if Ginny Davidson had invited me to expose what a fraud I was?

Then I remembered how puzzled Ginny looked at Holy Redeemer. Her surprise was genuine. But who had set me up?

Then it hit me. People hated toy scalpers so much, I bet someone saw the Davidsons on TV requesting a Sammy and thought they'd play a joke on a scalper.

Behind the leaded glass door, the barking grew louder. "I take it they have a dog?"

"Oh, yeah. Regina. She's very friendly."

A light came on inside, and the large man from the church opened the door. He was bent over holding on to the collar of a bulldog, whose massive jaws looked as if they could encompass my whole head. The dog growled and hunkered down.

"Regina, knock it off!" the man said as he nudged the animal with his leg. The dog snorted, reminding me of the way I used to grumble under my breath after my father yelled at me. "Go lie down."

Sulking, the dog lumbered away, but not before turning to look back at me with a snarl, telling me I was a marked man.

"Wow, what's with Regina?" Gloria asked as she stepped into the foyer.

"I don't know," the man said. "Usually she's so docile."

I walked into the house as if entering a lion's den, and the man closed the door behind me.

Inside the large entry, the woodwork—the hardwood floor and staircase—was partially stripped and sanded. The scent of sawdust hung in the air and the newly sanded floor felt slippery, smooth under my boots.

The man extended a hand. "I'm Joe Davidson." I shook it and knew from his callused palm that he must be doing all the labor. "It's great to finally meet you, Tom."

He appeared to be in his early forties, but as I looked more closely, I was stunned to discover that he was probably only thirty at the most. His hair was receding, and he wore a navy and gold striped rugby shirt that accentuated his belly.

Gloria looked around the entry. "You're redoing this? I thought—"

Joe put a finger to his lips. "Shhh. I told Ginny I'd have this done before Christmas. She's on my case."

Gloria turned to me. "Joe has his own business. He makes custom-made cabinets and furniture."

"Waiting drives me crazy," he said, running his hand over the staircase's bare wood. "So I keep busy sanding."

Gloria sighed. "I know. It's torture." She took off her coat and handed it to him. "Here, Uncle Joe."

Gloria, dressed in jeans and a gray TRU sweatshirt, looked like one of the beautiful girls featured in its admissions catalog. When I was a senior in high school, I used to sit for hours drooling over the babes in them, convinced that when I went to college, all the chicks would look like models. Then I entered the physics program and discovered that they looked like prison matrons.

93

"Cut that 'Uncle Joe' stuff out," he said as he took Gloria's coat. He turned to me. "I'm not that much older than Gloria, but she makes out like I'm older than dirt." Joe took my fatigue jacket too and hung both of our coats in the closet.

Joe closed the door and frowned. "I'll be honest, though, this waiting for a match ages you."

Gloria patted him on the back. "Ah, after Christo gets his transplant and he's well again, I'll watch him, and you and Ginny can take a cruise—visit an island and relax."

Joe rolled his eyes. "The only island I'll be able to afford will be Neville Island."

I laughed. Neville Island was a small plot of land in the middle of the Ohio River near Alcosan, the sewage treatment plant.

Joe led us through an archway into the living room. Family portraits hung on the wall. Most of them were of Christo. The boy I met at church looked markedly different from the healthy boy's pictures on the wall.

On a green plaid couch, sat Ginny Davidson. Christo lay sleeping on her lap with the Sammy I'd given him tucked under his arm. Already, the toy had been customized with love from Christo; the fur was matted and the vinyl face scuffed.

"Come on in," Ginny whispered. "Sit down."

I followed Gloria to the love seat directly across from Ginny. Regina, who was grousing under the coffee table in front of me, leaped to her feet and barked. I stiffened.

"Regina!" Joe bellowed. The dog came out and laid its enormous head in Gloria's lap. She petted the nasty beast; and it yammered with satisfaction.

"Don't worry, Tom," Ginny Davidson said, "Regina wouldn't hurt a flea."

I smiled and tried to relax, but the thought of that dog's teeth closing around my neck had me on edge.

The dog, the sick kid, and the possibility that somehow my deception might come out, made me anxious. Tense, my feet were pressed against the floor, my hamstrings taut like steel cables, and my back so stiff that I hovered above the cushions like an airfoil.

"Tom," Ginny said softly, "sorry for not greeting you at the door, but I was reading Christo a story, and he dozed off." She stroked her son's cheek. "He's so tired lately. Regina's barking didn't even wake him."

"That's OK," I replied, glancing to make sure the stupid dog was still nuzzling Gloria.

"And I want to apologize for falling apart on you at the blood drive" she said. "You see, we hoped we'd have 300 donors show up, but more than 750 came." Her eyes glistened with tears. "It was the largest turnout ever in Pittsburgh. We were overwhelmed, and then when you showed up . . ." She stopped for a moment to compose herself. "Well, I just lost it." She took her hand from Christo, wiped a tear, and then laughed. "You probably thought I was a lunatic."

My first appraisal of her at Holy Redeemer had been unfair. Ginny was pretty in an uncomplicated way. Her shoulder-length brown hair framed her dark eyes and straight white teeth. She wore little or no makeup, and I noticed dark circles under her eyes. I guessed her to be the same age as Joe, and like her husband, it looked as if her youthfulness seemed to be very fragile, that worry and fear had taken their toll.

"That's OK," I said. I didn't know what to do with my hands, so I massaged my knees that had begun to ache from the tension in my joints.

"No, Tom, thank you so much. You'll never know how much you've done for us."

I felt myself blushing. "You're welcome."

Ginny, sitting with her son's body draped over her lap, reminded me of a sculpture I'd seen in one of my mother's art books—Michelangelo's *The Pieta*. I shook off the image; it was too morbid to think of the kid as dead.

Ginny cocked her head and flashed her eyes at Joe, who leaned against the doorway. He caught Ginny's gestures and straightened up. "Hey, would you like something to drink?" He slapped his hands together. "We have Coke, coffee, tea." His eyes lit up. "I got great beer. Brewed it for Christmas. I've been waiting for a special occasion to break into it. How about it, Tom?"

"You brew your own?" I asked.

"Yeah, it's a hobby. What do you say?"

I threw my hands up. "Sure. Why not?"

I must have moved too suddenly for Regina's liking because she growled at me, baring her teeth.

"Wow, Regina, what is wrong with you?" Gloria exclaimed, grabbing the dog by her jowly face. She turned and looked at me. "Regina is usually so calm. Wow, Tom if I didn't know you so well, the way she's acting, I'd think you were the anti-Christ."

I laughed, but it was apparent that Regina had not been suckered by my hero image. Joe called the idiot dog over.

"Gloria, how about you, want a beer?"

"I'm driving—better not."

"Ah, Miss Goody Two Shoes," Joe said, dismissing her with a wave of his hand. He turned and walked out of the room. Thank God, Regina followed him.

"Oh, you'll make him so happy by drinking his beer," Ginny said. "Joe's not very good at saying things, you know, how he feels. This is his way of thanking you, Tom."

Now that Regina had left the room and it had become apparent that Ginny had no intention of exposing my lie, I relaxed, allowing myself to sink down into the love seat's cushion. With Christo asleep, I was able to keep my fear of him and his sickness under control. Ginny, Gloria, and I made small talk, until Christo moaned in his sleep.

Ginny stroked his brown stubble and kissed the top of his head. Suddenly, his eyelids flew up like a window blind whose springs were under excessive tension.

"Sweetheart," Ginny whispered, "Glooey's here."

I looked at Gloria and smirked. "Glooey?" Gloria put her hands on her hips. "He couldn't say Gloria when he was small, OK?"

Christo scooted upright on his mother's lap. "And guess who she brought with her?" He stared at me, wide-eyed, bewildered. "It's the nice man who brought you Sammy." Christo hugged the monkey to his chest. "Oh, no, honey," Ginny said, "he's not going to take Sammy away." Christo relaxed his grip on the toy. "His name is Tom . . . Tom Shepherd."

Something flashed in Christo's eyes, telling me that he was fully awake now. He made himself rigid, slid off his mother's lap, and walked over to the love seat, dragging Sammy along. The vinyl soles of his red fleece sleeper made soft swishing sounds on the carpet. Gloria hugged him. "How are you doing, honey?" She planted a kiss on his cheek.

He squirmed away from her, "Don't call me honey."

"Christo," Ginny said, "don't be nasty."

"Call me big guy," he said, raising his arms over his head in So Big Sammy fashion, "because I'm sooooo big."

Gloria tickled his ribs, and he collapsed like a folding chair in a fit of giggles. Picking him up, she sat him on her lap, so that he faced me. "Do you remember Tom?" Gloria looked into Christo's small face, and he nodded. But he was wary of me, and I was glad because I felt the same way about him. "Can you say 'hi' to Tom?"

"Hi," he said and then buried his face in Gloria's shoulder.

"Can't you say anything else to Tom?"

Christo turned his head and looked all around me searching for something. He screwed up his nose and asked, "Where's your *wams?*"

For Gloria's sake, I tried to be pleasant to the little guy, but I couldn't understand his babyspeak. Desperate, I looked to her for help, but she appeared puzzled too.

Turning to Ginny, I whispered, "I need an interpreter."

Ginny leaned in closer. "What did you say, darling?"

He sighed impatiently. "Where's his *wams?*"

"*Wams,*" Ginny repeated. She mouthed it again, thought for a moment, and then raised her eyebrows. Then her shoulders shook with laughter as she picked up a *Golden Book* sitting on the coffee table. She slapped it against her palms. "Do you mean lambs, sweetie?"

Christo smiled and nodded.

"Before you came," Ginny said, "we were reading the Christmas story. Your name is Shepherd. Of course, you must have lambs."

"Christo," Gloria said, "Tom goes to school with me. You know lambs aren't allowed to go to school. Remember, Mary? How they wouldn't let her keep her little lamb at school because it was against the rules?" Christo shook his head. "Well, Tom's lambs are on a nice farm."

I wasn't sure if it was a good idea to tell him such a tale, but then what did I know? Gloria believed in magic, and she had turned out better than I had.

Joe had been gone for quite some time when Gloria spoke. "Do you think Joe needs any help?"

Ginny looked disgusted. "He's probably out sneaking a smoke."

"A smoke?" Gloria cried. "He's smoking again?"

Ginny spoke cryptically. I guessed she didn't want Christo to hear her criticizing his father. "Started again in the summer." She nodded toward Christo, "When things got bad. Says it relaxes him."

"Relaxes him," harumphed Gloria. "It'll relax him to death."

"Please don't say anything," Ginny said. "He'll think I'm trying to turn everyone against him."

Joe returned carrying a tray of drinks, reeking of smoke. He passed out glasses and then returned to the kitchen with Ginny joining him.

Christo kneeled at the table, drinking apple juice from a sippy cup. "That infuriates me," Gloria whispered. "A year ago, he had some chest pains. It turned out to be nothing, but with his weight, and smoking, and all this stress from Christo's illness, the doctors told him he's a prime candidate for a heart attack. He quit then. Now he's started again. And I'm not supposed to say anything?" Gloria ran her finger under the rubber band on her wrist.

Joe and Ginny returned, each carrying a tray. One was filled with assorted cheeses and crackers and the other with heavenly-smelling Christmas cookies. That darn Regina strutted arrogantly behind them like a Nazi storm trooper. She took up her post under the coffee table, staring at me with cold brown eyes.

"You baked?" Gloria asked.

"It keeps my mind off things," Ginny said. "Christo helped me, didn't you?" Ginny patted her son on his shoulder. He nodded and eyed the cookies.

"Tell Tom and Gloria what you did."

A sly grin appeared on Christo's face. He stood up and giggled, "I ate all the buttons."

"When I turned my back," Ginny explained, smiling and shaking a finger at him, "he ate all the chocolate chips off the gingerbread men."

Christo covered his mouth with his hand and laughed.

Joe scooped Christo up into his arms and tickled his son's belly. "You didn't?"

"Help yourself, Tom," Ginny said.

I knew leukemia wasn't contagious, but I still didn't want to take any chances, so I avoided the gingerbread men that Christo had fingered and selected a nut horn.

As I reached for the largest one, crammed with nuts, Regina lunged from under the coffee table and snapped at me. Startled, I dropped the cookie. The dog pounced on it, scarfing it down.

Joe jumped up. "That's it, Regina! You're out of here!" He grabbed the dog by the collar and dragged her from the room.

Ginny apologized profusely for the dog's behavior and when Joe returned, he did too. Ginny was not out to get me, the stupid dog was banished to the basement, and Christo was keeping his distance. I could relax now. I reached for another cookie and settled back into the love seat to enjoy the beer and the spread set on the table. The Davidsons thanked me numerous times, pushed so much food on me, treated me so well, I waited for Joe to disappear into the kitchen and return carrying a fatted calf on a Christmas tray.

And as the evening progressed, a different Christo emerged. The shy, timid child gave way to a little boy full of personality. And to my chagrin, he took a liking to me. He sang songs, exhibited his expertise at reciting the alphabet, and showed me how he could wiggle his ears. His father had taught him how to do that. Then he produced a beautiful box, whose lid was made of inlaid wood. Joe had made it for him, and it contained Christo's rock collection—common stones and pebbles he'd found in the neighborhood.

From my father, I'd acquired a working knowledge of geology. Christo's eyes sparkled with delight as he held each rock in front of my face, and I classified it as either metamorphic, igneous, or sedimentary. Any eighth grader could have done the same, but he was nonetheless impressed.

Somewhere around nine-thirty, Christo began to tire, and he managed to wedge himself between Gloria and me on the love seat. The drowsier he became, the more he encroached until he nodded off with his head in Gloria's lap and his spindly legs draped across mine.

I really didn't want him on me, but I couldn't exactly dump him off my lap, now could I? After all, I had a hero's persona to maintain.

Gloria rubbed his hair. "He looks good," she said, her voice filled with hope.

"He does," Ginny agreed, but the look of concern that crept across her face failed to match the optimism of her words. "I just hope they find a match soon. This second round of treatments has taken a toll."

Gloria picked up the little guy's hand and held it. It was limp with sleep. "Maybe we'll have good news soon."

Joe, sitting next to his wife, stretched an arm across the back of the couch. "I certainly hope so. I don't think we could rustle up any more donors or dough."

"Dough?" I asked, pushing the hair back from my face.

Joe sighed and leaned forward. "Money. Our medical insurer, Hippocraticare, doesn't cover the cost of tissue typing the donors.

I shook my head. "I don't believe that."

"Oh, believe it, Tom. They say it should be covered by the donor's insurer. And that's not all—"

Ginny squeezed Joe's knee. "Let's not talk about it now. Tom doesn't need to hear—"

"You're always doing that. Don't tell me not to talk about it!" Joe cried, waving his arm wildly. Ginny withdrew her hand from his knee.

"But Joe," Ginny said, "Tom's not interested in our problems."

Out of the corner of his eye, Joe looked at Ginny. "Hey, I'm not the one who said it would be worth giving up our privacy to save Christo."

Ginny's smile flattened into a line. He sat back and put his arm around his wife and squeezed her shoulder. "Look I'm not complaining. I wish I was sick instead of Christo. The thing is I don't think that a family facing a catastrophic illness should also have to worry about winding up in the poor house.

"Doesn't your insurance cover anything?" I asked.

Ginny jumped in. "Hippocraticare. . . ."

Joe mumbled, "More like Hypocrite Care."

Ginny ignored his comment and continued, "Hippocraticare pays eighty percent of the medical costs, after we meet our deductible of $700. We pick up the other twenty, up to a cap of $5,000 per year."

Joe interrupted. "That doesn't sound so bad, Tom, but I'm self-employed and have to buy my own coverage. The premiums are already astronomical. Two years before Christo was born, we bought a house and wiped out our savings. And I was already in debt from starting the business. There wasn't much money to put aside for a rainy day. After a lot of fertility tests and stuff, Ginny got pregnant, and Christo was delivered C-section adding to the debt. When Christo was diagnosed, we were still paying on those bills. The first year of his treatments combined with our previous balances left us with nearly $10,000 in uncovered medical expenses. I know that doesn't seem like much, but it crippled us. And every year since, we've added more to the mountain of debt. I tell you, Tom, don't get sick. It's too expensive."

My hand froze when I noticed myself stroking Christo's back. His chest rose and fell rhythmically beneath my fingers.

This was what I'd been afraid of all along—getting caught up in their crisis. I only wanted Gloria, nothing else, but I felt myself being sucked into their atmosphere of suffering. As the air rushed out of Christo's lungs as he slept, I wondered what it would it be like if he stopped breathing? If he died? A lump swelled in my throat. I was no longer afraid of Christo but of what the future held for him.

"We checked into everything," Joe said, a muscle twitching in his jaw. He leaned closer toward me. "You tell me, Tom, what good are miracle drugs and medical breakthroughs when no one can afford them?"

I composed myself, swallowing the lump and said, "I don't know."

"But what really burns me up, Tom, is that in order to save my son's life, I've had to hold car washes and spaghetti dinners, like I was raising money to go to band camp." Joe's face was scarlet and a blood vessel pulsed near his temple. I wondered if high blood pressure was another reason why the doctors wanted him to stop smoking.

"Well," Ginny said, "if I've learned anything from Christo's illness, it is not to worry about tomorrow." She looked at Joe and patted his hand. He seemed to be calming down, the redness receding from his face. "Christo's still here, we're together, we have a roof over our head, and we're not starving. God's been good to us so far, and I'm trusting that He'll continue to be so."

I had to clamp my lips together to prevent myself for telling her she was an idiot to rely on God. But that would be too cruel. She would learn in time, like I had, what God was really like.

Gloria looked at the clock on the mantle. "Wow, it's getting late. We'd better be leaving." Ginny came and lifted Christo from her lap. Gloria stood, straightened her jeans and sweatshirt, and kissed Christo's cheek as his head rested on his mother's shoulder. "I ate so many cookies, I don't think I can walk," Gloria groaned.

I rose too, and stretched. "Yeah, thanks for the food and the great beer." I shook Joe's hand.

With his other one, he grasped my shoulder. "Take it easy, Tom. And stop by again."

Joe moved toward Ginny and held out his arms. "Here, I'll take Christo up to bed." Ginny handed the child to his father, and Joe headed upstairs, while Ginny escorted us to the foyer and retrieved our coats.

"Say goodnight to Christo for me," Gloria said, "and tell him I'll see him tomorrow night."

"Oh, that's right," Ginny said, grabbing Gloria's arm. "Can you be here at five-thirty?"

"Sure," Gloria said. Then she turned to me. "I'm babysitting."

Regina barked in the basement. "And say goodnight to Regina for me," I said. Everybody chuckled.

She hugged Gloria and whispered something in her ear and they both laughed.

"What's so funny?" I asked.

"Nothing." They spoke in unison.

Gloria opened the door and pulled out her car keys. Ginny surprised me by hugging me tightly too. "Please pray for us," she said as she released me. The desperation in her eyes frightened me. I never pray, but I couldn't tell her that. For her sake, I'd try. But as I left her house, I wondered if the prayers of an unbeliever to a nonexistent God would make any difference at all?

Chapter 14

Gloria started the Caravan. "I hope you had a good time."

"I did," I said.

Frost crystals like flowers had grown on the van's windows. Gloria fiddled with the knobs on the dashboard, and a powerful blast of warm air rushed out of the vents, wilting and evaporating them.

"I thought you would," she said. "They're amazing. I don't know how they keep their sanity."

"I don't think I'd be able to handle it. It seems so unfair."

"Seems? It *is* unfair, Tom. When Christo first got sick, that's all I thought about—the unfairness. Why him? Why not someone evil like Saddam Hussein?"

She drove cautiously; the snow had drifted across the streets making them narrower. "You can wonder and wonder until you go crazy. Then you've got to let the questions go." She looked at me. "Know what I mean?"

I nodded that I did, but I didn't. I can't let questions go. Maybe that's why I'm a science major. I need answers. I need to know.

Some of the slush had frozen. Gloria pumped the brakes, testing them. Then we came to the stop sign at the end of Cornell Avenue. "If you don't give up the questions, they'll destroy you."

That maybe so. But if nothing in this world made sense, then what reason was there for living anyway?

"Ginny and Joe found that out," she said. "For a while, they went through a bad spell."

I'd sensed an undercurrent of tension running between them. She adjusted the knob on the heater. "An illness like Christo's can be hard on a marriage."

"Have they had problems?"

"Some. They saw a marriage counselor." Gloria hesitated and glanced over at me. "I shouldn't be telling you this, but I have no one else to talk to. My mother and father—we're all too close to the situation."

"You can trust me." I raised my right hand and cringed, recalling my previous lies to her.

Gloria turned onto Highland Avenue. "They seem to be doing better now."

"Good."

Traffic was light and the van merged easily onto the interstate.

"You know what they say," Gloria said, "something like Christo's illness either makes or breaks you."

I looked out the side window. That was a lie! Sometimes tragedy doesn't make or break you, but cripples you so that you limp along through the rest of your miserable life.

The gusting wind sent a spray of powdery snow across the highway. Sadness washed over me as I compared Gloria's family to mine. The Davidsons' bond was strong like iron links of chain. Ours was as weak as the construction paper loop garlands I'd made in kindergarten. The least little tug and our lives ripped apart.

As we approached the Perry Highway exit, something ahead near the side of the road caught my eye—a patch of white dotting and dashing at the edge of the woods. Before I realized what it was, it darted onto the highway. I opened my mouth to warn Gloria, but the only sound I heard was the screeching of brakes.

Sliding on the snow-glazed highway, the van's front fender clipped the deer's hind legs. It fell to its knees as we skidded past it.

I flew forward, all the G-force concentrating in my forehead. The shoulder harness caught, kept me from crashing through the windshield, and jerked me violently back against the seat as the van spun around and then suddenly came to a halt.

Stunned, the deer lay on the road, twitching. Then it scrambled onto its unsteady legs and jumped into the brush. We were left sitting sideways, straddling the two southbound lanes of the interstate.

"Did I hit him? Did I hit him?" Gloria shouted.

My brain slopped around in my cranium. When it settled, I looked at her, and the sight alarmed me. Her eyes were clamped shut, and her face was corrugated with fear. She gripped the wheel so tightly the knuckles of her hands where white, and I thought her bones might pierce her skin.

"I killed him!" she shrieked. "Oh, please no!"

Past her out the driver's side window, a pair of headlights in the distance was rapidly approaching. My heart pounded like the hammer on a fire bell. We couldn't sit here in the middle of the highway in the dark. We'd get creamed.

"Pull over, Gloria."

"Oh, I'm going to throw up." Her abdomen undulated like a belly dancer's as she leaned forward and gagged. The headlights were closing in, their light shining into the van, beaming on Gloria while she dry-heaved.

"Gloria, listen! Pull off the road now!"

I unbuckled my seatbelt, knocked her hands away, and took over the wheel. The car's lights flooded the van's interior. Straddling the console, I pressed my foot to the gas pedal. Gloria's foot was frozen onto the brake. I kicked it aside and floored the gas. The tires chirped as a horn's blast filled my ears. Turning the wheel sharply, I swerved to the right, pulling the van into the slow lane. In less than a heart beat, the oncoming car zoomed by in the passing lane, nearly kissing the van's back bumper. The wake rocked us as if it we were in a canoe. Awkwardly, I steered the Caravan to the road's shoulder, threw it into park and shut off the ignition, collapsing into the passenger's seat, trembling.

My pulse pounded in my ears like the bass drum in the TRU band. Sweat trickled down the valley of my spine.

I stole a glance at Gloria. Her hands covered her face, and I heard her lip quivering. "You didn't hit him, Gloria," I said, my voice as thin as a filament. "The deer made it across."

No response. Worried, I grabbed her shoulder. "Did you hear me, Gloria?"

Her breathing was rapid and shallow. She dropped her hands from her face, her eyes bulging with terror. Clawing wildly at me like someone drowning, she gasped, "I can't . . . I can't breathe."

She was hyperventilating. What do I do? Why hadn't I paid attention when they taught first aid in health class? Then, from some remote recess in my gray matter, a thought popped into my consciousness: *Breathe into a bag.*

"A bag," I cried, rummaging through my pockets. "A bag. I need a bag!"

Gloria pointed to the one hanging from the cigarette lighter knob. I ripped it off and shook out the trash; wrappers and papers rained over the interior of the van. Putting it to her face, I clamped it tightly over her nose and mouth. "Calm down! Breathe, Gloria! It was a close call, but no one got hurt. Inhale deeply!" She struggled to catch her breath. "We're all OK." I was reassuring myself too. "Even Bambi."

Slowly, as the bag puffed in and out, her breathing became more regular and mine began to settle also. Then suddenly she became agitated again. I put a hand behind her head, sealing the bag even more tightly on her face. Twitching and struggling, she jerked her head away, reached up and tore the bag out of my hands, and let out a rush of air that sounded like she had risen from the bottom of a deep pool. "I can breathe fine, but now you're suffocating me."

"Oh, sorry," I said, settling back into the seat. An awkward silence fell upon the van.

And then she began to weep again.

"Aw, don't cry, Gloria."

"Oh, Tom, when I think about what could have happened." Her voice broke off as she leaned her head against the headrest and closed her eyes. Headlights from the cars heading north flashed on her face, illuminating the silver streaks her tears left on her cheeks. Then I heard a strange sound. *Snap.* I heard it again. *Snap. Snap. Snap.*

Gloria was frantically plucking the rubber band on her wrist. *Snap. Snap. Snap.* I flinched with each strike; the sound of it flogging her flesh sickened me.

"What are you doing, Gloria?"

"I've got to take control of my thoughts." She pulled the rubber strip out again and let it go.

I grabbed her wrists and held them. "Stop, Gloria! I won't let you do this to yourself."

"You don't understand," she said struggling to break free. "I have to."

"You're right. I don't understand."

My eyes caught hers and in their green depths I saw the poison of shame, and my heart went out to her. She ceased resisting and hung her head. Before I let her wrists slip from my grasp, I pulled the rubber band off. She draped herself over the steering wheel, her shoulders heaving with sobs.

"Listen, Gloria," I said softly, "it's too dangerous sitting here on the side of the road. There's a park and ride lot up ahead. Trade places with me. I'll drive there, and we can chill a bit. OK?"

She said nothing, but I heard her seatbelt click as she unlocked it. I crawled over her, into the driver's seat while she scooted beneath me. As we wrestled to change places, I made a joke. "Come to this mosh pit often?" No response—not even a hint of a smile. She slumped into the passenger's seat and stared out the side window. Reaching over, I drew the seatbelt across and buckled her in.

After what had happened, it was natural to be upset. But this was more than upset—this was despondency. And I was frightened.

The park and ride lot was deserted, and I pulled into a space under a lamppost and shut off the engine. Fearful to even touch her, I gently placed a hand on her shoulder. "You OK?"

She buried her face in her hands and sniffled, "I panicked . . . again."

"Again? You've hit a deer before?"

"No." She dropped her hands. Her eyes were rimmed in red as if she had lined them with a felt tip pen. "No, that's not it. It's just that it's such a disappointment."

"Disappointment? You wanted to kill that deer?"

She turned her head, looking at me like I'd been the one freaking out. "No, I didn't want to kill it." She shook her head and murmured, "I just thought . . . I just thought I was getting better."

Instinctively, her fingers reached for the rubber band, but it was gone. Better? Was she sick? Sirens wailed inside me. "From what?"

"I'm not sick in the way you think."

"I don't understand." She looked so fragile in the lamplight.

"I mean I relapsed." She sighed deeply and pivoted to face me. "I thought I'd put this all behind me, Tom, and I wouldn't have to tell you about this now. But since you've seen what a nut case I am, I guess I have to."

I braced myself for what I was about to hear.

She closed her eyes and blurted: "I suffer from an anxiety disorder—I have panic attacks." She opened her eyes and scrutinized my face for a reaction.

I knew the shock was evident on my face. "Panic attacks? Anxiety disorder? You? I—I don't believe it."

"Believe it."

I guess I had to. I had just witnessed one. In freshman year, I'd had a psych class, and I knew anxiety disorders ranked low on the mental

107

illness ladder. I ran my hands through my hair. "Well, at least it's not fatal."

She laughed sarcastically. "No, it only feels that way. And sometimes when things are really bad, I wish it were."

I reached across and grabbed her by the shoulders. "Don't ever say that, Gloria! I don't even want you to think . . . Wow, I mean . . . You're not serious, are you? You wouldn't try anything?"

She reached up and patted my cheek. Her hands were frigid, and I could see the red welts on her wrist. "Oh, Tom, you're so sweet. Relax! I'd never do anything like that. It's just that I'm so tired of battling this." She laughed wryly. "And besides, most of my anxiety stems from a fear of death, so you can be sure I'd never kill myself."

"Thank God," I said as I fell back in my seat. "I swear, Gloria, if I thought you were serious, I'd drive you right over to Western Psych."

"I'm fine—or I'll be fine. It's just that . . . I thought I had conquered this. But obviously, I haven't." She rubbed the red stripes on her wrist.

"Gloria, don't be so hard on yourself. I was afraid too."

"Yes, but at least your fear didn't endanger anyone. What am I ever going to do?"

I felt sorry for her. "How long have you had this condition, Gloria?"

"Since Christo got sick." She wiped at her eyes with the back of her hands like a child.

"So it's something recent then?"

She nodded. "Until then I was fine. Then he got sick and shortly thereafter the bottom fell out of my life."

"His illness trigged this?"

"Yes. He got sick in the spring of my sophomore year. When my mother phoned and told me that he had leukemia, I felt like I'd been shoved out a window. Things were never the same again. All that summer I watched him suffer through medical treatments, and when I started my junior year, everything caught up with me. "

"You just started panicking?"

"No, it snuck up on me. One night in the fall while I was studying, I noticed my heart skipping a beat, and it scared me. I thought I was having a heart attack. Frightened, I went to the infirmary, but they said I was fine. After that I felt like I couldn't swallow. Again, they found nothing.

"I was constantly checking my breasts for lumps, looking down my throat, or imagining that moles were turning malignant.

108

"Then right after Christmas, I began to experience these 'episodes.'"

"What do you mean 'episodes'?"

"Panic attacks—frequent excursions into hell. I looked normal, healthy, but my thoughts were shredding my soul and devouring me from the inside out. I felt like I was dying."

"Christ, I mean, cripes, I can't imagine." This was a new Gloria emerging before me. A vulnerable, frightened one. A Gloria like me. I wanted the old one back—the confident, outspoken Gloria who knew all the secrets to the universe.

"Tom, have you ever dreamed you were in a burning building?"

"Sure."

"Well, you know how real that terror feels? How everything you're made of cries out for you to run, run for your life?"

I nodded. I knew those feelings like I knew my social security number.

"That's the terror I feel when I'm having a panic attack. Everything—my mind, my body, my soul—screams for me to run, to save myself, to get out of the burning building. But I can't get out, Tom. And do you know why?" She pointed a finger to her heart and her voice caught. "Because I'm the burning building. I'm trapped inside me. My mind terrorizes my body, taking me as a hostage." Her eyes looked so sad. "I can't escape the terror of living inside me."

"Man, it sounds awful," I said, not knowing exactly how to respond.

"Oh, it is. But thankfully I finally realized what was at the root of this."

"What was it?"

"That I'd been blessed all my life."

"What?"

"I know it sounds crazy, but being blessed is scary. Christo's illness showed me how fragile my world was. Everything I loved could be wiped out in a blink of an eye."

I guess I never suffered from panic attacks because I had nothing to lose.

"Looking at you, I'd . . . I'd have never guessed."

"Nobody did back then either," Gloria said. "That's also part of my problem. I felt I couldn't tell anyone because they might think less of me. And with the family focused on Christo, I didn't want to add to their burden."

"But you seem . . . so perfect."

She covered her ears. "Oh, don't say that. I've always thought I had to be perfect for people to love me. But you know what, Tom?" She looked at her hands. "Perfection is loneliness decked out in good clothes. People resent it. When I began to admit that I had problems, I felt less isolated."

I admit it. I was less intimidated by her now. But she was still by far the most wonderful girl I had ever known. "All right then," I said. "You're perfectly flawed."

She smiled weakly.

"When was the last time you had an attack?" I asked.

"This severe? Six months ago. I dropped out of school for awhile, went to a bunch of different counselors and psychologist until I hit upon one who suggested cognitive therapy. Do you know what that is?"

"The rubber band?"

"That's a part of it. It's changing your behavior by monitoring your thoughts. All I thought of was gloom and doom." She clenched a fist in front of her stomach. "These thoughts were causing these horrible physical reactions. I've done a lot of soul searching, Tom, and learned that what I wanted most was assurance that everything in my life would be OK. But as you know, life comes with no guarantee. My parents, therapists, anti-anxiety drugs couldn't give me one. There's no one on this side of eternity that could guarantee that my life would be fine.

"Then I began to wonder how people who had terrible things happen to them coped. Why didn't they crack up? Why didn't Ginny?" She looked at me. "And you, Tom, how did you overcome your mother's death?"

Her question startled me. "Ah, Gloria, I was just a kid. I didn't know what was happening."

"You know what the secret to survival is?"

I shrugged.

"Faith." Gloria shifted, tucking a leg under her, sitting higher now. She leaned toward me. "I know you think I'm a pain with all this God talk, but I tell you, Tom. . . ." She picked up my hand and her tone was solemn. "Faith is what saved me."

"Well, if it helps . . . . " I started to speak, but she cut me off, and I noticed the fire in her eyes that first attracted me was blazing again.

"It wasn't like I hadn't known God before, Tom. I'd always gone to church, prayed, followed the commandments, believed in Him—jeez, I'm still a virgin."

I choked on my own saliva.

Laughing, she patted me on the back. "I know. I should be out the Carnegie Museum with all other dinosaurs."

I cleared my throat. "No, it's just that . . . well," I brushed the hair out of my face. "These days, that's unusual." And I quickly added, "but nice."

Really nice. I couldn't believe my luck. Finding a beautiful virgin these days is as rare as finding a Hollywood star with real breasts.

"What I'm trying to say is that even though I lived a moral life, something was still wrong. Then I came upon a Bible verse that changed my life. It said 'Fear is worthless. What is needed is trust.' Lack of faith was my problem. I let fear rule my life and keep me straight."

"Well," I interrupted, "if you'd like to overcome your fear of sex, I'd be willing to help you."

She tilted her head and grinned. "Somehow I thought I could count on you for that."

She dismissed my offer as a joke but I was serious.

"I copied that verse on a slip of paper and kept it tucked inside my pocket. When the waves of panic ambushed me, I pulled it out and read it over and over until the terror subsided."

She was staring at me, waiting for my reaction.

"How awful . . . I can't imagine." I squeezed her hand.

"Tom, I'm convinced everything stemmed from not having my head on straight spiritually. Faith is essential to my mental health. My belief in God has enabled me to get a handle on this and reclaim my life."

If God meant her being happy, I guess I could put up with Him.

"Tom, remember, when you said you'd never seen me on campus before? Well, I just transferred to TRU this semester." She shook her head and the corners of her mouth curled downward in sorrow, "Everyone has an Achilles' heel. I guess this is mine."

I envied her. At least she knew what her flaws were. I had no idea where to begin to rehabilitate myself.

"Look, Gloria. Six months is a long time. Don't be discouraged. You've made great progress." I smiled impishly. "And remember nobody is perfect."

She sighed. "You're right, I guess." She began gathering up the wrappers littering the car and stuffing them in the trash bag. "I think I've calmed down enough to drive now." We switched seats again and pulled back out of the park and ride lot.

We rode silently along while I tried to take in all that had happened tonight. As we rounded a bend, the sparkling skyline of the city came into view, and Gloria turned to me. "I hope you don't think I was keeping this from you, Tom. Mental illness scares people, and I know my religious beliefs annoy you too. I was just waiting to see how things progressed between us before I told you." Her voice fell to a whisper. "I'll understand if you don't want to see me anymore."

"No! No, I want to see you again!" Why would she think that? "Look, Gloria, I understand how screwed up life can make you. I told you about my relationship with my father, but I glossed over a lot of stuff."

I thought back to all those nights as a child I spent lying in my bed in the dark. "Gloria, I'm going to tell you something I've never told anyone before. And it's not something you'd tell a girl to impress her." I picked at a hangnail on my thumb. "After my mother died . . . well, I started wetting the bed."

I can still feel those clammy flannel pajamas as I lay in bed next to my father's room crying for my mother until I don't know if the bed was wetter from pee it or my tears.

"That's understandable," she said.

"I wet it until I was fourteen."

"Oh, Tom," she looked over at me, her eyes full of compassion, "that's so sad. When I think about your life—losing your mom at such a young age—I feel guilty even telling you about my stupid, imaginary problems."

At that moment when I had her sympathy, I should have come clean about how I had lied to impress her, how I never intended to give Christo the Sammy. But I couldn't. Under the surface of Gloria's terrible secret lay substance. She'd worked hard to fill the void within her with goodness. Beneath my surface lay nothing but a bottomless abyss.

We pulled into the dorm's parking lot around eleven-thirty. The campus was alive; lights burned brightly in the dorms. Gloria angled the van into a space and turned off the ignition. A group of guys pelted each other with snowballs as they walked across the lot toward the direction of the bars. The van's hot engine pinged as it cooled in the winter air.

I looked at her, my beautiful, fearful Gloria, and I felt a force pulling me to her, a force as natural and strong as the moon's tug on the sea. As I sat there listening to my breath rushing in and out, a tide of longing swelled within me. I needed to touch her, kiss her, have her fill me with her substance and goodness. I leaned over to kiss her, but she held her fingertips to my lips, stopping me.

"Thanks, Tom," she whispered, "for being so understanding. Not many guys would put up with the stuff I put you through tonight."

I said nothing but moved my lips to her wrist, where I kissed the angry welts. Then I took her hand and held it as I pressed my lips to hers. When she pulled away, her eyes shimmered like a moonlit ocean, and she raised her hand to my feverish cheek.

"Do you know what Ginny and I were laughing about when we were leaving?" Her voice was smooth and it lapped at my senses like waves licking a shoreline. I shook my head. "She said you were a keeper. Oh, and, Tom, you truly are."

She gave me a peck on the cheek and slowly withdrew her hand. Then Gloria turned the key in the ignition, signaling that it was time for me to leave. "Oh, I almost forgot," she said. "I'm babysitting Christo tomorrow night. You can come along, if you want."

I found it difficult to speak, now that my lips had discovered a higher purpose—kissing her. "Sure," I mumbled.

"Come to Ginny and Joe's anytime after five-thirty," she said. I felt for the door's handle, and stumbled out of the van. "Night, Tom."

"Night," I replied and shut the door.

Standing in the parking lot, under the bright lights, amidst flying snowballs, raucous laughter, and the thumping of far-off music, I watched her back out. She waved and honked her horn as she shifted into drive and pulled away.

When the glow of her red taillights faded from sight, I turned, leaped over the ridge of snow ringing the lot, and sprinted up the walkway. And to exhaust the blistering energy burning throughout my body, I ran the five flights of stairs to my room. If I hadn't, I swear I'd have burst into flames and been Three Rivers University's first documented case of spontaneous combustion.

Chapter 15

"You sleep with that chick tonight?" Rob was stretched out on his bunk balancing a can of IC Lite on his chest, his hand rustling through a bag of Snyder's potato chips. Some god awful grunge rock thumped out of the CD player.

I lowered the volume. "What'd you say?"

He pulled out a handful of chips, stuffed them into his mouth, and mumbled, "I said, you sleep with that chick tonight?"

"What? No—none of your business." I sat on the couch and bent to unlace my Doc Martens.

"Oh, come on. Sure you did." Rob stoked his mouth with more food. The chips shattered between his teeth, dropping crumbs all over his chest. "I've never seen you like this before. Since you've come in, you've been prowling around this room like a caged animal." He made his voice syrupy. "Why, Thomas, I declare you're positively glowing."

I looked up from undoing my shoes and pointed a finger at him. "And I declare you're an idiot."

He gulped his beer. "Come on, tell me."

"Look, knock it off. I don't like you talking about Gloria that way. She's not like the sleazes you know. She's special."

"Oh, did I offend you? She's different. She's special," he mocked me. "Yeah right. Next you'll be telling me she's still a virgin."

I ignored him. What Gloria was or wasn't was none of his business. I stood and pulled my sweatshirt over my head. My skin was still damp from sweating out the near collision.

Rob hopped out of his bed carrying the beer and bag of chips. He brushed the crumbs from his chest and came to stare into my face.

His breath smelled as greasy as a deep fryer. "She told you she was a virgin, didn't she?"

"Perhaps you didn't hear me," I said, as I walked to the dresser, "this is none of your business."

He followed, crunching chips. "I don't believe it." He laughed derisively, as he set his beer on the dresser. "She did tell you she's a virgin."

I ransacked the dresser drawers for a T-shirt. "So what if she did? What's it to you?"

He roared with laughter, potato chip crumbs sputtering out of his mouth like confetti. "And you believe her?"

I turned up my nose at him and flicked off the potato chip flakes that had landed on my chest. "Why would she lie?"

"Hello! Hello!" Rob said, waving a hand in front of my face. "Is there anyone at home in there?" I pushed his oily hand away. "For a guy with a 3.9, you're really dense. A girl tells a guy she's a virgin for only one of two reasons." He held up his index finger. "One. She's either done the whole football team and is now trying to appear pure or . . ." Rob smirked, rubbed my chest, and panted, "Two. She wants you."

"Get out of here," I said, shoving him. I pulled a T-shirt out and slipped it over my head. "You don't know what you're talking about."

"Oh, yeah? How many chicks you been with?"

"And how many have you that weren't bombed out of their minds?"

He put his arm around my shoulder. "I'm telling you man, she wants you." I threw his arm off me and walked away. "If this chick is so special, then what does she want with you? Ever think about that?"

Only constantly. I sat on the chair and slipped out of my jeans.

"If she's the sweet piece of meat you make her out to be, then my guess is that you're her 'walk on the wild side.'"

"Walk on the what?"

"You know, the wild side. She's slumming, Tommy. She's probably tired of jocks and rich dudes like Chaz and wants to do a different type guy, someone a little scruffy and dangerous. Someone like you."

"Where do you come up with these theories?"

"Don't believe me, but I'm warning you, man. If you want to keep this chick, then you better give her what she's after."

"You're out of your mind."

"Am I? Let me guess." He closed his eyes and lay his palm across his forehead like he was a psychic. "Judging by the color in your

116

cheeks, your sweaty clothes, and the way you came flying through the door, I'd say that just before you came in, you two were going at it hot and heavy. Right?" He opened his eyes, waiting for my answer.

"Well, yeah."

He slapped me on the back. "I'm telling you, you're going to lose her if you don't make a move and quick. She's given you an engraved invitation to a party in her pants. What more do you want?"

Maybe Rob was right. Maybe she did want me. She kissed me, and she did tell me I was "a keeper."

Reaching into his bag, I took a handful of chips. "I don't know." I didn't want to do anything to mess things up with Gloria. "She does seem to like me."

"Like you? I'm telling you, if you don't do something, she's going to drop you fast. Look," said Rob, "when are you seeing her again?"

"Tomorrow night." I put a chip into my mouth. "I'm helping her babysit her cousin, you know, the sick kid."

"You're a scientist. Test my theory."

"And how do I do that?"

"Here's what you do." He put his arm around my shoulder. "When the kid goes to bed," he said, "see how far you can get."

"What?"

"You know. See if she resists. If she doesn't, then I say move in for the kill."

"Where?"

"At the house."

"On the living room couch?"

Rob chuckled. "Why not? Worked for my mother. That's where I was conceived."

"Oh yeah, sure. Like I'm going to do it on a couch while we're babysitting—that's so . . . so high school. She'll definitely dump me."

"OK, Don Juan, then bring her back here."

"I'm meeting her there. She'll have her own car, and besides I can't bring her here . . . " I waved my hand around the room. " . . . with all the Sammys everywhere."

"OK, here's the plan," Rob said. "Sunday we'll clean out all the toys—stash them in our cars or something. Are you going to see her on Monday?"

"Probably."

"OK then, on Monday you find some way to lure her up here to the Pleasure Palace and have your virgin sacrifice."

As I walked to my bunk, the crumbs Rob had dropped on the floor stuck to the soles of my socks. I lifted my feet and brushed them away. "What if she gets mad? Then what?"

"Oh, that's easy. Flatter her. Tell her she's so beautiful, you couldn't control yourself. Chicks love a line like that." I crawled up into my bunk and folded my hands behind my head.

Rob walked over and stood next to my face. "You know, Tommy, I envy you. If she really does turn out to be a virgin, you'd get to break her in the way you want." He sighed and looked off into the distance. "Ah, there's something special about being the first," his voice was low and dreamy. "I remember one time, when I was a kid, we went to Sea World. It was the first time I'd ever been in a motel. Oh man, was I excited." A wistful look appeared on his face. "You know how they used to sanitize toilets seats and seal them with those little paper bands? Well, my mother let me be the first one to rip off the paper and use the clean toilet. I'll never forget it." He punched me in the arm. "Yeah, there is something special about being the first."

*****

By the time I'd left for work the next morning, Rob had orchestrated every move I was to make on Gloria and had code-named the whole operation, "The Big Bang." All during work on Saturday, I rehearsed my part in my mind, wondering if I should follow the advice of a moron who gets his kicks breaking toilet sanitation bands.

My shift at the bookstore ended at five-thirty, and I arrived at Ginny and Joe's a little after six. Before I even set foot on the porch, Regina started barking. I rang the doorbell, and the stupid dog took a run at the door like a canine battering ram. Gloria appeared behind the glass side panel and yelled, "Wait, Tom, until I put her in the basement."

A few minutes later a flushed-faced Gloria opened the door with Christo at her side. She pushed a strand of hair out of her face. "When that dog doesn't want to move," she huffed, "she just sinks to the floor. I had to pick her up and carry her down the basement steps. Goodness, she weighs a ton." Gloria opened the door wide. "Come on in the coast is clear now."

Christo stared up at me as I entered the house. "Regina hates you, Tom."

I patted his shoulder. "I think you're right, Christo."

Gloria closed the door. I didn't know whether I should kiss her or not. Remembering my mission, I figured I'd better start softening her up, so I gave her a little peck on the cheek. "How's it going today?" I asked. She was wearing jeans and a white thermal knit T-shirt.

"No problems." When I handed my fatigue jacket to her, I noticed she hadn't replaced the rubber band I'd removed. The red welts had faded to pink.

"You sure?"

"Yeah."

She seemed like she didn't want to talk about what had happened last night, so I didn't press her.

"Come into the kitchen. You're just in time for dinner." Ah, the magic word—dinner. The house was filled with the smell of frying beef, and I hadn't eaten since lunch. Christo slipped his hand into mine and dragged me into the kitchen.

Before taking a seat at the table, I dug around in my jeans pocket and told Christo to open his hand and close his eyes. He shut them tightly, and I dropped a rock into his palm, one that I'd found many years ago on a rock hunt with my father. It was the size of a ping pong ball. "You can look now."

When Christo opened his eyes, they nearly rolled out of his head. "Wow!" he said.

"You can keep it. Add it to your collection."

He held the rock up in front of his face, marveling at its golden luster. "Glooey, look. See what Tom gave me." While Gloria admired his treasure, Christo murmured. "Gold. I'm *wich*."

"'Fraid not, pal," I said. "That's not gold. It's pyrite. Also known as fool's gold because a lot of people have mistaken it for gold. It's not valuable. Glooey," I winked at Gloria as I said Christo's ridiculous nickname for her, "likes me to tell her amazing facts and maybe you'd like to hear one too?" Christo nodded. "Did you know every rock on earth is made of the same elements, or materials, that are found all over the universe? No matter where you travel in space, the moon, mars, the North Star, you'll always find the same elements."

"*Weally?*" Christo asked.

"Weally," I said.

Gloria rubbed my arm and smiled. "Even though it's not valuable, it's still pretty, and it's amazing to think that something like this rock could be found billions of miles away. What do you say to Tom?"

"*Fanks.*"

"No problem," I said. "I thought you'd like it."

I sat at the square wooden table. It looked handmade, probably one of Joe's creations. Gloria stood at the stove stirring. She looked so pretty, my mouth began to water, and I wasn't sure if it was from lust or hunger.

Gloria peered over her shoulder. "Christo, tell Tom what we're having for dinner."

"Chicken noodle soup and sloppy Josephs."

"Sloppy Josephs?"

"Yeah, they're so much better than plain old sloppy Joes," Gloria said, "that we call them by their formal name. Right, Christo?"

He put his hand to his mouth and whispered. "Glooey puts cheese on them and hot sauce."

"Hey," Gloria cried, as she set a sandwich in front of Christo, "you're not supposed to reveal the chef's secret ingredients."

Gloria set a plate in front of me too and then placed her hand on my back. "I know what you must be thinking—the girl can play the piano, cook gourmet meals—is there any limit to her talents?"

"I am impressed," I said.

She ladled out the soup into bowls. I wasn't used to being waited on and it made me antsy sitting there. "Need any help?"

"Nope, got everything under control." I think we were both recalling what had happened last night. She raised her eyebrows. "For now at least."

She seemed so much more relaxed than the previous evening. Thank goodness. I swear I'd never even attempt to make out with her if she had still been upset.

She brought the bowls to the table and took a seat. She and Christo prayed while I wondered what exactly were the limits of her talents? Would she be responsive to my advances I planned to make after Christo had gone to bed?

After dinner while she cleaned up the kitchen, I hoped to spend the time alone with her, but I was sent into the living room with the assignment of amusing Christo. We played a quick game of Candyland. It was quick because Christo had stacked the deck so that he drew Queen Frostine from the pile and won the game. He next suggested a Barney video, but I quickly nixed the idea. That dinosaur with the Dudley Doright voice irritated me.

"If you don't want to watch Barney, then what can we do?" he asked, one hand on his hip and the other outstretched. He pronounced Barney like it was "Bonnie."

"Ah, I don't know." I said, looking at the pile of toys. "How about Legos?"

"Nah," he shook his head. "Played them with Glooey before."

I picked up a case of small cars. "How about Hot Wheels?"

"Don't feel like it. Let's watch Barney."

"I've got it," I said. "Follow me." I led him into the dining room.

"We going to play ghost?" he asked. The whites of his eyes glowed in the dark room.

"No, something better."

At the bay window, I raised the blinds. Leaning against the pane of glass, I peered up into the sky. A smattering of stars winked back at me.

"Come here," I said to Christo. I stood him on the window seat, while I sat next to him. I was afraid he'd lean on the glass and fall through, so I put my arm around his waist. "Do you know anything about the stars?"

He looked down at me. In my arms, he was a wisp of a child, bony and wiry. "I know how to wish on them. Me and mommy do that. I always wish for Nintendo."

"What does your mom wish for?"

"That I get better."

I had to ask. Didn't Ginny know that wishes never come true if you revealed them?

"What I meant were constellations?"

"Is that when you can't go poopy?" He wrinkled his nose, "Cause I had that once."

I laughed. "No, that's constipation. Constellations are pictures the stars make in the sky."

He pressed his nose to the pane. "I don't see any pictures."

"There aren't really pictures up there," I explained. "See, long time ago people looked up at the sky and saw things—animals, people."

He scanned the sky. "I don't see any animals."

"Christo, have you ever done connect the dots?"

He looked down at me. "Sure, sometimes when I'm waiting in the doctor's office. I have an activity book."

"Well, that's what constellations are. They're connect the dots with stars." I pointed out the window. "See that group of stars right above that tree? That's a constellation called the Big Dipper." I traced the stars in the sky for him. "Doesn't it look like the ladle Gloria used to dish out our soup?"

"Hey, it does!" he cried. He put his hand on the top of my head. "Show me more, Tom."

We sat at the window, and I taught him how to locate Polaris off the lip of the Big Dipper, Orion the Hunter, and Betelgeuse. We found the twins Castor and Pollux in the sign of Gemini.

121

It was drafty sitting by the window, and I didn't want him getting cold. "That's enough for your first lesson, pal. Let's go see if Gloria is finished yet." I moved to stand.

Christo grabbed my shoulder. "Wait, Tom, show me the one you go to."

"The one I go to? I'm an *astronomer*, not an *astronaut*. I've never been to the stars."

"Not you. Me. My Christmas book that mommy read said a star appeared in heaven. Which one is Heaven?" He put his hands flat on the window, only the glass separating him from the blackness. "Show me where you go when you die, Tom."

I leaned my forehead against the cold windowpane.

He patted my head impatiently. "Show me, Tom."

"Ah, Christo—" That tightness was in my chest again, and it rose and constricted my throat.

Gloria switched on the light. "What are you two doing in here in the dark?"

The light from the dining room chandelier blinded me.

"Tom's showing me con—," He shoved me.

It took me a moment to collect myself. I whispered, "Constellations."

"Yeah, look, Glooey, that's the Big Zipper."

"Dipper," she corrected him.

"Look, I'll show you more."

Gloria took his hand. "Not tonight. It's time for your bath."

Glad not to have to answer his question, I volunteered to carry him upstairs on my back and run the water. Gloria took him to his room, got his pajamas, and undressed him. When I saw his scrawny naked body running into the bathroom, I had to turn my head. That was why I didn't want to get involved. It was too painful. How could this flimsy little body endure more medical treatments? How could this tiny body endure a transplant? How could I endure watching him endure?

Gloria bathed him and washed his sparse hair with Johnson's baby shampoo, treating it like it was the finest gold thread.

We dressed him in a pair of Snoopy pajamas and then he said he wanted a snack. I swear I thought he'd never go to bed. We sat at the table with him while he methodically ate his Lucky Charms, picking out all the marshmallows one at a time and eating them first. By the time he got to the cereal part, it had bloated to twice its size in the milk, and I had to throw it away.

Finally, at nine it was time for him to go to bed, and I helped Gloria tuck him in. His room was decorated in dinosaurs, not wimpy ones like Barney but nasty beasts with claws and fangs. How did he sleep with all these ferocious creatures roaming about? When I was his age, I'd have never been able to shut my eyes in a room like that.

Gloria tucked him under the covers. We sat on his bed, and he and Gloria recited some prayer. Then he "God blessed" I swear everybody in Allegheny County. Finally, he concluded his benediction with something that puzzled me. "And please, God, find a match for me and find the 'seminator' for mommy."

Puzzled, I looked at Gloria and her face was pale. She quickly pulled the covers up to Christo's chin. "I think you covered everybody. Now it's goodnight." She kissed him on the forehead. "Love you."

"Love you too, Glooey."

As Gloria walked away, Christo sat up. "Hey Tom, you're good at finding stuff. You found me a Sammy and all those stars. Maybe you can find the 'seminator.'"

"Seminator—what's that?"

"Christo, it's bedtime," Gloria said sternly. I'd never heard her use that tone of voice with him before.

"But wait," he cried. "Mommy was crying 'cause she wants to find the 'seminator.'"

Gloria snapped off the light. The darkness didn't silence him "She said if it'll help me, she'll find the 'seminator.' Daddy said no way. But Mommy wants to. Maybe you could help Mommy."

"Time to go to sleep, Christo," Gloria said sharply. She flicked on a dinosaur nightlight and left the room. We walked down the steps in silence.

I sat beside her on the plaid couch, and she fired the remote at the TV, flipping through the channels over and over until I interrupted her program roulette. "Hey, how about checking out the Pens' score."

She tuned in the hockey game, and we watched in silence. Christo's strange request had set her off again, but I needed to start making out with her before I ran out of time. Inching closer to her, I put my arm around her, and as I was about to lean over and kiss her, she bolted off the couch.

"Oh, what a mess things are," she said.

Before I fell onto the spot where Gloria had just been sitting, I caught myself. "What? What's a mess?"

"Everything." Her hand went to her wrist, searching for the rubber band. Not finding it, she began fiddling with her silver heart earring as she paced in front of me. "I'm sure you're wondering what Christo was talking about."

Actually, I was wondering if I would ever get my chance to kiss her.

"Well, I told you last night that Ginny and Joe had problems," she stopped and faced me. "But I didn't tell you everything. Now, since Christo brought it up, I guess I'll have to tell you the rest." She held up her right hand. "Swear to me, Tom. Swear you won't tell a soul."

I raised my hand. Right now, I didn't care at all about anything other than making out with her before Ginny and Joe came home.

"You look upset, Gloria. Why don't you sit down." I patted the seat beside me.

She took a deep breath. "OK, but don't worry I'm not having another panic attack." She sat and faced me. I rested my arm on the back of the couch and feigned an interest.

"Do you know what Christo meant by 'seminator?'" I shook my head. "Well, neither did I until a few weeks ago." She stared at her wrists. "When the doctors said that Christo needed a transplant, everyone in the family volunteered to be tested. Family members have the greatest possibility for a match. Ginny's an only child and both her parents are dead, so her relatives were a long shot. I felt certain that someone on our side of the family would be a match. But Ginny didn't want to wait for our test results. She insisted that we proceed with the fundraising and planning for a blood drive and tissue typing. It was weird. Like she knew none of us would be a match.

"As it turned out, we weren't. One day, this woman was on TV and her daughter needed a bone marrow transplant. The woman got pregnant and had a baby who provided the match for the daughter.

"I called Joe and suggested Ginny have another baby. He flipped out. I knew it took a while and fertility treatments to have Christo, and when I pressed the issue, he screamed at me. 'Look there's never going to be another baby. I can't get Ginny pregnant. Christo's not mine.'" He slammed the phone down in my ear."

"Ginny had an affair?"

"No, no. That's what I thought at first. Then later Joe called to apologize, and he reluctantly explained that he's sterile."

"What's wrong with him?" How ironic. The man could create anything from wood, but he could not create a child from his own flesh.

"He didn't really go into it, and I didn't want to ask. Anyway, he told me that Ginny wanted to have a baby of her own, and he felt guilty for depriving her. So he agreed to her being artificially inseminated but with one stipulation—that she never, ever tell how the baby was conceived."

"When none of our blood types matched, Ginny was so desperate she began to investigate the possibility of trying to find the sperm donor. When Joe learned that, he went nuts. He feared people would find out about the insemination. Ginny accused him of not loving and wanting to help Christo because he's not his biological father. That's not true; Joe loves Christo. That was a few months ago when they almost broke up."

"How did they resolve it?"

"Ginny agreed to hold off on locating the donor. But things were very tense. Everybody assumed it was the financial strain. They went to counseling, but I'm the only who knows the real reason."

I sighed. "Wow, that is a mess."

Tom, I'm so worried. She must still want to search for the sperm donor. If she does, it'll destroy their marriage."

Gloria leaned her head back and closed her eyes. Slowly and gently, I began stroking her hair, watching her breasts rising and falling as she breathed.

"Aw, what's going to happen, Tom? What'll we do if there's no match? What'll happen to Christo? What'll happen to Ginny and . . ."

"Calm down, Gloria," I crooned to her. "It'll all work out. They'll find a match. They won't have to find Christo's biological father. Ginny and Joe will be fine, and Christo will live to be an old man."

She relaxed, sinking into my arms. "Ah, I hope so."

I caressed her forehead and felt the muscles under her skin slacken. Leaning over, I kissed her. My lips must have surprised her because I felt her go rigid for a second, and then she relaxed once again into my arms.

We kissed until I was breathless. Then I moved to devour the delicate, sweet flesh behind her ear. As I was poised to make my next move, I heard the front door rattling.

Gloria quickly sat up straight, adjusted her clothing, and smoothed her hair. I moved a respectable distance away from her.

"We're home," Joe called, and it sounded as if he was warning us.

Oh, great. Now that they'd interrupted us, I wouldn't know whether to proceed with "The Big Bang" on Monday or not.

Ginny and Joe walked into the living room. Gloria stood. Her lips were rosy from kissing and her neck brush-burned from my beard. I'd have to remember to shave more often.

"Did you have a good time?" Gloria asked.

"Food was good, same boring people and conversation year after year," Ginny said. "It was the Woodworker's Society. What do you expect?"

Ginny had curled her hair and makeup concealed the dark circles under her eyes and brightened her cheeks. She unbuttoned her coat, and in the simple black dress that she wore under it, she looked attractive. If she and Joe broke up, I'm sure she wouldn't have any trouble finding another man.

"How was Christo?" Ginny asked.

"Good as gold," Gloria said. "We put him to bed about half an hour ago."

Joe loosened his tie and smirked. "So what were you two doing? Watching the Pens?"

"Yeah," I said.

"Watching the Pens," Gloria chimed.

"What's the score?" he asked, smirking and I knew he didn't mean the one from the game.

"I don't know," Gloria stammered. "I wasn't paying attention, we were too busy talking."

"Talking? Huh?" Joe grinned. "About what?"

"Well, we better get going," Gloria said. She dashed out into the hall and brought back our coats.

"Thanks for watching Christo," Ginny said, opening her purse and pulling out some bills.

"If you give me any money," Gloria said as she slipped on her parka, "I'll just put it right back in your mail box."

Perturbed, Ginny closed her purse.

They escorted us to the door and said goodnight. I walked Gloria to her van, and we stood under the streetlight. "Would you like to do something tomorrow?" I asked her.

"I wish I could," she said, unlocking the van, "but I have church, studying, my last piano lessons of the year, and a ton of Christmas shopping."

The disappointment must have shown on my face because she quickly interjected, "But I can see you Monday. How about I meet you up near the chapel again same time as last Monday?"

She was playing right into my hands. "Sure," I said. "That's fine." And between now and Monday afternoon, I'd have to decide whether or not to carry out "The Big Bang."

"Well, goodnight," I said and bent to kiss her, but she put up her hand, stopping me.

126

"Tom, don't look back at the house, but they're spying on us. How do you like Joe giving us the third degree? Ginny and my mother are always on the phone discussing me, my mental state, my love life. It's so annoying. How about kissing me really good so they'll have something to analyze."

"No problem." This was one request I could handle. I brushed my hair out of my face, planted my feet firmly in the snow, and with a sweep of my arms, I jerked her to my chest, pulling her off her feet. Shock registered in her eyes as I clamped my mouth on hers. Sighing, she melted into me. I opened my eyes and looked at her. Her lids were closed and she wore a blissful, dreamy expression. I knew this kiss had cleared the upper deck.

I released her, setting her feet back on the ground. "That good enough?"

"Wow," Gloria whispered. "Better than good." She started for her car and slipped on the snow. I caught her by the elbow. She giggled, opened the car door, and stumbled into the driver's seat.

"Night," I said and closed her door for her. I walked to my car and if I'd been wearing a cap, I would have tipped it to the astonished gallery behind the curtains. I unlocked my car, got in, and I knew instinctively that before I turned the key in the ignition, Ginny was dialing Gloria's mother.

Chapter 16

When I went to bed Saturday night, Rob was still at work. I had trouble falling asleep. The evening with the Davidson's had upset me. Christo's illness was like a small crack in a pane of glass. With time it expanded, sending out a web of fissures that threatened to shatter not only Christo's life but everyone else's as well. I sensed that it would exact a toll from me too.

"The Big Bang" was also on my mind. I still wasn't sure if I should go through with it. I wanted Gloria, but I didn't want to mess things up.

Rob came in around one-thirty and flicked on the light. I pretended to be asleep so that I wouldn't have to report the evening's events to him.

I eventually dozed off, but slept restlessly. Somewhere in a deep recess of my heart, part of me remained awake, burning like a pilot light for Gloria.

On Sunday morning the sound of rattling boxes and rustling plastic bags woke me. I pushed the hair out of my face, lifted an eyelid, and looked down from my bunk. Rob was struggling to stuff a So Big Sammy into a green garbage bag. He took the chill off the room with a profusion of profanity.

"Hey, what are you doing," I called, "playing in the trash?"

"No," he said, tucking one side of the bag under his chin while holding the other open with his hands. "I'm packing up my wares, Tommy." His words were distorted because his chin was welded to his chest. "I'm playing UPS dude today. I've got ten deliveries to make."

"Ten?" I slid down from the bunk and held the bag open for him.

"Yeah, while you were at work yesterday, I sold six more. After we unload these babies, we've only got eleven more left."

"It's only December 6, and that's all that's left?"

Rob opened another bag. "That's all. They're flying out of here. I wish we could get more."

I'd become so involved with Gloria, I'd lost track of the business. "How much do you think we've made so far?"

The tile floor was cold. I scanned the sea of dirty laundry on the floor, fished out a pair of socks, and slipped them over my icy feet.

Rob cinched the bag's drawstrings. "Excluding the cash from the ones I'm delivering today, we've got $5,255. But that's without subtracting what we shelled out to buy them.

He went to the desk, grabbed a pencil, and began figuring. All I wanted was a ballpark estimate, but he began calculating. He'll make a great accountant. He's never happier than when he's adding sums of money.

"So far," he said, "we've netted $3,755 but that's not counting the income from the ten we'll sell today and the eleven units still on hand."

He even talked like an accountant. "Don't forget to deduct the one I gave away from my share."

"I told you to forget it, Ebenezer. We're selling these babies," he pointed to the garbage bags, "for $500 each. By Christmas—I predict we'll be raking in $1,000 a piece."

"You really think so?"

He looked up from his figures. "Oh, yes!"

I whistled. "Then we'll have more than enough for Martinique." I could get my car's heater fixed and have enough dough left over to see me through grad school. Oh, this was fantastic!

"Didn't I tell you back in October that this toy was a gold mine? When I'm at the mall delivering these, I'm going to stop by the travel agency and get some info on Martinique so we can start making some plans. Hey, why don't you come with me?"

"I can't. Someone might recognize me."

"No one will recognize you."

"I don't know. . . ." I felt guilty that Rob had done all the delivering. He had very little free time.

"Come on," he coaxed, "you can sit in the car or walk around the mall. Hey, speaking of plans, you haven't told me about last night. Is 'The Big Bang' still on for Monday?"

I did want to discuss it. The morning had not brought me any closer to a decision.

"OK," I said, "I'll go with you."

I dressed quickly in flannel shirt, jeans, and Doc Martens. Then I helped Rob load the bags of toys into my car. Before I left the dorm, I grabbed the ski mask and tucked it into my fatigue jacket pocket in case I needed to disguise myself again.

After we were out on the road for a while, it became apparent that we should have taken Rob's car because his heater worked. But since his gas tank was on empty, I'd offered to drive. As we motored around the city, Rob wiped the foggy windows, and I updated him on last night's developments with Gloria. I spent four hours chauffeuring him around town. While he went inside the malls to deliver the toys, I sat in my car shivering, staring out the windows, making faces at dogs left in parked cars.

Our last appointment was at Ross Park Mall for two-thirty, and we arrived there forty-five minutes early. Because I was starving and freezing and tired of looking at dogs, this time, I went into the mall with him. We killed time at the food court. I ordered a cup of coffee to warm my hands, and we split a large pepperoni pizza. Then after checking out the new releases at National Record Mart, we rode the escalator to the lower level. Rob had arranged to meet our buyer in the center of the mall where Santa was holding court.

At two-twenty, we arrived in Santa Land and Rob quickly chatted up some ditzy-looking chick standing next to him who had just had her nails done. They were decorated with a little manger scene. Santa, enthroned on a green velvet chair in the center of the area, was attended by two middle-aged elves who charged $7 for a photo with Saint Nick.

Throughout Santa Land, a miniature train packed with children, chugged past mountains of fake snow, papier maché lollipops, and plastic gumdrops. The train traveled in a small loop, and I stared at it, watching it going round and round, letting it hypnotize me.

An intense sadness took hold of me, buckling my knees. To steady myself, I grasped the waist-high white picket fence that ringed and separated me from Santa Land. Why did watching the children make me feel so sad? Then I remembered Christo. Would he be here next year to visit Santa? Would he live another year to take a spin on the train?

Then I began to wonder if I'd ever ridden a train in Santa Land when I was small. I know my father never took me. I strained hard, trying to remember the years before with my mother, but was only frustrated. When my mother died, they not only buried her, they also buried my infancy and early childhood. I don't know when I got my first tooth, took my first steps, or if I ever had the chicken pox.

I felt like knocking over the fence. Christmas had never bothered me before, but for some reason this year was different. This year it angered me.

Feeling a tap on my shoulder, I jumped and snapped my head around. There, standing behind me, was Gloria.

"I thought that was you," she bubbled. The sight of her extinguished the anger flaring inside me. "I didn't know you were going shopping, Tom."

"Gloria, I didn't . . . I wasn't . . . I'm here with Rob."

When Rob saw that I was talking to a gorgeous girl, he ended his conversation with Miss Nativity Nails and began hovering behind me like a gargoyle, his breath hot on my neck reeking of garlic.

"This is Rob, my roommate," I said, pointing my thumb over my shoulder. "And this is Gloria." That was all the introduction he needed. He stepped forward and bowed.

"Nice to meet you, Rob," Gloria said, extending her hand.

He took it and kissed it. I felt sick, like I'd just handed over a Corvette to a sixteen-year-old valet.

"Charmed," he said, holding her hand much longer than necessary. Gloria wiggled it, trying to break free. "I can't tell you how nice it is to meet you," he said.

I swear he was licking his chops like the wolf lying in wait for Little Red Riding Hood.

Gloria freed her hand and smiled weakly.

When I remembered why we were at the mall, my heart started pounding like a jackhammer. At any moment our buyer would approach Rob and ask for the Sammy. I needed to get Gloria away from there. And fast. Taking her by the elbow, I exclaimed, "Rob was just heading down to Service Merchandise to exchange a Christmas gift his Aunt Myrtle sent him, weren't you?" I shot him a look.

"Oh, yeah," he said playing along. He nodded at the garbage bag sitting at his feet containing the Sammy. "It's a Tummy Tyrant," he lied and patted his abdomen, turning from side to side so we could admire his belly. "Tummy's in great shape, don't you think, Gloria?" She gave him a half smile, nodding politely. "I'm going to exchange it for a Butt Bully. Got to have a tiny heinie for spring break—"

Spring break? Before he could spill his guts about our trip to Martinique, I cut him off. "How about we meet you at the food court, Rob." I hustled Gloria to the escalator. "I'm starved. Have you eaten? I bet you're hungry too. Well, at least take a rest and get something to drink." I ushered her onto the escalator, pushing her from behind.

"Slow down, Tom," she said, tripping onto the rising metal stairs. "Is something wrong? You seem so nervous?"

I turned to face her, leaning my back against the handrail so that I could watch her and keep an eye on Rob. Behind her back, Rob was making gestures about how big her breasts were.

"Wrong? Me? No—I'm fine," I said, smiling a cheesy smile. I hoped my dimples would dazzle and distract her.

Midway up the escalator, I watched a young brunette woman wearing a black leather jacket walk up to Rob. Gloria turned to see what I was looking at. My hands dove into her bags. "What did you buy? Oh, GAP! Anything for me?" I said as I rummaged through her packages.

"Tom!" Gloria slapped my hands. "You're going to make me drop everything." She gathered her purchases together and cried, "What is wrong with you? Goodness, you'd think you were the one with the anxiety disorder."

Rob exchanged the garbage bag for an envelope the woman handed him. He counted the money, said something, and then the woman laughed and walked away with a pleased look on her face. The exchange over, my heart slowed, left my throat, and settled back into my chest.

I put an arm around Gloria's waist. "I guess I'm just excited to see you," I said as we stepped off the escalator and headed for the food court.

"Guess who was on the phone with my mother when I got home last night?"

"Let me see," I pretended to think hard. "Could it have been Ginny?"

"You guessed it. That kiss really started something."

I stopped, pulled her close, and nuzzled her neck. "Oh yeah? Like what? What did it start?"

She playfully beat me off. "Tom, calm down. We're in the middle of the mall. When my mother hung up, she quizzed me about you."

The food court was less crowded now, and we easily found a table. "So what did you tell her about me?"

"That you're a heathen."

"Oh, great." I collapsed onto a chair. "That ought to score big points."

Gloria set her packages on a vacant chair. She patted my head. "No, I told her you're the kindest, most understanding person I'd ever met."

"Did you really?"

"Yes. And I told her about the panic attack and how sweet you were. My mom and dad would like to meet you."

I didn't know if I was ready to meet Gloria's parents yet so I didn't answer her. "What are you hungry for?" I asked.

Gloria glanced around the food court. "Pizza. I could really go for a pepperoni pizza."

So I got her a pizza, and forced four more pieces into my already full stomach. As I sat there hoping the button on my jeans wouldn't pop off, I spied Rob's head towering over the other shoppers as he walked through the food court, scanning the place for us. I considered hiding from him. When Rob tries to impress girls, his mouth runs over like a foamy head of beer. Unfortunately, he spotted us and made his way over to the table.

"Where's your Butt Bully?" Gloria asked as Rob strode up empty-handed.

"Aw, they were sold out; they gave me a credit." Rob grabbed an extra chair and pulled it up to the wrought iron bistro table, right next to Gloria. His lanky body perched awkwardly on the dainty chair made him look like Frankenstein at a tea party. He leaned toward Gloria, whose hands rested on the table. "I am so glad we finally got to meet." He placed his hand on top of hers. "Tommy told me you were beautiful, but words pale in comparison."

Gloria smiled. "Thank you."

He looked her up and down, his eyes settling on her chest. "No, I'm not exaggerating." He seemed to be talking to her breasts; he was so enthralled by the curves under her red turtleneck.

Gloria smiled half-heartedly and slid her hand out from under his to cross her arms across her chest.

Not one to take a hint, Rob continued. "I've heard so much about you, I feel we know each other already." I sat listening in disbelief at the line of crap flowing from his mouth. He showered Gloria with compliment after compliment, and if you'd heard him, you'd have never guessed that minutes before in the car he was referring to her as a "sweet piece of meat." Where was he getting this stuff? Then I remembered that he was taking a course in English Lit this semester. I swear, he thinks he's Lord Byron or Robert Browning. My heart began thumping. What if he tries to impress Gloria and shoots his big mouth off about the Sammys?

"It's so crazy that we meet," Gloria said, backing away from his lascivious gaze. "During the Christmas rush, I avoid the malls on the

134

weekend, but I had to get a few gifts. I hate the crowds. All the jockeying for parking spaces. The pushing and shoving ruins my Christmas spirit."

"I know what you mean," Rob said, tapping her on the arm. "I love Christmas, but people have lost the true meaning. It's a disgrace."

I narrowed my eyes at him, warning him to cool it.

"Well, you're certainly not like your roommate," Gloria said. She laced her arm through mine, and although she was speaking to Rob, she stared into my eyes with a look so hot it could ignite kindling. "He has no use for Christmas, but I love it—all the magic and the mystery."

Rob watched the electricity circulating between us. He scratched his head. "Magic? Mystery?" Now that Gloria had so clearly turned her attention to me, he seemed to have lost his enthusiasm for her.

She turned to Rob. "Yes. The magic of the season and the mystery of how much God loves us. It's so fantastic—it's incomprehensible."

"Incomprehensible is right," he snickered. "Speak English, girl. I don't know what in the hell you're talking about."

Gloria straightened up. "I'm talking about God. And Christmas. How God loved us so much he came to earth—"

Rob's face looked like he'd just drank sour milk. "Wait a minute here. . . . You're not one of those Born Agains, are you?"

"Pardon me?" Gloria said.

"A Born Again? You know. A Jesus Freak . . . Holy Roller."

She tilted her head and clenched her teeth. "What if I am? What difference would that make?"

I'd seen Gloria upset and frightened, but I'd never seen her angry before. It was like watching a tornado sweeping across the countryside.

Rob ignored Gloria and turned to me. "You didn't tell me, Tommy, that she's a religious wacko."

Scarlet rose in Gloria's cheeks. I put my arm around her. "Look, Rob," I said, "Gloria has firm beliefs, and I really don't think it's your place—"

"Oh, this is hysterical," he said, pointing a finger at me. "You, Mr. Science, dating a Jesus Freak." He slammed the table with his fists. "What a match." Snorting like a pig, he clutched his middle as he roared with laughter. "Oh, this is a howl."

We were both furious at him now. "Rob—" I tried to stop him from doing any more damage, but Gloria stood and interrupted me.

"Listen, Rob," she snapped, "you can make fun of me all you want. But you . . ." She pointed a finger at him. "You have a lot of nerve ridiculing Tom. He may not believe what I do, but he's at least open-minded and kind and has the decency not to put me down. You could learn some manners from him."

Rob seemed shocked that she was offended. He wiped the tears from his eyes. "Hey, I didn't mean anything by it." He held up his hands like he was surrendering and looked from Gloria to me. "You got to admit it's funny that's all."

"Shut up, Rob." I stood and touched her arm. "Gloria, I apologize for Rob."

"You're not responsible for him," she said, and began to put on her coat. "Look, I've got to go anyway."

"Hey, I'm sorry," Rob said, still shaking his head and chuckling. "What say we forgive and forget, OK?" Gloria ignored him. "Hey, you people are supposed to be good at that forgiveness crap, right?"

Gloria stared at him. "Oh, I forgive you, Rob, but unfortunately, I doubt I'll ever be able to forget you."

She grabbed her packages, pushed in her chair, and said good bye to me. As she walked away, Rob shot her the finger behind her back.

I slapped the side of his head and followed after her. I didn't want her leaving the mall upset. "Let me walk you out," I called.

Gloria stopped. "No stay here, Tom. I'm fine. Really."

"Are you sure?"

"At first," Gloria said, "I was really mad, but the more I think about Rob, the more ridiculous it all seems. Actually, he's kind of pathetic, slobbering all over me then sticking one of his gigantic feet in his mouth."

"He is pathetic," I chuckled, looking back at him. He was rattling our paper cups to see if there was any Coke left.

She began to laugh and shake her head. "Don't be too hard on him when you go back to the table."

"OK," I said. "But I swear I'm tempted to just get into my car and strand him here at the mall."

I felt much better knowing she was no longer upset. "See you tomorrow," she said, giving me a peck on the lips before stepping onto the escalator.

As I walked back to the table, I was glad that the food court only stocked plastic utensils, because if I could have gotten my hands on a real knife, I'd have stabbed him.

When I returned, Rob didn't seem the least bit upset. Two slices of pizza remained on the silver pan and he was scarfing them down. As I sat on the bistro chair, he looked at me. A string of mozzarella dangled from his lower lip.

"You got your hands full with that one, Tommy," he mumbled. "She's gorgeous for sure, but complicated."

I stared at him, watching him inhaling the food without a care. He threw his hands into the air. "What?"

"You know what, doofus." I replied. "Did it ever occur to you that people don't like to be called names like 'Jesus Freak,' or 'Holy Roller'?"

He waved his hand while he chewed. "Ah, everybody's too sensitive today. But I'll say one thing. I envy you nailing her, Tommy boy. See how worked up she got. She's passionate—I bet she's a demon in the sack."

"That's just it. I think I should forget all about this 'Big Bang' plot of yours. I think it'd be a mistake. As you can tell, she's got deep moral convictions."

Rob grabbed my Coke and sucked on the straw until the cup gurgled. "Deep moral convictions, my ass! Religious nuts are the biggest hypocrites around. How many preachers have gotten busted with hookers? They're always telling everyone not to fool around but they're the first ones to do it."

"But she's not like that. She's sincere," I protested. "She really tries to live by her ideals."

He took the plastic lid off my drink and crunched the ice cubes between his teeth. "Yeah, yeah. That's what they all *say*. But what does she *do*? Ah, that's the key. Didn't you tell me she was all over you in the car the other night and while you had her on the couch last night?"

"Yeah, but—"

"What more do you want? A neon 'Welcome' sign hanging from her butt?" He spit a cube back into the cup.

I cradled my head with my hands. "Oh, I don't know."

"Look," Rob said, shaking the ice in the cup, "she's the one who threw down the gauntlet. Are you going to give it to her or are you going to let some other dude do it?" He wiped his greasy lips and fingers on a napkin. "Man, if you don't take a crack at her, I will."

"What?" I cried.

"Sure, I'd like to get my hands on her. She might be a religious nut, but I'd jump at the chance to nail her." He closed his eyes and moaned. "Oh, man I'd have her begging for more."

The thought of Rob touching Gloria, my Gloria, repulsed me.

137

We left the mall, and I drove back to the dorm in silence. Visions of Rob slobbering over Gloria, his greasy hands on her, his gangly body defiling her perfect flesh made me cringe. If he so much as looked at her again, I swear I'd kill him. It was then that I resolved to go through with "The Big Bang" for the simple fact that it would protect her from Rob. And perhaps he was right. Gloria was very passionate, and she did seem to want me. She even defended me to Rob. What could be the worst thing to happen? If she gets offended, I'll just apologize. I read somewhere that it's better to beg for forgiveness than to ask for permission. And besides, I really wanted her. And I didn't want anyone else to have her. Especially Rob.

"OK," I said, as we pulled in front of the dorm. "I'm doing it."

"Doing what?"

"'The Big Bang.' I've decided to go ahead with the plan."

Rob slapped me on the back. "You won't be sorry."

I hoped he was right.

Chapter 17

On Monday I waited for Gloria outside the Chapel. She arrived precisely at four, and this time she did not come to me out of sunshine. Gray light seeped through the Union's windows, draining everything of color—except her. Gloria's beauty radiated a spectrum that defeated the dreariness.

"Come here often?" she said as she approached. Then she looked behind me. "You didn't bring Rob, did you?"

"Oh no," I said, "I have better sense than that. I'm really sorry about yesterday. He's not a bad guy, a little thick-skulled."

"Well, in his defense, we are an unusual pair." Gloria took my arm. "So what's my amazing fact for today?"

"The Big Bang" had me so preoccupied I'd forgotten our little ritual. "Hmm. Let me think a minute. OK," I said, brushing the hair from my face. Ever heard of Hubbell's Law?"

"The guy with the telescope?"

"Yeah, they named it after him. Ever heard of his law?"

"Nope. Only his telescope."

"Well, his law came before that, and it states that an object in space recedes at a rate proportional to its distance."

"And that means?"

"That the further away you are from something, the faster you are moving away from it." Gloria looked puzzled. "OK, how about if I explain it this way."

I grabbed her by the shoulders and positioned her three feet from a chair. "Let's pretend you're a star. And that chair is a star and . . ." I moved three feet behind the chair so that Gloria, the chair and I were all in a line. "That I'm a star."

"Tom Cruise."

"What?"

"A star. You look like Tom Cruise."

"You think so?" Maybe Rob knew what he was talking about.

"Your eyes are brown and your hair is longer, but you're just as handsome."

"Thanks." I felt myself blushing. "Anyway, the chair is moving away from you,"

"You're taller than Tom Cruise but just as cute."

"Wow, if you keep complimenting me, I'm never going to be able to explain this."

"Sorry."

"Anyway, the chair is moving away from you. And I'm moving away from you too, but since I'm twice as far away from you, I'm moving away twice as fast. Get it? That's what's meant by an expanding universe."

"I get it," Gloria said walking toward me. "You explain things so well. But I hope you aren't moving away from me."

I slipped my arm around her waist. "After telling me I look like Tom Cruise? No way."

"Good. So Mr. Science," she had picked up on Rob's nickname for me, "what are we going to do?"

I couldn't tell her what I had planned. "How about I take you to dinner at The Parlor, as a celebration of the past week?"

"Sounds good to me," she said, and we headed to the elevator. While we waited for it to arrive, Gloria took my hand. "You know we really should celebrate. We are mismatched. Most people with such different beliefs would have never even lasted this long. They'd have bashed each other's brains in by now."

"Or start a Holy War," I added.

We stepped onto the elevator, and the button for the second floor was lit as some students were already inside. I whispered into Gloria's ear, "This is our one week anniversary." After the students got off on two, I crowded into the corner with Gloria and kissed her until I felt the elevator undulate under my feet as it arrived at the first floor. When I held her, I sensed no resistance, no hesitation, no holding back.

She grabbed my hand and led me out. It was time to execute "The Big Bang."

We left the Union and sleet, like hundreds of acupuncture needles, stung our cheeks. I put my arm around her, and we hurried toward The Parlor. "It's too nasty out here to walk," I said, my teeth chattering. "Let's take my car."

As we neared the dorm, I launched phase one. "Aw, I forgot." I said, slapping my forehead. "This morning at work, we got in a shipment—some children's books, *So Big Sammy and the So Big Surprise* and *So Big Sammy and the Christmas Miracle*. I bought them for Christo, but I left them in my room."

"Oh, that's so nice, Tom. He'll love them."

"Yeah, seems old Sammy is such a hit, he's spinning off all kinds of merchandise." I was trying not to appear anxious, but my blood vessels pulsed so fiercely, I thought one of them might blow, and I'd never live to consummate the plan. "Are you hungry? We could go to my room and get them now or after dinner."

"It's early yet and I ate a late lunch," Gloria said. "I'm not that hungry. We can get them now." She'd taken the bait. Suddenly, she grabbed my arm, stopping me. "But wait." The wind whipped her hair. "Will Rob be there?" She jerked her head, flinging her blond locks behind her.

"He's probably left for work, but I'll check before I bring you in. It won't take very long. We'll be in and out."

Taking her hand, I doubled our pace. When I opened the door, the room was dark, and an overpowering floral scent from Glade air freshener greeted me. After stashing all the Sammys in our cars, we had sprayed nearly a whole canister of the deodorizer around the room this morning in hopes of killing the stench of stale beer and dirty clothes that seemed to have permeated the walls and floors.

I went to the dresser and clicked on the Steelers helmet lamp but didn't turn on the overhead light. It would ruin the romantic mood I was trying to set, and even though we'd cleaned the room last night, our level of sanitation could not endure bright lighting. Gloria waited in the hall.

The night before, we'd planted a note on the dresser. I picked it up and pretended to read it. I held out the slip of paper and called: "Rob's gone to work. He won't be back until late. During the Christmas season, I hardly see him he's so busy working."

"Lucky you," Gloria said as she walked into my room. Her eyes darted all over; she wrinkled her nose. "I'd heard Foster Hall was pretty shabby, but I bet the inmates at the jail have nicer rooms."

From experience, I knew that my room was slightly better than the cells at the jail, but I couldn't tell her that.

"Couldn't you move to the new dorms?"

"We could have, but I'll show you why we didn't." I moved behind her. "Take your coat off," I said as I eased her parka off her shoulders, "or it'll seem twice as cold when we go back outside." She fluffed out her curls.

Gloria was wearing khaki pants and a forest green sweater. The sweater intensified the color of her eyes.

I walked to the chair near the door and draped our coats over its arm. While she looked at my solar system poster, I quickly reached behind me and locked the door. The bolt moved silently and held. Then I went to the dresser. "To get the best effect, it has to be dark." I turned off the lamp.

In the blackness, I made my way and found her standing in the center of the room. I put my arm around her small waist, led her across the floor toward the window, and pulled the cord, opening the curtains.

The drawn drapes would be my signal to Rob that we were in the room and not to disturb us. I didn't think we needed a signal since he'd be working until eleven. But he nudged me in the ribs and said, "You never know. If she's as hot as I think she is, you could be in there for hours."

As I drew the curtains, Gloria's breath caught and then escaped in a long "Ah."

"Wow. This is gorgeous, Tom," she said, taking in the glittering Pittsburgh skyline. The twinkling lights and the swirling flurries made the city seem like a town inside a snow globe. She looked at me, a galaxy of lights reflecting in her eyes, "Now I know why you stayed."

The moment had come to shift into the second, more precarious, phase of the operation—getting Gloria onto the couch. Before I left to meet her, I had stopped back at the room and carefully arranged the Sammy books on the couch to make it look like I had just tossed them there.

"I think the books are over there with my backpack," I said. "Let me turn on the lamp."

The bulb's soft light filled the room, and Gloria did exactly as I had hoped; she walked over to the couch. "Here they are," she said, as she moved my backpack to the side and sat. Crossing her legs, she began shuffling through the pages of *Sammy and the Christmas Miracle*.

I put my backpack on the floor and snuggled up next to her. Every nerve in my body was jangling.

She closed the book. "This is really cute, Tom. Christo's going to love them, but wouldn't you like to give them to him?"

"You'll see him before I will. No sense making him wait. He's doing enough of that as it is. He deserves a treat."

She patted my thigh. "Thanks, Tom. That was really nice." She tilted her head back against the couch and smiled up at me. "You're really nice."

The hour had come.

Her upturned mouth was begging to be kissed. I bent and touched my lips to hers. She responded and my mouth moved effortlessly, deftly on hers, kissing her the way I'd fantasized. I'd rehearsed this all a thousand times. Every touch, every movement had been choreographed. After about five minutes of making out though, I ran out of steps. Then instinct took over. I worked from pure desire, and I hoped that the rest of my seduction would come as naturally as these kisses had.

Gloria seemed to be enjoying herself. I wound my arms around her like ivy on a downspout, waiting for some clue that I should go ahead and make my move. How I wished Rob were standing in the corner, coaching me, feeding me signals.

It was now or never. Clamping my mouth over hers, and pushing off with my feet, I shifted all of my weight onto her. She fell backward onto the couch. Our lips still locked; I melted onto her like butter on warm toast and quickly stuck my hand up her sweater, fumbling for her breast.

Suddenly, my head jerked backward, and I heard my neck snap. Gloria had me by the hair. The scalp at the base of my head pulled away from my skull as she wound my hair around her fist and increased the tension.

"Ow," I cried, my necked arched and stretched like a swan's.

"If you don't get off me right now," she growled, "I'm going to head-butt you in the Adam's apple so hard, you're going to have to dig it out of your spine just to swallow."

Stunned and in pain, I couldn't move. With her free hand, she looped a finger through my earring and tugged. "I'm telling you. If you don't get your hands off me immediately, I'm going to rip this earring right out of your ear." She had a crazed look in her eye, reminding me of a commando threatening to pull the pin on a hand grenade.

"OK, OK," I said. My mind quickly ran an inventory. She had me by the hair and by the earring, and I thought I'd better move fast before she had me by a more vulnerable part of my anatomy.

"Please," I whimpered. "I can't get off you until you let go of my hair." Tears formed in the corners of my eyes. "Please let go," I begged. "I promise I won't do anything."

She relaxed her hold, and I scrambled off her. Gloria jumped to her feet as I massaged my scalp.

"What is wrong with you, Tom?" She was panting, and her face was blood red.

"I'm sorry." I checked to see if my earlobe was bleeding. "I got carried away."

"Carried away?" She straightened her sweater. "You call rape, getting carried away?"

Rape? "I'd never rape you!" I moved to touch her, and she backed away. "I swear, Gloria, I'd never ever do anything to hurt you." I raised my hands like I was surrendering. "I thought you wanted to . . . you know."

"What is it with guys?" she said as she straightened her sweater. "You tell them upfront that you're a virgin and you don't fool around so you can establish some ground rules and avoid this, but what happens? They act like they've been issued a challenge." She straightened her clothes. "I feel like Mt. Everest. Everyone wants to be the first to plant their flag in me." Gloria headed for the chair and picked up her coat. She shook her head in disgust. "I thought you were different, Tom, but you're just like all the others."

I ran to her and picked up her hand, clutching it to my heart. "No, I'm not. I swear I'm different. It's just that . . . Oh, I don't know. I mean you really fire me up. I never would have done anything unless I thought you wanted me to. The way you kissed me—I thought you wanted the same thing. Rob said—"

She wrenched her hand away. "Rob said what?"

Why did I mention his name?

"Nothing."

"No," she dropped her coat back onto the chair and put her hands on her hips, "I want to hear exactly what that idiot had to say."

I looked at my shoes. "Well . . . Well, I didn't know how far to go with you. And I didn't want to lose you. Rob said a girl only tells a guy she's a virgin because she doesn't want to be one anymore. And he said that I'd better accommodate you so to speak or I'd lose you."

She threw her hands into the air. "You told Rob I was a virgin? You told that moron my personal information?" Her green eyes boiled with bile. "That was between you and me. I can't believe you discussed intimate details—" She turned her back on me.

I scurried to face her. "No. No, I didn't tell him. He guessed."

"Guessed?" she shouted.

"Yes, he dragged it out of me."

She didn't hear me. She began pacing, moving so quickly, I don't believe her feet actually touched the floor. "They say women can't keep secrets. Hmph. I confided in you, Tom. I never dreamed you'd blab to that slimy creep." She turned and looked at me and her shoulders fell as she spoke. "You didn't tell him about my anxiety problems too?" Tears welled in her eyes as her anger morphed into hurt. Then suddenly her face blanched and her hands flew to her mouth. "You didn't tell him about the artificial insemination, did you?"

"No! No! I swear, I'd never blab about your problems or the artificial insemination." I put a hand on her shoulder. She flinched and crossed her arms in front of her chest. "Please listen to me. I am different, Gloria. You can trust me. I'd never hurt you. I'm so sorry. I just got carried away." I picked up the Sammy books that had fallen onto the floor and handed them to her. "Look, take the books. We'll get our coats. Let's go to dinner and forget this ever happened. OK?"

Her hands dropped to her side, and I could tell she was beginning to soften. "I promise I'll never do anything you don't want me to do again. You can trust me." I covered my heart with my hand. "Honest."

She stared at me for a long time. Then she sighed. "OK. Let's go to dinner and forget about what happened."

I handed her Christo's books and picked up our coats.

At that moment, fists pounded the door and laughter echoed out in the hall. Gloria turned toward the noise. Someone yelled, "Go for it, Shepherd." There was more laughter and running feet.

Gloria's head slowly turned to look back at me. Her bottom lip quivered as a large tear streaked down her cheek. "Damn you, Tom, for making me trust you." She flung the Sammy books at me. I dropped the coats to protect my face, but one of them caught me in the corner of my eye, in the mushy part above your cheekbone. She scooped up her coat from the floor, ran to the door, and turned the knob. Realizing that I had locked her in, she brushed the tears from her eye and fumbled with the latch. "You jerk, you locked me in."

I ran after her and put a hand on her shoulder to stop her. She knocked it off and opened the door. Then she turned and looked me in the eye. "You're a liar, Tom Shepherd." She slammed the door so hard in my face, I knew everyone in the dorm heard it.

I stood, cupping my injured eye, staring at the door. Rob and I'd never planned for this. Then a familiar, sickening feeling settled in the pit of my stomach. That feeling was abandonment. I'd been abandoned again.

I hurried to the window in time to see Gloria run out of the dorm, her white coat whipping in the wind as she dashed across the snow-covered lawn.

Opening the window, I stuck my head out into the cold December air and cried, "Gloria! Gloria!" My voice sounded like the strangled scream of a man falling into a bottomless pit. She kept on running and never looked back. The wind howled and took my breath away. I pulled my head inside, shut the window, and threw the drapes closed. There would be no need to signal Rob to stay away. I was alone.

Again.

Chapter 18

I hadn't been back to the Old Allegheny Tavern since that day three years ago when I was led out in handcuffs.

The checks coming from my father that first semester of freshman year were few and far between. To make some extra bucks, I had taken a job bartending there.

During the short time that I worked at the Old Allegheny, a regular who went by the name of Joey the T-Bone, took a liking to me. Joey the T was one of "those guys." Nobody was exactly sure for whom he worked, but everybody had suspicions.

Joey wore lots of leather and Brut, and Kaz, the owner of the place and its chief bartender, warned me the day he walked in to be careful around him. Seems Joey acquired the "T-bone" part of his name from poking some guy's eyes out with the bone from his steak.

A few weeks later while Kaz and I were joking around behind the bar, Joey called me over and ordered a Chevas Regal. As I set the drink before him, he pointed a crooked pinky finger, sporting a chunky gold nugget ring, at me. "You know what I like about you, Tommy?"

"What?" I asked, hoping it was everything because I didn't think a horse's head would fit into my bunk with me.

"You got an ascorbic wit."

I think he meant acerbic, but I wasn't going to correct a man who puts out eyes with food products.

"Yeah," he said, "you got an incremental ability to cut through bull."

Thank God Joey appreciated my wit and the Old Allegheny served nothing more deadly than pretzel rods. Yeah, Joey liked me for sure. In fact, he liked me so much, he helped me to earn a little extra money, setting me up booking numbers on campus. I ran numbers for three months—until I was busted.

Talk about a nightmare. I was handcuffed, fingerprinted, booked, and locked up. I understood why the guards confiscated my belt and shoelaces before they closed the bars. That place, with its rundown cells and the creeps that inhabited them, would drive anyone to suicide.

Luckily, that semester I was taking a course in Statistics and Probability, and my attorney was able to convince the judge that I wasn't really running numbers but conducting a statistical study on the lottery. The judge, a TRU grad and big-time bettor, bought my alibi and let me off.

I'm not sure why I headed back there. Maybe it was because I had nothing left to lose, and the Old Allegheny was a magnet for those who had lost everything.

Although it was dark outside, when I walked through the door, it still took my eyes a few seconds to adjust to the dankness. Curls of gray cigarette smoke floated above the customers' heads like dirty halos. The air was as old as the music coming from the juke box—a crackly version of "Kansas City."

Around the bar, all the regulars were seated upon the same chrome and red vinyl stools in exactly the same places I had left them years earlier. They were chessmen in a suspended game. Life had dropped these sorry creatures onto these stools and forgotten to move them.

Vinny the Vet, elbows resting on the Formica bar top, sat closest to the door. He was caressing the neck of an Iron City, leering at the bottle's curves as if it were a naked brown girl from an exotic island. A few stools away sat Lenny, who runs the newsstand round the corner. He was bending the ear of Manchester Mike. Mike was a legendary softball player on the North Side in the 70s. One night after celebrating a ninth-inning grand slam with massive amounts of beer, Mike made an even grander slam by driving into a telephone pole on Ohio River Boulevard. Mike was a paraplegic. He no longer drives, but he still drinks himself into oblivion most nights and then wheels himself over to the YMCA.

Behind the bar in a white Ban-lon Steelers shirt was Kaz. He hadn't changed much either since I'd last seen him. His arms still hung from his shoulders like sides of beef and his hair was the same—slicked back, Mike Ditka-style.

I hoisted myself into an empty stool, and Kaz, a bar towel draped over one shoulder, did a double take, walked over, and shook my hand enthusiastically as if he were pumping CO2 into a keg.

"It's been a long time, Tom." He was much too tactful a bartender to bring up my past problems, but I knew what he was referring to—my arrest.

In no mood to talk about the past or the present for that matter, I just mumbled. "Yeah, I've been busy with school and stuff."

Kaz tilted the tap's knob, filling a pilsner glass. "Hey fellas, look. Lulu's back in town."

Lenny interrupted his monologue long enough so that he and Mike could say "Hi," but then Lenny quickly began talking again before someone could wrest the conversation away from him. Vinny said nothing but gave me a small salute.

I nodded to them and said, "How about a beer, Kaz?"

"Sure thing."

On top of the scarred counter sat bowls of pickled eggs, pickled pigs' feet, and deviled crabs, and I wondered if they'd been sitting there for three years too. Kaz put a beer in front of me without placing a coaster beneath it—this wasn't a coaster kind of place. I pulled out my wallet, but he held up a hand. "It's on the house, Tom. Good to see you again."

I tucked my wallet back into my jeans, thanked him, and raised the glass to my lips, beginning my quest to get so blitzed that I would no longer care that Gloria had dumped me. The beer splashed in my empty stomach. I was hungry. Instead of listening to Rob, I should have followed my instincts and taken Gloria to dinner. The thought of the steak I was missing at The Parlor only brought more regrets. I drained the glass. "Say, Kaz," I called and motioned to the bowl in front of me, "these eggs fresh?"

He emptied an ashtray. "Sure are. Mum made them this afternoon."

Kaz's mother, a house dress-clad old crone lived upstairs of the bar. "I'll take three and while you're at it," I held up my empty glass, "I'll have another."

Vinny the Vet, sitting two stools down from me, mumbled without taking his eyes from his beer: "They sure are going down smooth tonight." There hasn't been a night for him yet when they haven't gone down smooth.

149

After a couple of hours, six more beers, and three more pickled eggs, Frank Gifford's face filled the screen of the TV suspended from the ceiling in the corner. *Monday Night Football* was coming on and the place was filling with workers coming off their shifts at Allegheny General Hospital.

The pain of losing Gloria throbbed like a stubbed toe, so I kept the beers coming and the eggs too. In my liquor-induced haze, time slipped by rapidly, and the next thing I knew, Kaz was sweeping up and cleaning off tables. He slapped me on the back. "Time to go home, Tom."

I climbed down off the stool, and when I stood up, I discovered that some jokester had come along and exchanged my legs with Slinkys.

Kaz wiped down the bar as I struggled to fish my wallet out of my back pocket and remain upright. Finally, I pulled it out and grabbed a bill. I thought it was a twenty, but I wasn't sure because my eyes had joined in on the rebellion of my body parts. Or I should say my eye. I could only see out of one of them since the one that had taken the corner of the Sammy book, was now swollen shut. When I touched it, it was tender. I slapped the bill down on the bar. Kaz picked it up and slid the bowl of pickled eggs in front of me. "Why don't you take these home with you, Tom? You seemed to have been craving them all night."

"Thanks, Kaz," I said, and I wanted him to know how much I appreciated his kindness, so I stood on the rungs of the stool, leaned over the bar, and hugged him. "You're a prince among bartenders," I said, resting my head on his muscular shoulder.

Kaz patted my back, then shoved me away. I stumbled off the stool. "Let me put them in a bag for you," he said.

"No," I put up a hand. "I've troubled you enough." There were nearly a dozen eggs left, and I stuffed all that I could into the pockets of my fatigue jacket. Two remained in the bowl. I put one in my mouth and the last I shoved into my back pocket with my wallet. Then I staggered to the door.

"Here's your change," Kaz said, walking over and offering me some bills.

"Ah, keep it," I mumbled, my mouth filled with egg. I waved the money off and nearly fell over.

He grabbed me. "How about I call you a cab?"

I jerked free of him. "No need, Kazy," I said, feeling egg yolk escaping from the side of my mouth. I stuck out my tongue to lick it up and it flopped all over my face. "You know I'm an astronomer," I slurred. "I could find my way to hell and back by the stars."

"OK then," Kaz conceded. He threw a meaty arm across my shoulder and guided me to the door. "I hope you drowned whatever was bothering you, Tom."

I walked out into the night air and gasped when I inhaled. The heat had left the earth's atmosphere; the frigid air made my nostrils feel like they were lined with boar's bristles and my lungs burn. "No chance of that," I laughed, but what I really wanted to do was sink to the stoop and cry.

It was a miracle that I wasn't robbed in West Park or that I didn't fall and freeze to death. But I made it safely back to the dorm. It was nearly three when I staggered into the room and turned on the overhead light. Rob let a string of expletives fly, grabbed his pillow, and covered his head. I kicked the door closed behind me and fell into the chair. Its legs scraped on the tile floor, letting out a sickening screech. Rob removed the pillow and arched his neck, looking at me with bleary eyes. "What are you doing?" Then he raised himself on an elbow. "Oh man, I forgot. What time is it?" He looked at the clock. "What happened? You two go to a motel or something?"

I stumbled over to the couch and flopped down onto it, smashing the egg in my back pocket. "Yeah, Heartbreak Hotel." The mushy egg seeped through my jeans. I stood and pulled my wallet out. Gobs of smashed egg fell on the floor. The leather was caked in yolk.

"What do you mean Heartbreak Hotel? Something go wrong?"

"Something?" I harumphed. "Everything." I began to unload my jacket pockets. Pulling an egg out, I popped it whole into my mouth. Then I offered one to Rob. It was covered with pocket lint and crumbs, and he made a face, declining my gift. "I followed the plan exactly the way you said to. She went ballistic," I mumbled, my mouth stuffed. "And dumped me." I pulled out the rest of the eggs one-by-one, laying them on the couch counting as I went: "six, seven, eight." They were slimy and one of them slipped out of my hand and rolled across the floor toward Rob's bunk.

He sat up. "What do you mean she dumped you?"

I was busy concentrating on my eggs. "Dumped me. The old heave-ho. Canned me. How else do you want me to say it?"

"You're kidding."

"I wish," I said, stalking my wayward egg.

"What happened?"

"I brought her back here and you know, stuck my hand in her sweater. She got mad."

"Well, did you tell her you couldn't help yourself?"

151

"Yeah, and she bought it until some jerk pounded on the door and screamed "go for it, Shepherd.""

Rob said nothing. He just pulled his blankets up to his chest.

"You told everyone, didn't you?"

"Only so they wouldn't disturb you."

"Well, they did. And then Gloria realized that this was no accident but a set-up. She stormed out of here and instead of enjoying a date with her, I spent the rest of the night at the Old Allegheny drinking with a bunch of derelicts." I crawled around, looking for my lost egg."

"Oh, man," Rob said lying back on his pillow. My egg had rolled under his bunk.

As I poked my head under his bed, I felt something building in my stomach. The rumblings inside me would have registered an 8.5 on the Richter scale. I sat back on my heels, burped a few times, and took some deep breaths. Suddenly, I lurched forward. Vomit gushed geyser-like out of me and splatted smack in the middle of Rob's chest.

"Aaahhh," he screamed as he squirmed under the barf-laden blanket. He threw back the covers and leapt out of bed, unleashing a flurry of curses at me. Resting on my heels again, I waited for my stomach to settle while I watched Rob jumping around the room. Then my stomach churned again, and I vomited down the front of my jacket. I retched until I'd purged myself of eggs and beer.

Now that the poison had left my stomach, I stumbled over to the couch and flopped onto it. I'd forgotten that I'd put my eggs there until I felt them under me. But I was so sick I didn't care.

"You moron!" Rob cried, standing in his Fruit of the Looms surrounded by puddles of barf. "Look at this place! Look at my bed!"

"I'm sorry, man," I said wiping, my mouth on my sleeve. But I really wasn't sorry. He deserved to be puked on. He had shot off his big mouth and now I had shot off mine so to speak. Even so, the score was still in his favor. He'd only been barfed on. I'd lost Gloria.

He grimaced. "What did you eat? It smells like a sulfur mine in here." Rob pulled the neck of his T-shirt over his nose to ward off the stench of the eggs and vomit. Then he ran to the windows and threw them open. A column of arctic air rushed in.

I stood. "I'll clean it up." I went to get a towel but my feet refused to cooperate. I fell into the CD player, knocking over a stack of CDs.

Rob grabbed me carefully by the shoulders and pushed me into the chair by the door. "Sit here, idiot, before you break something."

Rob stripped the blankets from his bed and started to mop up the vomit from the floor, swearing under his breath.

Noticing that my pickled eggs were smashed all over the couch, I crawled over to them. "My eggs," I cried, picking them up, regarding them with such reverence you'd have thought I had ovaries and they'd been harvested from me. "They're gone." I whimpered. "She's gone." And I began to cry. But it was not the hearty cry of grief but the syrupy, sloppy, maudlin cry of a drunk. "Everything is over," I yowled, letting the crumbled eggs fall through my fingers, "I blew it. I always blow it."

"Baloney!" Rob grumbled from down on his hands and knees sopping up the puddles. "Be glad she's gone. If she ain't giving it to you, then what good is she?" I couldn't explain to him because my brain was numb, but Gloria had been giving me something, something I really needed even though I didn't know exactly what it was.

Rob gathered the soiled linens into a ball, dumped them into a laundry basket, and put them out in the hall. He stood in front of me, his hands on his bony hips, his legs spread. In his underwear, he looked like a malnourished super hero. "Now we've got to do something with you. Man, you stink."

"I'm sorry," I whined, and I was so pitiful, I felt like my bones wouldn't even have anything to do with me. I was as limp as a jellyfish, and I rode each emotional wave that crashed upon me.

Rob dragged me to my feet and pushed me down the hall to the shower room. The door to Chaz's room was ajar, and as we passed by, I heard him mutter, "What *is* that smell?"

In the shower room, Rob turned on the faucet and propped me up in the corner under the spray, jacket, clothes, shoes and all. The water shocked me. I recoiled under the spray and gagged, but nothing more came up. He began stripping away my clothes until I was left standing naked in the shower.

Chaz walked in for a late night trip to the urinal, and when he saw Rob in his underwear and me naked together in the shower, a big smile overtook his face. "You boys always shower together?"

"Only when you're not available, Chuckie." Chaz may have disliked being called Chaz, but he absolutely hated being called Chuckie.

Standing at the urinal, Chaz made a face. "God, what smells?"

"Ah, he threw up," Rob said. They were talking about me like I didn't have a brain.

"What's he got? The flu?"

"Nah, idiot's drunk," Rob said, kicking my puke-encrusted clothes into a pile on the floor. "He nailed that gorgeous babe I told you about. Then he went out and celebrated too much. Tossed his cookies all over the room and himself." Rob threw a bar of soap at me. It was nice of Rob to try and salvage my pride. "Hey Chuckie, when you're done over there, watch him a minute for me, while I get him a towel?"

"I'm not watching him."

"Oh yeah, you are," Rob said, "unless you want to find these clothes in the backseat of your Lexus."

Chaz came over and stood outside the stall, while Rob disappeared. He stared at my naked, wretched body leaning in the shower. By the disgust on his face, you'd have thought he was looking at a hair on his bar of soap.

"He isn't conning me," he sneered. "I heard that girl slam your door and saw her run out of your room. She was grade A prime, and you got shot down tonight, didn't you?"

I didn't answer.

"She gave you that black eye, too, didn't she?"

It was humiliating enough being babysat by a freshman without having to admit that I'd struck out and was assaulted by a girl.

"You were an idiot for even thinking she'd ever go for a loser like you."

I was drunk but not so drunk that his words didn't land a direct hit to my solar plexus. *I am a loser.* Everyone knows it. I've been a loser all my life. My father didn't want me. My mother probably died to get away from me. And now Gloria. I thrust my face into the shower spray, so he couldn't see the tears rolling down my face.

Rob walked in with a towel, wearing a dry T-shirt and sweatpants. "He's all yours," Chaz said. And before he left, he shot me the finger.

Rob reached into the shower and turned off the water. I stumbled out of the stall and goose bumps rose all over my body. Rob handed me a towel, and I buried my face into it, pretending I was drying myself while in actuality, I was hiding my tears. Then I wrapped it around my waist, and Rob pushed me back down the hall to the room. *Loser.* Chaz's words rang in my ears, like I had sat too close to a speaker at a concert.

The room was frigid from the air blowing in through the open window, and I shivered as Rob sat me in the chair and helped me to put on some clean boxers and a T-shirt.

Loser.

I'd sobered up enough now that the liquor no longer blunted the pain of losing Gloria. Slumping forward, I covered my face with my hands.

"What is wrong now?" Rob asked, exasperation in his voice. "You got PMS?"

"I'm a loser," I blubbered.

"Knock that crap off."

"No, it's true. *I am a loser.* I always have been, always will be. Even Chaz said so."

Rob stood up. "Chaz said what?"

"That I'm a loser."

"When did that idiot say that?"

"When I was in the shower."

Rob began scraping smashed eggs off the couch. "Forget Chaz. What does he know?"

"He knows I'm a loser. And I am. Gloria knows it. Everyone knows it."

Rob walked over to me, his hands full of pulverized pickled eggs. I looked up into his face. "Admit it. You know it too."

"Listen," he said, "don't talk about yourself like that. It's not . . . It's not good." He threw the egg out the open window.

"But it's true. I am a loser."

"Man, Tom, if you want to know the truth, everybody's a loser. You're a loser. I'm a loser. Chaz's a loser. I haven't met anyone yet that's not a loser."

"Chaz? A loser? Yeah, right." I was entering the belligerence stage now.

"Yes, he's a loser! Why do you think he's up so late? He's over there," Rob nodded toward Chaz's room, "studying his butt off to please his daddy. Old Chaz is scared to death his old man will cut off the cash flow if he doesn't get straight A's. What's Chaz without his millions? Just another pimply-faced freshman. That's the kind of loser he is."

I wasn't convinced and Rob knew it.

"Look, Tom, deep down I know I'm a loser too. My old man abandoned me. My mom could hang a "billions served" sign off her back she's had so many guys. And I know I ain't no prince, but I'm not ever going to let you know that I know I'm a loser."

Maybe Rob wasn't as thick-skinned as he had let on.

"But you see," he said, "that's where Chaz and I differ. I know I'm a loser, and I don't care." He pointed a finger to his chest. "I answer to no one." He turned his finger on me. "Your whole problem, pal, is that you let everybody know you think you're a loser."

"And how do I do that?" I asked sarcastically.

He flicked my hair with his finger. "You hide behind that goofy hair, slouched over, with your hands in that scruffy jacket . . . " He hunched his shoulder and shuffled around the room, imitating me. "You might as well as get a tattoo on your forehead that says 'Kick Me.'"

While he went to the closet and rummaged through it, I thought about what he had said.

"Since you puked all over my bed," he said, "I'll sleep in yours." He pulled a sleeping bag out of the closet and threw it on the couch. "You can use this."

I walked over to the couch and unzipped the sleeping bag. "But, Rob, what you said. I can't deny what I am—the facts of my life."

"Yeah, but you're only focusing on your bad parts, man. You're forgetting all the rest."

"What 'rest?'"

"Man, you're the smartest guy I know. And when you're not covered in barf you're not too ugly. And basically you're a nice guy even though you can't hold your liquor." He threw my pillow at me. "Look, Tom, you couldn't have been a total loser to have attracted a beauty like Gloria, now could you?"

"Gloria . . . ." I shook my head sadly and crept down into the bag. "OK. So I'm not a loser. Big deal. That doesn't bring her back."

"Hey, Tom, I don't know what that chick has done to you, but if you really want her that bad, go after her. Get her back."

"Oh yeah. Right." I fumbled with the zipper. "And how would I do that?"

"I don't know, Einstein." Rob came over and zipped me into the sleeping bag. "You're the genius. Figure something out."

Rob closed the window and shut off the light. He crawled up into my bunk, his feet sticking beyond the bed. The room was quiet for a while then Rob spoke.

"Hey, Tom, I'll tell you something I learned a long time ago." His voice cut through darkness. "You've got to stop waiting for things to happen to you. You've got to go out, grab life by the throat, and make things happen for you."

156

Chapter 19

When I awoke Tuesday morning, my mouth was septic-tank fresh, and my abdominal muscles ached. I rolled over to check the time, and my head spun, as if my eyeballs had been set on a lazy Susan and given a whirl. I grabbed the couch's chrome arms to steady myself. It was eleven, and I'd slept through my morning classes. Glancing over at my bunk, I noticed that Rob's feet were no longer sticking beyond the bed. He'd probably gone to class. I hated to get off the couch, but my bladder was about to burst, so I eased myself out of the sleeping bag and started for the lav. Every step I took vibrated in my feet, rattled up through my body, and reverberated into my head.

As I passed Chaz's room, I noticed his door was closed. Thank God. With this hangover, I was in no mood for more of his wisdom.

Morning light streamed in through the bathroom's frosted glass windows, reflecting off the ceramic tile in shiny daggers that pierced my eyes. Squinting, I shuffled to the urinal and unburdened my bladder. I moved to the sink, put my mouth under the faucet, and gulped water down my parched throat. Then I splashed some on my face and looked in the mirror.

During the night, a bruise the size of a small plum had formed under my left eye. The whites of my right eye, the eye that was not swollen shut, were bloodshot. The purple bruise and the red spidery lines in my eyes were the only colors in my face; my complexion was the same sickly shade as oatmeal.

I trudged back to the room and deposited myself on the couch, wrapping the sleeping bag around my shoulders, and for a few minutes, I rested, trying to harness the energy to get on with the day. Every movement, every thought required effort. A post-alcoholic haze enveloped me, until a recollection of something Rob had said last night jogged my senses: *Your problem is that you let everybody know you know you're a loser.*

Was he right? Did I deserve a "Kick Me" tattoo on my forehead? Was I the incarnation of Charlie Brown? Was the only difference between me and the rest of the losers in the world was that I advertised my flaws? I wasn't sure, but it no longer mattered anyway. I didn't care what anybody else thought of me. I only cared what Gloria thought. But she was gone.

I ran my hand over my stubbly chin and found a piece of egg yolk sticking to my face. Oh, why hadn't I listened to my own instincts? I knew pressuring her was a mistake, yet I let Rob talk me into it. Only losers do things like that. Winners follow their guts. Why hadn't I been content to leave well enough alone? Why couldn't I accept what I was given and be happy? Everyone has a fatal flaw. I guess lack of acceptance is mine. I suppose that's why I'm an astronomer. I can't accept the universe as a mystery. That's why I'm an atheist. I can't accept a cruel God. That's why I hate my father. I can't accept what he's done to me.

Yeah, I was a loser, but I was not an accepter. And I would not accept that Gloria had dumped me. Rob was right. I had to stop waiting for life to happen. I needed to figure out what I wanted out of life and then go and get it.

What did I want?

Gloria.

Every particle in my body cried out for her. I wanted her, and I wanted her now. But how to win her back? How would a winner go about it?

For the really important things in life, there are no instructions. How did I learn to breathe? To walk? To talk? To kiss? Learning is doing. And I was about to start doing.

I rose from the couch, and my head reeled again. I only wish I didn't have to start doing with a hangover.

I cleaned myself up as best I could—brushing my teeth, shaving, and showering. There wasn't much I could do about my eye, and on my way out the door, I stole Rob's box of Tic-Tacs from the dresser in hopes of keeping my dragon breath at bay. I headed for Josie's Posies.

On Tuesdays, I knew Gloria had class somewhere on the second floor of Benson Hall. Peering inside classrooms looking for her, I made my way down the second floor corridor. Then as I neared the end of the hallway, I heard music. Piano music. My heart quickened. I increased my pace. The music was classical, although I didn't know what. It sounded intense like a Russian piece and whoever was playing, was striking the keys with fury. The sound grew louder as I came to Room 217. The door was open and I peeked in.

The classroom was set up like a small concert hall with rows of seats descending to the floor. At a black grand piano in the middle of the room, sat Gloria, running her fingers up and down the keys. Absorbed, she didn't notice me until I took a seat in the first row. When she glanced up and saw me, the music stopped.

"What do you want?"

I walked to the piano. I didn't know where to begin, what to say to win her back. Then a song from one of those $19.95 K-Tel record commercials came to mind. "Do you know how to play 'Who's Sorry Now?'" I asked.

"I don't take requests." She slammed her music book closed.

"But do you take apologies?" I held out a bouquet of yellow roses.

She ignored the flowers and began gathering up the sheet music on the bench beside her.

I lowered my arm and tried another avenue. "Then how about an amazing fact? Did you hear they just discovered the biggest jerk in the universe?" She glanced up. "Me," I said, pointing to my chest.

She didn't smile, but at least she was looking at me now. I moved closer; she stood and backed away. "I'm sorry, Gloria. I was a total idiot."

"I'll say."

"Please give me another chance."

"Why should I?"

"Because when I'm with you, I almost believe in God. Because when I'm without you, I do believe in Hell."

She bit her lip and hugged the sheet music to her chest. "You know, I can almost forgive you for grabbing me, but I can't excuse your telling Rob and all your fellow degenerates about my personal business." She unzipped her backpack.

"Ah, Gloria," I sighed and pushed my hair behind my ears. "Please forgive me. I'm so sorry about everything." I touched her arm and she jerked it away. I placed the roses on top of the piano. "Look, I was a selfish pig. Please forgive me."

She sat on the bench. "I'm not angry about that anymore. But I can't believe you told Rob—"

"Gloria, I never told Rob about your anxiety disorder or the insemination."

"But you did discuss my sex life."

"No. Not really—"

"What do you mean *not really*?"

"Like I told you before, he guessed."

"Guessed? And how did he do that? Were you complaining that you weren't getting any? Is that it?"

"No," I said, touching her hand. "I was so happy just being with you, he thought I was getting some. He kept badgering me for details, and when I wouldn't give him any, he guessed you were still a virgin."

She pulled her hand away. "But you told the other guys in your dorm."

"No! No, I didn't. Rob shot his big mouth off about me bringing you to my room." I sat on the bench next to her. "Look, Gloria, I'll be honest with you. This is not something a guy likes to admit, but I'm not very experienced."

"Experienced in what?" She knew very well what I was talking about, but she was making me pay.

"You know . . . " I glanced behind me to make sure no had come into the room, "sex," I whispered. "I haven't had that much experience with girls."

"How much experience is 'that much'"?

This was my penance. I hung my head and mumbled. "None."

"I knew it."

"Knew what?"

"That you're a virgin too."

"Shhh," I hissed as I tried to cover her mouth. "Someone might hear you," I checked the door again. "I'd be humiliated."

She pushed my hands away. "Like I was when I left your room and had to pass all those guys laughing in the hallway?"

I felt myself blushing from shame. "Ah, Gloria, I'm sorry. If I could go back and erase yesterday I would. I should have never done what I did, but I was so afraid of you."

She raised her eyebrows. "Afraid of me?"

"Yeah. I didn't know what to do with you."

"What we've been doing has been fine—going out to dinner, meeting for breakfast . . ."

"I don't mean it like that. Gloria, meeting you has been like hitting the lottery. You're the jackpot and I squandered my winnings. I admit I set the whole thing up to get you back to my room, but I did it because I was afraid of losing you. I listened to Rob's stupid advice and messed everything up."

"Let me get this straight," she said, tilting her head to the side, "you thought attacking me would keep you from losing me?"

"Gloria, you're the most beautiful, most talented, most extraordinary person I've ever met. And I know this is going to sound stupid because it sounds stupid to me now, but Rob said that the only reason you told me you were still a virgin is because you wanted me to have the honor of being the first."

I blushed again. Doing sexual things was a lot easier than talking about them. "He said if I didn't move in on you quickly some other guy would for sure." I took a deep breath. "He said if I passed up the opportunity, he'd take a crack at you."

She shuddered. "Oh gag. Not in a million years."

"Listen, Gloria, I'm so sorry. Please forgive me. What I did was stupid, but when you're afraid, you don't think straight. You know that. You said it yourself that your messed up thinking triggered your panic attacks. Well, my fear of botching things with you made me jump on you in my room. I apologize.

Gloria was silent for a moment, mulling over my words, then she spoke. "I'll tell you something, Tom. Last night, I didn't sleep at all thinking about what had happened, and I have to confess. I'm partly responsible. I was sending you mixed messages, telling you I'm a virgin and then making out with you. That was wrong." I saw that familiar twinkle in her eyes. "But I've never liked anyone as much as I like you. I should have cooled it before things got out of hand."

She was weakening. "I swear, Gloria, I won't ever touch you again. We can shake hands goodnight. Whatever you want. But please forgive me."

"Well, I don't think we have to be that extreme. But if you ever follow the advice of Rob again . . . " She was talking about a future. A death sentence had been lifted and my heart soared.

"You can trust me, Gloria." Bubbling over with enthusiasm at being granted a second chance, I hugged her. Then I thought I shouldn't touch her and pulled away.

"It's OK, Tom. I'm not going to bite."

"But you might pull my hair out or drive my Adam's apple into my spine."

161

She laughed.

"Did you take self-defense training, or something?"

"Nah, I told you I had an older brother. When you wrestle and fight with someone bigger than you, you learn to be clever."

"Speaking of being clever," I said, "how did you know that I've never . . . you know?"

"By the way you kissed me."

Embarrassed, I closed my eyes and groaned. "I'm that bad?"

I felt her patting my cheeks. "No. No, Tom. You're that good!"

My eyes flew open. "What? I'm good at it?"

"Oh, the best I've ever kissed. See a girl can tell the guys who've done it before. They're so impatient. They treat you like a piece of equipment. They think that if they kiss you for two minutes, adjust this knob, prime this part, manipulate this piece, then a girl will automatically give them whatever they want. They're like kids who hurry through dinner to get to dessert. But not you, Tom. Your kisses were never rushed. You've never had dessert before, so you enjoyed dinner."

"Ah, thanks," I said. "I didn't have any idea. That makes me feel better."

"Are you sick, Tom? You don't look so good?"

"Nah, I just had a restless night, too."

Gloria gently touched the bruise under my eye. "Did I do that?"

"Well, yeah. But I deserved much worse. I promise, Gloria, I'll never do anything stupid again. Honest."

And as those words left my mouth, I remembered the lie our relationship was founded on. She still did not know the true reason for my coming to Holy Redeemer that Sunday. Nervous, I began to finger the piano keys. In sixteen days it would be Christmas Eve, and I'd never have to worry about her finding out that I sold Sammys. I wouldn't tell her and would never get involved in such a thing again. Wasn't the intention to change enough to compensate for the crime itself?

"Do you play?" she asked, watching me tap the keys.

"Just 'Heart and Soul.'" I began pecking out the notes with my index finger. "My babysitter when I was a kid had a piano. We used to goof around on it. She taught me how."

"Can you play anything else?"

I laughed. "Oh no, this is as far as my musical talent goes."

Gloria began playing the upbeat, familiar song, accompanying my pathetic fingering. She leaned her shoulder into mine and smiled. We were back together. Rob may have been wrong about "The Big Bang" but he was right about one thing: You did have to go out and grab life by the throat.

"See Tom," Gloria said, "there's a lesson to be learned here. If you stop listening to Rob and everybody else and just follow your own heart and soul, and if I follow mine, then I know we'll be just fine."

I couldn't tell her that my heart and soul have always been unreliable compasses.

Chapter 20

Tuesday night the temperature plummeted, and freezing rain, snow, and sleet took turns assaulting the city. Wednesday morning, the campus resembled the moon—white, cold, and desolate. By midmorning, the snow had tapered off, but a fierce Arctic wind howled. As I hurried toward the library, I passed only a few brave souls. The wind blew head-on, bringing tears to my eyes. I broke into a jog, but the frigid air froze the insides of my nasal passages and stung my lungs. Cupping my gloves over my nose and mouth, I doubled my pace.

Gloria and I had planned to spend the afternoon together studying for finals. In front of the boxy brick library, I met her coming from the opposite direction. We didn't even pause to greet each other; I opened the library doors, and we escaped into the shelter of the foyer.

Once inside, Gloria threw back her hood. Her cheeks were red from the cold. "Oh, I'm frozen," she said through chattering teeth. She stomped the snow off her feet. From all the slush that had been tracked in, the mats in the entry lay like soggy rags on the marble floor. They splatted under her.

My jaw was stiff from the cold, making it difficult to speak. "So much for global warming, huh?" The foyer was only slightly warmer than the outside, so I opened the glass doors that led to the main section of the library, but Gloria grabbed my arm. "Wait, I want to tell you something."

Nothing could be so important to keep us in the freezer-like foyer. "Can't you tell me inside?"

"No. I can't wait. I have to tell you now. This will boggle your mind."

"Hey," I said, "you're stealing my thunder. I'm the one that's supposed to dazzle you with incredible facts. If you're going to tell me some music trivia, don't bother. It'll just go right over my head."

"No, no. It's not about music." She was ready to burst with excitement. A smile spread across her frostbitten face. Taking a deep breath, she then exhaled, and calmly said: "They found a match for Christo."

"What? You're serious?"

She threw her arms around my neck and squealed so loudly I was afraid the marble walls would crack.

"Yes, it's a miracle. Christo's tissue matched one of the first samples they tested." She danced with glee, swinging on my neck like it was a flagpole. "Oh Tom, I'm so happy."

I grabbed her arms, stopping her so that I could see her face. "That's incredible. I can't believe it."

"It was the prayers," she said, releasing me to prance around the vestibule. "I'm sure it was. I know you don't believe that, but I'm convinced. Everybody has been praying so hard."

Everybody but me.

"I couldn't wait to get here to tell you."

"When did you find out?"

"Ginny called right before I left." Gloria clapped her hands together. "Oh, I wish I had a bottle of champagne to pop or fireworks to light."

"That's wonderful," I said. "So what happens next?"

Gloria put her hands in a prayer pose in front of her mouth. "We just have to wait to find out if the donor will agree to the transplant."

"Well, of course, they'll agree. I mean, a kid's life is at stake."

A worried look crossed her face. "Well, donors are under no obligation. They can back out at any time."

"But that won't happen."

"I hope not. Sometimes people change their minds though."

"What kind of a person would back out after going to all the trouble of having a sample taken?"

"I don't know. People think they want to do something and then when the time comes, they get scared." Out of habit, her hand went to her wrist. But since that night in the car when I'd removed her rubber

166

band, she hadn't replaced it. "But let's not worry about that now." Gloria grabbed my arm. "Oh, pray that everything turns out OK."

"So if all systems are go, when will Christo get the transplant?"

"From what Ginny said, they'll do testing on both him and the donor, and if everything's OK, sometime after the first of the year."

"I hate to be nosy," I said, "but what about money? Can they afford it?"

"Oh, that's no problem. Way back in September when Christo's doctors recommended a transplant, Hippocraticare agreed to pay eighty percent. And through fundraisers, we've raised the other twenty percent. The money is sitting in an account waiting to be used."

"I'm so happy for you, Gloria." I hugged her. "I know how much you love Christo, and I hate to see you so worried about him all the time."

She gave me a peck on the cheek. "Ah, for the first time, Tom, I feel like everything is going to be fine. Christo will get well, no one will have to find out about the insemination, Ginny and Joe can rebuild their marriage, and we can all put this whole nightmare in the past and enjoy life."

I kissed the top of her head. I knew it was selfish, but I'd be glad when Christo was well too. His illness hung around, occupying Gloria's mind like the ghost of an old lover. Now maybe we could concentrate on each other.

"We'd better get studying," she said, "or I'll be flunking out."

The library was crowded, and it would get even more so the nearer it came to finals. We found a table in the rear and set up camp, unloading backpacks and spreading books and notebooks over the top. Gloria took off her coat, folded it and draped it over the back of her chair. She was wearing a bulky purple sweater and black leggings. She fluffed out her hair, took some Blistex from a pocket of her backpack, and applied it to her lips.

"You better make sure you protect those babies," I whispered as I took off my jacket. "I've got a vested interest."

She sat, puckered up, and planted a big kiss on my lips. "I'm insuring them with Lloyd's of London." Her fingers gently touched my cheek. "Your eye is looking better."

My shiner had turned a sickly yellow mottled with green. I was glad she felt free to kiss me. After the disaster in my room, I was afraid she would be less affectionate. She opened a notebook and pulled out a pen. "Oh, with the good news, I almost forgot. Are you busy Saturday night?" she whispered.

"No. Why?"

"Well, every year my grandma and I go to a Christmas production—*The Nutcracker*, or *A Christmas Carol*, or *The Messiah*. It's a tradition. I think she missed having a daughter of her own. See, Grandma is a music lover too. Anyway, Grandma's arthritis has been bothering her lately and in this cold, she doesn't feel up to going to the Christmas concert with me. Would you like to go?"

"Oh, I don't know." It sounded out of my league.

"She bought the tickets already. Aw, come on. Please, Tom. I'd really like you to come with me. And it's at Heinz Hall."

"But I'm afraid I'd be out of place there. I'm a cultural clod," I said. "I've only been to Heinz Hall once in my life, on a grade school field trip."

Gloria raised her eyebrows at me. "Don't worry, Tom. I guarantee you'll love it. Please say you'll go. It'll be a celebration of Christo's good news. We'll have a wonderful time. Heinz Hall is spectacular at Christmas. They decorate an enormous tree that's absolutely incredible. And the carols will be so beautiful, and when we stand to sing the 'Hallelujah Chorus—" She hugged herself. "Oh, it gives me chills just thinking about it."

"What's this *we sing* stuff?" I asked. "I don't sing."

"Not just you and me, silly. The whole audience sings along."

I laughed and arranged my books. "Obviously, you've never heard me sing. Joe could use my voice to strip the varnish off his woodwork."

"What your voice sounds like doesn't matter. Trust me." She put her arm around my shoulder and stroked my cheek with her finger. "We'll get dressed up, and then I'll take you out afterwards. My treat." She moved her fingers and grabbed a lock of my hair and began tickling my nose with it. "One of my piano students gave me a gift certificate to that new restaurant downtown, *Dolci*, for Christmas." She lowered her head and looked at me with puppy-dog eyes. "Please."

I swear I'm powerless around her. There should be a twelve-step program developed for resisting her charms. I pushed her hand away and scratched my nose. "How dressed up do I have to get?"

She kissed me on the cheek. "A suit or sport jacket and slacks are fine—no tuxes or anything that formal."

"I hate to sound like a geek, Gloria, but I don't have either."

She bit her lip. "Stand up, Tom."

"Huh?"

"Stand up."

I pushed out my chair and rose.

She looked me over. "You seem to be as big as my brother. Are you a 44 long?"

"I have no idea."

Gloria shook her head and rolled her eyes at me. "Hmph, you know the atomic weight of every element and the names and locations of a million stars, but you don't know your own size. I'll borrow a sport jacket from my brother." I sat down. "Wow, Tom," she laughed. "How would you function without me?"

After that night at the Old Allegheny and its terrible aftermath, I didn't find her question amusing. I knew how awful it was without her and to be with her, I'd do anything—including spending a boring evening listening to elevator music.

Chapter 21

"You look like that fruity poet," Phil said when I walked into the lounge.

"Who?"

"Aw, you know the one." He closed his eyes and shook his finger at me. "What's his name? He was always on 'The Mike Douglas Show.' Wore turtlenecks and read poems that made no damn sense." He snapped his fingers. "Rod McKuen—that's the guy. Where you going dressed like that?"

It was Saturday night. I'd decided to wait for Gloria in the lounge because Rob was in our room, and I didn't want to start a third world war. I felt stupid enough wearing a sport coat without Phil acting like Mr. Blackwell and critiquing my attire.

To the left of the security desk was the lounge. Five guys huddling around the TV watching the Penguin game were hurling their baseball caps and obscenities at the screen. A defenseman apparently had draped himself over Mario Lemieux like a feather boa and no penalty had been called. Around a gouged out wooden table in the back of the lounge, sat another group of freshmen—Chaz and his chums—who were playing Hearts.

"Where you headed?" Phil asked again.

"I got a date," I whispered.

"A date?" roared Phil loud enough to attract the attention of everyone in the lounge.

"With a girl?"

I clenched my teeth, "Of course, with a girl."

"Well, these days you never know." He shook his head and chuckled. "You guys with long hair and earrings confuse the crap out of me."

Chaz nudged the guy sitting beside him who had a complexion like a crispy Klondike and said loud enough so I could hear, "Bet Shepherd's got a date with a sheep. That's about the only action he'll ever get."

"Shepherd?" asked The Clearasil Kid. "Is he the dude you told me about—the one that blond chick shafted?"

Another freshman at the table, a jerk named Bobo, eyed me and snorted. Bobo looks like the Wolfman on a night with a full moon. "He's probably taking his 'little Lamby-pie' dancing," Bobo yelled. "Bet their favorite song is 'I Only Have Eyes for Ewe.'" He punched Chaz in the arm. "Get it?" The lounge erupted in hysterics.

Ignoring their comments, I walked over to the bulletin board to right of Phil's desk. The corkboard was plastered with notices, and I pretended to read them.

"Tom," I heard Gloria calling me. She was early. I was supposed to meet her in the parking lot in another five minutes. She had a lot of guts coming back into the place where she had been humiliated.

I turned around and when I saw her, my jaw unhinged.

Her curls were piled up on top of her head, a few corkscrews hanging seductively around her face and neck. She was wearing a black velvet cape that fastened at the neck with a large jeweled button. The cape gave her an air of royalty. But what really blew me away were her legs. I'd never seen her in a dress before. They were long and shapely and sheathed in sheer black hose. I caught myself before I drooled.

I wasn't the only one having jaw problems. Glancing over at the hockey fans, I saw that they were now silent, too, their mouths gaping.

As Gloria approached, Phil whistled and muttered, "Some dish, Shepherd."

I'm 6'2", but when I strutted over to her, I know I measured taller. Puffing out my chest, I bent over and kissed her. Then I gave Chaz a sidelong glance and flashed him a wicked grin. Who's the loser now, Chuckie?

Gloria stepped back, eyeing me. "Aren't you handsome?" she said loud enough for the whole lounge to hear. Chaz lowered his eyes and began rearranging the cards in his hand.

"Thank you," I said, beaming.

Gloria took my arm and teased, "Tell me something amazing."

I thought for a moment and leaned in closer to her. She smelled as good as she looked. I whispered, "Of all the heavenly bodies I've ever studied, you are the heavenliest."

She giggled and playfully tapped my arm. "You know, Tom, with your hair, and turtleneck, and sweet words, you could be a poet."

Phil, who wasn't missing a minute of this, called, "That's what I was just telling him. Don't ya think he looks like that Rod McKuen guy?"

Gloria turned to Phil. "Pardon me?"

"You know, Rod McKuen. That hippie poet. Was always on the *Mike Douglas Show* in the 60s?"

"Sorry," Gloria said, "but I wasn't born until the seventies."

"What?" muttered Phil. "Am I getting old?" Disgusted, he shook his head and went back to watching television.

"Well, if I were a poet like that Rod McKuen guy," I whispered in Gloria's ear, "I'd write all my poems about you." I knew that sounded lame, like dialogue from a soap opera, but Gloria and my audience seemed to eat it up.

She smiled. "I think that was poetry." A shiver made her body tremble, and she pulled the cape's collar tight around her throat. "I should have borrowed a coat for you, too, Tom. I wish this deep freeze would end." She nodded toward the door. "It's like the North Pole out there."

"I'll be fine," I said, putting an arm around her waist and moving her toward the door. And I knew I would be fine, for if I got cold, one glance at her would warm me. She could have melted a glacier.

*****

As we drove across the Fort Duquesne Bridge into town, the sign on Mt. Washington flashed the temperature—minus five degrees. The moon, a crooked grin, on the face of the black night, smiled down on us as we drove and walked the streets of downtown Pittsburgh. It was clear and much too cold to snow, but what little moisture there was left in the air crystallized, and as Gloria and I hurried to Heinz Hall, we walked in a swirl of diamond dust that sparkled in the light from the street lamps.

The gilded trim and twinkling chandeliers of Heinz Hall were just as Gloria said—beautiful. She was also right about the Christmas tree—it was breathtaking as was the climb up the stairs to our seats, which were in the last row of the Gallery. When we reached the top of the red carpeted staircase, I noticed that no one else had been seated in our section yet. Probably because no one wanted to buy seats in a tier that induced altitude sickness.

Gloria entered the row before me, and we stood for a moment, catching our breath, gazing out over the palatial theater.

"Grandma would have never made it up here with her knees," puffed Gloria.

I took the aisle seat and gradually my breathing slowed. Gloria unfastened the button on her cape and whisked it off. And then I lost my breath all over again. She was wearing a strapless burgundy velvet dress. No wonder she kept cinching the cape's collar together, she must have been freezing.

Gloria sat and crossed her long legs.

I swallowed hard. "Whew, that's some dress." My voice cracked like a thirteen-year-old boy's.

She smoothed the velvet skirt. "I borrowed it from my sister-in-law. She's eight months' pregnant. This dress is married to your sport jacket."

The urge to pounce on her again the way I had done back in my dorm room overwhelmed me.

Thankfully, my attention was diverted to the foot of the stairs where a swarm of elderly people had massed.

Gloria leaned over and said, "Grandma must have gotten these tickets through her senior citizens' group." We watched as they began their ascent up the long flight of stairs. Many stopped to clutch the velvet-covered railing and catch their breath, while others paused, leaning on their canes.

They began to fill our section of the hall. When they reached our row, both Gloria and I moved out into the aisle to let them pass. The men and women who shuffled by ranged in age from early seventies to some I swear must have been centenarians. Our heads were the only non-gray or bald ones in that whole section.

We took our seats, and I leaned over and whispered to her, "I hope you know CPR because chances are after that climb, one of them is going to need it."

She nudged me. "You're terrible."

A bald man, whose head shone like it had been waxed and buffed, had taken the seat next to Gloria. The lights from the chandeliers reflected off his dome and his thick glasses. Through his trifocals, the man eyed Gloria and smiled. "Are you by any chance Florence Davidson's granddaughter?" His old voice was as light as powder.

Gloria turned in her seat toward him. "Why yes, I am."

"Your grandmother told us you were using her tickets. I'm Mr. Gosnell and this . . . " He placed a liver-spotted hand on the old woman's arm sitting beside him ". . . is Mrs. Gosnell."

A tiny woman with tight, snow-white curls leaned forward. Her face was so old it looked like a piece of driftwood. She arranged her wrinkles into a smile as she removed a purple chiffon scarf from her neck. "Oh, Florence has shown us pictures of you, dear, but you're much prettier in person." With shaking hands, Mrs. Gosnell folded the scarf into a neat square and nudged her husband. "Isn't she much prettier in person, Clarence?"

He grabbed Mrs. Gosnell's bony knee. "Almost as pretty as my Genevieve."

Mrs. Gosnell batted his hand away from her knee. "Oh, don't pay any attention to him." She was blushing. "Is this your fella, Gloria? Your grandmother said you'd be bringing someone in her place."

"Yes," Gloria looked at me and winked, "this is my fella, Tom."

I leaned out and waved.

"You're the young man from the papers," Mrs. Gosnell said.

"That's him all right," Gloria said.

"Oh, the day I saw your picture in the paper," said Mrs. Gosnell, "I thought you were a girl with that long hair. Why a good-looking boy like you would want to have hair like a girl, I can't understand."

"Don't pay attention to her," Mr. Gosnell said with a wave of his hand toward his wife's direction. "It's the style. She forgets what it was like to be young."

Mrs. Gosnell stuck her tongue out at her husband. He turned to me and ran a bony hand over his bald cranium. "Listen, young fella, if I could have half of your hair, long or short—I'd be happy."

"Oh, don't bother these young people with your nonsense any longer, Clary," said Mrs. Gosnell. "They want to be alone."

Mr. Gosnell obeyed but Mrs. Gosnell continued to talk, asking about Gloria's grandmother's arthritic knees, Christo, and Gloria's grades and major. Then she gave a summary of her recent cataract operation and the specifics of Mr. Gosnell's last prostate exam. I thought she'd never shut up and let me enjoy Gloria.

But I was wrong. Fifteen minutes into the program, I looked over and discovered that Mrs. Gosnell had fallen asleep. Her chin rested on her chest, her glasses sliding down her nose. Mr. Gosnell had also drifted off. His head was tilted back, his mouth open, and a soft snore vibrated in his throat. I glanced around our section and while the symphony played Christmas selections from *The Nutcracker* many of the

175

seniors dreamed of sugarplums. I nudged Gloria. "Look, they've all zonked out."

Gloria whispered, "I think the climb up the stairs did it."

Mr. Gosnell shifted and let out a snore. Laughing, I leaned forward to make sure he was still alive. When I noticed his hand, I smiled. Mr. Gosnell's translucent, veiny hand was resting peacefully in his wife's. I don't know why but looking at their interwoven hands made me happy. Following Mr. Gosnell's lead, I took Gloria's hand in mine.

Our section mates only roused right before the intermission, when the soloist hit a high note that shocked them from their slumber.

After the intermission, the music began again and the majority of the elderly in our section dozed off once more.

Near the end of the performance, Gloria dropped my hand and began paging through the program. Gloria stood abruptly. "It's time for the 'Hallelujah Chorus,'" she whispered. "Stand up."

"What?"

"Stand up. It's a tradition."

"Oh," I shrugged and rose. Gloria and I looked out over the sleeping people. Only a few woke and stood in the rows below us. I leaned back to peek at the Gosnells. They were still snoozing.

"You know," Gloria said, "I once read that when Handel had finished composing *The Messiah,* his servant found him in tears. When the servant asked him why he was weeping, Handel replied that he had seen Heaven and God Himself."

"Jimi Hendrix said that too," I joked, "but he was tripping on acid."

She slapped my arm with the program. "Oh, you're terrible." She handed me the program with the lyrics to the "Hallelujah Chorus."

I handed it back. "I don't have a very good voice."

"That doesn't matter. Sing." She shoved the booklet into my palm. "This is a song you sing with the heart, not the voice."

I had no idea what she meant, but to please her, I tried to follow along in the program. I stumbled so many times I finally gave up to watch her instead. As she sang out, her face became flushed with joy, her breasts rising and falling with each breath. Then like Handel, I swear I saw the heavens open myself.

A pulsing began in me that swelled into a throbbing that escalated with each ejaculation of Hallelujah. It increased and intensified until my heart vibrated like the gong in the orchestra pit.

Gloria saw me staring at her and stopped singing. Tears, like the crystal droplets of the chandeliers, hung and sparkled in her eyes. And I

176

knew then that she felt the same emotions escalating in her that I felt. We were caught in a whirlwind of hallelujahs that swept us up and spun us into a cyclone of sensations.

As the chorus belted out "Forever and Ever," the light from her eyes shone forth, beaming at me, striking my quivering heart, piercing it and exploding it into a million fragments, unleashing a fireball of love that rolled throughout me and invigorated my body with a shower of rainbows. She was the light and I her prism.

Overcome, I swept Gloria into my arms. Peering deeply into her emerald eyes, I searched for the source of her light, looking into her soul. And there I found it, her goodness, glowing like the sun. I wanted that goodness. I wanted to possess it, to harness it, to own it.

Covering her lips with mine, I kissed her. I kissed her with all the beauty and passion and love that I could muster from my wreck of a soul. And I kept right on kissing her. I kissed her through the "King of Kings" and "Lord of Lords" and I didn't stop kissing her until the last "Hallelujah" reverberated throughout the hall and faded away.

After releasing her, we stood trembling, our lips numb, and our breathing coming in great gulps. Heat and passion had been in our previous kisses, but tonight we'd gone way beyond anything we had ever dreamed or known before. Our desire for each other was preordained, cosmic, metaphysical, based on some unknown principle, a principal that set the stars in orbit and governed the universe. I was in love.

The audience broke into applause at the conclusion of the piece, and roused the senior citizens. Quickly, I grabbed Gloria's cape from the back of her seat, flung it around her shoulders, and led her away. I didn't want anything to spoil this moment, not Mrs. Gosnell's diverticulitis—nothing.

"Goodnight, Gloria," they called as we started down the stairs. But Gloria did not speak. She only waved. In fact, neither one of us said a word as we made our way through the crowd and exited Heinz Hall. There was nothing to say; that kiss was more eloquent than any words could have ever been.

We flew out the doors, laughing at the involuntary gasps that escaped us as we inhaled the first shock of frigid air, and we jaywalked across the street and around the corner to *Dolci*.

In the bistro's crowded entry, we waited for a table. I know it's impossible for two objects to occupy the same space, but Gloria may have found a way to subvert that rule. Her hands were drawn tightly around her collar and she snuggled so close to me, she couldn't have gotten any nearer unless she stood on my feet.

A hostess led us to a booth near the window where we watched the other theater patrons hurrying in the cold, the limousines picking up passengers, and the traffic backing up at the red light. Staring dreamily into each other's eyes, we indulged in slices of chocolate cheesecake while a piano tinkled in background "The Christmas Song."

Afterward, we rode back to the dorm, in silence, simmering in our senses. Gloria pulled into the parking lot and shut off the engine. As I watched students entering and exiting the dorms, Gloria turned to me, her hand rubbing my arm. "Tom, what are your plans for the holidays?"

"Well, they leave the dorms open for the foreign students, so I guess I'll stay here."

"I'd like you to come home with me."

Flabbergasted, I wasn't certain what her invitation entailed, but I was pretty sure it didn't include what my hormones were screaming for. "What about your parents?"

"I talked it over with them, and they're all for it. You can stay in my brother, Rick's, old room."

I was disappointed when she told me where I'd be staying but not surprised. Still, the thought of being under the same roof with her for that many days delighted me.

"Sounds great," I said. "But what if your parents hate me when I get there?"

"Don't be crazy. They'll love you. Mom's been looking for another person to mother ever since Rick got married. And Dad . . . Well, he tries to be intimidating. I guess it's that Marine mentality, but underneath his tough exterior, he's a softie."

"Your father's a Marine?" I closed my eyes and rested my head against the seat. The cheesecake curdled in my stomach as I thought of my radical, draft-dodging father. What if her father found out about my scummy background?

"*Was* a Marine," she said.

Once a Marine always a Marine.

"He was wounded and then discharged."

"Wounded? In the War? In Vietnam?" If there is a God, He must be laughing Himself sick right now. First He sends me the girl of my dreams whose spiritual beliefs are completely opposite of mine, and then I find out her dad was a war hero.

"Yeah, he stepped on a mine and lost half of his right foot, but that was a long time ago. He doesn't talk about it."

I moaned. "Aw, I better get a haircut."

"Don't be ridiculous." She grabbed my hand. "Please say you'll stay, Tom." She was begging. Could you believe it? "We'll have a wonderful time. We'll go to the flower show at Phipps Conservatory, tour the Nationality Rooms at the Cathedral of Learning, visit Christo, and I'll kiss you at midnight on New Year's Eve."

"Only on New Year's Eve?"

She lowered her eyelids. "No."

I unbuckled my seatbelt so I could kiss her. As I held her, I shuddered and sighed. "Oh, Gloria, I love you."

The words just tumbled out of my mouth.

Gloria pulled away, and I waited for her to tell me that I was crazy, that it was too soon to have fallen in love, that I didn't know her well enough, that I'd confused love with good old-fashioned lust. But she snuggled in tightly. "I love you, too, Tom."

"What?"

"I said I love you, Tom."

I grabbed her by the shoulders and held her away. "Are you sure? You're not just saying that to be polite, are you?"

"Tom," she stroked my cheek, "I'm sure. I've never felt this way before."

"You really love me? Me? Tom Shepherd?"

She smiled and tapped my nose. "I really love you. Tom Shepherd."

I know I was supposed to act macho, but I started to tear up. "Ah, Gloria, you don't know how . . . I never dreamed. I can't believe." I clutched her hand, and she waited patiently while I took a few deep breaths.

"What I mean to say is from the moment I saw you, nothing has been the same. Things I thought were important mean nothing now that I've met you. And things I never cared about before suddenly mean a great deal. You've turned my world upside down and me inside out. I wasn't sure what was wrong with me, because I've never felt like this before. But tonight . . . Ah, when they were singing and I looked over at you, something happened to me and I knew. Even I knew it was love."

Our lips met and we indulged ourselves in a second helping of passion until it grew cold in the van and the windows fogged over. We laughed when we saw that. The condensation was the visible precipitation of two volatile elements—Gloria and me.

She rested her head on my shoulder and placed her hand over my heart. "Say you'll come home with me, Tom." Then she gazed up at me with her green eyes thick and rich, like the crème de menthe parfait at *Dolci*, and murmured, "And I promise I'll make you believe in the magic of Christmas."

Chapter 22

Rob walked into our room, groaned, and flung himself onto the couch. It was ten o'clock on Monday night, and for the past week he hadn't gotten in earlier from work than midnight.

"What is wrong with you?" I asked.

"I got that Chinese disease."

"Chinese disease?" Wouldn't it be just my luck to catch some foreign bug from him and mess up my holiday plans?

"Yeah, draggin' ass. Man, Tommy, I've never been so tired."

I felt like kicking him for worrying me.

"I knocked off early from work. Told them I was going to drop if I didn't." He stood and unzipped his leather jacket. "The only thing getting me through is Martinique." He flung the jacket into the corner. "So you been studying all night?"

"And most of the day." My necked ached from being bent over books, and my eyes felt dry and swollen like they had outgrown their sockets. I stretched and rubbed the knotted muscles in my shoulders.

"Thought so. You forgot to get your mail." He tossed a pile of envelopes on top of the desk. "Getting back to Martinique, what did you think of those brochures I picked up at the mall?"

I opened the desk drawer and pulled out the stack of travel brochures. I hadn't even thought about Martinique. These days my mind centered on Gloria, finals, and Christo. I spread the glossy brochures across the top of the desk. Each hotel and beach looked more luxurious than the next. I shrugged. "They all look fine to me."

"Well," Rob said, unlacing his Reeboks, "since we've made so much money, this year, I think we should go first class."

"Yeah, whatever. I know you'll find us the best deal."

He smiled, enjoying the compliment to his bargaining skills.

Rob removed his shoes and wiggled his toes. His joints snapped loudly, like someone cracking Alaskan crab legs. "Man, it feels good to get them off."

The smell from his sweaty feet, made my eyes water. "Aw, you're going to take the finish off the linoleum." He pulled a sock off, balled it up, and fired it at me. It landed on my arm. "You're disgusting," I said, flicking the sock off with my finger.

"The package deal sounds the best." He stretched and yawned loudly. "How long are you going to be out in San Diego?"

"I'm not going to San Diego."

Rob raised an eyebrow. "Why not?"

Picking up the stack of mail, I began shuffling through it. "My dad made other plans."

"Ah, too bad. Well, I was going to say when you came back, we should book the trip, but now you can come home with me, and we can book it any time."

"Thanks, but it'll still have to wait until after the holidays. I've got other plans."

"You don't have to act cool, Tommy. I know how your old man is. You're always welcome at my house."

"I'm not acting cool. I do have plans. I'm going to Gloria's for Christmas."

"No!"

"Yes."

Since I'd reconciled with her, Rob had lectured me regularly that I should dump her and move on to a more willing girl. Tonight, I was tired, and I didn't feel like hearing another sermon. I threw away three solicitations for charge cards.

"Now she's bringing you home for the holidays," he said, slapping his thigh. "I still say that chick wants it bad."

I opened an envelope containing information about grad school from Carnegie Mellon. "I'm sleeping in her brother's room."

"But what's to keep you from getting lost on the way back from the can and winding up in her bed?"

"You don't get it, do you?" I said. "Gloria's just not that way."

When I spotted a red envelope at the bottom of the pile, my pulse quickened. The handwriting was definitely feminine. Probably a card from Gloria.

"And besides," I said tearing into the envelope, "her old man's a Marine."

I pulled the card out and read the heading. Then I ground my teeth together. "To a Fine Son at Christmas," it said. Dad must be feeling guilty, I thought as I opened the card. A picture and a slip of paper fell out onto my lap. I picked them up and held them as I read the card.

No, Dad wasn't feeling guilty. Amber was. Written under the printed verse were the words: *Miss you this Christmas! Love, Dad, Amber, and Jeffrey.* Amber had written the card. My father probably didn't even know she'd sent it. I tore the stupid thing in half.

"Her old man's a Marine?"

Preoccupied with the card, I mumbled, "No, former-Marine. He was wounded in Vietnam or something. Now he works for the Post Office."

"Oh man, a vet that works at the Post Office! That's a lethal combo. Hey, you better watch yourself, Tommy. He could have that Post Traumatic Stress stuff, have a flash back, and freak out on you." He pointed a finger in my face. "I'm warning you. I'd sleep with the doors locked if I were you, man."

I hadn't thought of that before. Now I was not only afraid her father wouldn't like me, I was afraid he might kill me. "Ah, Gloria said he's a softie. And anyway he had half a foot shot off. I could out run him."

I unfolded the slip of paper that had fallen out of the card. It was a check for $50 that Amber had also gone to the trouble of writing. Since Jeffrey's birth, I've been getting Christmas cards. Amber had coerced my father into celebrating Christmas now that they had a child. At least I could use this gift, unlike the stupid geode they sent last year. I slid the check into my jeans pocket.

"You can't out run bullets, pal," Rob said, taking aim at me with his finger and firing. He held his fingertip to his mouth, blew on it like some Western gunslinger, and tucked his finger into his pocket. "So when do you join the set of *Apocalypse Now?*"

"I thought I'd stick around here for a few days after the term ends—catch up on my sleep, do the laundry, some shopping, and packing." I hadn't told Rob about my wish to go on to grad school. If I was serious about continuing my education, I'd need to start making some plans soon. I thought I'd take some time to research some graduate programs during the break too.

I examined the snapshot Amber had sent me. My father and Jeffrey were snuggled in a hammock while Amber kneeled behind them in the California sunshine. They were all tanned and smiling. I bet they spent more than fifty dollars on Jeffrey for Christmas.

"I'm going to the Davidsons' on Christmas Eve," I said. "I don't want to wear out my welcome by moving in too soon."

I scrutinized the picture. The paternal pride smeared across my father's face nauseated me. Is it rational to hate a two-year-old? Because I swear, I hate Jeffrey.

"Remember," Rob said taking off his jeans, "if her old man threatens you with a flame thrower, grenade launcher, anything, man, just give me a call. Although I don't blame you for not coming home with me. Old Fat Head will be slobbering all over the place and my brothers and sisters will be carrying on." He closed his eyes and folded his hands behind his head. "Man, I don't even want to spend Christmas there. I have to work right up until closing on December 24. I told my mom that I was going to stay at the dorm until then because it's easier to get to work from here than home, but she took a fit about hardly ever seeing me and made me feel bad. So I'm going home on the twenty-third."

"Hey, your family might be nutty," I said, "but at least they want you." I looked at the photograph of the happy little threesome again. How would I have fit into that picture? I tore the photo into little pieces and sprinkled them ceremoniously into the wastebasket.

"Well," Rob sighed and opened his eyes, "at least we have Martinique to look forward—"

A loud knock interrupted him. At first, I thought it was one of the comedians on the floor goofing around. But the pounding continued. We looked at each other.

"Who'd that be?" I asked. "No one ever comes to see us."

Just then the phone rang. "I'll get it," Rob said. "You get the door."

I opened it expecting to find Larry the maintenance man, standing there clutching a wrench, informing us that the toilets were broken again, but it wasn't Larry. It was Gloria. Her hair was disheveled and her eyes were swollen.

"Hey Tom," Rob called, "Phil says to tell you your honey is on her way up." Phil, our early-warning system had failed.

"I know," I said, panicking. "She's here."

"I need to talk to you, Tom," she said, the tremor in her voice telling me that something was terribly wrong. She put a foot in the room, but I remembered that I had taken our stock of Sammys back out of the closet.

Blocking the doorway, I blurted, "You can't come in here." Then I quickly added, "Rob's not dressed. Take it from me—it's not a pretty sight."

"Hey" Rob yelled, protesting the insult to his anatomy.

Gloria didn't even smile at my joke; she looked away. Alarmed, I said, "Wait, let me get some shoes."

I reached back into the room and grabbed the first pair I could find. Stepping into the hall and closing the door behind me, I realized I'd grabbed Rob's size 15 Reeboks. His shoes were three whole sizes larger than mine. As I bent over to put them on, a thought sprang into my head that terrified me. *She knows. She knows I lied to her.* Gloria knows about the Sammys. It's all over. I've blown it again.

I slipped my feet into the shoes. No, wait. Maybe it was something else. "Gloria, are you having another episode?" I know this sounded selfish, but as I tightened the laces, I hoped that it was a panic attack.

Before I could finish tying the other shoe, she took off down the hall toward the elevator. The distress carved on her face had me so scared I could hardly steady my hand to tie the other shoe.

"What's wrong? Please tell me," I called after her, but she just headed down the hall. I ran after her, the enormous soles of his shoes flapped on the tile floor like a circus clown's. I came to her side as the elevator doors opened.

Two guys from the seventh floor were already in the elevator. As I stepped inside with her, I grabbed her arm and whispered, "Did I do something wrong?"

She looked at the other freshman and said softly, "Can we go somewhere quiet where we can talk."

"OK, we'll try the lounge."

But when the elevator doors parted and we stepped out, the lounge was crowded with freshmen celebrating the end of their first term. Phil saw us and cried, "Hey Shepherd, she just stormed past me without signing in."

"It's OK, Phil,"

Gloria took a tissue out of her coat pocket and wiped her eyes. She looked like a water balloon filled to bursting. I knew any moment she would hemorrhage tears.

Searching for a quiet place, I grabbed her hand and led her outside. I curled my toes to keep the shoes from slipping off.

A warm front had pushed through last night ending the cold wave. The new weather pattern had brought an all-day rain that washed away much of the snow. Only patches of dirty slush dotted the lawn. The melting snow, together with the rain, had saturated the earth, turning the ground into a bog. Near dinnertime the rain had stopped, and now fog, in thick clouds, floated across the campus.

Traffic across the lawn was heavy; the excitement of the end of term and the balmy weather had brought the students out of hibernation. But as I looked for a private place to take Gloria, only muffled voices could be heard in the mist. Finally, under a great old oak half way across the lawn in front of the dorm, I spotted a secluded bench. By the time we got to it, I noticed that in my hurry, I'd forgotten to grab my jacket. Thankfully, the temperature was tolerable in my flannel shirt. I guided Gloria to the bench and took a seat next to her. It was wet and rain soaked through my jeans.

"Now what's wrong, Gloria? Another anxiety attack?"

She hung her head, her hair covering her face and muttered, "Worse."

I crouched in front of her, practically kneeling in the dirty slush and parted her hair to see her face. "What's worse? Tell me. Please."

She lifted her head. Tear tracks glistened on her cheeks. "It's back."

"What?" I grabbed her knees. "What's back? What are you talking about?"

"The leukemia." She bit her lip to stop if from quivering. Then she wailed, "Oh, Tom, Christo's out of remission."

My heart plummeted through the center of my body. "No. Are you sure?" I squeezed her knees. This can't be true. I wouldn't believe it.

"Yes. When my mother and I got home from shopping this evening, Ginny called." Gloria wiped her nose. "The doctors were doing routine tests, monitoring him for the transplant. His white count is way up. Ginny is devastated." She paused. "We're all devastated." Shredding the tissue between her fingers, she cried, "They can't do the transplant."

"No!" I pounded the bench. The blow stung my hand, but that pain was nothing compared to the pain I knew Christo's relapse would cause for Gloria and her family. And Christo? How much can you expect one little kid to endure? The unfairness of it all melted my bones, turning me into molten anger. Seething, I collapsed onto the bench beside Gloria, holding my aching fist.

"I'm falling apart, Tom," she sobbed. "I can't face this."

I stopped nursing my hand, momentarily forgetting my anger, and put my arm around her. She rested her head on my chest. "I didn't come here to upset you. I just needed to talk to someone."

"Don't worry about me," I said, as I held her tightly while she cried. Her tears soaked a spot on my shirt.

Then she raised her head. The light in her eyes that I loved was gone. I wanted the light back for her as well as for me.

"Can't the doctors do something?"

She closed her eyes and leaned back. Her forehead was rumpled. "Ginny and Joe are meeting with them tomorrow to discuss the options. If there are any." She sighed and opened her eyes. "Oh, Tom, I thought Christo was going to be all right, but now . . . I don't know."

I took her by the shoulders. "Gloria, don't give up. You can't. Remember your faith."

"But maybe that's just it, Tom. Maybe I don't have enough faith." She looked at her wrists, and I wondered if she was searching for the missing rubber band. "Maybe if I'd had more, he wouldn't have relapsed." She buried her face in her hands. "I feel like I've failed Christo."

I pulled her hands away from her face and held them. "Aw, Gloria, don't be ridiculous. You didn't fail Christo. I've never met anyone with more faith than you." I stared into her anguished eyes, wanting to seal this truth on her heart. "It's not your fault, Gloria. It's His."

Her eyes fixed on me. "Whose fault? Christo's?"

"Oh no. Not Christo's—God's. God did this to him. Don't be His scapegoat." I squeezed her hands. "Your only mistake, Gloria, was putting your faith in a God who's wicked enough to make Christo sick in the first place."

She sat quietly, absorbing my words, and by her silence, I thought I had reached her, had set her thinking straight. Then something sparked in her eyes and caught fire. My words had ignited it, but it was not the soft light of love that I'd grown accustomed to, it was a burning horror.

She jerked her hands away, shot off the bench, and began pacing in front of me. Frosty puffs huffed from her flared nostrils. Yes, get mad at Him, Gloria. God deserved your anger.

She stopped in front of me, her fists clenched tightly into balls at her side and opened her mouth to speak, but stopped suddenly. Closing her eyes, she took some deep breaths, choking back her fury, controlling it so she could speak. "Oh, yeah, Tom," she snarled. "Blame it all on God, you big coward!"

Coward? I felt like she had kicked me in the stomach. "What'd you call me?"

"A coward. You make me laugh. I'm the one with panic attacks, but you're the biggest wimp I've ever met. You're so afraid to feel anything, afraid to admit what's going on in there." She stabbed at my heart with a finger. "You hide—you hide behind excuses, you hide behind your father, you hide behind Rob, and you hide behind, God." She batted my bangs out of my face and cried, "You even hide behind that stupid hair." My bangs flopped back over my eyes.

I knew she was just lashing out at me because she was upset about Christo, so I clenched my jaw and steadied myself to avoid shouting back.

"Oh, but that's right," she continued, slapping herself on the cheek and taking a mocking tone, "I forgot, you don't believe in God." She threw her head back and laughed. Then she stopped and stared at me, her eyes laser sharp. "Unless there's something you want to blame on Him."

I stood up and a river of anger surged through my veins.

"Admit it," she cried. "Admit it. You do believe in God."

I pushed the hair out of my face. "OK, so maybe I do believe in God." I shouted. "So what?" The words dripped off my tongue like acid. "Let me tell you what I know about your great and wonderful God." I was in her face, toe to toe with her. "He's evil and cruel and he gets his kicks watching us suffer. He's the ultimate S&M freak."

She waved a hand in my face, dismissing me. I wanted to head-butt her. Grabbing her wrist, I yelled, "Oh, so you think I'm crazy, do you? Well, I'll tell you something else, sweetheart." I flung her hand away. "You're the one who's crazy. God doesn't care about any of us." My voice rose as we neared critical mass, my index finger poking at her face. "You. Me. Christo. Nobody. God doesn't listen to your prayers. He doesn't grant miracles. He couldn't care less whether Golden Gloria suffers from panic attacks! And He gave Christo cancer!"

Warning bells and flashing lights were going off inside my head. I grabbed her by the shoulders, shaking her like a rag doll and screamed, "And God killed my mother!"

MELTDOWN!!

My words echoed off the campus buildings and came back to me. Nearby, a girl walking through the fog looked over, and quickly scurried away. The radiation I'd been harboring in my soul spilled over; poison seeped out of my pores like sweat.

Gloria stared at me in horror. In her wide, frightened eyes, I saw the reflection of my tortured soul, and I was terrified. My pain was the fuel that fired my anger; the rage burned out of control, consuming me. I stood before Gloria quaking, self-destructing.

Ashamed, I turned and ran. I went ten yards before one of Rob's stupid shoes slipped off. My bare foot hit the mushy ground. I gasped at the shock of the cold wetness on my feet.

With a soggy sock, I turned back to pick up the shoe—like some loser Cinderella. The spell was broken. What I'd feared most had happened. Gloria had turned me inside out all right, and she'd revealed the waste dump that was my soul. Where was I running? I had no where to go. No home. No family. Nothing. No one. And now I no longer had Gloria.

The realization of what I'd destroyed set in. The clammy fog embraced me, closed in around me, swallowed me up like death. The wind gusted and sent a rush of cold air through my flimsy shirt. And as I bent to put on the shoe, I began to shiver and sob. I couldn't see through my tears to find the laces. Helpless, I wrapped my arms around myself to keep warm. I was alone. Again.

"Oh, Tom," Gloria called. "You forgot your jacket."

Startled, I looked behind me. Gloria hadn't left. Through the bales of fog swirling between us, I saw her grab the latch of her zipper and undo her parka. "Come here," she said holding her coat wide open. The wind stirred again parting the fog, and catching the sides of her coat. It billowed and rose behind her like white wings against the black night. "Come here, Tom," she commanded, I'll keep you warm."

She was inviting me back?

"Come on, Tom," she called again. In disbelief, I wiped away the tears with the backs of my hands and slipped my wet foot into Rob's shoe, not bothering to retie it. And I slowly rose and stumbled, laces streaming, shoes slapping back to her.

I stood before her not knowing what to do.

"Put your arms around me," she insisted. Slowly, I slid my arms around her waist, beneath the lining of her silky white wings, and she wrapped the coat around my freezing body like a mother bird protecting her chick.

What kind of girl was she? Who could welcome such a wretched person as me?

"Oh, Gloria," I whispered, "what I said. . . ."

"It's OK, Tom," she hugged me tightly and patted my back.

I collapsed onto her shoulder, burying my face in her curls and began sobbing. Eighteen years' worth of pent-up tears and grief flowed out of me. I cried for the frightened little boy who'd never gotten over the death of his mother. I cried for the child rejected by his father. And I cried for the misguided young man I'd become. I cried so long and hard, I felt as though I'd wept away the liquid part of my body, leaving nothing but the worthless residue of dried minerals that I was.

She let me cry until the sobbing wore me out. Then I rested silently in her arms.

"Tom," she said softly in my ear, her warm breath caressing my damp cheek, "I'm so sorry. Sorry about everything. About taking out my disappointment and anger on you—"

I raised my head. Her green eyes were full of the love and compassion that I had missed so much, that had gone into the ground along with my mother's body. Gloria stood on her toes, stretched, and kissed me on the forehead. "And I'm so sorry about your mom."

I bit my lip to stop a sob.

"Ah Tom, I understand your anger. You have a right to be angry. Death, sickness, cruelty—they anger me too. I don't know why God allows bad things to happen." And then she laughed though I saw that she, too, had tears in her eyes. "But of course, as always, I have an opinion. Would you like to hear it?"

I nodded and waited for her to make sense of the world for me once again.

"I think God allows bad things to happen so that we can become more than ourselves, so that we can become more like Him. Terrible things test us, give us the opportunity to rise above our selfish nature, to be divine, to be God for one another.

"If God had not allowed Christo to get sick, Tom, all those people who donated blood and money would have never had the opportunity to give of themselves. And you, you'd have never had the opportunity to give of yourself by giving Christo the Sammy." The tears were free falling down her face now, but I could tell they were tears of joy. "I never wanted Christo to get sick. But if he hadn't, Tom. . . ." She hesitated, her voice faltering. "I would have never found you." She wrapped her arms tightly around me.

"You mean you still want me?" I asked, hugging her tightly. "After all the awful things I said?"

She pulled away and looked up at me. "When I told you I loved you, I meant it."

"Oh, I don't deserve you," I sighed and snuggled up to the heat of her body, trying to absorb her goodness. "You know," I said, "this feels so good, I may give up coats all together." I kissed her on the top of her head, and she squeezed me even tighter.

I thought for a moment about what she'd said, reconciling it with the circumstances of my life. I ran my hand over her curls. "But my mother's death, Gloria . . . I still can't understand it. I can't see any good in it. I don't know if I ever will."

"Perhaps you haven't discovered it yet. Perhaps *you* haven't made the good come out of it yet."

This was her subtle way of telling me to get my "act together," that it was time to stop living in the past.

She looked into my eyes. "But, Tom, I believe this with all my heart: We're all evolving, you, me, the world—we're all evolving toward something greater."

Ever since that day when I pulled in front of Holy Redeemer, I sensed that I had started on some journey, that I was beginning my evolution. As I clung desperately to Gloria in the damp night, I only hoped that she was right, that I was evolving toward something greater and not toward something more terrible.

Chapter 23

"Thomas?"

"Ahhh," I cried, jumping as if I'd touched a live wire. The stack of books crashed to the floor as my hand flew to cover my palpitating heart. "Rajiv, what are you doing? Trying to scare me to death?"

It was Tuesday, December 15, and Rajiv had caught me staring out the window instead of stocking shelves. Yesterday's balmy weather provided only a brief respite. Through the night winter returned with a vengeance. Anything that had been liquid was now frozen solid, providing a foundation of ice for the big, fat flakes that had been steadily falling since early morning.

Watching the snow falling and the cars moving sideways over the slick roads had hypnotized me. The store was quiet as the term was over and books were the last things on the minds of TRU's student body.

"I did not mean to frighten you, Thomas." Rajiv's lean brown figure hovered so closely I could feel his hot breath on my neck. I didn't believe him. He's always scaring me. Americans are too big and loud to be really good at skulking. Rajiv was smaller and treaded more lightly. He insists that if I lived in the "present moment" instead of letting my mind wander, I'd be aware of him and not be startled when he approached.

My mind wasn't wandering today. It was fixed on Gloria. I needed to talk to her, but with this weather, she'd never be able to drive over and see me.

"What is it?" I growled as I knelt on the floor and began collecting the books I'd dropped.

He held a magazine in his hand. "I hope you do not take offense, but I feel it is my duty to point out your error."

I'd probably dog-eared the magazine while I was stocking the racks, and now he was here to nag me about it. I rose. "What error?"

"Do you recall our conversation the day the news reporters came seeking you? When I said you are negative and that one day you will meet your positive?"

"Yeah, what about it?"

"You will remember that you stated that when a positive and negative meet, they annihilate each other."

"Yeah? So what's your point?"

"Please forgive me, Thomas. But you are wrong."

Wrong? What did he mean wrong? Who was the physics major here? Annoyed, I put my hands on my hips and adopted my wise-guy tone of voice. "OK, Rajiv, you tell me how I'm wrong."

"You have heard of antimatter, I presume?"

"Yes, *of course* I've heard of antimatter."

Antimatter is believed to have been formed alongside regular matter when the universe was created. In an environment of high energy, matter is created in pairs—one particle of matter and one of anti-matter.

"What about it?"

"What happens, Thomas, when matter and antimatter meet?"

This conversation was an insult to my intelligence. I rolled my eyes. "I told you before, Rajiv. They annihilate each other. When a positive and negative collide, they obliterate each other, wipe each other out. Got it?"

"Then why do you and I exist?"

"What's that have to do with antimatter?"

"Thomas, why do we exist?"

"I thought we were talking physics here, Rajiv, not philosophy."

"Ah, but I am." He licked his fingers and began leafing through the magazine. "I was reading this article on antimatter and it stated that for every billion antiparticle-particle pair created, there was one extra particle. A positive particle. If there had not been that one extra positive particle, the universe would not exist." He looked at me. "You and I would not exist."

"Let me see that magazine," I said, grabbing it from him. Pushing the hair out of my eyes, I looked at it. "I can't read this." I shut the magazine. The stupid thing was written in a foreign language—Hindi or hieroglyphics, or something.

"So you see you were wrong," he said.

I thrust the magazine back at him and walked toward the stockroom to get more books to shelve. I didn't need him explaining the universe to me.

Mr. Persistence, Rajiv, followed after me, practically skipping as I doubled my pace to get away from him. "When a positive and a negative meet, Thomas, it is not annihilation—but assimilation and creation. It is destiny that positive wins. It is woven into the fabric of the universe; it is preordained in the stars. Good must triumph over evil, love over hate."

I stopped in the stockroom's doorway and turned to tell him to get lost, but when I looked at him, he beamed his blinding white smile at me, "the cowboys in the white hats over the ones in the black."

"OK, OK," I said, throwing up my hands in surrender. "I get it. Positive wins. Big deal. What's that have to do with me?"

"It has everything to do with you."

"How?"

He placed a hand on my arm. "I tell you this as a friend, Thomas. Do not be afraid to embrace the positive. Open yourself to it. It will not destroy you. It only desires to unite with you to create something beautiful."

I jerked my arm away. I didn't want to hear this garbage. I was still hell-bent on annihilation.

*****

Liberation day came the next day on Wednesday, December 16. Finals were over, and I was exhausted from studying and the emotional upheaval of the past few days. Christo's failing health and my confrontation with Gloria had plowed up buried feelings, leaving me feeling raw and vulnerable. Even now, two days later, I was having trouble dealing with my emotions. Seeds of anger, fear and sadness sown in my childhood now sprouted under Gloria's warming light like dandelions in spring. I was afraid my emotions would choke the life out of me.

I slept in Wednesday morning, and when I awoke at eleven-thirty, the roads were still dicey. I hoped that by evening, they would improve so that I could see Gloria.

I dressed and hoofed it across the Sixth Street Bridge into town, where I picked up a Big Mac and fries at the McDonald's on Liberty Avenue. Then I spent the rest of the day Christmas shopping. The stores were empty because of the bad weather.

I arrived back at the dorm close to three. As I wrapped the gifts that I'd bought, something that Gloria had said during my meltdown festered in my mind. Was it true? Was I afraid to feel? Was I hiding from my emotions? Myself?

Deep down, I had to admit I was. I had no other choice. My emotions left me powerless.

Thinking back to those years after my mother's death, I remembered the sense of abandonment, the loneliness, and the loss of comfort and security. When she first died, I felt all those emotions sharply, and I remember expressing them as any child would have. But when your cries are met with an icy stare, and your tantrums are met with a "Knock that off," you learn to deny your emotions.

But now the feelings that I had put on layaway were threatening to ruin my life.

On my way back to the dorm, I'd picked up a seafood hoagie at Subway, and after wrapping my gifts, I sat at the desk to eat my dinner. The phone rang, breaking the solitude. I swallowed quickly, gulping a large chunk of sandwich and picked up the receiver.

"Hello," I said cheerfully, expecting Gloria's voice. The roads had improved, and I hoped we'd be able to go out later.

"Hey T.P., glad I caught you." The cheeriness drained from me. My father was the last person I wanted to hear from. I took a bite of my sandwich.

"You there, T.P.?"

"Yeah, I'm here," I mumbled, my mouth stuffed with imitation crabmeat. I knew it was rude to eat while on the phone, but that was the whole point of doing it, wasn't it?

"How's it been going?"

That's what gets me the most. He acts like we're the best of buddies. He's too stupid to realize that I hate him.

"OK. Why?" I picked up a napkin and wiped the sauce dripping from the corner of my mouth.

"Hey, guess what I got in the mail today?"

A Father of the Year citation? I took a sip of my iced tea. "I don't know."

"A Christmas card from Kathy O'Halloran."

Kathy O'Halloran was the woman who babysat me when I was little. "Yeah, so. I got one too."

"Guess what was in the card?"

What was this "twenty questions?" I sighed. "I don't know."

"A clipping from the *Post-Gazette* of you giving one of those Sammy toys that everyone's going wacky over to a sick boy." I didn't respond. I was tired of Sammys, tired of my father, tired of everything.

"Why didn't you tell us, T.P.?"

"Look, I know Jeffrey wants a Sammy, but I can't get anymore. They're all sold out."

"That's not why I'm calling. Why didn't you tell us you were in the paper?"

I shifted in the chair. "What do you mean?"

"Well, you should have told us. Amber's making copies for all our friends. She's so proud of you." He paused, then he tacked on, "We all are."

"It was no big deal."

"Not according to Kathy. Her note said you were on the news and everything. You know, T.P., you should have sent me that clipping, so I could brag." He laughed.

"Brag? About what?"

"About what a wonderful dad I am. You know, how well you turned out. All you hear about are poor single mothers. How about us single fathers? I think I deserve a little pat on the back."

What an arrogant jerk! "You called me all the way from California to tell me what a wonderful dad you were?" I screamed into the phone. "What planet are you from?"

"Hey, what's your problem?"

Pressure, like someone had injected me with extra pints of blood, strained every vessel in my body. My heart felt like it was about to explode. "You. You're my problem. You've always been my problem."

"I'm your problem?"

"Look, I'm 22. I'm not a kid anymore. Don't you think it's time to cut the crap? You know why I didn't tell you about the clipping, why I don't tell you anything. Because you're not my father."

"What do you mean?"

"Just what I said. I never had a father. A father cares about his kid and knows what's going on his kid's life. You never cared about me—"

"You ungrateful little bastard."

"Bastard is right. You saw to that too. You didn't even care enough to marry my mother after you knocked her up."

The way he sputtered, I could tell that if he'd been in the room with me, he'd have had me jacked up against the wall. "I rearranged my whole life for you. Took you in. Gave you a home."

"Took me in?" I screamed. "A real father doesn't take his kid in—a real father is there from the beginning."

197

"OK, so I wasn't there when you were young. Cut me a break. I did my best."

"Well, your best sucked."

"Sucked? Who took you to the doctors every time you had a snotty nose? Who spent their life-savings on braces? Who washed ten years' worth of pissed sheets?"

"Oh, yeah, you took me in, fed me, dressed me, but you never cared about what happened to me. What I felt like."

"That's a lie."

I was breathing heavily like I had run a four-minute-mile. "All you did was maintenance. You maintained me. You raised me like I was a house plant, like I was a frickin' philodendron or something."

Silence. Then after a moment he spoke in a controlled tone. "Well, then call me a fool for spending thousands to send a philodendron to college."

"Oh, yeah. You sent me to school and sent me money, but you made such a stink about it, you'd have thought I'd asked for one of your kidneys instead."

"Didn't stop you from taking it though."

"I guess I learned something from you."

"Oh yeah?"

"To look out for yourself and forget everyone else."

"OK, then wise guy. You know so much, when you graduate, don't come crying to me, asking me to save your hide. Get your spoiled ass out and get a job."

"If it means I'll never have to speak to you again, I will." I slammed the phoned down.

Exhilaration, as if I'd plunged into frigid water tingled and electrified my body. I was brilliant. That line about the philodendron split his spleen. I've never heard him so angry.

For years I'd dreamed of this day, when I would let my father have it, when I would rattle off his list of sins that I kept filed in my memory, when I would tell him what a jerk he'd been all my life. And now I'd done it.

Euphoria, that I had finally stood up to him made me lightheaded. I crossed my hands behind my head and gloated.

But as I sat there, the excitement slowly faded, and I began to wonder exactly what I had done. Telling off my father felt nothing like the way I had dreamed it would. There was no satisfaction. What satisfaction is there in declaring your father is an idiot? In declaring that your own dad hated you?

Chapter 24

"Why don't you pick," Gloria said. "We've done something that I like. Tonight, let's do something you enjoy."

Thirty minutes after hanging up on my father, Gloria called. When the phone rang, I was still contemplating what exactly I had done in severing my relationship with my father. Preoccupied, I found it hard to concentrate on what she was saying.

"What do you like to do, Tom?"

"Huh?"

"What do you like to do?" she repeated, her tone emphatic.

"Ah, I don't know." I'd been so busy with work, school, selling Sammys, and trying to impress Gloria, I'd forgotten what I liked to do.

Darkness had fallen since I'd gotten off the phone with my father, and as I stared out the window at the city, it glowed white under the layer of snow. Cars were moving across the bridges and streets without much difficulty. I checked the sky, and the moon shone brightly. Then an idea hatched in my brain. "OK," I said. "I know what we can do."

"What?"

"It's a surprise. I'll pick you up in an hour. Wear boots and bundle up."

"Your car's not that cold."

"No, but you'll need to dress warmly for what we're going to do."

"Come on, tell me what it is."

"*No.* I told you, it's a surprise."

"We're going sledding. I know it."

"No," I said trying to be mysterious, "it's not sledding."

199

"Then what? Oh, I know. Ice skating."

"I'm not telling, but I think you'll like it. At least, I hope you will."

*****

I had layered on the clothes, made a quick stop, and within an hour of hanging up, was cruising down Countryside Lane looking for Gloria's house. I had no trouble finding it; a large, illuminated Nativity scene sitting on the lawn shined like a beacon and led me to the two-story red brick home.

Pulling into the driveway, I noticed that the house was well tended and cozy. Ruffled curtains framed the windows, and a miniature barn on a wooden post served as the Davidsons' mailbox

Gloria opened the door and stepped outside. She had taken my advice to dress warmly seriously. Waddling down the red brick walk, in her white coat, Gloria looked like the Pillsbury Doughboy. I leaned across the front seat and unlocked the door for her.

As she got into the car, she groaned. "I've got so many layers on, I can barely move." She leaned over to give me a kiss and grunted. "Now I know how Maggie must feel."

"Who's Maggie?"

"My sister-in-law. Remember, I told you she's pregnant. I'll be an aunt for the first time the beginning of January."

"Oh yeah. Right." She had told me. I'd have to pay closer attention if I was going to spend the holidays with her family.

"I would have invited you in to meet my parents, but they're out at a Christmas party," she said.

Gloria reached up and dragged the seat belt across her chest, but I had to fasten it for her because she couldn't reach the buckle over her bulky clothing.

I was so used to seeing her dressed nicely, it seemed strange to see her looking like a bag lady. "Just what do you have on?" I asked as I backed out.

She pulled a knitted Penguin cap off her head, smoothed her hair, and popped the snap at her collar. "Well, I've got on thermal underwear, a T-shirt, a sweatshirt, and a wool sweater. And on the bottom," she patted her thighs, "pantyhose, three pairs of socks, thermal undies, and my ski pants." She extended her leg, modeling black mid-calf boots with a fur cuff. "Aren't these stylish? They're my grandma's. I don't have boots. Every September Grandma leaves a pair at our house in case it snows. If a flake falls and she doesn't have boots, she panics. When I was little, I used to think she was like the witch in the Wizard of Oz, that touching snow would make her melt."

I chuckled. "Well, you should be warm enough."

We entered I279 at the Camp Horne exit. As we merged onto the highway, Gloria clapped her mittens together, making a muffled thud. "So where are we going?"

"You'll see."

"Tell me." I shook my head no. "Oh, you're rotten, Tom." She crossed her arms in front of her chest, pretending to pout.

The interstate was bone dry; I took the car up to 65. "So, what's the latest with Christo?"

She let out a deep sigh. "Oh, you wouldn't believe it. I watched him this afternoon while Ginny and Joe met with his oncologists. It seems there's a hospital in Wisconsin that is pioneering transplants for patients who have relapsed. I don't understand all this medical stuff, but even when chemo and radiation wipe out the leukemic cells, some cells may hide undetected in the spine and testicles. Then later they trigger a relapse—that's what's happened to Christo. Do you know what graft-versus-host disease is?"

I wiped the windshield with an old T-shirt I'd brought along. "Yeah, I'm no bio major, but isn't it when the donated marrow, the graft, attacks the host? It's like organ rejection. It's not something you want to happen. Right?"

"Yeah, well," Gloria said, "evidently, this doctor does. Ginny explained the new procedure this way: The doctor transplants the marrow into the patient and then tries to trigger graft-versus-host disease. Along with the donor marrow, the doctor transfuses genetically altered T-cells, they're the immune system's killer cells. Before transfusing the T-cells, Ginny said the doctor alters them by giving them a 'suicide gene' that is sensitive to the drug Acyclovir. As I understand it, the T-cells trigger the graft-versus-host disease and attack the hidden leukemic cells in the process. But before the T-cells also destroy the donated marrow, the patient is given Acyclovir to cut short the T-cell reaction and save the transplant."

I looked over at her. "So in other words, the altered T-cells go in and clean up on the leukemia, and then just before they get out of hand and completely wipe out the new bone marrow, Acyclovir moves in, kicks butt on the T-cells, and the bone marrow is saved?"

"I think that's the basic idea. Sounds like the plot of an Arnold Schwarzenegger movie."

201

"Hey, well that's great," I said. "Christo can still get the transplant."

"It's a long shot. The success rate isn't very high."

"But at least he's got a chance. So what's the next step?"

"Friday, Ginny and Joe are meeting with the doctor who does this procedure. Fortunately, he's in town for some conference so they won't have to fly to Wisconsin. We'll know more then."

We exited the interstate and drove down Zelienople's main drag, past Seneca Valley High School, until we turned onto a one-lane, asphalt road that meandered through rolling snow-covered cornfields. At a fork in the road, we headed left, down a narrow county lane, Orange Creek Road. Snow piled high along either side made me feel like I was navigating a luge run.

The road hugged the winding path of the Connoquennessing Creek, and after a mile or so Gloria turned to me. "You're not having delusions of Dr. Zhivago, are you? You're not kidnapping me, and taking me to an Ice Palace?"

I laughed. "No."

"Good, because if you were, I'd demand a sable coat to keep me warm instead of all these clothes."

To the left, there was a gap in the trees lining the road, signaling the turn off. I quickly swerved and pulled into a secluded clearing.

"I guess I can tell you now," I said as I shut off the car's engine. "We're having a picnic."

"In December?"

I turned off the headlights, and the night swallowed everything.

"It's so dark. Where are we, Tom?"

A trace of anxiety was noticeable in Gloria's voice. I didn't want her to be afraid. I wanted us to relax, to forget our problems, my father, and Christo.

"This place belongs to Rob's family. They said I can come here anytime I want." I reached under the front seat and brought out a flashlight.

"Is Rob here?"

I shined the light on her. She looked perturbed. I patted her hand. "No, I might be crazy enough to have a picnic in December, but I'm not crazy enough to bring the two of you together again."

I got out of the car and walked to the trunk. The snow was deeper here than in the city; it came midway up my shins. Gloria got out and joined me at the back of my car. I opened the trunk and took out a case and my gym bag.

"What's all this?"

"You'll see," I said, slamming the trunk shut. "Can you hold the flashlight and shine it where I'm walking?"

She took the light from me and beamed it all over, scouting out the area. The small arc of light cut a path across the lot. She held my elbow tightly. "Is it OK to be here, Tom?"

"Trust me, Gloria. I wouldn't bring you here if it wasn't safe."

"OK," she held on tighter to my arm. In the more thickly forested area surrounding lot, it was darker, but as we left the cover of the trees, the moon shone brightly giving everything the appearance of having been dipped in platinum. Gloria, stopped, and squeezed my arm. "I hear water."

She shined the light in my eyes. I squinted. "Yeah, there's a stream in front of us; we have to cross a wooden footbridge. Turning the flashlight ahead, she illuminated three small steps that led up to the bridge. "Be careful the boards might be slippery," I said as I guided her up them. I neglected to tell her that the bridge was a suspension one.

On each of the stream's banks two sets of steel poles were anchored into the ground and two sets of cables were strung across the stream between them. The bottom set had planks secured to it, composing the bridge's deck. And the other set of cables ran chest-high and served as a railing. The bridge looked like something from a Tarzan movie. Thankfully, this span was only twenty feet above the stream rather than hundreds of feet from the bottom of a jungle gorge.

When we stepped onto the bridge, it bounced like a trampoline. Gloria shrieked and froze. "Is this thing sturdy?"

In the stillness, the water rushing over the rocks in the creek sounded as loud as the thunder of Niagara Falls. She shined the light on the water below us.

"I swear, Gloria, these cables could hold a herd of elephants." But by the way she clung to me, I could tell she was still frightened. I sat my case on the deck of the bridge. "Look, I'll take the flashlight. You hold on to my arm and the railing." I stuck the flashlight's end in my mouth, picked up Gloria's free hand, and placed it on the handrail. I felt the fingers of her other hand curl around my arm. Then I grabbed the case and went on. The bridge was only about one hundred fifty feet long but Gloria shuffled so slowly and cautiously across, it seemed much longer.

In the middle of it, she said, "I don't know about this thing, Tom. It looks like the rickety bridges on holy cards, where a Guardian Angel watches over children as they cross."

"Trust me." I mumbled around the flashlight in my mouth.

Safely on the opposite bank, Gloria pulled the flashlight out of my mouth. "You're going to have to drug me to get me back across that thing."

In front of us on a small knoll sat a three-room, white frame cottage with green shutters. A porch spanned the front of it. Thirty yards to the right was a matching outhouse. And to the left, a clearing as large as a football field ran parallel to the creek.

"This is Rob's family's summer place. His grandfather was raised here. When he died, he left it to Rob's family."

"Summer place? His family doesn't live here then?" asked Gloria as she surveyed the area.

"No, they live in a trailer in Mars."

"In a trailer? Why don't they live in this house?"

"I asked that same question the first time I came here. I thought it was strange that they lived in a trailer all year but spent their summers in a house. Seemed backwards to me. But the place has no running water and sewage, and Rob said it never will. Something about it being too expensive to run the lines across the creek."

We trudged through the snow to a picnic table sitting twenty yards from the house. I brushed the snow off and sat my things on it. Then I took Gloria up onto the porch. While she shined the flashlight, I wrestled to free a chaise lounge from the pile of porch furniture stacked in the corner. Old leaves that had pooled there last fall crunched under my feet as I wrenched it free. Gloria spotlighted the steps as I carried the lounge chair down from the porch.

"We're not going inside?" she asked as I set the chaise lounge down in the snow. Away from the cover of the trees, the moonlight was much brighter, and I could make out a puzzled look on her face.

"No, this is a picnic, remember? And it's bright enough that we don't need the flashlight any more." Taking it from her, I turned it off and stuck it in my jacket pocket. I tucked the chaise lounge under my arm and picked up the case. "How about you carry the gym bag."

Gloria grabbed the bag and followed me in the moonlight. We cut a path through the pristine snow, walking out into the field. The air was cold and fresh and felt alive in my lungs.

"This isn't one of those snipe hunts, is it?" Gloria asked.

"No," I laughed and in the middle of the field, stopped. The moon had bathed the snowy landscape in light; the field stretched out before us like it was a giant sheet of aluminum foil. "This looks good." I set up the chaise lounge.

Dubious, Gloria stood watching me, her arms crossed in front of her chest. "Good for what?"

"You'll see." I opened the gym bag, pulled out a sleeping bag, and threw it over the chair. Then I pulled out my battered thermos. "We have hot chocolate and . . ." I took out a box of Dunkin' Donut Munchkins. "Doughnut holes." I placed the box on the lounge chair.

"You're serious about this picnic thing."

I bent over my case, and pushed on the silver buttons of the locks, releasing the case's latches, and lifting the lid. "And we have a telescope."

Gloria's arms dropped to her sides as she stepped near. "Oh, cool! We're going to stargaze."

"Yeah, you said we should do something I like, and this is my favorite thing to do when I have the time." I planted the tripod firmly in the snow, making sure it was stable.

Gloria pulled the hat from her pocket and slipped it over her ears. Then she looked up at the black night studded with stars and sighed. "Oh, this is great, Tom. I've never stargazed before. At least not with someone who knows about astronomy."

I fixed the telescope on the tripod, looked through the eyepiece, and adjusted the focus. "What I know about up there," I pointed toward the sky, "is very small. Most of the universe is still a mystery."

"Aren't you glad?"

"About what?" I asked, focusing in on Polaris.

"That the universe is still a mystery. Don't you think life would be boring if everything was figured out?"

I thought of my father. Maybe it would be boring knowing everything, but I'd be happy knowing more than I knew now. I'd like to know how my father could be the way he was.

"Yeah, I guess so," I said. The telescope properly focused, I raised my head and touched her back. "Here, have a look."

Gloria stepped up to the telescope, closed one eye, and pressed her other one to the eyepiece. "Ah, this is fantastic," she exclaimed.

"Ideally," I said, "it should be darker. The moon is too bright tonight. You see light best when it's darkest. That's the only disadvantage of living in the city. I can never use this on campus. All the background lighting makes it too hard to see anything."

"Looks good to me," Gloria said, staring through the tube. "Do you know the names of all these stars?"

"Some. Not all." For the next ten minutes, we stood at the telescope while I located stars and showed them to Gloria. I was introducing her, my newest passion, to my oldest. Our brief tour of the heavens began with the Big Dipper. From there we identified Polaris, the North Star, in the handle of the Little Dipper then Cassiopeia, and the Andromeda Galaxy. We skipped across the sky to the Pleiades and the Hyades and the constellations of Taurus, Orion and Gemini, pointing out the twin stars of Castor and Pollux.

Then I backed away, leaving Gloria to explore the sky on her own. Sometimes it's more exciting not knowing where you're going or what you're seeing, making discoveries on your own. I grabbed the thermos. "Want some hot chocolate?"

"No, I'm fine for now," she mumbled, not taking her eye from the eyepiece. "When did you become interested in astronomy, Tom?"

"Oh, I don't know." I said, as I capped the thermos. "Maybe when I realized that there wasn't much here for me on earth."

She looked up and put her hands on her hips. "Hey."

"That was before I met you."

"OK," she said and went back to the telescope.

"I guess I've always liked the stars. I can't remember a time when I didn't. I like their constancy." Steam rose from the cup. Before I took a sip, I held the cup under my cold nose to warm it. "Everything else changes but the stars never do."

I reclined on the chaise lounge. Gloria turned to me. "But, Tom, even the stars change." She was watching me now.

"You wouldn't believe how upset I was when I learned that bit of information." Pulling the sleeping bag over me, I took another sip of my drink. As the hot chocolate slid down my throat, warming me, I put an arm behind my head and looked up. The beauty of the night never failed to overwhelm me. In a lot of ways the heavens were like Gloria. I don't think I'd ever get tired of looking at either of them. I inhaled deeply wanting to take this night and all its beauty into my lungs, to spread it through my blood stream, and absorb it into every cell of my body like oxygen. Nothing could be more perfect than sitting out in a dark field watching the heavens with Gloria, and I wanted to always remember how I felt being here with her.

"I'm sorry," Gloria said, standing next to me. "I'm hogging the telescope."

"No, that's fine." I said. "Sometimes I like to just look up without it. It's purer. For thousands of years, that was the only way there was to stargaze, and sometimes it's better when there's nothing to separate you from the sky."

Gloria opened the little doghouse-shaped doughnut box sitting at my feet and popped a doughnut hole into her mouth. "Want one?"

"Sure," I said.

She picked a cinnamon-sugar one out. I sat up and she fed it to me. Then she took a seat between my legs at the foot of the lounge, holding the box of doughnuts in her lap.

"That's a fantastic telescope—so powerful. My brother had this really cheap one when we were little. You could barely see the moon."

"Yeah, this one was expensive. My dad—" I stopped.

"Your dad, what?"

"He bought it for me." I took a gulp of the hot chocolate, but it was near the end of the cup and it was way too sweet. I pitched the dregs out onto the snow.

"You seem upset, Tom. What's wrong?"

"Nothing." I lay back on the chaise.

"Come on. What's wrong?"

I brushed the hair back from my face. "Aw, I just had a fight with my father. That's all."

Gloria picked out another mini-doughnut. "From the tone of your voice, I take it that it was a bad one."

I lifted my head toward the sky. The stars seemed to be pulsing at me. "Yeah, it was. The worst . . . and probably the last. I told him what I thought of him, told him he was a lousy father. I'll never hear from him again."

Gloria looked over her shoulder wearing a frown. "He was that bad?"

"I don't want to talk about it." She pivoted to face me, with a look that said she didn't believe me. "Really, I don't."

She put a hand on my knee and spoke softly: "He didn't abuse you, did he, Tom?"

I shifted in the chair. "Well, no . . . He never knocked me around or anything. I don't know how to explain it, Gloria. He was . . . cold. That's it. He was just cold."

"In what way?" Lying there on the chaise, I felt like I was having my head shrunk by Sigmund Freud.

"I don't know."

She waited for a better answer. "Come on, Tom."

"OK, OK. I don't think he ever cared for me." I sat up. "If you want to know the whole truth. He doesn't love me. Never has."

Aghast, Gloria exclaimed, "He actually told you that? Your father told you that he didn't love you?"

"Well, no. Not exactly. But all the while I was growing up, he never ever said he loved me or ever gave any indication that he cared about me at all." I leaned forward. "Look, Gloria, I wasn't asking for Howard Cunningham for a dad, but my father has made it pretty clear that I've been nothing but a burden to him."

Gloria stood, lifted up the sleeping bag, and wedged herself into the chaise lounge beside me. She held the box of doughnut holes. "You know, Tom, just because someone doesn't love you the way you expect them to, doesn't mean they don't love you at all."

I lay back and pulled her close. With all her extra clothing she felt like a pillow, and she smelled like powdered sugar and cinnamon. She selected another donut hole from the box resting on her chest, held it up to the moonlight to see what kind it was, and then put it to my lips. I took a bite. "Take us for instance," she said, finishing off the rest of the doughnut. "I'm sure you expected the girl who fell in love with you would hop into the sack with you the first chance she got. Right?"

I couldn't lie. I pushed the hair out of my face. "Well, yeah."

"But just because I didn't fulfill your expectations of love, doesn't mean I don't love you at all, does it?"

"So what you're saying is that I'm wrong."

"No," she looked into my eyes. "What I'm saying is that maybe you've got to let go of your expectations. You've got to open yourself to other expressions of love."

"Let me get this straight. You think my father does loves me then?"

"I don't know. Maybe. I hope. Have you ever asked him?"

"Oh, I couldn't do that."

"Why not?"

I pulled the sleeping bag up to my chin. "I don't know. Maybe because I'd be too afraid to hear his answer." It sounded so illogical, but whoever said fear and emotions were logical?

We snuggled in the dark, warming each other, listening to the gurgling creek and the wind whispering in the trees. Then Gloria raised her head onto her elbow. "You said something before, Tom. About how you see the light best when it's darkest. Well, that's true of love too, you know. Perhaps this black spell between you and your father will finally allow you to see the love he has shining for you."

"Ah, I wouldn't count on that."

"No, I'm serious. It was during my darkest time, when I found love to be the brightest. That's when I found God."

"I don't know Gloria," I said. My nose was cold and I pressed it to her cheeks to warm it. "Whenever I'm engulfed in darkness, there's never anything there but interminable blackness."

"Well, maybe that's because you're too busy noticing how dark it is. Next time, start searching for the light. Who knows? Maybe you'll find it."

She selected another doughnut, bit it, and powdered sugar went all over her face.

"Oh gee, what a mess," she said, brushing the white dust from her cheek. She tilted her face toward mine. "Did I get it all?"

"You missed a little," I said, and I leaned over in the black night with the stars twinkling around and kissed all the powdered sugar from her mouth.

Chapter 25

The bookstore was open until noon on Friday, the eighteenth, then it closed for the holiday break. I spent that morning making sure everything was in A-1 condition—stocking shelves, straightening magazines, and readying the place for the mobs of students who, after the break, would swarm the store to purchase next semester's books.

Promptly at noon, Rajiv made a final inspection, sauntering up and down the aisles, his hands behind his back like a general. When he reached the front of the store, he smiled, locked the door, and led us to the stockroom where he hosted a small Christmas party for the staff.

Although Rajiv was not a Christian, and I was not a Christmas-lover, that didn't stop him from throwing a party and me from filling up on free eats and drinks. Rajiv had purchased a sandwich ring from the Giant Eagle, while everyone else brought a side dish or dessert.

Willis opened a tin of cookies that his wife Yvonne had baked. As he sat the container on the folding table covered with a paper Christmas cloth, he told everyone to make sure they had one of the cookies because Yvonne's are the best. She only baked "with butter and not that margarine slop," he boasted.

Dolly, the cleaning lady, brought an elaborate Jell-O salad, layered with thin ribbons of different flavored gelatins. On my plate, it looked like a cross section of rainbow-colored sedimentary rock. Bob and Jeanne, the other students who worked at the bookstore, pitched in and brought a tray of hot wings they'd picked up at one of the local bars. The wings were so spicy, they stripped my throat of its mucous membrane lining. After eating them, I dashed into the restroom and ran

211

my tongue under the faucet for a while. My contribution to the party was a bag of Doritos.

When I had sufficiently stuffed myself and spent a reasonable amount of time making chitchat, I glanced at my watch: one-thirty. At two o'clock, Ginny and Joe were meeting with Christo's doctor and the oncologist from Wisconsin to discuss the possibility of Christo's receiving this new type of bone marrow transplant. Gloria had volunteered to watch Christo, and I was to meet her at their house after the party. After Ginny and Joe came home, Gloria and I planned to grab something to eat and then go to the movies to see *Unforgiven*. I put on my fatigue jacket and said my goodbyes. Everyone wished me a Merry Christmas and Happy New Year. I returned their volley of greetings, and then I was out of there.

When I arrived at the house, Christo was elbow-deep in glue, felt, rhinestones, and beads. To amuse him, Gloria had brought along a supply of materials and patterns for making Christmas ornaments. Wisely, before I came, Gloria had exiled Regina to the basement.

As I walked into the kitchen, Christo, who was kneeling at the table, wearing a Steelers sweatsuit, was pressing a rhinestone with all his might onto what I assumed was one of the Three Kings crowns. When he saw me, his eyes lit up. "Hey, Tom, look what I'm making." He lifted his hand to show me his creation, but the felt ornament stuck to his tacky fingers.

"I think you might have over done it with the Elmer's there, buddy," I said, peeling the glue-sodden ornament from his hands. The felt left a haze of purple fuzz sticking to his fingertips. "How about I wash your hands?" I took off my jacket, picked him up, and carried him over to the sink, sitting him on the kitchen counter.

Gloria watched as I rinsed his sticky hands under the faucet. "You know Christo," she said, "I think you should be the one called Glooey." Standing him on the floor, I dried his hands on a kitchen towel, and then he was right up at the table again.

Gloria leaned her back against the counter. Glitter, like iridescent freckles, stuck to her cheeks and sparkled in the sunlight coming in the kitchen window.

"He was so excited you were coming," she said, motioning her head toward Christo. "I think I've been deposed."

She was wearing one of those frumpy long sweaters and stirrup pants. Putting my arm around her waist, I nuzzled that delicious, tender spot just back of her jawbone. "Then he has lousy taste." She shuddered and gently pushed me away. We stood in the kitchen,

212

Christo's back to us, watching him working diligently, his head bent over as he cut, glued, and decorated. He was oblivious to Gloria and me, and I wondered if he was as unaware of the precarious fate of his health.

"Does he have any idea what's going on?" I whispered to Gloria.

She titled her head toward me. "He knows he's out of remission," she said softly, "but I'm not sure if he understands what that means and how desperate things are." She glanced over at Christo, who was squeezing the glue bottle, pumping it between his palms. The bottle wheezed and spluttered glue. She rested her head on my shoulder and murmured, "And for that I'm grateful." I wrapped my arms around her and kissed the top of her head.

"Hey, I heard a noise," Christo said. "You better not be kissing."

Caught, I let my arms fall to my side. Gloria moved away. Christo looked over his shoulder with a devilish grin. "Daddy said I'm supposed to make sure you two don't do any kissing." When he said the word kissing, he wrinkled his nose.

Gloria blushed, walked over to the table, and sat. She placed her palms flat on the table and looked Christo in the eye. "Did your dad really say that?"

"Sure, Glooey," he said, sprinkling sparkles over a pond of glue. "He said I was on kiss patrol."

Gloria slid her palms to the edge of the table and pushed herself away, looking at me. "Do you believe that?"

I laughed and walked over to the table, taking a seat across from Gloria. "Well, Christo," I said, "you can tell your dad, that I wouldn't dream of kissing Glooey. Girls are yucky." I kicked her under the table. "Have you ever kissed a girl, Christo?"

He picked up a piece of felt and began cutting. His tongue moved like a rudder between his lips, shifting with each turn of the scissors. When he stopped, he looked at me and said, "Mommy."

"Mom's and family don't count."

"Nah, girls stink. Daddy says I'll like 'em when I'm old."

I patted his back. "Yeah, you will, buddy." And I hoped Christo would have the opportunity to grow older and make that most wonderful discovery—that girls don't stink.

Since Christo was on kiss patrol, I had to behave myself. They insisted that I join them in making ornaments. Gloria inserted a Johnny Mathis Christmas disc into the CD player in the dining room. As she walked back into the kitchen she was humming along to "It's the Most Wonderful Time of the Year." I've never been a crafty type, so I sat for a minute wondering what I should make. Then a flash of creativity came over me, and I selected a piece of yellow felt, traced a star on it, cut it out, applied glue to the edges, and wrote GLORIA across it. As I was shaking glitter over my ornament, Regina began barking in the basement, and we heard the front door rattling.

"They're back," Christo cried. He picked up the ornament he'd made, hopped off the chair, and ran out of the kitchen, heading for the front door.

"So soon?" Gloria said as she glanced at the microwave clock. She shrugged her shoulders and rose to follow Christo. "I didn't expect them for a while." As we passed through the dining room, she shut off the CD player.

When Gloria and I came into the living room, Ginny and Joe were already inside. They looked pale like the meeting with the oncologists had drained them of their blood.

"Look! Look, what I made!" Christo cried, dancing in front of his parents, shoving the ornament in their faces. Ginny touched the ornament, and feigned a smile. Joe, looking distracted, patted Christo on the head and said, "That's nice."

Ginny took off her coat and hung it in the closet and waited for Joe to take his off so she could hang it up too. The tension was unbearable. I wanted to scream. I wanted to know if Christo had any hope, but I was afraid to hear the results of their meeting. Joe took off his coat and huffed as he threw it over the newel post. Ginny frowned and closed the closet door.

"Hey, Christo," Joe asked, "did you make an ornament for Regina?"

"No."

"Then why don't you go out into the kitchen and make one for her while mommy and I talk to Gloria and Tom?"

"OK," Christo said. "I know. I'll make her a bone and put sparkles all over it," he plotted as he walked out of the room.

We all sat, Gloria and I on the love seat, Joe in the chair, and Ginny on the couch. It felt as cozy as an interrogation room. We sat there looking at each other, not knowing where to begin. It wasn't my place to ask, so I waited for Gloria to get the ball rolling, but she said nothing.

Joe clutched the chair's arm and pushed himself out of it. "Anybody thirsty? I could go for a beer."

"No, no." Gloria and I both cried. Joe slowly sat back down.

Gloria leaned forward and looked at me. I put my hand on the small of her back. "So how'd it go?" she asked.

214

The muscles around my eye sockets tensed like I was expecting a punch, as I braced myself for their response.

Joe jerked his head to the side. "Terrible." My muscles slackened as my face fell with disappointment.

"Terrible?" Gloria cried. Her hand reached for my knee.

"Not terrible," Ginny said, aiming a perturbed look toward Joe.

"Yes, terrible," Joe shot back.

Gloria squeezed my knee. "Why? What did they say?" The alarm in her voice shook Ginny and Joe from their bickering.

"Christo's a candidate for a bone marrow transplant under this new procedure," Ginny said.

"Good, good." Gloria sighed, and I felt her back sag beneath my hand as she exhaled in relief.

Joe jumped out of the chair. "Yeah, but our stupid insurance company won't pay for it."

"What?" Gloria cried. "But they agreed to pay—"

Ginny massaged her temple. "That was when he was in remission. Because he's relapsed, this kind of transplant is considered experimental. They don't cover experimental."

Joe's arm slashed through the air. "Everything's experimental in the beginning. But try to tell that to those morons."

"So what are you supposed to do?" Gloria asked, looking from Ginny to Joe.

"Raise another one hundred sixty grand."

"What? But there's no time," Gloria said. She turned to me. "It took forever just to raise what money we do have."

"So in effect," I said, "they told you to—"

"Got to hell," Joe yelled.

Ginny gasped. "Joe, my goodness. Don't get so upset."

His face turned purple. "Will you stop telling me not to get upset."

Ginny stood and placed a hand on his arm. "It won't accomplish anything, Joe. I hate to see you—"

Joe jerked his arm away from her. "OK, Ginny, you tell me. When can I get upset? Tell me? I got a kid who's dying—"

Gloria sprang from her seat. "Joe, stop it! Christo'll hear you."

". . . And no one cares," Joe continued. "Isn't that reason enough to get upset? Huh, Ginny?" He was in his wife's face. "Or do I have to wait until Christo's taking his last breath to get upset? Can I get upset then? Or do I have to wait until he's dead?"

Ginny covered her ears. "Stop it! Stop it!"

Gloria, who was in tears now, ran and put her arms around Ginny.

"Look, you're upset," Joe laughed pointing at Ginny. Then he turned on Gloria. "And she's upset. Why aren't you harping on Gloria? Why are you two allowed to be upset, and I'm not? Huh?"

Gloria pleaded to me with her eyes to do something.

"Joe, man, you've got every right to be upset." I put my hands in the air, talking gently to him the way you'd do to a guy out on a ledge threatening to take a swan dive. "But this is getting you nowhere. Why don't you sit down, have that beer, and we'll figure something out? There's got to be something we can do."

"Oh, there is," he said calmly. But I knew he was not quieting down but gathering more fury. Stomping to the bookshelves, he threw open the glass doors. The panes rattled in the casements. He riffled through the shelves, throwing books on the floor, until he pulled out the phone directory.

Ginny broke free of Gloria's protective embrace and went to him. "What are you going to do, Joe? Who are you calling?"

Joe ignored her as he flipped wildly through the pages. He stabbed his finger at the book. "Ah, here we go." He walked to the phone, the book draped over his hand. Ginny grabbed him. "Who are you calling?"

He knocked her hand away. "Sandra Creighton."

"No, Joe. Don't."

"Why not? You're the one who thought it was a great idea to air our personal problems on TV."

"But you're upset. You're not rational."

"Rational? What's rational about your kid dying? What's rational about inventing new procedures and then refusing to let you use them?" His voice was rising and his breathing was heavy. Beads of sweat formed and glistened on his forehead. "What is rational about any of this?" He punched numbers into the portable phone as we closed in around him. "If I'm going to be upset, then I want everyone upset too." He waved the receiver madly in the air as he shouted, "I want Ginny upset! I want those pinheads at Hippocraticare upset! I want the whole city upset! I want the country upset! I want the whole damn universe upset!"

Then he was quiet, and I thought he was waiting for someone at the TV station to answer. But instead he pressed another button, disconnecting the call, and handed me the phone. Suddenly, his eyes bulged out of their sockets as his face twisted in pain.

"Call an ambulance," he gasped. The words sounded like they had been wrung out of his lungs. Then his hand clawed at his chest and he collapsed.

Chapter 26

"Joe," Ginny shrieked, sinking to the floor beside him. I fumbled with the phone, my hands trembling so badly I had trouble pressing the numbers.

"Oh, dear God, help me," Ginny cried. She looked from Gloria to me and then clutched Joe's shirt, shaking him.

As I gave information to the dispatcher, I watched a white-faced Gloria drop to her knees and push Ginny aside. Gloria felt for a pulse. Then she put her ear to his chest and looked up. "He's not breathing." Ginny wailed. "Loosen his shirt, Ginny," Gloria commanded. Ginny struggled with the buttons at Joe's neck.

I hung up the phone and stood by helplessly. A possessed look appeared in Gloria's eyes. It was the look of an adrenaline rush that enabled the body to override the mind.

Gloria quickly tilted Joe's head back, opened his slack jaw, and clamped her mouth over his. She puffed air into his lungs, counting to herself, then she left his mouth, put the heels of her hands over the center of his chest and pumped. She did six repetitions of CPR, and it had only been a few minutes that Joe had been lying on the floor, but between the seconds that ticked by, I swear great loops of time had been inserted.

Gloria looked up at me as she pumped the blood through his body for him. Her hair was stuck in matted curls to her face, "You gave them the right address?" she said breathlessly. I could tell she was tiring.

"Yes."

"I can't keep it up, Tom. I'll do the respirations and you pump his chest."

"I don't know how," I cried.

"I'll show you," she counted and compressed. Then her mouth was back on Joe's blue-tinged face again.

I knelt beside her, and she grabbed my hands. Her power surprised me as she placed them over Joe's heart. "Right there," she said. I felt Joe's sternum under my palms, and I began pushing on his chest. "Harder," she commanded. I increased the effort and Joe's rib cage sprang up and down under my hands like a wicker basket. Gloria looked at Ginny who was slumped against the doorframe, whimpering. "Ginny, call the paramedics again." Ginny stumbled toward the phone, but the faint wail of a siren stopped her.

Since the day my mother died when the police came to inform my grandmother, sirens and flashing lights have always frightened me, but today the piercing squeal was the most beautiful sound I'd ever heard. Regina began freaking out in the basement. Ginny shot through the door onto the porch. The noise grew louder and finally settled in front of the house, where it went silent.

The siren had not only brought the paramedics but Christo from the kitchen. He stood in the doorway, holding a felt bone, with confusion and terror reflecting on his small face. Spying Joe, he screamed, "Daddy!"

Ginny led the paramedics, a young man with a military-style haircut and a girl whose man-tailored uniform pants didn't fit her female-tailored shape very well, into the living room. They quickly relieved Gloria and began working on Joe. I scooped Christo up and carried him back into the kitchen. He didn't need to see his father like that. Regina was charging the basement door.

"Knock it off, Regina," I screamed into the doorframe. "Stupid dog."

Christo beat my chest with his fists and wriggled in my arms. "I want my daddy. I want my daddy." I held him tighter.

"You can't go back in there, buddy. They're fixing him." He wrestled with me for a few more seconds, then the fight left him, and he buried his face into my neck, clinging to me.

Minutes later, Gloria appeared in the doorway. "They're taking him to the hospital now. Can you stay with Christo?"

"Yeah, sure," I said, rubbing his back.

"I'm going with Ginny."

"Is he . . . ?"

"I don't know."

I held onto Christo with one hand while my other searched my jeans pocket. "Do you need my keys?"

"No, I'll take their car."

As I let my keys drop back into my pocket, Christo broke loose, slid out of my arms and ran toward the living room. Gloria and I chased after him and found him standing at the front door, watching as his father, strapped to a gurney, was being loaded into the back of the ambulance. Its red light alternately flashed on Christo's ashen face. I pulled him away from the door and Gloria rushed past.

"I'll call as soon as I know something," she said.

The ambulance doors slammed shut and the siren blared. Regina started barking again. Christo latched onto my leg like he'd done at Holy Redeemer. I picked him up again and this time he was crying. As I held him tightly, he covered his ears to block out the siren's wail. After I made sure Gloria got Ginny's car started, I closed the front door, shutting out the cold air and the noise. And for the longest time, I stood in the foyer just holding Christo, trembling. I didn't know what else to do for him.

Eventually, Regina quieted, and then my arms began to ache from clutching him so tightly. As the aftershock of what had happened hit me, my legs grew incredibly shaky. I carried Christo into the living room, where minutes before Joe had begun his tirade, and sat on the couch. Thinking of him so out-of-control made me angry. If he died, he deserved it for being cruel to Ginny. Oh, God, he can't die. What was I thinking? Christo hung onto me, his small hands strangling my neck. Then he pulled away and looked at me, his nose was running. I wiped it with the tail of my flannel shirt. "Is Daddy dead, Tom?"

"I don't know."

"Tom, who will take care of me and mommy if he dies?" I wanted to reassure him, to tell him that fathers were expendable, to explain that it was mommies you couldn't live without. At least that's how I've always felt. Until now. Holding Christo and witnessing Joe's collapse, the impact of losing my father hit me. He wasn't dead but he might as well have been. Grief for Christo as well as for myself, weighted my heart.

"Look, Christo, I hope your dad is going to be OK. But I don't know. I do know that no matter what happens, you'll be fine. Lots of people love you—your mom, Gloria . . ." His sad eyes broke my heart. "And me," I said, patting him. "Listen, little pal, my mom died when I was about your age, and I wasn't lucky like you. I didn't have anyone to love me, and I still turned out fine, didn't I." Christo gave me the once over. "Hey, didn't I?"

"I guess so."

I nudged him. "What's this 'I guess so' stuff?"

Christo looked serious. "You're better now, Tom, but when you gave me Sammy, you was a scared of me and sad."

"I was?"

"Uh-huh. You was afraid of me. That's why you runned away." The kid was more perceptive than I had given him credit. "That's OK," he said. "The counselor lady at the hospital? She says lots of people are a scared of sick kids."

"Yeah," I said, "I guess you're right. But now I'm better?"

"Yeah," he smiled, "I think Glooey's kisses made you better. Mommy's always make me better."

"That and having a nutty little friend like you," I said.

The light was fading. In winter, nightfall always seems ominous, but when it falls and you're not sure if by the next sunrise you'll be mourning a death, it seems twice as menacing. I looked at the mantle clock four-forty. "Are you hungry? How about I order us a pizza?"

"OK," he said. "Pepperoni, no *mushwooms*."

"Got it no *mushwooms*."

I turned on all the lamps in the living and dining rooms as if the extra light would ward off death. Maybe it was my pagan attempt at a vigil light. I picked up the phone book from where it had landed when Joe collapsed, and I paged through it for the phone number of the nearest pizza shop.

Before calling, I gave in and put a Barney tape into the VCR for Christo. He easily became engrossed in it, forgetting all about his father. It amazed me how kids live in the moment. I swear, I was beginning to sound like Rajiv.

Forty-five minutes later, the pizza delivery guy finally showed up, and we ate out of the box in front of the TV. Then I let Christo watch more tapes. I wanted his pain anesthetized so I didn't have to deal with it.

After eating, I went out to the kitchen to throw away the empty box and get Christo some apple juice. With all the confusion, I'd forgotten about the ornaments we'd been making. Blisters of glue had dried on the table, as well as felt and glitter. I gave Christo his juice, wiped the sauce off his face, and got busy cleaning up the kitchen, scrubbing and scrubbing, while I waited to hear from Gloria. I found the star I'd made for her and tucked it into my shirt pocket. All the others, I set aside on the kitchen counter.

Often when you're expecting a call, the ringing of the phone is the most shocking sound. When it trilled, I jumped and ran to answer it. The blood pounded in my ears so loudly, I could hardly hear.

"Tom?"

"Yeah?"

"He's alive."

I drooped against the wall, my body limp with relief. "Oh, good."

"But they think it was a heart attack. We don't know how bad yet. He's in the ICU."

"How's Ginny?"

"Dazed. Is Christo OK?"

"I calmed him down. He's watching Barney. We just finished a pizza."

"Good. It took a while," Gloria said, "but I finally got in touch with my dad. He's on his way to the hospital now. When he gets here, I'll leave. Is that OK?"

We're both fine. No rush."

The pay phone clicked, momentarily cutting off Gloria. Then I heard her voice again, "Hello . . . Hello?"

"I'm still here."

"My money is running out; I've got to hang up. I'll be there soon. Thanks Tom." The phone went dead.

I walked into the living room and gave Christo the good news about his father. He said "great" and went back to his tape while I returned to cleaning the kitchen.

As I opened the cupboard doors to put away the dishes, I marveled at how intimately involved I had become with the Davidsons. Now I was doing their dishes, rummaging in their cupboards, taking care of Christo.

After the kitchen was straightened up, I joined Christo. While he watched TV, I read the newspaper. I reread the *Drabble* cartoon three times, I was having such difficulty concentrating. A little after seven-thirty, I noticed that Christo had fallen asleep on the floor in front of the television. Taking an afghan that was draped over the back of the couch, I covered him.

Twenty minutes later, Regina began barking. I pulled the curtains back and looked out the window. Gloria had parked in front of the house, and I went to the door to open it for her. She had left without her coat.

"Sorry it took so long," she said as she ran up the steps, rubbing her arms. She looked wiped out. Even the glitter still sticking to her cheeks looked dull.

"No problem," I said, putting my arm on her shoulder and leading her into the living room. "Christo just fell asleep on the floor. The only thing you might want to do is let Regina out. She keeps scratching at the door, but I was afraid she'd take my leg off if I tried to do it."

"I'll do it now." She walked into the kitchen. "I'll let her out through the basement."

"Are you hungry? I saved you some pizza."

"Thanks, but my dad made me take Ginny to the cafeteria. I ate with her."

"How about a cup of tea then?"

"Yeah, I could certainly use one."

Gloria opened the basement door a crack and quickly slipped behind it before Regina could break through and go for my throat. I took a teacup, filled it with water, and popped it into the microwave.

A few minutes later, Gloria slithered from behind the basement door and locked it behind her. "I'm so cold," she said, as I dunked a tea bag in the hot water. I suspected that it was not the winter air that had chilled her but the shock. I removed the bag, put the cup on a saucer, and handed her the tea. We walked into the living room and sat on the love seat.

"So how's Joe now?"

"Resting. They let me see him for a minute. Do you know what that idiot said to me?" She sipped her tea. "Be sure to call Hippocraticare. They need authorization for emergency admissions. Wouldn't want them to deny a claim. Do you believe him?"

I went to say something, but Gloria spoke again. Then I understood that this was one of those listening conversations. Gloria had been through so much, she needed a sympathetic ear, so I shut up.

She set the cup on the coffee table. "I could just kill him. Getting himself so worked up. And where were his brains smoking again? With all this stress, he was a heart attack waiting to happen. Oh, and he was so mean to Ginny." She shook her head. "I'm going to stay here with her. She's going to have to be at the hospital a lot." Gloria had run out of steam. She picked up the tea and drank again. When she returned the cup to the saucer, she sighed.

"How bad was the heart attack?" I asked.

"It's too early to tell. The tests haven't come back."

She was quiet for a long time, and then she spoke. "The paramedics told me I saved his life."

"Really?" She looked at me and now in her green eyes I saw the fear in them that was absent when she was performing CPR. Tears spilled over the edges of her lower lids. She couldn't speak. She simply nodded.

"Where'd you learn CPR?"

"High school health." Her lip quivered as she spoke. Thank God somebody paid attention in high school health. "I don't know how I remembered," she said. "Next thing I knew I was on the floor listening for Joe's heartbeat." She gulped. "I've never listened to a silent chest before." Her hands shook; the teacup chattered on the saucer. I took it from her and put it on the table.

Picking up her trembling hand, I held it to my chest, where my heart was not silent, but beat with pride and love for her. "You were amazing, Gloria. Do you realize that when Ginny and I lost it, you kept your cool?" Her eyelids fluttered trapping tears in her thick lashes. She looked so fragile now, it was hard to imagine her a few hours before, straining and sweating, beating Joe's heart for him. "You didn't panic. You didn't hyperventilate. You didn't let fear get to you."

"I guess that's because I had no time to think. Sometimes it's easier to help somebody else than it is to help yourself."

I pulled the ornament out of my pocket. "Here I made this for you. You really deserve a gold star. What you did, Gloria, was one of the most courageous things I've ever seen."

"Courageous?" She wiped her eyes with her fingertips. "Then why when I think of it, do I feel like throwing up?"

I put the star in her hand. "Because that's what courage is. It's doing something even though you're scared to death."

She looked at the ornament. "Wow, I feel just like the Cowardly Lion."

"All those other times when you panicked, Gloria, it didn't matter. Nothing was at stake. But when the chips were down, when everything was on the line, you hung tough."

She smiled at me as the flow of tears rolling down her cheeks increased. "You sound like a football coach or something."

I laughed. "I'll tell you something else. I'm jealous."

She looked surprised. "Of what?"

"That awesome liplock you put on Joe."

She hit me in the chest. "You're awful, Tom." Then she reached up and pulled my head down, and her mouth latched on to mine. No wonder Joe lived. I swear her lips could breathe life into the dead.

Chapter 27

The medical tests revealed that Joe had indeed suffered a heart attack, but he'd been lucky; it'd done minimal heart damage.   If he stopped smoking, dropped forty pounds, exercised, and reduced the stress in his life, his doctors predicted he could expect to live a normal, healthy life.   For a man like Joe, those were some very big "ifs."

Ginny spent the weekend before Christmas with Joe at the hospital.   By Monday, he had been moved from the Cardiac ICU into a step-down unit, with the hopes that he would be released from the hospital by Christmas.

I saw very little of Gloria; she was too busy pinch-hitting for Ginny and trying to devise ways to raise money for Christo's transplant. We kept in touch by phone, but the withdrawal of her physical presence was painful.   Methadone therapy would have been appropriate.

Sunday evening, December 21, marked the winter solstice—the darkest night of the year.   That night the heavens shifted, and we began the slow climb toward light.

The heavens weren't the only things shifting.

With Joe out of danger, Gloria told me that Monday morning Ginny had called Sandra Creighton to update her on Christo's quest for a bone marrow transplant, how he had relapsed, the experimental procedure, and how Hippocraticare had refused to pay for it.

On Monday's evening newscast, a segment Ginny had taped earlier in the day with Sandra Creighton aired.

I watched the report at Ross Park Mall, in Service Merchandise's electronics showroom. A wall of Ginnys surrounded me and the other shoppers who had gathered to catch the nightly news.

Ginny held Christo on her lap while she told how Hippocraticare had denied the only treatment available to Christo to save his life. At the end of the interview, the camera focused in on Christo who was watching his Barney tape, while Ginny spoke. "I wish someone at Hippocraticare would please tell me how I'm to explain to a four-year-old that policies and money are more important than his life."

To balance the piece, Sandra Creighton invited Hippocraticare to reply. Of course, some talking-head-PR-guru appeared to explain their side.

My angry response to the report was not unique. A gray-haired man wearing a Sheet Metal Workers ball cap, looked at me and said, "That's pitiful. To let a kid die."

A young mother with an infant strapped to her chest in a baby sling, patted her kid's bottom, and walked away shaking her head as Hippocraticare's Patient Relations chick tried to put a palatable spin on their denial.

I knew this was going to be a public relations nightmare for Hippocraticare. And by nine the next morning, Hippocraticare knew it too. Their phone lines were jammed with people calling to voice their outrage.

Before lunch on Tuesday, Ginny received a call in Joe's hospital room from Hippocraticare inviting her to a meeting the next day at their offices to discuss the situation.

Although I missed Gloria, her absence freed me to concentrate on the Sammy trade. The last few days before Christmas, people went berserk for them. Our phone rang incessantly as desperate shoppers scrambled to snag one before the holiday. Prices soared and Rob and I were overwhelmed with business. And money.

Tuesday evening, two days before Christmas, we sold the last one to a red-haired woman wearing a full-length beaver coat. Rob had arranged this deal. I sat on a wooden bench in Station Square, just out of sight, watching the manicured hands of the woman as she forked over an envelope to Rob. Gold bangle bracelets crashed on her wrist as she picked up the bag containing the last Sammy and walked away.

Rob sashayed over to me doing his George Jefferson walk, arms swinging, head bopping, singing, "We're Movin' On Up." When he plopped down next to me on the bench, he slapped me on the back.

"Merry Christmas, Ebenezer, my man." Then he held open the envelope so I could peek inside. Ten portraits of Ben Franklin stared back at me.

"Holy hell!" I cried. Then I lowered my voice. "That's a thousand bucks."

"Yes, Tiny Tom, it is. And I say God bless us everyone. Didn't I tell you we'd break a thousand?" He tucked the envelope inside his denim shirt pocket. Then he shook my hand. "What's say we splurge, partner? Celebrate a successful holiday retail season?"

We went next door to the Grand Concourse restaurant, where Rob ordered champagne. Hoisting his glass, he toasted me, "Here's to Scrooge & Marley." Then we both ordered whole lobsters and I felt like a weight had been lifted off me. Now Gloria would never find out about the Sammys or my lie.

After dinner, Rob dropped me back off at the dorm. Then he left for his mother's with his half of the Sammy profit, $10,575, and the snorkel gear that I had given him for Christmas. He also left with two promises: that I'd meet him at the travel agency on December 30 to book our trip to Martinique, and that I'd call him if Mr. Davidson turned Rambo on me.

Wednesday was Christmas Eve, and I spent the morning doing last minute things for my stay at Gloria's. As I drove around the city, the whole world had gone mad with Christmas craziness. Traffic was backed up everywhere, lines of people spilled out of the post office, and throngs crowded the stores.

When I returned to the dorm, the contrast was remarkable. The only person I saw on my way back to the room was Phil dozing at the front desk.

In the stillness, every rattle and ping from the boiler seemed louder. It was so quiet in my room, I felt like my thoughts could be heard outside my head.

After lunch, I decided a nap was just what I needed. So I crawled into my bunk and crashed. I had just nodded off, when the phone rang. The noise startled me, and I quickly jumped out of bed and picked up the receiver to silence it.

"Hey, Shepherd, Phil at security." His voice sounded deep and full of authority like he was head of the CIA instead of an old fat guy snoozing at the desk while watching soap operas.

"Yeah? What do you want?" I was annoyed that he'd interrupted my nap.

"There's a delivery here for you at the desk."

"You sure it's for me?"

"You think I can't read or somethin'? The slip says Tom Shepherd. That's you, ain't it?"

Who would send me something? My curiosity piqued, I said, "OK, be right down."

At the security desk, only the top of Phil's bald head was visible. He was bent over, staring at his TV. When I approached, he looked up. "Oh, that Oprah," he said. "Makeovers again. I hate makeover shows. You ever notice, Shepherd, that the person in the 'before' shot always wears a hangdog look? Then in the 'after' one they're always smiling? That's not fair. They should make those broads wear the same face in both pictures. Don't you think?"

"Yeah," I said, "I guess." What did I care about makeovers?

"See there," Phil cried, pointing at the TV screen, "in the 'before' picture, the broad's making a puss, like someone just told her they quit making estrogen, and in the next, boy, you'd think she won the Publisher's Clearinghouse."

"Ah, Phil, the delivery? Where's my package?"

"Oh yeah." Phil reached below the desk, brought out a cocoon of tissue paper, and placed it on the counter. I examined the tag stapled to the top of the tissue paper. It was from Josie's Posies.

"Your honey send you flowers?" Phil asked in a mocking tone.

"Looks like it."

He snorted. "Boy-oh-boy, in my day, if a guy got flowers you'd a thought he was a sissy. But hey, you kids today. . . ." He shook his head.

"It's probably a poinsettia or something for my room." I tore the tissue paper, and as soon as the paper fell away, my hands began to shake. I plucked the card from the small plastic trident stuck in the center of the arrangement, but didn't open it. I knew who'd sent it.

"What is that?" Phil asked. "I ain't no botanist, but that don't look like no poinsettia to me."

I scooped up the plant. "It's a joke," I stammered, hurrying away.

I ran into my room, set the philodendron on the desk, and quickly backed away as if it were some exotic man-eating plant. I stood, my back against the door, staring at it. Then I moved to the desk chair and sat. Slowly, I raised my hand and touched the plant's heart-shaped leaves. They were supple, glossy, green, and vibrant and the rich smell of fertile soil filled my head.

The card was still in my hand. I was afraid to read it, but I knew I must. Opening the small white envelope, I felt as nervous as a presenter at the Academy Awards. I pulled the card out and winced. It said: "I do know the difference. I've never loved a philodendron."

I slumped forward, leaning my elbows on the desk and covered my eyes, the card resting against my forehead. There it was in writing. My father loved me. I thought I'd never hear those words from him. And now that I had, I didn't know what to do. For ten minutes, I sat there holding the card against my head, as if the words would be absorbed into my skull and inspire me.

What do I do now? Should I call my father? What would I say? How would I begin? The idea of confronting him had always terrified me, but now, that seemed easy compared to this.

As I picked up the phone, my tongue was dry as a sheet of parchment and stuck to the roof of my mouth. I dialed, hoping that he'd already left for Mexico. The phone rang once before it was answered. I heard heavy breathing and garbled sounds.

"Jeffrey, it's Tom. Get your dad. . . . I mean get our dad." I heard a thunk and noises that sounded like balloons being twisted. "Jeffy, get—"

"Hello?"

". . . dad. Dad?"

"Tom?" He sounded startled too.

"Yeah, it's me." I wanted my voice to sound deep and confident, but it had sounded like a frightened child's. Just talking to him reduced me to a four-year-old boy again.

"I'd hoped you'd call." His voice was different too; it was deferential; it lacked that casual, flippant tone that irritated me so much. And he called me Tom. "I suppose you got the delivery." He sounded like a guy from Federal Express checking on a package.

"Yeah, I got it." I said. Then the conversation stalled; we both hung on the phone breathing like Jeffrey had done for an uncomfortable length of time. "Well, you're probably getting ready for your trip," I finally fumbled some words. "We can talk when we you get back."

As I went to hang up, I heard him yell, "Wait, Tom." I put the receiver back to my ear.

"Yeah."

"Don't hang up. Not yet. I need to tell you something." He cleared his throat two or three times, like he was getting ready to sing an aria. "Ah, what you said about how I treated you?"

"Yeah?"

"Well, you were right."

"Aw, dad—"

"Please don't say anything, Tom. Let me finish." He inhaled so deeply, I felt like he was going to suck me through the phone. "Ah, this is hard. . . . When you hung up on me last week, I was so mad. If I could have gotten hold of you, I'd have beaten the living daylights out of you. When Amber heard me swearing and stomping through the house, she asked me what was wrong. I exploded, unloading on her everything you said. She listened to me rant about you, and when I finally shut up, she looked at me and said 'you don't get it, do you?'"

"Get what? I screamed. What's there to get?"

"'All Tom wants is for you to love him,' she said. Tom, Amber's right. That's all you've ever wanted from me, and I've always known it. I did maintain you; I never raised you." His voice cracked like the shale I'd seen him extract from the earth. "Tom, I'm sorry."

I thought of how helpless I felt when I tried to comfort Christo after Joe's heart attack. Perhaps my father had felt as inadequate with me. "It was a bad situation, Dad. I was thrust upon you. I wouldn't know what to do with a four-year-old either."

"But you weren't just any four-year-old, Tom. You were my son." He hung on the other end breathing deeply, trying to go on. "I deliberately kept a distance between us Tom."

"Why?"

He began to cry. "Oh, Tom, when your mother. . . When she was killed, I thought I'd die too. I loved her so much."

"If you loved her, dad, why didn't you come after her? Why did you leave us in Wyoming?"

There was silence.

"It was me, wasn't it? You wanted mom, but you didn't want me."

"No! No, that's not it. I couldn't come."

"Couldn't? Oh, I know you were too busy with changing the world." The resentment was apparent in my voice.

"No," he sighed. "I was . . ."

"What? You were what?"

"In prison."

"Prison? You were in jail? When? Why?"

"Right before you and your mother left for Wyoming, a bunch of us broke into the Federal Building and threw blood all over the draft records. I went into hiding, but was caught. My parents had already disowned me, and without money and a good lawyer, I was sent to jail for three and a half years, Tom. I had just gotten out two weeks before your mother was killed. I was looking for a job. Your grandmother had only a few months to live and after she died, your mother planned on moving back to Pittsburgh."

His words were like a sledgehammer to my heart. "All my life I thought it was me," I said. "I thought you stayed away because you didn't want me. Why didn't you tell me you were in prison?"

"Ah, Tom, I don't know. When I first came and got you, you were too little to understand. And then later, nothing I could have told you would have made a difference anyway. All you wanted was your mother."

"But why didn't you tell me when I was older? When I could understand?"

"By then, you thought I was such a screw-up, if I'd told you I'd done time, that would have only confirmed your opinion of me."

I hated to admit it, but he was right.

"Ah, man," he sniffled into the phone, "if your mother hadn't died, things would have been so different." He broke down. "I still miss her."

"Me too." My voice sounded like the peep of a chick. Hearing him crying about my mother, dredged up the sorrow I had carried all my life, but it was comforting to have someone who shared my grief. I had always assumed that I was alone in mourning my mother.

He blew his nose. "I thought she'd be there when I got out, but I never got to see her again. I left her to raise you alone. It couldn't have been easy for her." I heard the ache in his heart. I may miss my mother, but at least I carried no regrets about her.

"And then when I could be there for her, she was gone. I failed her and I've kept on failing her. The one thing I could have done for Linda was to love you, but I couldn't even do that right. I pushed you away, Tom, and I knew it messed up your life."

"Why dad? Why did you push me away?"

"Oh, I don't know. Fear."

"Of me?"

"No, Tom. The pain. Every time you looked at me with those lost brown eyes, I saw Linda in them. You're so much like her. The way you moved and spoke made me hurt all over with wanting her back." He began to sob. "I knew all along what you wanted, needed, but I couldn't give it to you, because there was nothing inside me to give. I was empty. Those nights you cried yourself to sleep, Tom? I heard you. But I couldn't comfort you, I was crying in my bed too. Oh, I'm sorry. So sorry. And there's nothing I can do to make it up to you."

"Oh, but you already have," I whispered.

"Have what?"

"Made it up to me. Look, Dad, I can understand that you don't love me. I'm just glad that you don't hate me and that you loved mom. I always felt that you blamed me for everything that went wrong."

"Ah, Tom," he sighed. "But that's the tragedy. I do love you. I always have, but I just couldn't tell you."

Even though thousands of miles separated us, I never felt closer to my father. Instead of seeing him as the demon I'd always thought he was, I now saw him as a scared, weak human being. Just like me.

"Why couldn't you tell me, dad?"

"I don't know. I guess holding you at a distance was my way of keeping the pain away. It was easier to deny I had a heart, than to try to fix a broken one. I screwed up both of your lives."

"Oh, Dad, don't blame yourself. You couldn't have stopped mom from dying. Things happen."

"But you, Tom—I could have done something for you."

"Look, I didn't turn out so bad. I'm doing well in school. I'll be graduating soon, and I met a really great girl. I'm spending Christmas with her and her family."

"Oh, there's another failure." He sounded despondent. "What kind of father goes off and leaves his kid alone for the holidays?"

"Don't take this the wrong way," I said. "But I'd rather spend the holidays with her." He managed a chuckle.

Then I told my father about Gloria and Christo. I told him everything except how I sold Sammys. I swear I told him more about me that night than I had in all the time I'd lived with him.

"This Gloria, Tom, is she the one?"

I smiled, feeling a warmth grow in my heart and spread throughout my body. "Yeah, she's the one."

His voice sounded louder in the receiver, and from the confidential tone he'd taken, I knew that he'd cupped his hand around his mouth and was whispering into the phone. "Don't get me wrong. I love Amber, Tom, but you know your mom was the one."

It was good to hear about his love for my mother. I'd always assumed my conception was the result of some drug-induced random coupling. For the first time, I felt like I'd been born into a family.

"Ah, there's no love like your first love, Tom," he said. "I don't have to tell you there have been a lot of other women over the years. But every one of them I measured against your mother. They all fell short."

Funny, I'd been doing the same thing all my life too. Every woman I ever met, I measured against the mother I remembered or had invented in my mind.

"I have so many regrets," he said. "Don't make the same mistakes, Tom. Let nothing stand in the way of love. Not ambition. Not distance. Not fear. Nothing."

There was nothing I'd ever let stand in the way of my love for Gloria. I was certain of that.

"I won't, Dad. I promise."

"I've learned another thing, too, Tom. Kids need stability. Thankfully with Jeffrey, I've been given a second chance. I guess now is a good time to tell you. Amber's pregnant again, and we've decided it's time to get married. Hey, maybe you and your girlfriend could come out over spring break. We could get married then. I'd like you to be the best man."

I was flattered. "Sure Dad," I said. I couldn't tell him about the trip to Martinique now. We could deal with that later.

"I'd better be going," he said, "before I have to take a second job to pay for this phone bill."

I laughed. It felt strange, but good. I can't ever recall a time when I laughed with my father. It was always at him or behind his back.

"And, Tom, what I said about paying for your schooling, I didn't mean it. I just flew off the handle. Money's tight, you know that, and finding out that Amber's pregnant again, I was just stressed."

With another baby on the way, I knew now that I couldn't count on him for financial support for grad school, but I didn't care. If I was careful, with the money I had made from the Sammys, I wouldn't have to.

Before he hung up, he said, 'Hey Tom, enjoy the holidays," and then he added, "I love you. Always have."

A lump swelled in my throat so large that I was shocked the words, "me too" squeezed past it. And then I gently hung up the phone, and with it the hate I had held for my father for so long.

Chapter 28

The wad of money fanned out in my hand reminding me of a tiny palm tree—a money tree. Having accumulated such a phenomenal sum with such ease made it seem as if the Sammy money had grown on a tree.

I shoved the bills into an envelope and stashed it inside my jacket pocket.

After my conversation with my father, I took that much-needed nap and slept more soundly than I could ever remember. I awoke at two-thirty, took a shower, and got ready for my first Christmas Eve.

Standing at the window now, I looked out over the campus, watching for Gloria's car. Since the end of term, the university had slowly transformed into a ghost town. While I napped, light snow had fallen, freshening what was already on the ground. No footprints spoiled the clean whiteness of the walkways, and eddies of snow skipped across the lawn like mini tornadoes. My snow-covered car was the only vehicle in the parking lot.

When I said before that Christmas was no big deal, I was lying. That was envy speaking. When you can't have something, it's easier to pretend that you didn't want it in the first place. I'd always envied people who had homes, and families, and love, and I especially envied them at Christmas. But tonight would be different. Tonight I'd share in all of that.

I looked at my watch—four o'clock. At any minute, Gloria would arrive and the anticipation of seeing her heightened the sense of euphoria that had been building in me since this afternoon when I reconciled with my father. My body hummed like I had been thrown into a particle accelerator, every cell inside of me vibrated with excitement.

I walked across the room to check myself in the mirror, and I hardly recognized the person staring back. My hair had never been this short before. On impulse while at the mall today, I hopped into a salon chair and had it cut. I hoped Gloria would like it.

I adjusted the cuff of my beige turtleneck and brushed some lint from the shoulder of my new green sweater. Looking at my reflection, I had to laugh. I appeared wholesome, like a background singer from a Barbara Mandrell Christmas special. The only remnant of the old me was the gold loop hanging from my earlobe.

There was a soft knock at the door; my heart quickened and I opened it. Gloria stood before me, her head tilted to one side, smiling. "Merry Christmas," she said, her voice frothy with glee, as she stepped inside.

As I closed the door, her hands flew to cover her mouth. "Oh wow," she cried, "you got your haircut." She moved back to take a longer view of the new me and then her face fell. "I hope you didn't cut it because of what I had said that night out on the lawn. I didn't mean it when I said your hair was stupid."

"No," I said, passing my fingers over my head. "It was always hanging in my face. It got on my nerves." She circled me, examining the back of my head. "Do you like it?"

"Oh, yeah. You look like a new man. Not that I didn't like the old one, but now I can see your eyes. You have such kind brown eyes." She stroked the closely-cropped hair at my nape and giggled. "Ooh, it feels soft—like velvet."

I wrapped my arms around her waist, pulling her close. "Know what else feels like velvet?"

"What?"

"Your lips."

"Wow, you're certainly in the Christmas spirit," she said after I kissed her. The gleam sparkling in her eyes told me that tonight she, too, felt the same excitement.

Even the way she'd dressed was festive. She had gathered some of her hair into an ivory bow, and ringlets dangled from it like streamers of gold curling ribbon. She looked like a gift waiting to be unwrapped.

I buried my face into those curls, hugging her. "I have every reason to be." Her hair smelled wonderful—fruity and smoky. "Oh, you smell good."

"Matthew, one of my piano students, gave me a bottle of Passion for Christmas."

I inhaled deeply, drawing in her scent. "Ah, it smells fantastic—like pineapples and camp smoke."

She pulled back. "Pineapples? Camp smoke? Passion doesn't smell like. . . ." She raised her arm, sniffed her sleeve, and then twisted her face. "That's ham you smell." She shoved me away. "My mother has one baking in the oven."

"So, you still smell great."

"Oh yeah, my new fragrance—Eau de Sugardale." She walked to the window. "So why are you so full of Christmas cheer? I thought you weren't into the holiday scene." She looked over her shoulder and grinned devilishly. "Jacob Marley visit you in a dream?"

"Almost. Guess who I talked to this afternoon?"

"Who?" she asked admiring the view of the city.

I walked over and stood behind her. "My dad."

She whirled around. "He called? See I told you he cares about you—"

"No, I called him."

"*You* did? Why?"

I led her to the desk where the philodendron sat. "He sent me this."

She fingered the plant's leaves and raised her brows. "A philodendron?"

I explained the plant's symbolism and related this afternoon's phone conversation. "You were right, Gloria. My dad does love me."

She patted my cheek. "Aren't I always? I'm so happy for you, Tom. Oh, this is the start to a great Christmas." She moved her hand to the nape of my neck and began playing with the back of my new haircut. "So are you ready to meet the rest of the Davidsons?"

"I don't know. I'm nervous. I've never gone home to meet a girl's parents before."

"They're going to love you."

"You might have to teach me some of your relaxation techniques." I pulled her hands from my neck. She was rubbing against the grain of my stubble, and it was giving me the willies. "Do we have a few minutes before we go?"

"Tom, you know how to breathe. I taught you before. Inhale deeply, hold it, then—"

"No, that's not what I meant. There's something else."

She glanced at her watch. "Sure, we've got plenty of time. It's only four-fifteen. Dinner's not until five-thirty."

"Hey, what happened to your coat?" I asked. Instead of the white parka that I had grown to love, she was wearing a cream-colored wrap-style one. "You didn't give it away, did you?"

"No, since it's Christmas, I thought I'd wear my dress one."

"Good. I'm glad you didn't get rid of it." I undid the loose knot in the belt and eased the coat from her shoulders. Underneath it, she was wearing an eggnog-colored dress that had shiny gold buttons running up the front of it. I draped her coat over the couch. "I really like that other one better."

Certain times of the year accentuate natural beauty, and Christmas was definitely Gloria's season. It was as if she absorbed all the energy and light of the holiday, concentrated it within herself and reflected it back.

I sat on the desk chair and pulled her onto my lap. "I want to give you something."

She titled her head and a playful look crept over her face. "I believe you wanted to give me something the last time you had me in this room and it turned into a disaster."

I laughed, my face turning red. "No," I said, as I produced a small gift from the desk drawer, "this time I really do have something for you." I handed her the present.

"Wow, you're just like Santa," she giggled, holding the box to her heart. "Should I open it now?" But her question was pointless; she was already attacking the bow. She tore off the wrapping paper, revealing a square jewelry box. Putting the crumpled wad of paper on the desk, she then opened the hinged box. When her eyes fell on the gold watch inside it, her lips puckered and she emitted a small "oh."

She removed the watch. "It's so pretty, Tom."

"Look on the back."

She turned it over, draping it across her palm. "It's too dark in here to read it. What does it say?"

She held the watch closer to her eyes, and I repeated the inscription softly in her ear: "When I'm with you, I believe in magic."

She clasped the watch to her chest and turned to me. "Oh, Tom, it's . . . " But she didn't finish the sentence because her bottom lip began to tremble. I hoped she was crying because she liked it. "Oh, it's so beautiful." She put the watch on her wrist, and I fastened the clasp while she brushed away the tears with her other hand. "I'm sorry," she said.

"You must think I own stock in a handkerchief factory, the way I'm always bawling."

Blinking through teary eyes, she admired how it looked on her wrist. "Christmas always makes me sentimental, Tom, but this year it's worse. It's so crazy. I'm incredibly happy and sad at the same time." She patted my cheek. "I'm thrilled that you're coming home with me, but when I think about Joe and Ginny and Christo, I feel so guilty being happy when this could be Christo's last—" She stopped. She couldn't bring herself to utter the words. I could tell by the set of her jaw that she had banished that thought to the dungeon in the mind where all unspeakable thoughts are chained.

I patted her knee. "I know. Christo's been on my mind a lot too."

"It's beautiful, Tom. I love it." She kissed my forehead. "And I love you."

"Do you really? I still have trouble believing it."

She took my face in her hands and gave me a look that seared my flesh. "Don't ever doubt it." Then she lowered her eyes and pressed her lips to mine. At first she kissed me slowly, tenderly, reinforcing her love. Then the longer our lips touched, the more urgent our kisses became. My hands desperately kneaded the flesh of her back like I was trying to grab a piece of her that I could keep always for myself. Our passion built and intensified until I feared something in me would snap.

Gloria and I were venturing into unknown territory, leaving the atmosphere, leaving this world behind. We were about to fall off the face of the earth. She sensed it too, because suddenly she pulled away. Breathless, I rested my head on her chest, listening to her heart hammering and her breath rushing in and out.

"Oh, Gloria," I moaned, "when you kiss me like that I can almost feel your love. I can almost believe it."

She squeezed me tightly. "Oh, Tom, please believe it. Please. I want nothing more than for you to know how much I love you. I want you to feel it with all your heart."

I looked up into her face. Her eyes were closed and her cheeks flushed. Then she opened her great green eyes and her feverish hand began stroking my face. "I'd do anything for you to know that. If I thought making love to you, Tom, would convince you, I would."

"Really? You'd do that for me?"

She nodded.

I'd never been so moved or offered a greater gift. "I love you," I said as I took her face in my hands and began to kiss her hungrily, like my life depended on it, like I was anemic and she was whole blood. Then I stopped.

Her eyes flew open. "What's wrong, Tom?"

"This is, Gloria. We can't do this. As much as I want you, I won't allow you to jeopardize your sanity. I know your faith in God is what has kept your anxiety at bay. If you compromise your morals, it may compromise your mental health. I won't risk that. I love you enough to wait."

She seemed moved by sacrifice, but if truth be told, I wanted more than her body. I wanted all of her. Forever.

I eased her off my lap. But what I wanted would jeopardize more than her sanity, but her life and her very soul.

Chapter 29

"We'd better get going." I said. "Your parents are going to wonder what's happened to you."

And as I gathered my things, she fluffed her hair and picked up the frame on my desk and stared at the photograph. "Is this you?"

"And my mother," I said relieved to make small talk instead of dissecting what had just occurred. "When I was packing, I came across some of my mother's art books that were in the closet, and that picture fell out of one of them. I thought I'd better frame it before it gets lost."

While I put on my fatigue jacket, she glanced at me and then back at the photo. "You were a sweet baby."

"Thanks."

She sat the frame back on the desk. "You have your mother's dimples."

"I know," I said and the notion that I had some lasting connection to my mother made them bloom in my cheeks. They felt as deep as the craters on the moon. Gloria put on her coat, and I felt inside my jacket pocket to make sure the envelope with my share of the Sammy money was still there.

As I patted the wad, Gloria said, "She'd be very proud of you, Tom."

I felt a stab of guilt and quickly pulled my hand out of my pocket. Would my mother be proud of me? Of how I had acquired this money? Of how I had lied to Gloria? I didn't like thinking about that.

We pulled out of the lot and headed for her house. Christmas carols streamed out of the radio and they seemed inordinately loud with

243

the lack of conversation. A few times, as we drove up I-279, she glanced over at me and smiled, trying to appear confident, but I knew her well enough to know that what had just transpired back in my room was troubling her. I knew she was mulling over how close she'd come to chucking all her morals for me, and she was plagued by guilt and confusion.

As we neared the McKnight Road exit, I could take the silence no longer. "Gloria, what happened back in the room—I don't think we should place ourselves in such temptation like that again. It's too dangerous."

She looked over at me, the color draining from her face. "What are you saying, Tom? You think we should break up?"

"No," I said, "you know I can't live without you. What I'm saying is there is another solution."

She stared at me puzzled. "Like what?"

"Marriage."

"Marriage?" she gasped. The car swerved as she momentarily lost control of the wheel. Then she sucked in some air and quickly righted the car. "Did you say marriage?"

I was silent for a moment. "Yeah, I did."

"Are you asking me to marry you?" Her eyes were bright.

Yes, marrying her would be the only way to ensure she would be mine forever. Gloria took the exchange of marriage vows seriously, and after we were married if she ever found out that I had lied to her, her moral code would prevent her from leaving me. I knew it was selfish, but I needed to lock her up as mine forever.

"Yes, I am, Gloria." I felt like Satan asking her to sign her soul away.

She put on her turn signal. "I've got to pull over," she said, "because I'll be answering 'yes,' and I can't kiss you and drive at the same time."

She stopped the car near the spot where the deer had darted across the highway and shut off the engine. In the glow of the dashboard lights, she looked frightened and joyous at the same time.

I plucked her hand from the steering wheel and held it next to my heart. My ribs felt like they were going to split apart and my heart leap out of my chest. I cleared my throat. "Gloria, I love you," I said. "Will you please marry me?"

She squealed, "Yes."

I have never been so relieved. Soon she would be all mine, and I would never have to fear losing her again.

244

We lunged for each other, but our seatbelts caught and held us back. Laughing, we quickly unbuckled, and fell into each other's arms, and I smothered my future bride with kisses. Who would have believed it? I had reached for the brass ring and snagged it. We sat there by the side of the road for nearly ten minutes, bubbling over with joy, making plans for the future. Cars whizzed past us, but we didn't notice them. They could have been space ships for all I cared.

"One thing, Tom, you will marry me in church, won't you?"

"If you want."

"I do. I know God brought you to me, and I want Him to bless our marriage."

"OK, then," I said, "how about after Christmas, we go shopping for a ring. Go the whole nine yards," I said. The extra Sammy money would come in handy for sure now.

"Oh, could we?" she asked. "But let's not tell anyone until we get the ring and it's official. Maybe we can tell them on New Years Eve—wouldn't that be a great way to start the New Year? My parents are going to be so surprised." She frowned. "Wow, you haven't even met my parents yet." She looked at her new watch. "We'd better get going." She turned on the ignition. And before she shifted gears, she patted my knee. "Time to meet your future in-laws, Tom."

Suddenly, I felt sick.

Chapter 30

If I said I was nervous about meeting Gloria's parents, that would be putting it mildly. I swear an astronaut on the launch pad waiting for final countdown was calmer.

Gloria pulled into the driveway and shut off the van's engine, and I opened the door and stepped out into a freefall of fright.

Standing in the driveway, I stared up at her house as if it were the Bates Motel.

Although I wore gloves and my fatigue jacket, I was cold. The fatigue jacket! Oh no, I never thought of it before. What would a combat vet, a bona fide war hero, think of me wearing military garb? What would he think of my earring? Worse yet, what would he think of me?

I reached into the back seat, retrieved my bags, removed my jacket, and stuffed it inside my gym bag. Then I waited for Gloria to lead the way.

She came around the car. "Tom, are you OK? You look pale."

"What if they hate me?"

She put her hands on her hips. "Now why in the world would they hate you?"

I was an earring-wearing, scheming, lying, heathen, son of a draft-dodging felon. "Oh, any number of reasons."

"Give me one."

"What if they find out that I nearly attacked you in my dorm?" I whispered as if her family could hear through brick walls.

"But nothing happened." She closed the van's door.

"OK, tell that to your father when he gets his shot gun out. They never shoot the daughter, it's always the boyfriend who gets blown away."

Gloria started up the walk. "My dad doesn't even own a shotgun. The best he could do is weed whack you to death."

"Wait," I said standing in the driveway. "There's something else."

She stopped and looked over her shoulder. "Now what? Wait, let me guess. You pulled the 'Do not remove under penalty of law' tag off your pillow."

I hung my head. "It's much worse than that." I wasn't sure if I should tell Gloria but I couldn't contain so many secrets and so much anxiety in the same mind. Something had to be dumped. "Well, when I called my dad this afternoon, I found out something terrible."

"Yeah?"

"The reason he never came to Wyoming was . . . " If this had been a soap opera, the organ would have played right now. "Because he was in prison. My father's an ex-con."

"Really? What'd he do?"

"During an anti-war protest, he broke into the Federal Building and splashed blood on the draft records."

"OK?"

"Didn't you hear me? My father is a criminal. He did time. In the 'big house.' The 'slammer.'"

"I thought he did something serious like armed robbery or murder."

"Your father might think it was serious."

"No, he won't, Tom. He ministers to the inmates. And besides, everybody went a little loony back in the sixties. How else do you explain lava lamps?"

I couldn't.

She patted my cheek. "Remember, you aren't your father. Take deep breaths. They calm the nerves."

With my lungs expanding and contracting like a bellows, I followed her up the walkway to the front door. As she reached for the knob, I cowered behind her like the Cowardly Lion hiding behind Dorothy when she knocked on the gates of Oz.

As soon as Gloria's hand touched the knob, the door flew open, startling me. A middle-aged man stood inside the house. Holding my breath, I followed her. The man moved to the side, and I detected a limp as I carried in my bags. I assumed he was Gloria's father. Inside the entry, he leaned on a cane. It was wooden and looked heavy. He could probably bludgeon me to death with it if he couldn't get to his weed whacker.

Mr. Davidson's sandy hair was thinning and wire-framed glasses muted his brown eyes. A tall man, he at one time probably had been thickly muscled, but now those muscles had softened and migrated southward to his belt, where an inner tube of flesh ringed his waist. He was hardly the crew-cutted, hard-bodied Marine that I had expected. I let out my breath, knowing that I could outrun him. Nonetheless, Rob's comment about not being able to out-run bullets still made me wary. He closed the door behind us.

Standing ill at ease, I looked at my shoes. White salt lines had formed on the toes of my boots. Why hadn't I seen them before? Surely, Mr. Davidson, spit shine and all, would notice the marks.

While I tried to brush away the salt marks with the toes of my other shoe, I heard a voice call, "Is that Gloria?" Ahead down a short hallway, a woman, wearing a red apron and wiping her hands on a Christmas dishtowel, appeared in the archway. She flipped the towel over her shoulder. "I was starting to worry."

"Traffic was heavy," Gloria said, covering the true reason why we were late. Now she was lying. I had corrupted her. "Mom, Daddy," she said proudly, "this is Tom."

Her father thrust out a meaty hand. "Tom."

"Nice to meet you, sir," I barked as I pumped his hand heartily.

Mr. Davidson pulled his hand away and massaged his knuckles. "It's nice to meet you, too," he said.

"I'm Gloria's mother, Ellen." She looked like an older, faded version of Gloria. Seeing the two of them together, reminded me of those soap commercials that aired when I was kid, where you had to guess which was the daughter and which was the mother. Gloria was bright, fourteen carat gold while Mrs. Davidson was gold with a rich patina. "We're so glad you could come for the holidays." She stared at me making me feel self-conscious. "There's something different about you."

"He got a haircut," Gloria said.

"I thought something was different," Mrs. Davidson said. "It looks very nice."

"See the beautiful watch Tom gave me," Gloria said, pulling up her sleeve. While her parents admired the gift, I quickly spit on my fingertips and tried to wipe the salt marks from my shoes.

"Well, come in," Mrs. Davidson said. "And Gloria, introduce Tom to the rest of the gang. They're all in the family room. Dinner will be ready in ten minutes. Hon," she said touching Mr. Davidson's arm, "I need you to slice the ham." Gloria's parents disappeared into the kitchen.

"Where'd your jacket go?" Gloria asked as she removed her coat and hung it in the closet.

"It's in there," I whispered, pointing to the gym bag sitting next to my Hickory Farms shopping bag on the floor. Then I remembered that the envelope with all the Sammy money was still in my jacket pocket. When Gloria wasn't looking, I'd have to sneak the envelope out; I hated to leave that much money unattended.

Gloria shut the closet door. "What's it doing in there?"

"Fatigue jacket?" I raised my eyebrows. "Your father's a vet. He might not like me wearing military clothing."

"Wow, Tom, you worry more than I do."

Gloria dragged me down the hall and into the kitchen. The smell of ham and baking dinner rolls made me glad that I hadn't run away. As we entered, Mrs. Davidson was stirring a pot on the stove while Mr. Davidson stood at the counter, his back to us, holding something. He opened a drawer, pulled out a large fork and speared a ham studded with pineapple rings and cherries.

"Everything smells great," I said, trying to get in their good graces.

Gloria led me into the family room. "Merry Christmas, everybody," she said as we walked in. Her family was scattered throughout the room. "I'd like you to meet Tom Shepherd." Joe and Christo were near the Christmas tree in the corner bent over examining the miniature homes and Lionel train on the platform underneath it.

As Joe stood, walked over, and extended his hand, I noticed how drawn and pale he looked. Christo followed at his heels. "Good to see you again, Tom," he said offering his hand. I shook it, and it seemed smoother than when I shook it a few weeks ago. Probably from the lack of work. I don't know if it was my imagination, but he seemed uncomfortable when he greeted me. Perhaps he was embarrassed by the way he behaved before he collapsed.

"Good to see you again, too," I said. "You're certainly looking well." Thoughts of his motionless body lying on the floor flashed in my mind. That was something I never wanted to go through again.

"Yeah, well, I'm feeling pretty good. They say it was a heart attack, but I'm not so sure. I think it might have been low blood sugar or something."

"Oh, come on, Joe," Gloria said. Joe's eyes became steely. The last thing I needed was for him to get upset and keel over again, so I changed the subject.

"Christo, you ready for Christmas?" I reached out and rubbed his stubbly head. Christo seemed paler too. He was dressed in black corduroy pants, white shirt, and a tartan plaid vest and matching bow tie. The festive holiday attire seemed out of place, almost cruel, on such a sick little boy.

"You bet! Hey, Tom," Christo pointed to my shorn head, "you lost your fur too!"

"Well, pal, you looked so handsome with that 'do' of yours I just had to copy."

Gloria moved me further into the room and continued the introductions. "This is my brother, Rick," she said pointing to a man in his late-twenties. Like his father, Rick had sandy hair and it was already thinning. Crouched, poking the fire with a brass fireplace tool, he stood, put the poker back into the rack, and patted me on the back. "You're the guy who's given my sport jacket a social life." He stuck out his hand.

"Oh yeah, that's right," I chuckled as I shook it. "Thanks for the loan."

"No problem," he said. "It probably fits you better now anyway. The last time my wife took it to the dry cleaners, I think they shrunk it."

"Oh, don't blame it on the cleaners," laughed a dark-haired pregnant woman relaxing in the chair next to the fireplace. "It couldn't be that you've gained weight?" She turned to me. "I'm Maggie." Her hands grasped her enormous belly. "Forgive me for not getting up, but I've sunk so far down in this chair, I think I'm going to need a forklift to get me out."

"Nice to meet you." I said, having difficulty imagining Maggie's swollen body ever fitting into the velvet body-hugging dress that Gloria had worn to Heinz Hall.

Gloria took my arm and led me over to Ginny and a small elderly woman sitting on the love seat. "And you remember Ginny, of course."

Ginny stood. "Merry Christmas, Tom," she said and gave me a hug. She whispered in my ear, "Thanks for taking care of Christo. You're an angel."

Funny how things change. A few weeks ago, when she had hugged me, I felt so uncomfortable. Now, it felt natural. I grasped her arm and winked, signaling that she was welcome.

Gloria turned to the old woman and kissed her lined cheeks. "Grandma," she said, her voice louder, "this is my friend, Tom."

Gloria's grandmother wore thick glasses that magnified her eyes, making them look incredibly large. "So this is Tom." She picked up my hand and held it as she studied me. "Jenny Gosnell said you were a big, handsome fella." She nudged Gloria. "Oh, kiddo, if I was younger, you'd have to fight me for him."

Grandma cackled, and I blushed. The skin on her hands was loose, and if I tried to pull mine out of her grasp, I was afraid I'd come away with some. She patted the back of my hand with her other one. "Oh, I made him blush, Gloria. You gotta watch out for the ones that turn red easily. Your grandfather was a blusher too." Grandma squeezed my hand. "I think they turn red easily because they have a fire burning inside." Everyone in the room laughed. Except me. The fire inside me made me blush more intensely.

To save me from any further speculation from Grandma on what was burning inside me, Gloria suggested that we take my bags up to my room before dinner. We passed through the kitchen where Mrs. Davidson, called, "almost ready" as she pulled something out of the oven. In the hall, I picked up the gym bag and tried to take the shopping bag, but Gloria grabbed it.

"I got it, hot stuff," she said as she headed up the stairs in front of me swinging her rear-end.

"Very funny."

"Your face was so red, you looked like you'd been scalded."

"OK, keep it up," I said, "And I'll see if Grandma is interested in keeping me for the holidays."

Gloria laughed. "She probably would too."

At the top of the stairs, the bedrooms spread out like a fan. Mr. and Mrs. Davidson's room lay between Gloria's and the one I would be occupying—Rick's old room.

His room looked like a typical boy's room, blue carpet, double bed with a tan chenille bedspread. Old trophies rested on a shelf along with other sports memorabilia. The rest of the room had been stripped. Sitting on the dresser was a picture of a younger Rick and Maggie at some dance.

I put the gym bag on the floor, and Gloria deposited the shopping bag beside it. On the bed sat a large, wrapped box, and Gloria took the gift and handed it to me.

"Merry Christmas, Tom." She sat on the bed; it squeaked like an old piece of machinery.

Curious, I took the box from her. "Wow, this is heavy." Then I sat beside her on the noisy bed and removed the wrapping paper, wading through layers of tissue paper until I found a navy blue stadium coat with plaid flannel lining and wooden toggle buttons. "Can I use this?" I said, pulling the coat out of the box.

"It'll keep you warm when I'm not around." She searched my face for a reaction to her gift. "Try it on."

I stood and slipped my arms into the sleeves. The coat was wool and felt very warm. Gloria stood a few feet from me, assessing the fit. "You must have spent a fortune on this," I said.

"Don't worry about it. I had some money saved for Christmas."

"It's great," I said, walking toward her, "but I'd much rather have you keep me warm." I wrapped my arms around her. "Thank you." I kissed her and I felt deliciously wicked stealing a kiss in her home. I gave her a great bear hug, picking her up off her feet. We lost our balance and toppled onto the bed. It screeched, and we both laughed.

"We'd better go downstairs," I said. "Your parents are going to be wondering what's going on up here."

At that moment, Mrs. Davidson called up the stairs. "Gloria, Tom, dinner's ready."

"We're coming," Gloria called back. She kissed me and said, "Just think, Tom, soon we'll be married, and we'll have a license to roll all over any bed we want."

"I don't know if I can wait," I said. "Think we could get married tonight?"

She dragged a finger across my lips. "They're a little busy at church tonight. Come on, we'd better go before my dad come up with his weed whacker."

While I took off the coat and lay it across the bed, Gloria stood in front of the mirror on the dresser, straightening her dress and smoothing her mussed hair. While she primped, I sneaked the envelope of money out of my jacket and shoved it into my front pants pocket. Thank God they were pleated and loose fitting because the bulky envelope would have been noticeable in a tighter pair of pants.

She took my hand to lead me downstairs. "Wait," I said, "I need my bag. I did a little Christmas shopping."

"You didn't have to buy gifts."

"But I wanted to."

We returned to the family room as Mrs. Davidson was trying to round everyone up for dinner.

"Mom," Gloria said, "Tom's coat fit."

"Did you like it, Tom?" Mrs. Davidson asked.

"Oh, yeah. It's great. Speaking of gifts . . ." I pulled a present out of the shopping bag. "Ah, Mrs. Davidson, this is for you." I said shyly.

"Why, thank you, Tom. But you didn't have to do this."

"Well, it's nice of you to invite me here for the holidays."

Mrs. Davidson peeled away the paper. "Oh, candy! You picked the right gift for me."

"I hope you're going to share," Joe called.

"You're not allowed to eat candy anymore, Daddy," Christo said. Joe patted his son on the head, dismissing his words of warning.

Mr. Davidson opened the basement door and emerged with two folding chairs under his arms. "Share what?"

Rick took the chairs from his father. "Tom brought me some candy," Mrs. Davidson said. Mr. Davidson limped over and inspected the box.

"Turtles," he said and looked at his wife. "You better believe she's going to share."

"Got any presents for me?" Christo asked.

"Christo," Ginny cried, "that's not polite."

"Well," I dug in the bag. "Let me see." I pulled out a gift and made a big show out of reading the tag. "This says Christo. Is there anyone here named Christo?"

"Me! Me!" He clapped his hands. "That's me!"

I handed him the gift, and he tore the paper.

Ginny called, "What did you forget to say?"

"Oh, yeah, fanks, Tom," he said, his tiny arms flailing at the paper.

"It's a wamb," he cried, pulling the present out of the box. "Look, mommy, it's one of Tom's wambs." Christo held the fleecy stuffed animal up to his mother's face.

"Isn't that cute," she said and jingled the bell fastened to its collar. She placed a hand on my arm. "What an appropriate gift, Tom."

"I swear, I was all over town trying to find him a lamb. Everywhere I went, they tried to talk me into a reindeer or snowman."

Digging in the bag again, I pulled out another gift. "And this is for you, sir," I said, handing a present to Gloria's father.

He took the gift from me, held it, staring me down. The look in his eyes alarmed me.

"Gloria told you that I was a Marine, didn't she?"

"Yes, sir."

"Well, Tom," Mr. Davidson said, placing a hand on my shoulder. "I'll accept this gift on one condition."

I froze. "What's that sir?"

"That you knock off that 'sir' stuff. It makes me feel really old."

Relieved, I laughed. "Sure."

Mr. Davidson tore away the wrapping paper. "Ah, Hickory Farms." He held the box up and examined the contents. "Sausages . . . cheese, crackers and those little strawberry candies. I love those things." He looked at me. "Do you like football, Tom?"

"Yes."

"Well, this will be great for munching on while we watch all the bowl games."

Gloria tapped her father on the shoulder. "Oh, Daddy, Tom is my guest, not yours."

"Aww," Mr. Davidson whined, "can't I enjoy a little male companionship in this house?" Mr. Davidson draped an arm around my shoulder. "Since Rick left, I've been outnumbered. I never get to watch anything good on the big TV anymore. Every time there's a hockey game on, they vote me down and insist on watching what they want to watch. It's always that silly figure skating. I spend all my time watching that old nineteen-inch set in the basement. You don't like figure skating, do you, Tom?"

"Can't stand it," I said with a smile. I felt like I had just aced an exam. "It shouldn't even be classified as a sport."

"I feel the same way about synchronized swimming," Mr. Davidson said as he ushered me into the dining room.

Here I had feared Mr. Davidson as some "Lord of Discipline," yet he wasn't even lord of his own manor.

Chapter 31

I ate two helpings of Mrs. Davidson's dinner and that seemed to please her more than the box of candy I'd given her. Oh yeah, my appetite was in fine form. It was what happened during dinner that ruined my digestion.

Mrs. Davidson pulled out a chair. "Sit down, everyone."

Mr. Davidson and Joe took the head and foot of the table respectively, while Mrs. Davidson sat to the right of her husband, nearest the kitchen. Gloria directed me to a chair. When I pulled it out, it already had an occupant—Christo's So Big Sammy.

"I feel like one of the Three Bears, Christo," I said. He was seated directly across from me, perched atop a booster chair like a little king on a tiny throne. "Because somebody's been sitting in my chair."

I picked up the toy. Christo held out his hands, and I passed it across the table to him.

"So that's where you left him," Ginny said. "How about we put him over here until after dinner." Ginny propped the stuffed monkey in the corner.

I took my seat, sandwiched between Grandma and Gloria. The envelope, thick with money, rested like a brick on my thigh. When everyone was settled around the table, Mr. Davidson bowed his head. Not wanting to appear to be too much of a rebel, I folded my hands in my lap and bowed my head, but I felt really stupid.

Gloria's father cleared his throat and prayed: "Dear Lord, on this Christmas Eve, we thank you for all the good things you have blessed us with—delicious food, a loving family, good friends." I felt Gloria's elbow in my rib. I guess "friend" meant me. "And on this night of miracles—" His voice grew softer.

I stole a look at Mr. Davidson. His eyes were clamped shut and furrows formed below his receding hairline. "We ask you to remember Christo and keep him in your loving care."

I shifted my gaze to the others gathered at the table. Their eyes were closed as well and the muscles in their faces were tight too as if they thought by concentrating deeply, God would grant their miracle.

At that instant, I knew all of the adults were united in the same thought—that this could be the last Christmas dinner ever shared with Christo.

Mr. Davidson stopped, opened his eyes, and smiled. But candlelight reflecting in puddles of water gathering in the corners of his eyes, betrayed his brave face. The rest of the family took a long time opening and spreading their napkins over their laps, buying time to blink away tears and compose themselves.

Until this moment, I'd never realized how Christo's illness had touched them all. Ginny and Joe suffered, I knew that. And I knew Christo's illness had planted the seeds of anxiety that had blossomed into Gloria's panic disorder. But until now, I'd never thought about how Grandma felt, or Mr. Davidson, or even an in-law like Maggie. Christo was not only a son, but a grandson, a nephew, a cousin—and a little boy. His age magnified their pain. If he died, how would they ever cope with the loss?

Gloria rubbed her foot against my ankle and winked at me. Underneath the table, I squeezed her knee and worried how she'd cope if Christo died.

And I knew something else too. Christo was a friend, my friend. And I wasn't at all sure I'd be able to handle his death either. But it was my first Christmas, and I didn't want to spoil it with morbid thoughts, so I turned my attention to the food steaming on the table.

Mr. Davidson picked up his glass. "How about a toast? To the best Christmas ever." Everyone around the table returned his wish, clinking their goblets. "Now, let's see if this all tastes as good as it smells," he said, selecting a roll from the basket. "Yikes, they're hot!" he cried, juggling it and dropping it onto his plate.

Christo burst out laughing while Mr. Davidson fanned his hand. "You think that's funny, down there in the peanut gallery?" he asked with a smirk.

Christo's shoulders shook with laughter. "I thought you were playing hot potato, Uncle Dan."

"Nah," Mr. Davidson said. "Didn't I tell you, Christo, I've taken up juggling?"

"Weally?"

"Yes," Mr. Davidson said with a serious face, "and right after dinner, I'm going to juggle you."

"Oh, stop teasing him, Dan," admonished Mrs. Davidson. She then turned to me. "I hope you like ham, Tom." She held a platter stacked with slices while Grandma selected a piece. The look on Gloria's mother's face told me that she cared desperately if I liked her food.

"I like everything," I said.

"Speaking of food," Gloria interrupted, "I haven't gotten a chance to tell anyone. I spoke with Vic from the Umbria Restaurant this morning, and he's agreed to host another lasagna dinner to raise money for Christo's transplant. We made about $2,500 the last time, didn't we?"

"Oh," Ginny cried, jumping a little in her seat and quickly swallowing. "Now that we're all together, we have good news too. We wanted to surprise you. Hippocraticare called right before we came. They've agreed to pay 75 percent of the transplant."

"Yeah," Joe grumbled, harpooning a green bean with his fork. On his plate lay only a small slice of ham and beans. I guessed that his diet had been restricted. "Sandra Creighton's report shamed them into it."

"More like Ginny shamed them," Gloria said brightly and smiling at Ginny.

"I saw you on TV, Ginny," I said. "You really gave it to them."

"Oh yeah, Ginny can be a real shrew when she wants to be," Joe said.

His remark made me sorry that I'd complimented her.

I wasn't the only one bothered by Joe's sharp words. A look of collective shock registered on the faces around the table. Seeing their reaction, Joe laughed and tried to cover it over. "You ought to see her when I try to eat some candy or potato chips."

The Davidsons seemed eager to forget Joe's comment. Grandma clasped her hands together. "Oh, Ginny, that's wonderful."

Mr. Davidson leaned on an elbow. "They wouldn't pay for all the expenses?"

"No," Joe said before Ginny could open her mouth to speak. "They gave us some song and dance about setting a precedent. If he gets his transplant, it'll still be considered experimental because Christo's not in remission."

Gloria put down her fork. "What do you mean 'if' he gets his transplant?"

"Well, we still have to come up with the rest of the money before we can move ahead," Joe said.

"We can start raising it with the lasagna dinner," Gloria replied.

"I don't like *basagna*," Christo said, plucking a gob of butter from his roll and eating it like a chunk of cheese. "I like *basghetti*."

"You'll like this lasagna, darling." Grandma winked at him. "It'll help you to get better."

"*Basghetti* can make me better, too," he declared.

His mother tapped his arm, instructing him to eat.

"The only problem is," Gloria said, "the restaurant isn't available until the end of January. It's booked with playoff and Super Bowl parties."

Joe waved a fork around. "See that's the problem. We're working against the clock. We need to raise the money as fast as possible before . . ." Joe's fork froze in midair. He looked at his plate. "Before it's too late. It's going to be really tough raising money at this time of year. People will have already given to charities at Christmas and then by January their credit card bills will start rolling in. Today, I called the bank and asked for another loan to tide us over until we raise the money, but they wouldn't budge. With our previous loans for medical expenses, mortgage, and my business loans—"

Ginny chimed in, "and now with Joe's medical condition and his being out of work." When she mentioned his heart problem, Joe looked wounded. "They said we're overextended as it is—"

"I'd put our house on the market," Joe interrupted Ginny. He wanted control; you could sense it. "But we'd never get enough out of it. And besides it could take months to sell. We don't have the luxury of time."

Mr. Davidson picked up his glass and stopped before drinking. "I told you before, Joe, I have some money put aside for retirement. I can go to the bank as soon as they open on Monday, and get you the cash."

"No," Joe said. "That's your retirement. You've already given too much." He looked down at his plate and carved his measly piece of ham. "No, this is my problem."

Mrs. Davidson looked thoughtful. "Joe, exactly how much more money are you talking about?"

"Well, the transplant is $200,000. They'll pick up $150,000 of it. We've already raised $40,000. We're shy ten-thousand dollars."

I choked on my Parker House roll. *Ten thousand dollars?* The amount of money I had in my pocket meant the difference between life and death for Christo? Gloria handed me my glass and instructed me to take a drink. I gulped the wine.

"Ten thousand dollars," Mr. Davidson said, mulling the figure over, "the price of a child's life."

As I cleared my throat, I wondered what would Gloria say if she knew I had $10,000? I didn't want to think about that so I took another slice of ham.

Mrs. Davidson said, "You know you could borrow the money. We're years from retirement. And you're wrong, Joe. This isn't just *your* problem. We're a family. You'd do the same thing for us if it were Gloria. Take the money."

Joe unconsciously tapped his knife against the rim of his plate. Even now, anger simmered in him. "There's no way, I'll ever be able to repay everything I owe as it is," he said. "I can't do it. I won't."

"Good grief," Mr. Davidson said, "you are the most stubborn person I know. Do you think I could ever enjoy my retirement, spending money that could have helped Christo? I'd rather work another five years and know I did everything I could. How could I ever sun myself on some beach knowing I could have done something to save him and didn't? Don't choose your pride over your son's life for goodness sake."

Joe stiffened and set his jaw in anger. "Don't you tell me about pride." He pointed a finger at his older brother. "Wouldn't you just love to come to the rescue again? Big brave Dan, the war hero, saves the day again."

"Please don't argue," Ginny cried, looking pale. "You just got out of the hospital."

"I can take care of my own family," Joe shouted.

"Tom's a guest," said Mrs. Davidson. "He doesn't want to listen to you arguing."

Mr. Davidson looked sheepish. "We're not arguing," he said, smiling and trying to defuse the emotions. "Arguments are when you're on opposites sides of an issue. We're all on the same side here— Christo's side. You see that don't you, Tom?"

The spotlight fell on me. "Yes," I said timidly. I was sorry I'd taken a second helping of ham; the conversation had upset my stomach.

Everyone became quiet and interested in their food. I moved some green beans around and wished Joe would accept Mr. Davidson's money so I could spend mine with a clear conscience.

261

Next to me, Grandma put down her silverware. I thought she was rubbing her arthritic knuckles, but she nudged me and whispered, "Here, pass this to Joe." Then she dropped something into my palm. I opened my hand and saw a diamond ring resting in it. Shocked, I raised my eyebrows. She nudged me harder and motioned with her head. "Go on."

I cleared my throat, "Ah, Joe . . . ah, Grandma said to give you this." I extended my hand across the table, and I may as well have lobbed a grenade across it.

"What's this?" Joe asked. I lowered my eyes, wishing I had my long hair back so I could hide behind it.

"My engagement ring," Grandma said.

"Your engagement ring?" Joe cried.

"Take it for Christo and sell it." Grandma calmly cut her ham.

"Mom, I can't take it." He pushed his chair away from the table. "I won't take it."

"What good are diamonds when I could lose a more precious gem." Grandma smiled at her grandson, who was unaware that his life had become the topic of Christmas dinner conversation.

"But that's from Dad," Mr. Davidson interrupted. "Keep your ring, Mom. Joe can have my money."

"Baloney," Grandma said, dismissing her son with a wave of her hand. "Your father would want me to give it to him."

My arm ached as I held it outstretched across the table while the Davidsons bickered. Gloria looked at me apologetically and shrugged. Red blotches crept up Ginny's neck, spreading to her cheeks as she sawed at her ham like it was a two-by-four.

Rick and Maggie, who until now, had remained out of the battle, were huddled at the end of the table. "We're a little low on cash right now," Rick said, "with the baby coming and Maggie not working, but maybe I could see about a home equity loan on our house."

Ginny dropped her utensils. They clattered on the plate. She whipped the napkin off her lap, stood, snatched the ring from my hand, walked it over to Grandma, and deposited it into Grandma's hand. We all sat dumbfounded watching her.

Behind me, Ginny gripped the back of my chair, and said firmly: "I know you all love Christo, and we love you too for your good intentions, but please . . . Please can't this wait until after Christmas? There's nothing any of us can do now, and I'd like tonight to be special." She inhaled deeply, and squared her shoulders. "So everyone, let's concentrate on having the merriest Christmas possible."

She walked back to her seat, sat, lowered her head, and whispered a postscript that made the hydrochloric acid in my stomach bubble up, and burn my esophagus, "at least for Christo's sake."

Chapter 32

The tension between Joe and Gloria's father was thicker than the pecan pie Mrs. Davidson served for dessert. So after dinner, I opted to stay with Gloria and the women clearing the table instead of retiring to the family room with them, Rick, Grandma, and Christo.

As I shuttled a stack of dirty dishes into the kitchen, Rick walked in and poured himself another cup of coffee. Mrs. Davidson called him aside. "Rick, why don't you take your dad and Joe down to the basement? Show Joe the new band saw I got your father for Christmas."

Rick stirred cream into his coffee. "Are you sure you want those two around sharp objects with the mood they're in?" Rick looked at me and made his eyes wide with mock terror.

Mrs. Davidson moved to the sink, turned on the water. "Oh, you know those two. As soon as they get around a piece of equipment, they'll forget all about what happened at dinner." She squirted Joy into the dishwater.

Rick carried his coffee into the family room, and I heard him call, "Hey, Dad, how about showing me that new band saw mom got you." Joe and Mr. Davidson took the bait and headed downstairs with Rick.

Call me liberated, but I didn't mind helping in the kitchen. After clearing the table, Gloria handed me a tea towel and began drying the dishes her mother had washed. Maggie asked for some aluminum foil to wrap leftovers. When Mrs. Davidson handed the roll to her, she spied Maggie's puffy ankles and relieved her from any further kitchen duty. She dismissed Maggie to the family room with the command to keep off her feet, keep an eye on Christo, and keep Grandma company.

Ginny set a stack of dirty dishes on the kitchen counter top. "Ow," she cried, jerking her index finger to her mouth.

"What'd you do?" Mrs. Davidson asked.

She took the finger from her mouth. "I cut myself."

"On what?" Gloria asked, tossing her towel over the back of a kitchen chair and coming to Ginny's aid.

"The electric knife blade," Ginny said with a wince. "It slipped when I put the dishes on the counter." Blood ran down her finger. I looked away.

Mrs. Davidson wiped her hands on the front of her apron. "Is it bad?"

I knew how I reacted around blood, so I continued drying dishes while Mrs. Davidson tore a paper towel from the roll and handed it to Ginny.

"I don't think it needs stitches," Ginny said. Her statement was more a request for our opinion on treatment rather than a definite declaration. "I don't want to spend Christmas Eve in the emergency room."

I stole a glance at her finger and blood had soaked the paper towel. With the argument at dinner and now the blood, it'd be a miracle if I survived the night.

Mrs. Davidson and Gloria examined Ginny's finger. "What do you think, Tom?" they asked. "Does she need stitches?"

They forced me to look the cut. As I gazed into the gaping flesh, I felt lightheaded like someone had opened a valve in the top of my head and let my air escape. I quickly averted my eyes. "I don't think so," I said. She could have needed twenty stitches for all I knew.

"Gloria," Mrs. Davidson said, "take Ginny upstairs. In the bathroom, I think we might have some of those butterfly bandages from the time your dad cut his hand on the lawn mower blade."

Since we'd lost three helpers, the speed of the clean-up operation was drastically diminished. Mrs. Davidson washed much faster than I dried, and soon a mountain of clean dishes had accumulated.

I stood next to her at the sink. As she stacked another plate in the drainer, she tilted her head toward me, and talked out the side of her mouth. "If I didn't know any better, Tom, I'd think Ginny and Gloria plotted that little accident to get out of dishes. Hope you don't mind helping."

"Oh, no" I said, "I've got to earn my keep." I tried to increase my drying speed to keep up with her.

"Seriously, Tom, we're very happy to have you here for the holidays, and I hope you'll feel at home. And I want to apologize for that nasty scene at dinner. We're all upset about Christo. Everybody wants the best for him, but we all have different opinions on how to attain it. Before you came along, something like what happened at dinner would have really upset Gloria. You've been so good for her. I can't tell you how much she's changed since she's met you."

I wiped a dish, staring into the soapy water. If Mrs. Davidson only knew what I was really like, would she still be as kind to me?

She rinsed some silverware. "Sorry to make you dry all this by hand," she said, "but this was my mother's china, and I no longer trust it to the dishwasher. One year, I put it in there and a plate shifted and was chipped."

My hand stopped in mid-swipe. "Maybe I shouldn't be drying. I'm afraid I'll break something." I held the plate so tightly I thought it might crack under the pressure.

"Don't be silly," she said, pushing a stray hair into place with the back of her wet hand. "They're not valuable, they're just sentimental."

Mrs. Davidson scrubbed at some sticky ham glaze on the platter, then stopped, and looked absentmindedly out the window above the kitchen sink. The darkness outside trapped our reflections in the pane of glass. "I like to use the china, especially on holidays, because it reminds me of my mother and all those who aren't here to celebrate anymore. Every year, every holiday, these were the dishes we ate from." She turned and looked at me. "My mother was a horrible cook—lumpy mashed potatoes at Thanksgiving, dry ham at Christmas. I spent a lot of time staring at these plates when I was a kid wondering how I was ever going to stomach her food."

We laughed.

"It's funny," she said, "how with the passage of time, bad things don't seem so awful any more."

"It's nice that you have something to remember her by." All this talk about her deceased mother was making me sad. How different my life would have been had my mother not been killed. The only consolation was that had my mother lived, I'd probably not be in the Davidsons' house tonight, and I'd have never met Gloria.

When Mrs. Davidson finished washing, she picked up a towel and began to help me. As if she could read my mind, she said, "Gloria tells me you don't have much family."

"Yeah, my father moved to California when I started college, and my mother is dead. She died when I was four."

Mrs. Davidson frowned. "I'm sorry. It's hard losing a parent. My father died when I was a baby. And even though I never knew him, I still felt the loss."

Ginny interrupted the melancholy state that taken hold of Mrs. Davidson and me. "I'm off the injured reserve," she said. "Where's my towel?"

"How's your finger?" Mrs. Davidson asked.

"Oh, it'll be fine." Ginny held up her hand. The wounded finger looked like a cocoon. It was now two times its size from the gauze and tape Gloria had wrapped around it. "I think Gloria went a little overboard."

Mrs. Davidson chuckled. "Good thing she's not studying to be a nurse."

Ginny picked up a towel and began drying.

"Where's Gloria?" I asked.

"With Christo. He came upstairs. She's helping him with a surprise," Ginny said mysteriously.

"Well, we're almost finished here," Mrs. Davidson said. She patted me on the back. "Tom did a fine job. He didn't break a single dish."

"Thanks," I said, "and if I don't get a job as a physicist at least I know I can get one washing dishes at Eat 'n Park."

Mrs. Davidson looked at the clock. "I think we better get moving. I want to be sure to get a seat." She pulled Ginny's towel out of her hands. "I'll finish these when I get back. Keep your finger dry."

Just then, Christo ran into the kitchen, shouting "ta-dum" as he presented himself to us. He wore a plaid flannel bathrobe and striped hand towel on his head, looking like a pint-sized extra from the set of *Lawrence of Arabia*.

"You're not ready yet," Gloria called, chasing after him.

He handed his mother something. "I don't want to wear this."

Ginny held up the object. It was a mask. "If you want to go to church," she said, handing it back to her son, "then you'll have to wear it."

"I have an eyebrow pencil," Gloria said bending down to Christo's level. "How about we draw on the mask so it looks like a beard? No one will ever be able to tell that you have it on."

Christo thought a moment then said, "OK."

"Here," Gloria said handing the pencil to Ginny.

"Oh, you do it, Gloria. I can't draw with my finger bandaged like this."

"What are you supposed to be?" I asked Christo, watching Gloria attempt to draw a beard on his mask.

"I'm going to be a shepherd like you," he said. I saw the excitement in his eyes, but I wanted to warn him not to be anything like me.

"Oh, this isn't working," Gloria said. "How about if I put the mask on Christo's face and hold it in place while Tom draws on the beard." She handed me the pencil and slipped the mask over Christo's mouth and nose. "You're the only one here that has experience with beards."

"Don't expect too much," I said as I knelt before Christo. "I got C's in art. Remember I'm a scientist." That remark made Gloria snort.

I took his bony chin in my hand and drew short black strokes over his baby-soft cheeks and over the mask, giving him a beard, mustache and dark brows. He reminded me of a toy I had as a kid— Wooley Willie, the picture of the bald man on whose face you arranged iron filings to form hair. "There," I said rising. "No one will ever know you're wearing a mask."

Christo tried to see his reflection in the oven door's glass.

"I didn't know you were going to church," Mrs. Davidson said, undoing her apron. "I thought you had decided to stay here."

"We had," Ginny said. She put her hand on Christo's head. "Sweetie, Gloria will take you and show you your face in the mirror. Then go show Daddy."

Gloria picked Christo up and carried him from the room. I didn't leave with them because I still had silverware to dry.

Ginny waited until Gloria and Christo had left the kitchen before she spoke. "I know we risk infection by taking him in crowds, but he found that costume yesterday. Remember, he wore it last Christmas? He begged me to let him dress up again and go." Ginny looked at her hands and twisted her wedding ring. "It's so hard to refuse him. I couldn't say no. I want this Christmas to be extra special . . . his best ever." Her mouth was tight, and she worked her ring more rapidly as if it were a pump that filled her with courage. "This might be our last—" She stopped. The words, "Christmas together" were distorted by her quivering lips. She covered her face with her hands and began to cry.

While Mrs. Davidson pulled Ginny close to her, I finished drying the silverware and began quietly stacking the clean dishes. Ginny cried into Mrs. Davidson's chest. Sobs wracked her body, making her shoulders heave like they were being jerked from above by a hidden rope. Ginny tried to stifle them, making the sobs that did escape even louder and more desperate. Each sob whacked at my heart like a tire iron. I wanted to slip out of the room, but I knew it would be more awkward for me to leave than it would be for me to stay. So I worked at making myself invisible, busying myself stacking and rearranging the clean dishes.

"Oh, I'm so sorry," Ginny sniffed and raised her head. "I don't want to ruin everyone's holiday."

Mrs. Davidson patted Ginny's back and used her free hand to wipe away her own sympathy tears. "Nonsense. It's good to let it all out. I don't know how you've held it in this long."

"Until now, I've been able to handle it, but since Joe's gotten sick," Ginny said, "I feel like it's all coming down on me."

"Well, of course. You're trying to care for Christo and protect Joe. It's only natural not to want him to get upset. But you'll be fine, Ginny," Mrs. Davidson said. "You know God doesn't give you more than you can handle."

Now there's a bunch of bull, I thought.

"Maybe," Ginny said, "but He sure likes to take you right to the edge." They both chuckled, and I could tell Mrs. Davidson's words had soothed her. Ginny's breathing settled into a regular rhythm. Her sorrow for now was passing like a brief, violent summer storm. Mrs. Davidson ripped a paper towel from the roll and handed one to Ginny, who blew her nose. Gloria's mother sopped up the tears in the corners of her own eyes with another towel.

I think they forgot I was in the room, because when Ginny looked above the paper towel and spied my face, she groaned. "Oh, Tom," she said with a sad smile, "bet you're so glad you decided to spend Christmas with us. First we argue at the dinner table. Then I'm always blubbering. And to top it off, Joe takes a heart attack on you. You must think we're a pack of lunatics." When she mentioned his name, she looked from me to Mrs. Davidson. "Please don't tell Joe," she begged. "It upsets him when I lose it."

Her red, swollen eyes tore at my heart. I certainly didn't think she was a lunatic. I liked her and admired her, but I knew if I told her that, she'd probably start crying again and would make me cry too. I didn't know what else to say. But then I didn't have to because Mrs. Davidson came to my rescue. Ellen Davidson's pruney, soggy hand felt for mine, found it, and squeezed it tightly. "Tom, doesn't mind. Do you, Tom?"

I shook my head no. I really didn't mind Ginny's crying. What I minded was that I had no way to comfort her, and that I felt I was being sucked further into their problems. It was fine to care about Christo and the Davidsons' dilemma from a distance, but I didn't want to be caught up in it. I had enough troubles of my own.

Mrs. Davidson dropped my hand and put her arm around Ginny, squeezing her like a coach giving encouragement to a discouraged player. "I'll tell you the same thing I told Gloria when she was battling her panic attacks," Mrs. Davidson said. "You are much braver and stronger than you think. What do they say, 'if it doesn't kill you, it makes you stronger?'"

I'd never though of myself as brave or strong. Was Mrs. Davidson right? Had the experiences of my life made me courageous? I hoped she was right. I hoped I was brave and strong, because tonight, more than any other night in my life, I had a feeling I'd need to be.

Chapter 33

When I accepted Gloria's invitation to spend Christmas with her, I didn't realize it entailed an encore at Holy Redeemer. Had I known church was in the plans, I'd have arranged to come to Gloria's house afterwards and start my holiday with her then. But as I snipped the tags from my new coat, I took consolation that at least I'd get to snuggle up beside her in the van on the way.

But even the ride to church didn't turn out as I'd thought. Grandma's arthritic knees kept her from crawling into the back of the van, so I was forced to climb into the third seat and ride to church by myself while Gloria sat in front of me with Grandma..

And as we rode along, a feeling of isolation and despair swept over me. My new coat was very warm, and I began to sweat. I unbuttoned it and wished that it was tomorrow and this little visit to church was over.

Mr. Davidson pulled in front of the building and let Mrs. Davidson and Grandma out. Then he drove down the driveway and pulled into the parking lot behind Holy Redeemer.

Gloria rolled open the van's door and stepped out. I emerged and took a few deep breaths to clear my head.

"You should button up," Gloria said. "It's cold."

"I'm fine. It was a little hot in the back of the van."

Ginny pulled into the spot next to us. Joe was not yet allowed to drive, and he sat up front with a glum look on his face. I recognized that look. I'd seen it once before when my babysitter's dog returned from the vet's after being neutered. Christo, sitting in a booster seat in the back, waved frantically at us as if he hadn't seen us for months. Rick had also dropped Maggie off up front with Mrs. Davidson and Grandma, and he parked his Cavalier three spaces away.

Our small group, led by Christo in his shepherd's costume, mask, and Penguin jacket, walked to the front of the church with Gloria and me bringing up the rear.

As we neared the front entrance, snowflakes began to fall. They floated in slow motion through the air as if they were afraid to complete their procession to the earth. Like the snowflakes, I was in no hurry to get to my destination either.

On the church steps, we reunited with Grandma, Maggie, and Mrs. Davidson. Gloria's father held open the glass doors to Holy Redeemer, and as I crossed the threshold, my heart froze, waiting for a lightning bolt. When I cleared the doorway without any zigzagging down on me, my heart resumed beating. God loved Gloria, I reasoned. Maybe he'd grant me immunity because I was with her. All I knew was that I wanted this evening to be over and to get out of there.

As I stepped into the vestibule and saw all the people gathered there, the jelly legs I experienced the first time I came to Holy Redeemer returned. I felt for Gloria's hand and clung to it like it was a lifeline.

In the corner, a crowd had gathered around Christo and his parents. Gloria and I stood on its fringe watching as people asked about Christo's health, patted his head, or grabbed Ginny's arm to wish her Merry Christmas. Many people stopped to tell the Davidsons that they were praying for them. I watched the look of shock register on people's faces as Ginny told many of the well-wishers about Joe's heart attack. She requested prayers for him too. With every person that Ginny told about Joe's recent illness, Joe seemed to shrink beside his wife.

By the number of people who had stopped to wish Christo good health, it was obvious that this congregation had a vested interest in him. No wonder. They'd given their own blood for him. They treasured him. How they would hate me if they knew I had $10,000 in my pocket right now, the amount needed to save his life.

Mrs. Davidson tugged on Gloria's sleeve. "I'm going to take Grandma and Maggie in. I don't want them to have to stand."

"We'll be there in a minute," Gloria said. "Save us a seat." Gloria grabbed my arm. "Come on, Tom, I want to introduce you to someone." She dragged me across the back of the vestibule to a doorway where a pudgy, white-haired man, dressed in a robe, was giving some last minute instructions to a pair of girls. He looked familiar, but I didn't know why.

When he saw Gloria, he broke into a big smile. "Ah, Gloria," he said.

"Father Bob Moran, I'd like you to meet my friend, Tom Shepherd." The way she beamed, you'd have thought she'd grabbed the prodigal son by the scruff of the neck and dragged him to church or something.

Father Bob extracted a hand from the wide sleeve of his vestment and shook my mine. "Welcome back, Tom," he said, the flesh around his eyes crinkled as he smiled. "It's nice to see you again."

Gloria and I exchanged puzzled looks.

"You don't remember?" He turned to Gloria. "Tom and I met the day of Christo's blood drive." He looked back at me. "I showed you the way into the church hall."

Oh, no. Now I knew why his face seemed familiar. He was Fatso, the man who had sneaked up on me, scared the daylights out of me, and led me into that nightmare at the blood drive. My instincts were right that day. I should have never followed him, and if my instincts were right again, I should get out of this church now, before something terrible happened.

I laughed to cover my nervousness. "Oh, I thought you looked familiar."

"That day, I assumed you came to donate blood like everybody else." He put his arm around my shoulder. "I never got to tell you how impressed I was with what you did for Christo. Gloria's one lucky lady to have found a young man like you. It's not often that you come across someone so generous." I felt myself blushing but this time not from embarrassment but from shame.

"You don't have to tell me how lucky I am," Gloria said. "I'm well aware of it. I guess we'd better go take our seats. Mom and Dad and the rest of the family have gone in already. The place is going to be packed."

Father Bob rubbed his hands together and rocked on his feet. "Ah, standing room only—I love it." He patted us both on the back. Merry Christmas, you two."

"He's my buddy," Gloria said. "He counseled me when I was sick."

He seemed nice, but I didn't trust him. You never know what he might be capable of or what tricks he had hidden in those wide sleeves of his.

Gloria opened another set of etched glass doors that led into the main part of the church. As she led me up the center aisle, I noticed most of the seats were filled and that the ushers were beginning to instruct people to stand along the side aisles. With this large an audience, to Father Bob, this must feel like a performance or show. My unfailing instincts, however, told me that this was not a show but a showdown.

Chapter 34

Although the church was flooded with light and was open and airy, walking up that aisle I felt as if I were descending into an abyss. Was my anxiety apparent on my face? Keeping my eyes straight ahead, I avoided the stares of the people in the pews. At the foot of the altar, sat a large crèche in a field of red and white poinsettias, and I fixed my sight on the empty manger. The aisle seemed endless.

Gloria's parents and her grandmother were seated up front, and Gloria slid into a pew next to them. I took a seat on the end behind Joe, who was seated with Ginny, Christo, Maggie, and Rick in the pew in front of us.

Gloria prayed while I checked out the rest of the church. Evergreen garlands tacked up with red velvet ribbons festooned the walls. To the left of the altar, in an alcove, a choir of chubby-cheeked children sang in high-pitched voices "It Came Upon The Midnight Clear."

Excitement mingled in the air with the scent of beeswax candles and pine. As we waited for the service to begin, even I felt the adrenaline pumping through me. But I reminded myself that there really was nothing to be hyped about. It was just church.

Christo spied us and crawled over his father to sit in front of me. Joe shifted closer to Ginny. The little nomad turned around, looked at me, and waved. I crossed my eyes.

"Baa," he bleated loudly from behind the mask, thrusting the lamb that I had given him at me.

Joe shushed Christo, grabbed him, and sat his son on his lap.

Gloria settled back into her seat and heaved a sigh. What was she feeling now? She reached for my hand, and I slid it into hers. Our fingers dovetailed, our hands resting on my thigh, inches from the bulging envelope of money.

She stared straight ahead, softly singing along with the choir. As I watched her, I was amazed. A month ago, had you told me that I'd be attending church on Christmas Eve with the most beautiful girl in the world, the girl who only a few hours before I'd become engaged to, that I'd be sitting with my hair cut short with more than $10,000 in my pocket, I'd have said you were out of your mind.

The church was hot; I took off my coat. Father Bob was correct—it was standing room only. The choir stopped singing and the church fell eerily silent. A bell chimed and Gloria squeezed my hand. Everyone stood. I looked around, not wanting to make a false move, and then I stood too. The organ pumped out "O Come All Ye Faithful."

Gloria sang loudly and magnificently, and I watched her, her voice and beauty overwhelming me again.

In front of me, Joe pointed up the aisle, and Christo hung out from the pew, his eyes growing wide. And from the way the mask moved over his cheeks, I knew he was smiling beneath it. I looked back to where Joe was pointing, but saw only a heavyset woman in a Christmas sweater carrying a Bible, and the priest holding aloft what looked like a porcelain doll.

"Baby Jesus!" Christo exclaimed, and he shuffled across the pew to his mother and tugged on her sleeve. When she bent down to tell him to be quiet, he grabbed her by the chin and forced her to turn her head. "Look, it's Baby Jesus, Mommy!"

Father Bob processed past us to the nativity scene, where he bowed his head, knelt down, and placed the porcelain figure in the manger. Then he rose and moved behind the altar as the last notes from the organ vibrated and faded away. He raised his arms and invited everyone to pray. I pretended to cough so I wouldn't have to join in. Then, I shoved my hands into my pockets and clutched my money.

"On this most holy of nights," he said, "we welcome all who come seeking the Savior."

He was so melodramatic I had to stifle a laugh.

Gloria and those around me made the motions and recited the prayers while I stared blankly ahead. She pushed the prayer book in front of my face. I took my hands from my pockets and shared the book with her, following along in the text, but resisting participation.

My feet ached from standing. I was glad when it was finally time to sit. The fat lady who'd carried the Bible into the church went to a podium and began reading. Gloria picked up my hand again and inched closer to me. My mind wandered as the woman droned on.

When the congregation suddenly rose, my thoughts sprang back to the present. Father Bob strode to the marble pulpit. "As this service is for children," he began, "I ask all of you to please be seated while we read the gospel." We all sat. *Again.* With all the up, down, up, down, I felt like I was in an aerobics class. Settling back into the hard pew, I unleashed my mind to wander again, daydreaming about how Gloria and I would spend the holidays.

Then Father Bob descended from the pulpit and began hovering near the front of the church only five pews away. His presence unnerved me and drew my mind back to the church. Straightening up, I kept my eye on him while he began to read out of a large red leather book.

"A reading of St. Luke's gospel," he said. "At that time, the Emperor Caesar Augustus ordered all people to return to their hometown for a census." He stopped and looked up. "Is there a Caesar Augustus here tonight?"

What was he talking about?

Across the aisle, a boy of six stood, climbed over the people in his pew, and made his way to the aisle. He was wearing a toga fashioned from a white bed sheet, and a wreath of silk ivy on his head. A plastic Star Wars sword dangled at his side. The boy ran up the aisle, and the Pastor directed him where to stand in the sanctuary.

Father Bob resumed the reading. "So Joseph took his wife Mary, who was going to have a baby very soon, to his hometown of Bethlehem to be counted. He raised his head. "Do we have any Josephs or Marys?"

A small girl popped up. Pink-rimmed glasses perched on her upturned nose and a blue veil framed her heart-shaped face and matched the blue robe she was wearing. She shot out of the pew and bustled up the aisle carrying a baby doll.

A boy, two rows in back of us, in a brown velour bathrobe, carrying an upside down hockey stick as a staff, was prodded by his parents, and then finally pushed out of the pew.

Gloria leaned over and whispered, "That's Matthew. I give him piano lessons. He's the one who gave me the bottle of Passion."

The boy hung his head and dragged his feet as he plodded to the front of the church. When he turned and faced the congregation, he scowled. He looked so lifeless the kid could have used a dose of Passion himself.

When Father Bob saw the look on Matthew's face, he laughed. "A true portrait of Joseph if I ever saw one," he said. "The poor man was shoved into a role he didn't want."

Gloria whispered again. "He shows the same enthusiasm for the piano."

The Pastor went back to the reading. "'And Mary gave birth to a little baby boy. She named Him Jesus, wrapped him in warm clothing, and laid him in a manger because there was no room for them in the Inn.' "Do we have an Innkeeper?" He asked.

People murmured and turned their heads, searching the congregation. "An Innkeeper?" he repeated, scanning the crowd. "Going once. Going twice." He paused a moment and then shrugged. "Hmm, no Innkeeper." After taking a few steps, he stopped. "Oh well, that's fine. Innkeeper is a lousy job." Then his eyes sparkled with devilment as he added, "You always have to work Christmas Eve."

The congregation broke up in laughter, and I admit so did I. One thing for sure, Father Bob knew how to work a room.

I looked at my watch. The kids were cute, but man, this little pageant was taking forever.

"'There were shepherds in the field that night watching over their flocks,'" He read. He looked up from the book. "Do we have any sheep?"

Three small brothers, about a year apart in age, dressed in white wooly lamb costumes, ran from the back of the church, racing up the aisle wanting to be the first to reach the front. They plowed into Father Bob, nearly knocking him over. Laughter erupted again as he grabbed Joseph's hockey stick and herded the reckless sheep-boys to the side.

After the place settled down, he said, "I know we have one shepherd here tonight." He pointed at Christo then looked at the other side of the church. "Are there any others?"

"That's you," Joe whispered to Christo.

Christo jumped off his father's lap, and Ginny handed him Mr. Davidson's cane to use as his shepherd's crook. Christo bounded out of the pew, but instead of walking up the aisle, he pivoted and grabbed my hand. "It's our turn," he exclaimed. "Come on, Tom."

Our turn? Panicked, I looked to Gloria as Christo yanked my arm. "What's he talking about?" I whispered. Every eye in Holy Redeemer was focused on us. Heat burned in my cheeks, and I knew my face must be the color of the poinsettias in front of the altar.

"Christo, leave Tom alone," Joe barked.

"But it's our turn," Christo said, his voice rising. He dug in his heels and jerked harder, nearly dislocating my arm.

Father Bob walked over. He placed his hand on his veiled head. "What seems to be the problem here, Shepherd Boy?"

Christo looked up at him. "He's a shepherd. And it's our turn." Then Christo dropped the cane, using both hands to tug harder on my arm.

Father Bob looked at me, awaiting an explanation.

"My last name is Shepherd," I whispered, "but he thinks I'm a real one." I rolled my eyes, in an appeal for him to tell Christo to knock it off.

But Father Bob said nothing. He only smiled and headed back to the front of the church.

"Friends," he began, "Christo Davidson has been kind enough to bring to my attention that tonight we're fortunate to have an authentic shepherd—Tom Shepherd—with us. You may recall that Tom was the young man who brought Christo the So Big Sammy during the blood drive last month. We'd be honored to have a certified shepherd grace our altar on Christmas Eve, wouldn't we?"

The congregation broke into applause.

This was it. What I'd feared. The tips of my ears were on fire, burning with embarrassment. Gloria nudged me. "Go on up, Tom."

"No! I can't!"

"Go, Tom," she said, pushing me. I resisted. "Go," she said again and pushed harder. I stumbled out of the pew, and when I stood up straight, the applause grew louder. Christo never let go of my hand. He picked up the cane, and led me proudly to the altar like he was presenting his prize lamb for slaughter.

Under Father Bob's direction, I took my place with the children. Standing in front of the church, I towered over the midget biblical characters surrounding me. Mary titled her head and eyed me with a look of disgust. Humiliated, I stared at my salt-stained shoes until the applause subsided.

I wanted to kill Christo for doing this to me. If he hadn't clamped himself onto my hand and Gloria hadn't been sitting there, I'd have bolted out the door like the last time.

When the church quieted, he continued the reading. "Suddenly, angels appeared. And the shepherds were very afraid."

How appropriate—a shepherd afraid. It's in my bloodline; I'm genetically programmed to be scared. I stole a glance at Gloria. She beamed me a smile.

Seven little girls from various places in the church left their seats. Most wore white gowns, diaphanous wings, and golden halos. They flew to the altar, surrounding Christo and me. One little girl's set of wings was green with spots. She'd probably been an insect for Halloween.

Father Bob read on: "'Do not be afraid, the angels told the shepherds.'"

The girl with the green wings smiled up at me. Her front teeth were missing.

"'I have good news for you,'" He continued. "'Your Savior has been born. You will find the baby sleeping in a manger in Bethlehem. Then the angels sang a beautiful song: Glory to God in the highest and peace on earth to all. After that, the shepherds left in search of the baby the angels had told them about.'" Father Bob closed the red leather book: "This is the Gospel of the Lord."

"Thanks be to God," the congregation replied.

He instructed those of us standing in the front of the church to have a seat. I detached myself from Christo's death grip and started for the pews.

But Father Bob grabbed my arm. "You can remain up front." Not wanting to draw further attention, I followed the priest's directions and sat down cross-legged on the floor beside Christo.

The Pastor thanked all the children who had participated in the gospel reading and their parents who had gone to the trouble of making costumes. Then he held out a hand toward me and added: "I'd like to especially thank our distinguished shepherd, Tom, for being such a good sport."

The crowd applauded again. Father Bob stood before me clapping too. I did a full-body blush this time. If this was Christo's last Christmas, it surely would be a memorable one. No one in Holy Redeemer tonight would ever forget the big geek with all the little kids.

I looked beyond Gloria and her family who were smiling and waving at us, and what I saw surprised me. Face after face in the church, male and female, old and young alike was smiling at me. Their faces radiated a goodness toward me that told me I was wrong, that I was not an alien here, that I was welcome. That I belonged here. This Christmas Eve the church was filled with joy. It was alive on everyone's faces, and I felt it too. It surrounded me, wrapped me in its arms, and filled my heart so that I could hardly contain it. This was the magic Gloria had never lost, the element that I loved most about her—this joy, this radiant love.

She'd made good on her promise. I had come home with her, and she had made me believe in the magic of Christmas. Oh, God, how I loved her for that.

"Boys and girls," the Pastor said as the applause subsided, "I have a question. Who in our gospel story was the first person that God told about the birth of His son, Jesus?"

Immediately, the little girl dressed as Mary's hand shot up followed by a smattering of children's hands throughout out the congregation. He called on a red-haired boy in the second pew. The boy stood and said timidly, "The shepherds?" The boy's face turned as bright as his hair, and he melted back into his seat.

"Right!" the Pastor exclaimed, bringing a grin to the boy's face. Then he walked to the center of the church. "God could have announced the birth of his son to the kings first, or the rich people first, or to the holy people who prayed every day in the temple first, but he didn't. Of all the people on earth He could have told, He told the shepherds first."

He let that bit of wisdom sink in while he walked to the side of the altar where Christo and I were sitting with the three brothers in sheep costumes.

"Let me tell you a little something about shepherds, boys and girls," Father said. "They weren't rich. In fact, they slept outside with the sheep so they didn't even have a bed. And they weren't educated, because you didn't have to be a genius to tend sheep. And they didn't even smell very good because they lived with the stinky old animals." The sheep brothers giggled at that comment.

Then he walked over, put his hand on my head, and looked down at me. "No offense to you, Tom, but shepherds weren't the movers and shakers in society." A chuckle rippled through the pews.

I'd never thought about the origin of my name before—how appropriate it was. I was an undesirable. I deserved none of the joy I felt tonight. I didn't deserve Gloria, and I certainly didn't deserve the warm reception I'd received from the people in this church.

Father Bob walked back to the center aisle. Christo, restless, stood. I whispered for him to sit.

"God told the shepherds first for a reason," he said. Christo plopped into my lap. His fuzzy hair smelled like baby shampoo and his breath was sweet from the Christmas cookies he'd eaten for dessert. Even though he felt as light as a bag of feathers in my lap, he weighed heavily on me.

His tiny hand clutched the cane. A fine network of blue veins lay beneath his milky-white skin. Were there killer cells marshaling their efforts inside those vessels now preparing a final assault on him?

"God told the shepherds first, boys and girls," boomed Father Bob, "because God loves shepherds. He loves the lowly and will do anything, go anywhere, to the ends of the earth if necessary, to get them to love him back."

Christo played with his cane, hooking one of the sheep boys by the ankle. I tapped his arm, warning him to stop it. He set the cane on the floor and put his hand on my thigh, right on top of the stack of bills concealed in my pocket. I flinched. He looked up at me and grinned under the mask.

It was over. Right then, I knew that the trip to Martinique, grad school, my car heater, everything I had planned to spend the money on was gone. Christo had staked his claim to my cash.

When I thought I could lie on a sandy beach while the Davidsons scrounged for dollars to save his life, I was kidding myself. Maybe Rob was right. Maybe I did have too much of a conscience. I didn't know about that, but I did know that I had to give the Davidsons my money to finance Christo's bone marrow transplant. I'd have no peace until I did.

But how to get the money to Ginny and Joe without Gloria finding out? If she found out that I've been lying to her from the very beginning, she'd never forgive me, especially after putting herself on the line by pledging to marry me.

Gloria was the bright spot in my life. She was my hope, my future. It was too much to ask of me to relinquish my money and her too. I'd give the money to the Davidsons, but Gloria must never find out where it came from.

As if to reinforce my decision before I wavered, Father Bob continued with his sermon. "Boys and girls, not only does God love shepherds, He loves us all." He walked over and stood near me. "God calls all of us to be His children, not just the pure and holy, but the sinners too. If you haven't noticed before, God has a soft spot for shepherds. Why it was a lowly shepherd boy who slew Goliath, saved his people, and became the greatest king of Israel. And it was another lowly man, who called himself the Good Shepherd, who slew death, saved the world, and became the King of Kings."

Then he looked down at me, and I felt as if he were speaking the words solely for my benefit. They soaked into my soul like rain on parched earth. "We are all sinners, lowly shepherds, called to rise above our fears, slay them, and take our rightful place in His Kingdom."

Chapter 35

There were many things in life that I did not understand: Why Richard Simmons was famous. Why guys with beer guts are always the first ones to take off their shirts. Why anyone watched auto racing. Why my mother died. Why Christo got leukemia.

But as Father Bob dismissed us from the altar, I did understand this: I'd been sent to Holy Redeemer that Sunday after Thanksgiving to save Christo's life.

As I held his small hand, we walked back to the pew, and suddenly it all became clear. Fate had conspired for me to meet Christo so that I could supply the extra $10,000 he would need for his transplant.

I slid into the pew next to Gloria, and she leaned over and whispered, "Thank you, Tom. You made Christo so happy. I'm so proud of you."

I was proud of myself too. Having a sense of purpose for your life gives you that. Yes, I would sacrifice my money for Christo, but I would not, absolutely could not, give up Gloria too.

Then I thought of Rob. He'll freak when he finds out that I gave the money away. How could I ever make him understand? Some things you can't understand, you just have to deal with them.

But how to get the money to the Davidsons without Gloria finding out? I didn't know how I would do it, but I would get it to them someway.

Pleased with myself, I picked up Gloria's hand. She turned and smiled, and I don't know if it was the way the light struck her hair, or if it was the Christmas magic, or if the words that the priest had spoken had touched me, but when I looked at her smiling at me, something shifted. The earth titled a few degrees on its axis.

I found the pencil.

Gloria was the pencil. Her beauty and goodness proved God's existence. I had been sent to save Christo, and she had been sent by God to save me.

The congregation stood. Energized by this revelation, I sprang to my feet. Gloria handed me the prayer book, and before I realized it, the words of the creed were rolling off my tongue. "I believe in God, the Father Almighty, Creator of Heaven and Earth," I declared. I could hardly believe I was admitting this. The weight of the moment struck me, overwhelmed me with emotion. My voice trailed off. I could no longer read the words on the page because tears distorted my sight.

An awareness that I couldn't explain took hold of me. It was as though I had been brought outside myself to view my life from a distance. The telescope had been turned on me, and I watched as my life unfolded before me. I witnessed myself repeatedly grasping, fumbling, and failing in all my attempts to understand the universe. I had always looked outside for answers, when the secrets were locked within me.

Lowering my head, I looked to the side and secretly wiped the tears away before they ran down my cheeks. I listened to the rest of the creed, and although I was too choked up to speak, my heart spoke them for me. *Oh, God, I do believe, and I'm so sorry.* And as the prayer continued, each word echoed in my heart and dropped like a stone into the pit of my soul, piling up, filling me, plugging the hole.

Then I felt the love. All of it—Gloria's, God's. Everyone's. Love flowed into me, rose, saturated me and overflowed my banks. Giddy and unsteady on my feet, I was grateful to be able to sit when the prayer was finished.

As I sat there pondering what had just happened to me, a thought bubbled up, tickling my brain like a Pepsi bubble that rises in your nose. And I had to suppress my laughter. I had been converted. God hadn't knocked me off a horse, or struck me by lighting, or sent me a vision. No, I'd been waylaid by a sick kid dressed as sheep herder and a beautiful girl.

I looked for Christo now, and he had fallen asleep on the pew. After kneeling for a long time, we rose and Father Bob asked us to turn to each other and share a Christmas greeting. Gloria took my hand and kissed me on the cheek. "Merry Christmas," she said and the love dancing in her eyes told me that she knew what was happening to me.

Then I watched Joe Davidson bend over and kiss the sleeping Christo on the cheek. Ginny bent over him too, gently placed a hand on his back and kissed him. When she raised her head, she was wiping away tears. Joe put his arm around her.

How much had they lost? Joe's manhood? Their marriage? Their son? Their grief was so private, I felt as if I were snooping. No matter how much any of us cared about Christo, or how much his illness haunted me, no one could touch the depth of his parent's pain. To let them suffer one second longer than necessary, would be unconscionable. I had to get the money to them tonight, someway, somehow.

Row after row of people filed out of their pews for communion, while I sat there analyzing my problem. Maybe I should tell Gloria. Perhaps I could tell her that I'd give Ginny and Joe the money only if she forgave me. No, blackmail wouldn't work. I didn't want her to love me out of obligation. Perhaps I should throw myself at her feet and beg for mercy. She'd be furious to learn that I'd been lying to her since we met. There was no way I could tell her.

Gloria's eyes were clenched tightly, absorbed in prayer, looking more luminous than ever. I was a negative held up to her light; she exposed all my dark spots.

A heaviness settled in the center of my chest. It was the lie I'd have to carry and hide from Gloria for the rest of our lives together. Although I wanted to marry her more than anything else in my life, I knew she'd never truly be mine unless I told her everything. We would never be totally unified; the lie would forever separate us.

Could I live with partial love to keep her and spare myself pain? And if I told her, could she live with the knowledge that she had wasted herself on a self-centered liar?

I ached all over as I watched her beautiful face in prayer. I owed her the choice of either forgiving me or dumping me.

I would tell her.

I closed my eyes tightly, and prayed my first prayer as a believer: *Please God, please, don't let me lose Gloria.*

As the service drew to a close, Christmas spirit swelled in the church. But I only felt sadness swamping me. Better to tell her now before I settled in at her house. Before I chickened out. The organist went to town playing "Joy to the World" as Father Bob strolled up the aisle. I leaned over and took Gloria by the wrist. "I need to talk to you."

"OK," she smiled and waved to Matthew.

"No, I mean now—alone."

"What is it, Tom?"

In the back of church, we shook hands again with Father Bob. He patted me on the back and said he'd hoped that he hadn't embarrassed me too much. He wished us Merry Christmas again, and said, "I hope to see you again, Tom."

After I told Gloria about what I had done, I knew there was no chance of that.

Chapter 36

Snow had fallen, covering everything like a shroud, and large, lacy flakes were still coming down. On the front steps, people gathered in small groups, wishing each other Merry Christmas. I was so weighted by sadness, I could barely move my feet. Gloria looked up into the sky. A snowflake came and rested on her lashes and then quickly melted. After I tell her how I lied, that's all I'll have been to her. A snowflake, here and gone.

"A white Christmas," she sighed and wrapped both of her arms around mine, looking dreamily into my face. "Everything is perfect, Tom."

"I'll get the car," Mr. Davidson said, taking his cane from Christo. "Stay here with Grandma." He shuffled down the snow-covered steps.

Mrs. Davidson and Grandma quickly struck up a conversation with another woman. Maggie, as well as Joe and Christo, lingered on the church steps while Rick and Ginny went to get their cars. Joe looked embarrassed to be standing with the women, the elderly, and the pregnant, but I didn't care anymore about how he felt. He still had a life. Mine was over.

Gloria must have sensed my distress because she interrupted her mother's conversation. "Mom, Tom and I are going to walk home. We want to look at all the Christmas lights."

"Are you sure? It's slippery."

"You're not wearing boots," Grandma cried.

"It's only a few blocks," Gloria said, "and we'll be careful."

"Don't be too long," Mrs. Davidson said. "We still have Christo's gifts to give him."

Gloria took my arm as the sidewalks were slick and her dress shoes gave her no footing. How I would miss her, the feel of her, the smell of her, her clinging to my arm. We walked along in silence for a while. Red taillights from the traffic leaving the church glowed and were strung down Perry Highway like a strand of rubies.

We passed by the businesses and shops in Perrysville that were all closed for the holiday. At the light, we crossed Route 19. The snow intensified as we made our way back Good Lane. Gloria chattered away, pointing out the homes of children to whom she gave piano lessons, and admiring the Christmas decorations.

At the top of the hill on Grandview Avenue, she pointed to Ross Park Mall. It was only a few hilltops away. "Maybe we can go there and look for rings the day after Christmas?"

"Yeah," I said. It pained me to hear her talking like this when we had no future.

At the entrance to Sharmyn Park, she said, "Let's cut through here. It's shorter, and it will be so pretty in the snow."

I made no reply. I was too busy composing my confession in my mind. There was no way to soften the lie.

"Tom, you're scaring me," Gloria said. "I thought you wanted to walk home so that we could be alone for a while. But you haven't said a word, and your face is as white as the snow. You're not sick, are you?"

We stepped over a chain that was strung across the entrance to the park. "No, I'm not sick."

Inside the park, it was calm. The branches of the trees and bushes were laden with snow, and it muffled the sound of our footfalls. It was so still it seemed that everything in the park was holding its breath. We walked on the pathway, past the playground, toward the softball field.

Gloria stopped, let go of my arm, and looked up at me. "I can't take it anymore. What's wrong, Tom? What do you want to talk to me about?"

I began to tremble.

"OK," she said. "I get the picture. You're sorry you proposed."

"No!" I cried.

"Then you're upset because I dragged you to church and Christo embarrassed you."

"That's not it either," I said weakly. I walked over to a bench outside the shuttered concession stand and slumped onto it. A motion-detection light clicked on and shone down on me like the strobe of an interrogator. I blinked and ran my hands over my face, into my hair, steeling myself for what I was about to do.

"Gloria," I said, my teeth chattering, "I have something to tell you . . . something terrible about me."

The Christmas cheer drained from her face. I bent over, holding my head in my hands, staring at the slush on my shoes, searching for the right words while my resolve melted like the snow under my feet. The terror of being alone again closed in on me.

Tears stung my eyes. Burying my face in my hands, I cried out, "Oh, God, but I'm so afraid." My voice cracked like an ice-coated limb.

"Don't be afraid, Tom," Gloria said softly.

Droplets fell from my eyes and splashed onto the slush while I fought for strength. Inhaling deeply, I began my confession. "I'm not what you think I am, Gloria. Not what I led you to believe." My voice was barely audible, and the words came slowly. Then like a painful medical procedure, I wanted it over and the words came spilling out. "I lied to you. I lied to everyone. That day I came to Holy Redeemer? I didn't come there to give Christo that Sammy. I came there to sell it to Ginny, but things got messed up. I'm no hero. I'm a toy scalper. A lousy, rotten toy scalper. I only pretended to be a hero to impress you. The whole time I've been seeing you, I've been scalping Sammys—"

Gloria tried to interrupt me, but I couldn't stop now. "I'm a loser, Gloria. I was a fool to think I could ever be worthy of someone like you. And you were right. I am a coward. I'm such a coward, I can't even look you in the eye when I tell you this." With my thumb and index finger, I pinched back the tears dripping from my eyes.

"Tom—"

"No, wait let me finish. I never meant to hurt anyone, especially you. But I have more than $10,000 in my pocket right now that I made selling Sammys this year."

Gloria gasped. "Ten-thousand dollars?"

"Yes," I covered my head with my arms. "I'm really sorry, Gloria. You'll never know how sorry."

Gloria's hand on my cheek startled me. "Tom, will you shut up and listen to me?" she yelled. "I know. I've known all along—"

"But I love you too much to lie to you," I blurted. "And I want Christo to have the money."

Gloria took my face in her hands and raised my head. The security light behind me illuminated her face, cloaking her with a golden light, and shining on the snowflakes that swirled about her like celestial bodies in the dark night. Her magnificence enraptured me and stilled my rambling tongue.

"Tom! Oh, Tom, listen to me. I've known you were lying since our first date at the Parlor."

"What? You knew?"

"Yes, I knew. You see," Gloria said, smiling down on me, "the G. Davidson who made the arrangements to buy the Sammy for Christo was not Ginny, but me. I'd saved up money from my piano lessons. I wanted to buy him one as a surprise. When no one showed up at the church by three-twenty to sell it to me, I went back downstairs to help at the blood drive. I assumed the scalper sold the toy to someone else for more money. The person I made the arrangements with was very pushy and told me that if I didn't want to pay $150 to forget it."

"That was Rob."

"I know. When I ran late for our lunch date at the Parlor, I called your room to tell you I'd be late. The number seemed familiar. Then when I heard the recording on your answering machine, everything clicked, and I knew you had to be involved too."

"You weren't upset with me?"

"Upset?" Gloria echoed. "Oh, Tom, I was beyond upset. When I met you for lunch, I planned to give you a piece of my mind." Her voice lowered and became as soft as the falling snow. "But then when you told me about your mother and how you'd never experienced the magic of Christmas," she said, wiping the tears from my cheeks, "I knew what you really needed was not a piece of my mind, but a piece of my heart."

She placed her hands on my shoulders and looked deeply into my eyes just as she had done that first day in the Student Union. "Tom, you may not have been a hero then, but you are now."

"But why did you take a chance on me? You didn't know I'd change?"

She smiled radiantly. "Remember, that day I told you that I sensed beauty and passion in your soul. I needed to learn to trust God that he would be able to reach you, and help you become the person I sensed you could be. I love you. Do you hear me, Tom? I love you."

Now I believed it.

I leapt from the bench and fell into her arms. "Oh, I love you too," I cried. "I've loved you since that first day when you walked out of the light and came to me." I hugged her tightly. She loved me in spite of everything I'd done, in spite of all my flaws and weaknesses. I felt whole.

Burying my face in her golden curls, I clutched her to my heart, kissing her and crying, "Gloria, Gloria. Oh, Gloria!" My words rose like a chant from the heavenly host into the dark, silent Christmas night.

Chapter 37

Like that first Christmas Eve nearly 2,000 years ago, when Glorias filled the night sky, and shepherds were led to a child, I, Tom, a shepherd in the truest sense, was led back to a child-Christo— who through his pain and suffering had brought me the fullness of love.

When we arrived at Gloria's house, everyone was gathered in the family room. Torn wrapping paper and strands of ribbon littered the floor. Mrs. Davidson, who was bent over gathering the trash, looked up. "Oh, you're here," she said, and I could see she was relieved. "I was beginning to worry. Hope you don't mind, Gloria, that you weren't here to see Christo open up the gifts we bought him. I couldn't make the poor child wait any longer. He's getting sleepy."

He won't have to wait for anything now, I thought.

"That's fine," Gloria said. Excitement spilled over in her voice and colored her cheeks.

Christo was on the floor with his father playing with a fleet of Matchbox cars. "I hope he's not too tired to open one more gift," I said.

Christo ran to my side, and began jumping up and down, clapping. "I'm not too tired!"

"But you've already given him a gift," said Ginny, who was sitting on the hassock.

"Well," I said, "I saved this one—the best—for last." I pulled the wrinkled white envelope from my pocket and handed it to Christo. He stared at the odd gift, and screwed up his face. "Why don't you let your mommy open it for you."

Christo scampered over to Ginny, and handed it to her. She looked at me quizzically. "Open it," I said.

She lifted the envelope's flap and peered inside. And like that first time at Holy Redeemer, her mouth dropped open and her hands began to shake. Her eyes shot to mine. I smiled. Tension melted from her face. Clutching the envelope to her heart, she whimpered.

Alarmed, Joe rose. "What is it, Ginny? What's in there?"

Ginny Davidson's tear-filled eyes never left my face as she handed the envelope to Joe. He pulled out the stack of bills, and fanned them. His eyes grew larger and by the way he was breathing, I was afraid he was going to have another heart attack. "There must be a couple thousand dollars here!" he exclaimed.

The rest of the family rushed to Ginny and Joe's side. "There's $10,204 to be exact," I said. "Enough to buy a bone marrow transplant."

Eight sets of eyes were glued on me.

"Where did you get all this money?" Joe asked.

"You two didn't knock over the 7-11 after church, did you?" Grandma asked.

"No," I laughed, as I put my arm around Gloria, who gazed up at me with those Christmas green eyes full of love and admiration. I squeezed her tightly and smiled. "I believe it's Christmas magic."

I hope you enjoyed **A Shepherd's Song.** *If you did, would you please post a review wherever you purchased the novel.*

Also, be sure to sign up for my newsletter at www.janicelanepalko.com

Thanks!

Janice

Read a preview of Cape Cursed, a romantic suspense novel, which will be released in spring 2013.

CAPE CURSED

By

Janice Lane Palko

Chapter 1

"If you want to know anything about the lighthouse, Miss," Parker heard Ernie say as he grasped the screen door's metal handle, "then Parker, there is the fella you should be talking to."

Parker Swain stepped inside The Seafood Shack. The door's spring squeaked, and then the door slammed shut behind him. Hot, greasy air enveloped him. How did Ernie endure working behind those deep fryers on days like this? Parker wondered. If it was ninety-three degrees outside, it surely must be more than one hundred inside.

"Ma'am," Parker said, as the woman leaning against the counter turned and fixed her black eyes on him.

"I was just asking about the lighthouse," she said, tucking a lock of long, lustrous raven-colored hair behind her ear.

What little air there was seemed to have been suddenly sucked out of the place, and Parker felt short of breath. She was heart-stopping beautiful in an exotic way that he'd never seen in person but only on the faces of women from faraway lands in the *National Geographic*.

It was nearly sunset; the dinner rush over. She must be a vacationer who had just arrived at Crystal Shoals and was looking for a bite to eat, he thought.

He brushed his sun-bleached hair off his forehead and used the pretense of being responsive to her interest in the lighthouse to take in the sight of her. Her skin lacked a tan, but that was about all she lacked. "I'd be happy to answer any of your questions," he said feeling desire for her overwhelm him. He'd assumed that he was dead to the wiles of beautiful women, but the quickening of his pulse told him otherwise.

Maybe physically he was alive, but emotionally he knew he was as lifeless as the stagnant air.

Steady, Parker, he chided himself and turned to the man behind the counter. "How you doin' today, Ernie?" he asked, trying to regain his composure. Ernie's face was a leathery cross-hatch of wrinkles, indicating that he'd lived every day of his life, except for those spent in Korea during the war, under the bright North Carolina sun.

"Fine. What can I do you for?" Ernie drawled.

The Seafood Shack was an appropriate name as it was nothing more than a small wooden structure with a few Formica booths. For a fast, delicious meal, however, it couldn't be matched. Taking advantage of the long June days, Parker had worked through dinner. Famished now, he'd planned on picking up a bite to eat and spending the rest of the evening organizing his research material.

Parker scanned the menu above Ernie's head. "How fresh are the crabs?"

"Fresh as them kids you teach."

Parker raised a golden brow. "That fresh, huh? Then, I'll have the platter. And would you be kind enough to slip me a couple extra hushpuppies for Beau?"

"Sure thing. You want somethin' to drink?"

"I'll talk a large."

"What have you been working on?" Ernie asked as he wrote Parker's order on a slip of paper and passed it to Skip Jeffers, the young man behind him who was perspiring over the deep fryer.

Parker pulled his wallet from the back pocket of his well-worn jeans, fished out a ten, and handed it to Ernie. "Porch roof."

Ernie rang up the tab, closed the cash drawer, and gave Parker his change. "Bet that was toasty."

Holding out a muscular forearm, Parker assessed his skin, which was the same deep brownish-red shade of a well-worn baseball glove. "I'm about as cooked as your clams."

Ernie set two paper cups down on the counter. "Here, ya'll go. Why don't you talk to this pretty young lady. Tell her about the lighthouse, Parker, and I'll call you when the orders are up."

"Drinks are over here," Parker said nodding toward the soda fountain. He watched as the woman in the white capri pants and lime tank top scooted past him and grabbed some napkins and a straw. She certainly filled out her clothing nicely. The graceful curves of her back and derriere reminded him of the gently sloping dunes hugging the beach.

"Ladies first," he said motioning to the soda machine.

"Thank you."

Her accent was definitely not southern. Yet Parker couldn't quite place its origin.

The ice rattled into her glass. "I was just asking about the lighthouse."

"Well, what would you like to know?"

"Is it really cursed?" she asked as the Dr. Pepper streamed into the cup.

Parker froze. The bluntness of her question startled him. He felt his defenses rise, then he forced himself to exhale and told himself to let it pass. Looking at his work boots, he answered, "There's been some tragedies, and such. But no more than any other place. Just local folklore. That "Cape Cursed" b.s. draws tourists."

She held her glass to her temple and closed her eyes. "I also heard the markings have some significance."

Who is this woman? Most visitors only wanted to know how tall it was or how old. Why is does she want to know this?

She opened her eyes, and he fell into the depth of them. Canted exotically above her high cheekbones, they were black like the mermaid's purses that washed up on the beach, and seemed to hold fathomless mysteries. Resist, Parker. He'd been down the summer romance road before, and it had lead to only one destination: heartbreak. Besides, at thirty-two, he knew better and was too busy for that kind of silliness. He needed to focus on preserving The Keeper's House.

"They're so unusual," she said as Parker held in the ice button.

"Not another one in the world like it," he said, filling his glass two-thirds full with cubes. "Originally, it was to be painted like a barber's pole."

He loved talking about the Cape Destiny Lighthouse, but the vacant stares and yawns that often greeted him when he tried to enlighten others about it warned him to temper his enthusiasm. He figured he'd better be polite and not monopolize the conversation. "Where are you from?"

She seemed to stiffen. "What do you mean?"

"Nothing, just that I've never seen you around before. Take it you're not a local?"

"No," she said appearing to relax. "I'm from Pittsburgh," but then she quickly changed the subject. "What do the markings signify?"

His eyes fastened on hers, and he paused a moment as his throat suddenly went dry. "Eternal love," he rasped.

Quickly, he filled his glass with lemonade, took a long sip that cooled his parched throat, but did nothing for the heat this woman was generating in him.

"Eternal love . . ." she repeated wistfully.

"Legend has it," he continued, "that the first keeper insisted it be painted with the two intertwining stripes to symbolize he and his wife—their love spanning their lifetime and reaching into heaven."

She sighed, her small, firm breasts rising and falling. "Now that's what I call romantic." Then she looked pointedly at him. "How do you know so much? Are you a lighthouse aficionado?"

Aficionado? No, she definitely wasn't from Crystal Shoals.

"Order's up," Ernie called, breaking the spell that had come over Parker. They walked to the counter, and Ernie handed each of them a bag.

"Thanks, buddy. You take it easy now," Parker said.

"You too. Enjoy your stay, ma'am."

The young woman gave a small wave to Ernie. "Bye."

Parker held the screen door for her. They walked outside together into the thick June air and the slanting sherbet-colored rays of the setting sun.

"I like lighthouses," Parker said, "but I'm particularly attached to Cape Destiny." Now that they were out of the greasy air, he could smell her scent. Honeysuckle. His mouth began to water, and he wasn't sure if it was from hunger or desire.

She pointed over her shoulder. "I'm parked around the side."

"Mind if I walk you over?" he asked, not wanting to let someone so interested in the lighthouse get away. She shook her head no.

A dog barked. They both turned. A large Golden Retriever leaped from the back of a pickup truck parked in front of The Seafood Shack and came bounding over.

"Beau!" Parker said sharply. "You know better than to do that."

The dog reached out with his paw and hit Parker's bag. Shaking his head and holding the bag higher, Parker said, "He knows I have hushpuppies in here." Taking out a golden fried ball of cornmeal, Parker fed it to the dog, which gobbled it in one bite.

The woman crouched and petted Beau's silky coat. "Aren't you a pretty boy." The dog yammered and stared adoringly at her.

"This is Beau, and my name is Parker Swain. The Swains have always been lighthouse keepers at Cape Destiny."

"How charming," she said stroking Beau under the chin.

Charming? Definitely not from Crystal Shoals.

Beau responded to her affection by giving her a slurpy lick on the cheek that made her giggle.

She rose and smiled coyly. "Are you as romantic as your ancestors?"

Good lord, she's flirting with me.

Beau nosed around the bag. "Get in the truck now," Parker said. The dog snorted, meandered back to the pickup, and jumped into the bed.

Parker grinned at her. "I can be. When I'm properly motivated." *What am I doing flirting with her?* This is no good. This can only bring trouble.

She laughed and began walking. Parker followed along. "Well, Parker Swain," she said looking coyly over her shoulder, "if you're ever feeling motivated to talk about the lighthouse, I'd love to hear more. I'm staying up the road. The Destiny Cove." She stopped and turned toward him, offering her slim hand. "In case you're wondering, I'm Bliss—"

He shifted his dinner to his left hand and shook hers. "Did you say Bliss?"

"Yes. It's a long story."

"I'm a history teacher. I love long stories." He was still holding on to her slim hand.

She smiled and slid it out of his grasp. "Well, I have five older brothers. When I was born, they put me in my father's arms, and my mother asked him what he thought of a daughter. He replied, 'This is bliss.'" She shrugged. "That's how I got my name."

It sure would be bliss to hold her in my arms, Parker thought. They walked around the back of her black Ford Explorer.

"My last name is—

"Sherman?" he cried, reading the lettering on the side door: B. C. Sherman Engineering. Moving Heaven and Earth for You.

He looked at her, his face burning scarlet with anger. "You're Sherman Engineering? You're the destroyer of my lighthouse?"

St. Anne's Day

By

Janice Lane Palko

Chapter 1

"Come on. Move it." Anne Lyons slapped the steering wheel, her green eyes darting to the Malibu's digital clock. She was to be there by nine. If the traffic on the Fortieth Street Bridge didn't soon move, she was going to be late on her first day.

Her shoulder muscles kinked as she berated herself for not allotting time for traffic. Anne hadn't yet mastered estimating allowances for Pittsburgh's gridlock. She sighed. The rush of air from her lips ruffled a rust-colored curl that had slipped from her headband.

The previous night's thunderstorms had chased away the sultry July air. Beneath the bridge, the Allegheny River, a shimmering glass path, coursed toward downtown Pittsburgh, which gleamed like the crystal in Macy's Bridal Registry Department.

Ahead, an orange-vested worker flipped his "Stop" sign to "Slow," waving Anne's car through. "Finally." Her nose wrinkled at the odor of hot asphalt. There were only two seasons for Western Pennsylvania roads—snow removal and pothole patching.

The clot of cars flowed over the bridge. She turned left onto Butler Street, entering the heart of Lawrenceville. Anne had never been to this section of the city before. She was amazed at how much life had been packed into so little land. Bars, restaurants, doctor's offices, banks, and repair shops were crammed together, and where they left off, row houses took over, running perpendicular from the main street, up the hill to the site of the new Children's Hospital.

Anne slowed the Malibu, reading addresses. There it was on the corner—518 Butler Street. Bold brass letters above the entry spelled out MAC'S PLACE. "Oh, great," Anne snarled, "they gave me the address of a bar.   That can't be right."   She'd have to call the agency to get the correct one.   Anne felt the pocket of her scrubs and groaned when she realized that she had forgotten her phone at home.

A block down Butler Street, she found a parking space.   She hoped no one was watching as she did hand-to-hand combat with the steering wheel, fighting to wedge her car between two others parked at the curb. Having grown up in nearby rural Westmoreland County, she'd not yet mastered on-street parking.

Anne's jaws ached from clenching her teeth.   She shut off the engine, quickly gathered her file and her medical bag, and stepped out of the car.   The clock on the bank flashed 9:03.   She felt as if the large digital numerals were timing her.   Quickly, she fed a few coins into the parking meter and bustled up the sun-drenched street.

She scanned the old brick building for a side entry to a residence but saw none.   Large plate glass windows, shrouded by tan and white striped awnings, wrapped around both sides of the corner.   A forest green façade trimmed in brass framed the windows and the doorway.   In comparison to some of the other storefronts, the bar looked as if it had been renovated.   She'd heard other nurses in the office mention Mac's Place as having good food.   Anne hoped it was open this early.   Perhaps someone inside could direct her to her patient.

She pulled on the brass handle of one of the double doors, passing through a small vestibule and another set of doors, entering the dark, cool pub.   A scent of pine, as if the floors had been freshly mopped, masked a trace of spilled liquor.   In the dimness, she made out the shadowy figure of a man working behind the bar that ran the length of the far wall.

Anne crossed the scuffed plank floor, weaving between tables, the rubber soles of her tennis shoes not making a sound.   She had to stand on the foot rail, leaning across the counter to find the man who had stooped below the counter.

She cleared her throat and rapped her knuckles on the top. "Excuse me . . ."

The man startled, jerking upright.

When he turned to face her, she heard her breath catch with a small squeak in her throat.   Before her brain could register that he was handsome, her body reacted by sending a rush through her as potent as if she'd been given an injection of adrenaline.   Thick, wavy black hair contrasted to his light eyes that were as blue as a gas flame.   As she gazed into them, something ignited inside her.   Something that surprised and alarmed her.

"I'm looking for ⸻   ⸻he was embarrassed at how breathless her voice sound⸻

The man leaned ⸻   ⸻in. "You can take care of me anytime."

Anne stepped o⸻   ⸻d laughed nervously. "No, I'm serious."

"So am I." R⸻   ⸻ prop up his head, he smiled wickedly.

Anne felt h⸻   ⸻d to flattery. What she wasn't used to was   ⸻ for it.

Focus, An⸻   tucked the straying curl behind her ear an⸻   studying the file in her arm. "Really. I'm loo⸻   ⸻r," she said, tilting her head, reading from t⸻   ⸻er listed at 518 Butler Street, but that is obv⸻   where I can find her?"

Silenc⸻

She ⸻   ⸻ing herself up to her full four-feet, eleven ⸻   ⸻d demanded, "Well, do you?"

"W⸻   to you?"

Everyth⸻   *job.* "Please," Anne said, "this is important."

"What could be more imp⸻ ⸻tant than you and me?"

What am I a jerk magnet? Anne felt the all-too-familiar anger building in her gut, the rage that waited like a coiled cobra for the opportunity to strike back at men who reminded her of Zach. What did that counselor say that she'd been forced to meet when she worked at the hospital? *Take a calming breath.* Anne inhaled deeply, trying to speak calmly. "Look, do you or don't you know where my patient lives?"

He smirked. "Oh, I know."

When he didn't volunteer any more information, Anne looked at her watch, huffing. It was already nine twenty-one. "Is there a phone I can use?"

"There might be."

"You don't understand. I'm late. I don't have time for games." Anne spun on her heels, starting for the door.

"Wait! Why, it's your lucky day," he said, as he caught up to her at the doorway, placing a hand on her shoulder.

"Don't touch me!" She jerked away.

He threw up his hands. "Whoa, sor-ry."

Seething and embarrassed that he been able to provoke her temper, she turned and pushed on the door. It opened a foot then stuck.

She shoved it again, putting all her one hundred and two pounds behind it. It didn't move. She drove her shoulder against it, and as she did so, she looked up and discovered that he was holding the door in place. Out of breath, her face as red as her hair, she glowered up at him. "Let me out now!"

He smiled. "She's here."

"What?"

"I said she's here."

"Who's here?" Anne glanced around the bar.

He leaned in closer, so close she thought he might kiss her. And half of her hoped he would. But he stopped, just inches from her lips. "Your patient. Mrs. McMaster. She lives upstairs."

"What? Why didn't you tell me?"

"I was having too much fun."

Anger erupted in Anne, a mushroom cloud of rage roiling throughout her. Grimacing, she curled her fingers into a fist and swung at him.

Before she could connect with his jaw, he caught her wrist

"Let me go." She struggled to wrench herself from his powerful grasp until her fury subsided and logic took over. He was much bigger and stronger; she could not get away from him. *Perhaps if I play on his sympathies.* "Please let me go. I have a very sick patient who is waiting for me."

Still clutching her wrist tightly, he pulled her closer until she was nearly smack against his chest. Anne could see each individual black whisker of his beard.

At that moment, she decided that whoever he was, no matter how handsome he was, she hated him.

He laughed, dropping her hand. "Aren't you the little hothead."

"Hothead? Who do you think you are?"

He tilted his head, smiling smugly. "Only the person who hired you."

Made in the USA
Charleston, SC
28 November 2016